ALSO BY HAROLD COYLE

HAROLD COYLE

GOD'S CHILDREN

FORGE®

A TOM DOHERTY ASSOCIATES BOOK
NEW YORK

This is a work of fiction. All the characters and events portrayed in this book are either products of the author's imagination or are used fictitiously.

GOD'S CHILDREN

Copyright © 2000 by Harold Coyle

www.haroldcoyle.com

A Tor Book
Published by Tom Doherty Associates, LLC
175 Fifth Avenue
New York, NY 10010

www.tor.com

Tor® is a registered trademark of Tom Doherty Associates, LLC.

ISBN: 0-812-57538-5

First edition: February 2000
First mass market edition: April 2001

Printed in the United States of America

0 9 8 7 6 5 4 3 2

This book is dedicated to

NATHAN CROW

And all the young men and women of:
The Virginia Military Institute
West Point
Annapolis
The Air Force Academy
The Coast Guard Academy
Norwich
The Citadel
and
Texas A&M.
These youths, past and present, have freely chosen
to endure personal sacrifice and hardship by
dedicating their lives to defend and uphold the
ideals and principles that have made this nation and
its people unlike any other.

PROLOGUE

They didn't bother to wait for the cover of darkness. There was no need to. There would be no one to stop them, no one to stand between them and what they had to do. They knew the routine of NATO units in that sector better than the NATO troops did themselves. So the soldiers went forward with the same casualness that millions of other men around the world assume as they commute to their work. They exchanged idle chitchat, smoked a last cigarette, or dozed off as best they could on the stiff, uncomfortable seats of the military vehicles in which they rode. There was little to be excited or anxious about. As the village they were headed for was rather small, it promised to be a short and, from their perspective, uneventful day.

For the people of the village, however, this day would be unlike any they had ever known before. For some it

would be their last. That is not to say that they were
unprepared for what was about to happen. Most had by
now taken in relatives and strangers alike from other
villages that had been "relocated." The horror stories
that these poor souls related to their hosts in the confines of their modest homes caused the owners to look
about the room, wondering not if, but when.

The piercing, high-pitched squeal of steel track pins
pulled through the teeth of drive sprockets polished
smooth by heavy use, followed by the deep-throated
rumble of diesel engines, was all the warning the villagers had. Though every man and woman of the village
had lived for months with the fear that such a thing
could happen, when they were finally faced with the hor-
rible reality of the moment, few knew what to do. Like
a pending death in the family, almost no one had dared
speak of the danger that haunted them. To have done
so would have been to invite the dreaded event to in-
vade their simple lives. This appalling lack of conscious
thought left each and every member of the small farm-
ing community pretty much alone to react to the approaching calamity in his or her own way.

Slowly, with the ominous sounds of the approaching
Slovakian Army column drawing nearer, the inhabitants
of the doomed village responded to the threat. Instinctively, they ceased whatever they were doing and fled.
Many turned to their homes in the misguided belief that
their presence in their houses would deter the soldiers
from destroying them. Others, who saw them as potential death traps, sought to put as much distance between
themselves and the soldiers by whatever means came to
hand. For some, this was a private car or a farm truck.
One frantic farmer took flight on a tractor dragging a
wagon of old straw laced with manure. A few, for whom
any rational thought was impossible, even fled on foot
through the small private gardens that surrounded the
village toward the nearest stand of trees that promised
them protection from what was about to happen.

The young, who had been out playing or tending to chores away from their elders, were not as quick to respond to the crisis. The older ones did best. Though they didn't understand why this danger was being visited upon them, they knew enough to gather in smaller brothers and sisters. Like many of their parents, they turned and made for the only sanctuary they knew, their homes. Many of the younger ones, still unschooled in the ways of the world in which they lived, were overwhelmed with fear. Stunned, they failed to respond in much the same way a person is compelled by curiosity to linger a bit too long to watch a disaster unfold before them. Like sailors drawn to their doom by the song of the Sirens, they eagerly sought vantage points from which to watch the unfolding drama. The more fortunate of these stray children were retrieved long before the coming danger appeared. A few had no saviors. Not every parent and older sibling was able to overcome their own personal fears and pressing desire to save themselves. Left on their own, these waifs watched as the soldiers, now roused to full readiness by their officers, deployed in fields before the village and prepared to punish those who had the audacity to be descendants of a different lineage.

Whatever hope there was that divine intervention or an uncharacteristic show of pity on the part of their foes would spare them was dashed even before the first infantry fighting vehicle entered the village. Though the aged BMP was all but obsolete by the standards of any first-rate military power, the 73mm gun and 7.62mm coaxial machine gun was more than enough to overawe the people of the village, who had nothing but their prayers with which to defend themselves. Without halting, the lead BMP prepared to fire a high-explosive round into the first house that just happened to come into the gunner's field of vision. A small boy, standing in the doorway of the house the gunner had selected, was pounding on the sturdy door with his fists. By now the gunner no longer allowed himself to see such things. His only concern was to match each target he selected with the appropriate weapon. His commander, a demanding soul and a professional soldier to the core, insisted that they not waste ammunition.

The sharp crack of the BMP's main gun, followed almost immediately by the deafening explosion of the impact on the house, paralyzed those villagers who were already teetering on the edge of inaction and quickened the steps of those in flight.

Only after the round from his vehicle had impacted did the commander of the lead BMP order the driver to halt. With the vehicle's engine idling, the gunner slowly traversed the turret, first to the right, and then, just as slowly, to the left, watching for any reaction to their bloody provocation. Only when he was sure they would not be challenged by the local militia did the BMP's commander order the driver to continue on, into the village. The gunner, switching weapons, slew the turret to one side and opened fire, spraying the street with rounds from the BMP's PKT 7.62mm machine gun. Known as recon by fire, this indiscriminate mayhem was meant to either cause foes waiting in ambush to shoot before they were ready or discourage them from shooting at all.

There was no response, however, to the lone BMP's brazen dash through the village. By themselves, or in the company of their immediate families, the villagers had stayed huddled in the corners of their homes. With each new burst of machine gun fire, those who prayed did so more loudly and recited their pleas for salvation or atonement faster, as if they were in a race to finish the Holy Scriptures before their turn came. The instinctive gathering together of families made it easier for the soldiers who followed in the wake of the BMP to execute their assigned duties. It also left little for the BMP's crew, now posted on the far side of the village, to do.

Having completed his initial task, the commander of the BMP maneuvered his vehicle into a position from where his crew would be able to cut down anyone foolish enough to seek refuge in the nearby woods. Their nerve-racking charge through the village completed, the crew of the BMP opened the hatches of their combat vehicle and crawled out. Now it was their turn to relax and watch as the company of infantry they were attached to went in.

There was little that was exciting about this. The soldiers moving through the village did not rush about willy-nilly, spraying bullets about like drunken cowboys. Rather, they made their way from house to house slowly, taking their time flinging satchel charges or grenades into whatever convenient opening they could find. Only when it was necessary did they use their small arms to cut down survivors or those who attempted to flee. When they did so, the soldiers preferred to engage their victims at the greatest possible range. This made it easier for them since they could not see the expressions of fear or panic of a target that was moving and in the distance. The soldiers, after all, were humans who, like everyone else, were plagued by memories and occasional doubts.

All told, it took less than an hour to finish their sweep of the village. While his soldiers were dealing with the last row of houses on the far end of the village, the commander of this small combat team looked at his watch, then turned his face up to the chalky gray sky. They had plenty of time, he decided, to make one more sweep through the village before they had to leave. Even if the nearest NATO unit had been notified that the attack was in progress, it would take time for news of the incident to travel all the way to Brussels, and then on to Washington, where the graveyard shift was still on duty. By the time a decision was made as to what to do and transmitted back to units in the field and a respectable response could be mounted, the commander knew that he and his men would be long gone. Odds were, they would be back in their cantonment, eating lunch and enjoying a well-deserved rest. Of course, sometimes NATO units did respond faster then expected, either because the Slovakian commander was careless about the timing of his attack or there was a NATO commander in the area who had the balls to act on his own initiative. But such occurrences were rare. NATO forces, the commander had discovered, were like so many jellyfish, unable to do anything but drift to and fro at the mercy of the fickle tide known as public opinion.

After making one more quick scan of the gray, cloudy sky and seeing no sign of attack helicopters, the commander clapped his hands and shouted to his second in command. The young lieutenant, who was hovering over the radio in the command vehicle, lifted an earphone off one ear, faced his commander, and waited for his orders. "Pass the word," the commander shouted. "All teams to make their way back through the village and check each house. I want to make this a clean sweep." Then, fixing his deputy commander with a hard and uncompromising glare, he added, "And tell the commander of 2nd Platoon no excuses, no exceptions. I had the devil of a time getting rid of the last group of children the fool brought back. I will not be embarrassed like that in front of my battalion commander again."

Without comment, the deputy commander nodded in acknowledgment, replaced the earphone he had been holding, and passed the word on. A clean and thorough sweep. Those were his commander's orders. That was their duty. Simple, clear, and uncompromising, as things should be for a soldier.

1

The coming of dawn brought little warmth to the cold, desolate countryside. Turning his face toward the east, First Lieutenant Nathan Dixon sat on the hood of the battalion S-3's Humvee. With his feet planted firmly on the vehicle's front bumper and his arms held tightly across his chest, he watched as the pale sun grudgingly began its ascent into the eastern sky. Like everything else in this part of the world, Nathan thought, even the sun is dragging its tail.

With a sigh, the young officer closed his eyes, leaned his head back, and slowly rotated it in an effort to get the kinks out of his neck. The day had hardly begun and yet he had been up and on the road for better than three hours. Breakfast, and Fort Apache, his unit's base camp, was still an hour away. Opening his eyes, the young battalion staff officer looked out over the abandoned farm fields that surrounded them. These liaison trips back to brigade, he decided, were no longer much of a diversion from the daily grind that had come to dominate his life. They were six months into their deployment with nothing to look forward to but another six months of doing the exact same thing, day in, day out. He, and the rest of the 2nd Brigade, would have to go through the motions of performing a mission that no longer made sense, using rules of engagement that kept them from having any effect, in a country no one much cared about, while living among a people who weren't particularly interested in having them there.

Assigned to the 2nd Battalion of the 13th Infantry just as it was in the throes of deploying to the Slovak Republic, Nathan Dixon was sent to the place where all surplus combat arms officers are dumped, the unit's S-3 shop. Chiefly responsible for planning the operations of a unit, S-3 sections are notorious for being the home of an eclectic collection of officers and NCOs. In just about any unit's operations section, you'll find one or two stallions, primarily officers, waiting for a chance, any chance, to charge off to a new, more challenging assignment somewhere else. Working side by side with these are the nags of a unit, officers and NCOs who had not quite measured up to the demands of their last duty position, but were not bad enough to warrant elimination. Holding this mismatched assortment of personalities together is the primary function of the operations sergeant. This man, by necessity, is something akin to a miracle worker, expected to do anything and everything, with absolutely nothing, by yesterday. If stress, frustration, overwork, and too many demands put forth by too many people were the primary cause of baldness, the head of every operations sergeant in the United States Army would be as smooth as a cue ball.

At first Nathan didn't much mind being thrown into

this mix of professional fast movers and has-beens. Having just left an airborne unit, the young first lieutenant was somewhat out of his element in a mechanized infantry battalion. Distances that had required his footborne parachute infantrymen the better part of a day to march were covered in less than an hour by soldiers mounted in Bradley fighting vehicles. Even the sharpest young officer required a bit of time for his view of the world, and in particular the battlefield, to make this sort of adjustment. So his assignment to the S-3 shop had been, even in his own opinion, not all bad. Slowly, however, as Nathan mastered his duties and became familiar with the idiosyncrasies of mounted warfare, the limitations of his post began to press in upon him. Like any young eagle that had learned to fly, he did not take well to being caged.

The people he worked for, having been there themselves, helped make Nathan's stay in staff purgatory as painless as they could. Major Jon Sergeant, the operations officer, was quick to see that Nathan had a keen eye for terrain, an intuitive grasp of tactics, and a habit of being brutally honest. Whenever he needed someone to check out a reported incident, to recon a site for a new checkpoint, or to run to brigade or other units, the S-3 sent young Dixon. On occasion, he even allowed the energetic officer to slip away and attach himself to one of the line companies as they went about trying to enforce a peace accord that only the peacekeepers seemed interested in. Yet these diversions from the daily routine were only that, diversions. At the beginning of each day, Nathan found himself right back where he had been the day before; a third-echelon staff weenie commanding nothing more than a folding chair and half of a field desk.

Glancing over into the field where his driver had wandered in order to relieve himself, Nathan was about to ask if the man was having problems when he heard tracked vehicles coming down the road. Sitting up, he looked to the front, toward the east, to see if they were coming from that direction. When he saw nothing, he stood up, carefully balancing himself on the Humvee's fender and looking to the rear, over the roof of the vehicle. There, off in the distance, he saw a squat, full-tracked vehicle headed down the road toward them. Behind it were several trucks, two, perhaps more.

"Hey, Harvey," Dixon called out to the driver, "you'd better pick up the pace and finish whatever it is you're doing. We have company."

Turning his head, the Humvee driver looked over at Nathan, then down the road in the direction his passenger was staring. When he saw the approaching column, the young soldier began to do his best to bring his business to a conclusion.

When the lead vehicle was about a thousand meters away, Nathan recognized it for what it was, a BMP. Hopping down off his perch, he walked over to his side of the Humvee, reached into the vehicle, and pulled out the hand mike to the radio. Keying the radio by depressing the push-to-talk button on the side of the mike, he called brigade operations. "Foxtrot niner seven. Foxtrot niner seven. This is Kilo eight five Bravo, over."

Releasing the button, he waited for the NCO on duty at brigade to acknowledge. "Kilo eight five Bravo, this is Foxtrot niner seven. Send your traffic, over."

"This is Kilo eight five Bravo. Are there any Slovakian Army units scheduled to be operating or moving about in sector today, over."

"This is Foxtrot niner seven. Wait one, over."

While Nathan waited for the radio telephone operator, or RTO, at brigade to pass the question on to a duty NCO, Nathan reached into the Humvee to fish out his rifle. Even though the Slovakians showed American soldiers little in the way of respect, they were even more contemptuous of one who was unarmed.

From the speaker, the voice of the RTO at brigade called out. "Kilo eight five Bravo, that's a negative. No authorizations have been approved for the movement of any Slovakian units in our sector, over."

Drawing in a deep breath, Nathan keyed the mike as he contemplated what he knew would follow. "Foxtrot niner seven, be advised, we have a column of Slovakian Army trucks, number unknown, led by a BMP-1, moving east on the road at grid . . ." Then, realizing that he hadn't bothered to check their location before starting his report, Nathan quickly added, "Wait, over."

Leaning inside the Humvee, the young officer looked up at the GPS that was attached to the frame of the windshield. Hitting the display button for their current location, Nathan watched as the letters and digits representing their location on the ground flashed across the tiny screen. These he passed on to brigade. In return, the RTO dutifully read off instructions as to what Nathan was expected to do. "You will halt and detain all violators of the Munich Accords. You are to provide this headquarters with the name, rank, and unit of the senior officer in charge of the force violating the Accords. In addition, you will provide this headquarters with the number of troops present, how they are armed, and the vehicular composition of the unit in violation of the Munich Accords and await further instructions, over."

Without bothering to use the call signs, and with a bit more sarcasm in his voice than he meant to use, Nathan came back, "I do hope you realize that it's just me and my driver out here."

To this, the RTO came back with, "*Vaya con Dios, amigo.*"

Angered by the stupidity of their standing orders as well as the hopelessness of enforcing any sort of peace in this region, Dixon threw the hand mike back into the Humvee just as Harvey, the driver, was climbing into his seat. "I see brigade gave you the standard 'Hold until relieved' spiel."

"Yep," Nathan replied in disgust as he watched the column draw closer.

"So what do we do, LT?" Harvey asked as he prepared to start the Humvee. "I hope it's pull pitch and get the frog outta here."

Drawing a deep breath, Nathan began to make his way around to the rear of the Humvee.

" 'Fraid not, GI. We got our orders."

"If you ask me, sir," the concerned driver went on as he followed Nathan's movement around his Humvee, "the poor shmucks who followed Custer had their orders too. But that didn't mean they were smart to follow them."

"Well, Harvey," Nathan said as he stepped out into the road, "I didn't ask you. Now, get on the radio with brigade. Stay with them, and keep alert."

The driver was still trying to think of a snappy comeback when the lead BMP came trundling up to Nathan. As with so many incidents like this in the past few weeks, the driver of the BMP continued forward, refusing to hit his brakes until it became clear that Nathan wasn't going to give way. High risk games of chicken such as this, between the Slovakian Army and the NATO peacekeepers, had become the order of the day. For the NATO troops deployed in southwestern Slovakia, it was the only option they had under rules of engagement that had done nothing to keep the Slovakians from carrying out their program of ethnic cleansing. For the Slovakians, it was their way of demonstrating their total disregard for the NATO troops and their mission, a mission that had, to date, failed to accomplish any of its stated goals.

Nathan, like his fellow American peacekeepers, had no desire to lay down his life trying to enforce an accord that his own government was anxious to see fade away. Unlike Bosnia, where a one-year commitment had become an albatross that hung around the Army's neck for the better part of a decade, the American role in this NATO mission to Slovakia would be for one year and one year only. If, in that time, the conflict between the Slovakian government and its ethnic Hungarian minority had not been sorted out, the Americans, at the behest of their Congress, were prepared to walk away from it and leave whatever else needed to be done there for the Europeans to finish. Still, while they were there, soldiers like Nathan were expected to carry out their assigned duties, no matter how ridiculous, or hazardous, they sometimes became.

When the BMP finally came to a full stop, it sat little more than a foot away from where Nathan stood. For his part, the young battalion staff officer, having been prepared to leap out of the way, relaxed, but only a little. The commander of the BMP, hanging out of his open hatch, waved furiously at Nathan as he ordered the American to get out of the way. Sprinkled in with his demands were threats and a few curses that Nathan was able to pick out. This only reinforced Nathan's resolve to stand firm, presenting his own demands in English. "This troop movement has not been sanctioned by NATO. I demand to see your commanding officer." Ignoring Nathan, the commander of the BMP continued to wave his arm wildly, adding more and coarser expletives to his dialogue.

This pointless exchange continued for several minutes, until a Slovakian officer, flanked by half a dozen soldiers clutching AKs to their chests, stepped out from behind the BMP. "What seems to be the problem here?" the Slovakian captain demanded.

"Sir," Nathan stated in a crisp, commanding tone. "This troop movement has not been sanctioned by NATO. If you are the commanding officer of this unit, I must have your name, rank, and the identification of this organization."

The Slovakian captain forced a smile. "I think not, lieutenant."

"Sir," Nathan insisted, "these demands are not negotiable. They are spelled out in the Munich Accords and must be obeyed."

"If you had bothered to study those Accords, lieutenant," the Slovakian officer explained, "you would find that not a single official of my government affixed his signature to them. Therefore, your precious Accords have no meaning to me. Now, you are blocking the road. You will step aside."

"I cannot do that, sir."

The smile disappeared from the Slovakian's face. "Then you leave me no choice but to remove you."

Seeing that the moment of truth was at hand, Nathan tightened his grip on his M-16. This action caught the attention of the six soldiers who were backing the Slovakian captain. In response, they took one step closer to their officer, lowering the muzzles of their weapons as they did so.

From behind him, Nathan heard his driver call out. "Sir, brigade is on the radio. They need to talk to you right now."

Nathan stood there, glaring at the Slovakian captain for another moment before pivoting about smartly on his heels. Hoping that the other officer hadn't seen the beads of sweat that were beginning to form, the young staff officer walked away from the Slovakian and his consorts. Taking his time, Nathan walked over to the Humvee, going around to the passenger side. Taking advantage of his absence, the Slovakian captain signaled the commander of the BMP to move out.

At the Humvee, Nathan stuck his head into the vehicle, but made no effort to take the hand mike from his driver. "Does brigade really want to talk to me?" the young officer asked quietly.

Shaking his head, Harvey whispered, "No, sir."

Nathan smiled broadly as he looked out the rear window. The Slovakian captain and his men had already mounted up and were preparing to follow the BMP. "Good move, Harvey. I owe you one."

※

FORT APACHE
AFTERNOON, FEBRUARY 4

By the time the convoy made its way past the sandbag
bunkers that flanked the main entrance to Fort Apache,
Second Lieutenant Gerald Reider's spirit had pretty
much been beaten to death. Thus far, nothing he had
experienced during his long journey even came close to
matching his expectation. The infectious high that had
inflamed Reider and his fellow officers after they had
completed the rigors of Ranger training had been followed too closely by their introduction to the "real"
Army.

The long road that took Gerald Reider from Fort Benning, Georgia, to the gates of this battalion outpost in
south central Slovakia had been slow and tortuous. It
started with the charter flight that transported Reider
and some four hundred fellow soldiers, airmen, and
their families from the United States to Germany. While
the young second lieutenant of infantry had no delu-
sions that he was about to become a rather small fish in
the overall scheme of the military universe, Reider was
not prepared for the indifference, bordering on disdain,
that he ran into as he began his travels. It seemed that
no matter what line he stood in, Reider found himself
waiting between a mother with small, impatient children
and an enlisted soldier who had somehow managed to
make it though basic training without even learning how
to wear his uniform properly.

While there was absolutely nothing he could do about
the kids, Reider felt no compunction about making on
the spot corrections whenever an errant soldier strayed
into view. This continued, despite the glares his efforts
earned him, until a major pulled him aside. "A word of

advice, lieutenant," the major stated in an easy, friendly sort of way. "Take it easy on the uniform stuff. This is going to be a long, uncomfortable flight for all of us. There's no need to make it more miserable for the enlisted men than it has to be. Save all that gung-ho stuff for your platoon."

Though he felt like standing up to the more senior officer, Reider said nothing. He was too shocked to respond. Instead, he just stared at the major as the older, experienced officer smiled, turned, and walked over to where his family was waiting for him. Just what kind of Army, Reider thought, was he joining? Only the fact that the major was an aviator kept the young lieutenant of infantry from sinking into total despair.

They were a good two hours into the flight, after a meal that made Reider long for an MRE pork patty meal, when he began to see the light. Crunched between a maintenance warrant officer who had somehow managed to evade the Army's overweight program and an unaccompanied mother and her two small Ritalin-deprived children, Reider broke down and loosened his tie, unfastened the top button of his shirt, and slipped his shoes off. Though this did nothing to hush the three-year-old next to him who chanted the words to "Itsy Bitsy Spider" until Reider wanted to scream, it did make reclining in his seat a bit easier.

Arrival in Frankfurt, a way station along the long and tortuous road to 2nd of the 13th Infantry, brought little relief and no comfort. There, waiting for the plane load of tired, bedraggled soldiers and family members, were more lines, more briefings, and for some, like Reider, no ride to their units. Most of what Reider and his fellow wanderers heard from the personnel who greeted the plane passed into one ear and went straight out the other without making the slightest impression. All Reider wanted to do at this point was find a place where he could lie down, in peace and quiet, and get some sleep. The fact that this was still somewhere off in the distant future was disheartening.

As bad as it had been to be reduced to a mere manifest number and absorbed into the faceless mass of newly assigned personnel headed to Germany, the idea of arriving in country to find that no one cared enough to be there on time to pick them up was even more devastating. Though he tried to fight the feeling, Reider's sense of self-esteem and worth was beginning to ebb. He was even beginning to believe the cynics in his graduating class who had warned him that West Point was not the Army. "No one in your platoon is going to give two shits that you were a cadet battalion commander and wore academic stars," a classmate who had never managed to stay off academic probation during his four years warned him. "The little gold bar you wear isn't going to shine any brighter than mine and your ability to solve complex math problems isn't going to impress your troopies. You and me," his classmate told him with a broad smile, "will be starting out all over again, at ground zero, the day we walk into our first company orderly room."

At the time, Reider had chosen not to believe his classmate's words. The man was obviously jealous and bitter that he had not been able to excel during his four years at the Academy. Yet now, as he sat slumped down in a plastic chair, blurry eyed and feeling as rumpled as his uniform, Reider found himself wondering if there wasn't some truth to his classmate's bitter prediction.

The continuation of the trip, from Frankfurt am Main to division headquarters in Würzburg, did nothing to brighten Gerald Reider's outlook on his immediate future. The rank of the sergeant who drove the van didn't seem to match his age. Even at West Point, Reider had come to learn that a staff sergeant with gray hair was a sure sign that the man had, somewhere in the past, screwed up badly. Either that, or the man was somewhat less than brilliant. It didn't take long for the young officer in his rumpled uniform to figure out that the latter was the case here. A friendly and amiable man, the staff sergeant quickly struck up a conversation with one of the enlisted men. The man, who wore the blue disk around the brass infantry insignia on the collar of his uniform, had been one of the individuals whom Reider had reprimanded for a minor uniform violation the previous day before their departure from the States. Taking their cue from this soldier, the other four enlisted men in the van did their best to ignore Reider, which, the young officer thought, was fine by him. He wasn't in the mood for conversation, especially with people he really didn't have anything in common with.

Talking fast and using street slang, half of which Reider didn't understand, the enlisted man Reider had reprimanded began to pump the older NCO for information. In the beginning the soldier's inquiries were innocent enough, and the sergeant's responses quick and quite informative. But slowly, the nature of the interrogation changed. The subject of women, drinking, and, eventually what Reider thought were references to drugs, popped up. Each time a new and potentially sensitive subject was broached by the enlisted soldier, the man glanced over to Reider immediately after asking the question. The staff sergeant, sensing the delicate nature of the matter, would look up, into the rearview mirror at Reider before answering to see if the young officer showed any sign of reacting to the soldier's question. Only when he was sure that the only officer in the van wasn't going to, did the sergeant reply, as cryptically as he could manage.

For his part, Reider continued to ignore the pair, as well as his other fellow passengers. Instead, the exhausted and bewildered young man, who had yet to have an opportunity to use his commission and authority in any meaningful way, pretended that he was dozing off. As he did so, two thoughts kept spinning around in his mind. The first was the hope that this long and excruciating odyssey would soon be over. The second one concerned the soldier who was engaged in a nonstop conversation with the driver. "Dear God" Reider found himself praying. "Please don't assign that man to my platoon."

Arrival in Würzburg brought a bit of relief, but not much. Since the duty day was just about over by the time they arrived, the van driver dropped Reider off at the BOQ. With little more than the sketchiest of directions and a time that he thought the young officer should check in, the van driver bade Reider adieu and took off to deliver the enlisted men to their temporary quarters for the night.

With the division deployed in Slovakia, the in-processing of newly arrived personnel was consolidated at division level. For Reider and his fellow travelers, this meant several more days of filling out forms, turning in records and orders, and drawing personal field equipment that included everything from a flak vest and protective mask to a sleeping bag and wet weather gear. Along the way, Reider was subjected to another battery of shots, most of which he thought he had received at Fort Benning. His efforts to inform the medic at the records desk came to no avail. "Well, sir, if they did, they never marked it in your records. We can't send you forward unless you have all your shots, now can we?" The medic's innocent smile did little to hide the mischievous laughter Reider thought he detected in the man's eyes.

These shots, coupled with jet lag, and the mind-numbing running from one station to the next with no clear end in sight, did nothing to boost Reider's flagging morale. In the back of his mind, Reider began to wonder if this wasn't some sort of test, a perverted effort to see if he was as dedicated to his profession as he claimed to be. In a demented sort of way, it sort of made sense. West Point had its plebe system, during airborne training there had been zero week, and Ranger school had, well, Ranger school. In every instance the cadre had intentionally applied unreasonable and unremitting pressure in an effort rapidly to weed out those who were weak in either body or spirit. Though he refused to believe that the Army would resort to this sort of thing this late in a young lieutenant's journey, the alternative was to accept the obvious, which was that the system used to process, move, and integrate replacements was totally screwed up.

Of course, it wasn't. Like all large bureaucracies and institutions, the United States Army suffers because of its size and complexity. Created to accomplish big things, like winning wars, the Army tolerates minor inefficiencies in the process. Organizations operating with unlimited funds and dealing with fewer individuals, like a corporation, can tailor the personnel services it must deliver. They can also contract such services out to other corporations. Microsoft, AT&T, Citibank, and GM don't need to worry about setting up and operating their own systems of hospitals to care for their workers. They have no requirement to move their employees every few years. And when they do, they simply buy the tickets and pay the bills for any expenses incurred in such moves. Few corporations and companies have the requirement to equip their employees with everything they need to survive in a barren, hostile environment, let alone one in which other people are hellbent on killing them. And corporations have the ability quickly to shed antiquated computer systems and programs without staffing requests for new systems through layer after layer of bureaucracy and begging for funds from a tax-conscious Congress. Like its sister services, the Navy and the Air Force, the Army does the best it can during peacetime to meet worldwide commitments operating with funds that are inadequate and relying on equipment that is aging, overused, and often begging for spare parts. When all is said and done, it is nothing short of a miracle that the Armed Forces of the United States actually accomplish what they do.

Such grand and philosophical thoughts did not even occur to young Gerald Reider. With all the narrow focus of an inexperienced infantry officer equipped with what the Army considered the bare essentials necessary to lead a platoon, Reider was concerned with only one thing: reaching that platoon and taking charge of it. During the long train ride from Würzburg to Bratislava via Munich and Prague, and then in the cab of a truck that was part of an armed convoy, Second Lieutenant Reider rehearsed, over and over again in his mind, exactly what he was going to say and how he was going to make his presence known. Everything, including four years at West Point, better than half a year's worth of military schooling, and the ungodly ordeal of his journey from the States to here, was but a precursor to that event. It was all a prologue written by others that would be the start of a career that Reider fully expected would carry him to the stars.

Of course, like all too many new second lieutenants, Gerald Reider hadn't learned from his military experiences to date. Nothing, not even those things one is trained for, ever really unfolds as one expects. And that, for an officer like Nathan Dixon, is what makes the military such an exciting profession to pursue.

2

In the closed, isolated community of Fort Apache, one of the highlights of the day, at least for the officers, was the evening briefing. It was more than a means of marking the end of the duty day and providing a forum for the exchange of information. For officers who are, by virtue of their rank, isolated from the bulk of the people they worked with throughout the day, the evening briefing was an opportunity to spend time with those who were their peers, if not in rank, then in the responsibility that their commissions and position bestowed upon them. Lieutenant Colonel Rob Miller, the commander of 2nd of the 13th, understood the strain his officers were under. Like the soldiers who served under them, they daily faced a situation that they could do nothing about. Yet Miller expected them to maintain a positive, professional attitude at all times. "I don't give two hoots what you think about our reasons for being here or the rules of engagement that we're forced to operate under. You're supposed to be professionals, each and every one of you. Even if you don't believe it, at least try to act as if the future of the free world depends on the job we're doing here. Remember, your men are watching everything you do and hanging on every word you utter."

While that was true most of the time, few enlisted men participated in the evening briefing. So Miller used that gathering as an opportunity for his company commander and staff officers to relax and, as best they could, enjoy themselves with their fellow officers in a relatively nonthreatening environment. In this, the battalion commander was greatly assisted by some of the secondary staff officers, those senior first lieutenants and junior captains who still hadn't lost all their boyish longings for mischief and fun. When provided an opportunity to brief, these free spirits pushed the envelope in an effort to lighten up an otherwise drab and mundane existence. Among the junior officers, an unofficial "can you top this" competition had sprung up. For everyone else, it was better than watching an old-time vaudeville show.

Occasionally, a briefer would go a little too far, or allowed the fact that his real purpose was to provide critical information in a timely manner to slip his mind. When this happened, it normally took nothing more than a frown by Lieutenant Colonel Miller to bring the errant officer back into line. Only once did it become necessary for Miller to pull an officer off to the side and counsel him for losing sight of his responsibilities.

Not every evening briefing provided the junior officers with an opportunity to indulge their own particular sense of humor. Like his fellow staff officers, Nathan Dixon knew when he could deviate from the straight and narrow and when it was best just to present his briefing without any embellishments. Tonight was one of those occasions. Captain Peter Westover, the battalion intelligence officer, set the tone. Known throughout the battalion for his razor-sharp wit and silver tongue, the military intelligence officer was presenting his ominous overview of Slovakian raids and ethnic Hungarian responses straight-faced. Though he already suspected what the response would be, Nathan Dixon looked over at his boss, Major Jon Sergeant. Sergeant rotated the nightly briefing responsibilities among his officers in an effort to develop their skills and keep them on their toes. As it was Nathan's turn in the barrel, and the intel briefing was, to say the least, ominous, the young first lieutenant turned to Sergeant for guidance on how best to present. The battalion operations officer took note of Nathan's glance and gave him one of those 'Be clear, be concise, and get out fast' looks. The younger officer acknowledged the major's expression with a slight nod, indicating that he understood, before jumping to his feet to take the place just vacated by Captain Westover.

Nathan's briefing followed a formula that the battalion commander insisted upon. Whereas the battalion intelligence officer addressed the activities of non-NATO forces that posed a threat in and around the battalion's sector of responsibility, it was Nathan's task to present the friendly situation. This included a quick review of operations and significant incidents that the battalion's next higher headquarters was involved in as well as those units whose sectors adjoined that of the 2nd of the 13th. This was followed by a brief review of the 2nd of the 13th's own tactical operations during the last twenty-four hours and a detailed description of battalion operations planned for the next twenty-four. Any additional tasks, mission, and long-range projects were discussed after that.

Unlike Peter Westover's briefing, Nathan's was quite routine and undramatic. Since the most recent round of Slovakian operations were in the 2nd Brigade's area

of operations, Nathan's litany of patrolling, shows of
force, and roving security operations, both for his own
battalion and the other units of the 2nd Brigade,
needed little elaboration. Nathan described each patrol
and pointed out where they had gone on the operations
map hanging on the wall. He summarized the results of
their efforts with phrases like negative contact, routine
civilian and commercial activities and traffic, or no apparent change in the activities of Slovakian units in sector.

Three months ago this would have brought a smile
and a nod of approval from Lieutenant Colonel Miller.
The spate of hostile actions in the Second Brigade's sector, however, coupled with the rumblings throughout
the region, changed that. Now Miller viewed the blatant
violations by the Slovakian Army in the areas surrounding Fort Apache, and his unit's inability to stop them,
with growing concern. So when Nathan announced that
he had finished his prepared spiel by asking, "Are there
any questions?" Lieutenant Colonel Miller stood up and
turned to face his assembled company commanders and
staff.

"Gentlemen," he stated briskly, "I am becoming nervous, and you all should be too." Without looking, he
waved his hand at the map behind him. "There's some
serious shit bubbling up out there, things that we, here
on the ground, are unprepared to deal with. The nature
of the situation in Slovakia, vis-à-vis the open hostility
between the Slovakian government and the ethnic Hungarians living in the Slovak Republic, is changing faster
than our ability to deal with it." This was as close as
Miller would come to telling his officers that he didn't
have confidence in their current rules of engagement.

"Until such time as the situation clarifies itself," he
continued, "and we receive new guidance that will permit us to deal with it effectively, we must, and we will,
continue to execute our assigned duties as laid down by
the agreements that established this peacekeeping force

and in accordance with the mission statement that governs its operations. That does not mean, however," Miller stated in a low, but firm voice as he placed his hands on his hips, leaned forward, jutted his jaw out, and stared at the faces of his company commanders, "that we will conduct business as usual. On the contrary. I expect each and every one of you to impart upon every man in your company that now is the time to redouble our vigilance. Now is the time that we must be on our guard and ready for damned near anything and everything."

Relaxing his stance somewhat by straightening up, but making no effort to soften his tone, Miller went on. "We've been here for over six months. Our soldiers have walked the same traces, stood watch at the same bridges and road intersections, and paraded around through the same villages and towns without a single shooting incident in that time. In the process, they have become, in my opinion, lax and inattentive. I am not comfortable with the bland reports concerning the comings and goings of Slovakian Army units in our area of operation that come back to me stating simply, 'No contact,' or 'only routine activity to report.' While others may find comfort in hearing All Quiet on the Western Front, I do not."

Pausing, Miller turned sideways and began to pace in front of his commanders and staff, looking alternately down at the ground, then back up at them, as if he were thinking. Nathan, of course, was aware that his battalion commander already knew what he was going to say. He was just giving his company commanders an opportunity to absorb the mild, if thinly veiled, rebuke they had just been given.

When Miller was satisfied that he had made an impression on the captains who commanded the battalion's line companies, he continued. "As I was saying, now is the time to redouble our efforts. Now is the time to review the manner in which we carry out our tasks to ensure that we are not only doing everything that we're supposed to, but that we are not missing anything in the process. I want your patrols to be more than sight-seeing tours of the countryside. I want them probing, looking behind every tree and bush that time permits. I have a feeling," he stated as he folded his arms and raised an eyebrow, "that we've allowed our routines to become, well, too routine, if you know what I mean."

The assembled officers took this as a cue that their commander had finished his chastisement of the company commanders and was trying to strike a lighter tone. A few of the more secure officers, such as Nathan's superior, even chuckled. After a nod to thank Major Sergeant, Miller continued. "Having said all that," the lieutenant colonel went on, "I want to impress upon you all the need to be careful, to be very, very careful. There's something afoot out there, something that I fear we are not ready to deal with. Some of our brethren along the Danube are already starting to suffer from the change in the military and political climate in this country. I suspect our turn is coming. While there is little that we can do, proactively, to stop this, we can be careful. You," he stated, fixing his gaze again upon his company commanders, "can impress upon all your subordinates the need to remain vigilant and be thorough in everything they do. This is especially true when they are getting ready for a mission and while they are actually out there," Miller thundered as he pointed toward the door of the briefing tent. "Check everything, twice if necessary. Leave nothing to chance. Make sure your people know what they're suppose to be doing and have the wherewithal, whether it be ammo or comms, to get themselves out of a tight spot. Is that clear?"

In unison, the company commanders came back with a crisp, clear "Yes sir!"

Fort Apache had few social venues. It was a base camp, a place from which the soldiers of 2nd of the 13th Infantry sallied out to patrol the peace that existed only on paper. It was also a strongpoint, a dirt and sandbag fortress that lived up to its name. Lieutenant Colonel Miller, who knew when to be cautious, had rearranged the battalion's priority when they had been establishing Fort Apache. Rather than seeing the base camp's main purpose as a platform from which he could project military power, Miller viewed it as a sanctuary where his battalion could hunker down and protect itself should that become necessary. Now, with the Slovakian government opting to take a hard line against the ethnic Hungarians in their country, and the Hungarians themselves showing teeth despite the odds against them, Miller's farsightedness and the hard work required to make the battalion's base camp defendable seemed to be paying off.

To that end, everything within Fort Apache was laid out with an eye toward defensibility. There were no large clearings that served as motor pools where a company's Bradleys could be lined up, dress right dress, as if on parade. When not on a mission, every combat vehicle had a fighting position along the base camp's outer perimeter. The only time a Bradley came out of its hole was when the squad that it belonged to was going out or the vehicle required maintenance. Even the battalion's support vehicles were scattered about in small clusters rather than grouped together in one, huge holding area. This was especially true of the fuel trucks, which were segregated as far from the living areas as possible and parked in their own individual revetments, much in the same way the Air Force scatters and protects its aircraft.

This defensive posture, naturally, made for cramped quarters within the base camp. A tight perimeter, after all, is easier to defend. Wherever possible, tents and the few cobbled together wood and tar-paper structures that

made up Fort Apache served more than one purpose.
The battalion's main mess tent was one case in point.
First and foremost, it provided the troops a place to eat
that was as dry and warm as the weather of Central Europe permitted. When not being used as a dining facil-
ity, the mess tent became a movie theater, an all ranks
club, a chapel on Friday nights and Sunday mornings,
and on occasion, an auditorium where mass briefings
could be held. On this particular night, since there was
nothing special scheduled, the mess tent was a social
club. Soldiers who wanted to escape the confines or
company of their squad mates were gathered there to
buy a soda or candy bar from the small exchange run
by the battalion sergeant major, chat with friends from
another company, or watch one of two TVs that had a
satellite down link and VCR attached to it. It was here
that young staff officers, finished with their day's duties,
migrated after the evening briefing.

Nathan Dixon headed off to the mess tent as soon as
he could and before his boss could think of something
else for him to do. There he met the battalion's bugs
and gas officer, a name given the chemical officer assigned to the operations section. Like Nathan, she had
not waited around for fear that Major Sergeant would
remember something at the last minute that he needed
her to tend to, as he was prone to do. Since there was
little threat of nuclear, chemical, or biological warfare,
Christina Donovan, the chemical officer, was assigned
whatever duties and responsibilities one of the other officers in the ops section didn't have or want. This meant
that she handled a myriad of diverse duties, for none of
which she had any formal training. She liked to joke that
if everything she did were listed on the section on her
officer's evaluation report where her assigned duties
were enumerated, her rater would need a continuation
sheet. Nathan's predicament was not much different. As
the junior officer in the ops section, he found himself
inheriting all the operationally related duties and tasks

none of the other officers in the section wanted. Like Donovan's litany of labors, these were often varied, boring, and multiple. So when either Christina or Nathan had reached the saturation point, the two would conspire to sneak off and seek whatever break in the routine they could find.

There was more to their mutual attraction, of course. For one thing, Donovan, like Nathan, was not West Point. Her desire to serve her country and her South Carolinian heritage had drawn her to the Citadel, where she had graduated with honors a year after Nathan had finished at VMI. Together with Major Jon Sergeant, a graduate of Texas A&M, these collegiate foes formed their own little mutual protective society. As Major Sergeant explained to his battalion commander, a man who believed that West Point was the center of the Army's universe, "It's important that those of us who graduated from a state military college stick together. After all, sir, you'll never know when you'll need someone with a college education."

Tonight, the former Keydet and Bulldog settled into the corner of the mess tent, where the two engaged in an innocent game of chess. Since Nathan was not schooled in the traditional strategies of the game, he played it the way he had run his airborne platoon at Fort Bragg, aggressively and fast. Having survived four years at the Citadel, not to mention working in close quarters with combat arms officers day in and out, Christina Donovan was unintimidated by Nathan's approach to the game. She met Nathan's lunges and drives on the chessboard with equally devastating advances and moves of her own. That these moves sometimes took on sexual overtones was not missed by either player, or by anyone else who bothered to watch their games. As neither was married and both found gratification in the attention and mutual respect given by the other, both junior officers spent as much time together as they could.

Nathan, reduced to his king, a rook, and two pawns,

was in the throes of trying to escape a check by Christina's queen and rook when Major Sergeant and Captain Charles Andrew Pierpoint found them. Like Nathan's father, Pierpoint's was a serving officer. But that was where all similarities ended. It was more than the simple fact that Pierpoint had attended West Point, or that his father was a colonel whereas Nathan's was a general. Rather, it was the way in which Pierpoint conducted himself and performed his duties that told the difference. Instead of being a source of pride and inner strength, the rank that Pierpoint's father wore and the reputation he had built for himself were a burden to the son. They hung over Pierpoint like a threatening storm cloud. More than once the other officers joked that Pierpoint ran his company not as he thought it should have been run, but rather as the young captain believed his father expected a company to be run. "It must be hell," Captain Andrew Andronette once commented to Nathan after watching Pierpoint deliver a briefing to his company, "to live in the shadow of a father who's made a mark on the Army."

In his usual manner, which sometimes crossed the line that separated brashness from insubordination, Nathan shot back. "I wouldn't know, sir. My dad never served in a real Army. He was a tanker." Such comments were more than simple repartee meant to deflect embarrassing comments or comparisons. They were a statement, by Nathan, that he was not his father. In that, and numerous other ways, Nathan took great pains to make it known that he was not a carbon copy of a man he admired above all others. "Though I'm proud of my old man," he confided to Chris Donovan one night when they were engaged in one of their more serious discussions, "I'd be a fool to try to be like him. To start with, I'm not him. Second, the Army he joined isn't the same one I did. And third," he added with a chuckle, "he'd draw and quarter me if I tried."

Captain Charles Andrew Pierpoint's own views on the

world in general, and the Army in particular, didn't do anything to soften an instinctive dislike that had sprung up between the two men on the first day they had met. Nathan, the son of a general, did not behave as a Pierpoint believed a general's son should behave. For Pierpoint, this meant living on the straight and narrow and upholding a mythical tradition in which few in the society they defended, or even in the Army itself, put much stock. That, coupled with a reputation that already marked Nathan as a rising star, annoyed Pierpoint.

Chris Donovan, who was facing the direction from which the operations officer and company commander were approaching, saw Sergeant and Pierpoint first. Quickly she took note of their demeanor.

Looking up from the chessboard, Nathan saw his opponent looking over his shoulder with a concerned expression. Turning, he caught sight of the major and captain. "Do you think we can make a break for it?" he asked, looking back at Donovan.

The chemical officer shook her head. "Don't think so, comrade. We've been made."

Twisting about again, Nathan looked Sergeant in the eye. Even at this distance, Nathan could see that his boss was wearing "The Look" as he continued to march toward them. "No good can come of this," he whispered to Donovan.

Sergeant waited until he was standing over the two young officers before saying anything. Looking down at the chessboard, he smiled. "Nate, I sure hope your ability at chess is no reflection on your tactical expertise."

The major, of course, knew that Nathan was a proven commodity. He had, as they say, "been there, done that," and come out looking good. The fact that Nathan had been used by the battalion commander to lead patrols assigned sensitive missions was a reflection of the confidence the battalion's chain of command had in him. Which was why Nathan already knew, without Sergeant having to say a word, that the major had another winner of an assignment for him.

In an effort to break the tension she could already feel building, Donovan chimed in. "Why, sir, must you always assume that he's in a bad spot because of his poor playing? Why can't you permit yourself to acknowledge that his foe is a person gifted with superior intellect and tactical abilities?"

Looking at Donovan, Sergeant smirked. "Because, lieutenant, I've known too many Chemical Corps officers." Then, Sergeant dropped his smile as his gaze fell back on Nathan, who was still seated and looking up at the medium-built major. "Captain Pierpoint has a problem that I thought you might be able to remedy."

Without waiting for a response from Nathan, Sergeant turned to Pierpoint and gave him "The Look."

If the West Pointer's countenance had not already communicated the great displeasure he took in having to seek outside help, then his crisp, almost curt tone did. "As you know, *Lieutenant* Dixon, my company is scheduled to run a dismounted patrol through the hills north of Modrany tomorrow."

Though Pierpoint's tone and manner irritated him, Nathan maintained his composure and nodded. "Yes, sir. I know. I covered that in my briefing."

"Well, yes, of course," Pierpoint mumbled. "I also have to conduct a show of force in Komarno. Since things have been touchy there in the past few weeks, and the battalion commander wants a company commander to lead those, I have no choice but to go with Lieutenant Gerhard's platoon on that mission."

Though Nathan was dying to say "So?" he held his tongue.

"Lieutenant Jefferson and his men have just finished five days' worth of patrols and convoy escort," Pierpoint continued as he awkwardly shifted his weight from one foot to another like a schoolboy delivering a weak excuse to a teacher. "They're due for a one-day stand down before assuming responsibility as the battalion's ready reaction force. That leaves the 3rd Platoon for the dismounted patrol."

Irked by Pierpoint's roundabout manner, Sergeant cut in. "The problem, Nate, is that the platoon leader of that platoon is new to the battalion. In fact, he just arrived today."

A mischievous smile lit Nathan's face. "Gee, they finally got around to replacing poor Fulham." Turning to face Donovan, Nathan winked so that Pierpoint couldn't see. "Rotten luck to get pinched between two Bradleys. Kind of puts a crimp in an officer's career, if you know what I mean."

From across the table, Chris Donovan gave Nathan a look that could cut through steel while Pierpoint clinched his fists and struggled to hold back his anger. Despite the fact that the death of Second Lieutenant Hank Fulham had not been his fault, Pierpoint, as the company commander, viewed the incident as a black mark against him. The mere mention of the accident was normally enough to set him off. To have someone like Nathan Dixon make fun of the dumb bastard's death was too much. Were it not for the fact that he didn't feel comfortable sending a newly arrived lieutenant out on a patrol on his own, Pierpoint would have turned and walked away from the operations trio right then. But he didn't. He stood there and waited for Sergeant to continue.

"When Captain Pierpoint asked to be relieved of the Modrany patrol, I turned him down. It wouldn't be fair to the other companies," Sergeant snapped as he turned to look at Pierpoint for a moment. "Everyone has got their problems."

"Well you don't need to tell me that, sir," Nathan stated in an effort to break the tension. "After all, you have me."

After bowing his head, so that Pierpoint couldn't see the smirk he could not suppress, Sergeant looked back over at Nathan. "Well, Nate, not tomorrow. You see, you're going with Pierpoint's 3rd Platoon."

All business now, Nathan thought for a moment. "What about Eugene? It would seem to me that this would be a perfect job for the company executive officer."

Sergeant shook his head. "Lieutenant Fung isn't back from court-martial duty at division yet. The S-1 doesn't expect him back until the end of the week."

"Bummer," Nathan stated absentmindedly. While he understood the need to execute the normal duties and responsibilities associated with military organizations, even when in the field, he, like so many other combat arms officers, became peeved whenever some additional duty, such as serving on a court martial, took them away from their unit.

"That's not exactly the same word I used," Sergeant replied, "but it captures my sentiment. Anyway," he continued, "that leaves Captain Pierpoint in a pickle. Like the battalion commander, he's uneasy about sending the new man off on his own, especially with the way things have been going. That's why you were elected to go along with him."

Though the prospect of going out on a foot patrol was exciting, Nathan gave Pierpoint a hard, damning look. While he didn't know what song and dance the captain had used to convince Major Sergeant why it was so important for the 2nd Platoon to make the Komarno show of force, Nathan understood the real reason. The 2nd Platoon was Pierpoint's best. Everyone knew that. Just as everyone knew that the 3rd Platoon was his worst. But rather than personally take the 3rd Platoon in hand and sort things out himself, Pierpoint opted to ignore the problem by assigning that platoon every low-visibility tasking and no-brainer he could manage. When there was the need for an officer with more experience to oversee the activities of the 3rd Platoon, Eugene Fung was normally assigned to do so. But Fung's absence placed Pierpoint in the onerous position of having to seek help from battalion.

Persistent rumors of weapons caches hidden someplace in the hills north of Modrany by Hungarian militias made that piece of terrain an item of interest to NATO command and, therefore, the object of further investigation. The operation scheduled to work those hills required that the platoon conducting the patrol split. After dropping the dismounts off near Modrany, the Bradleys would move along the roads that encircled the hills, setting up roving checkpoints as they went. This element was normally led by the platoon sergeant. The dismounts, under the control of the platoon leader, had the task of combing the hills on foot, kicking over rocks and shaking the bushes as they did so. Though nothing of substance had been found to date, enough evidence of clandestine operations had been uncovered by previous patrols to warrant return visits.

Had the operation permitted the platoon to remain together, the platoon sergeant, Sergeant First Class Eddy Taylor, would have been able to handle the mission. But the requirement to split the small command, coupled with the growing tension between NATO forces and military forces on both sides of the dispute, made the battalion commander, as well as Captain Pierpoint, nervous about sending out any patrol without at least one experienced officer accompanying it.

"What, sir, are my duties while out there?" Nathan finally asked Pierpoint.

Relieved that he wasn't required to go through his song and dance as to why he wasn't using 2nd Platoon for the Modrany patrol, the company commander relaxed. "I want the new lieutenant, Reider, to do everything. This is his first time out of the chute and I want to see if he can handle it."

"And if he can't? Or if the nasties show their plug-ugly little faces and decide they want to start some trouble?" Nathan interrupted.

"You're the battalion commander's insurance policy," Sergeant responded before Pierpoint could.

Looking at the major, then over at Pierpoint, and finally back, Nathan nodded. "Understood. When," Nathan asked Pierpoint, "is Lieutenant . . . ah . . ."

"His name is Reider, Gerald Reider. He's a West Pointer," Pierpoint added with pride.

"Well, sir, when and where is Lieutenant Reider going to issue his patrol order. I'd like to be there when he does."

"Oh, there's no need for that," Pierpoint pointed out. "I'll take care of that. Unless something out of the norm goes down, you're just along for the ride, Lieutenant Dixon. Nothing more." Then, as an aside, or perhaps as a warning, Pierpoint added, "I can train and handle my own platoon leaders."

Nathan felt like making another remark concerning Lieutenant Fulham's death, but deemed this neither the time nor place to do so. "Well," Nathan quipped after being put in his place, "I guess that's fair. Now," Nathan went on, winking at Sergeant, "if neither of you gentlemen has anything else for me, I've got a chess game to win here."

Across the table, Chris Donovan made a face. "Fat chance, grunt," she snorted.

"Hey, hey, young lady," Major Sergeant admonished. "Watch your language."

Changing her expression, as she was prone to do when goofing around, Donovan flashed a broad, toothy smile and batted her eyelashes. "Why, sir," she stated in the thickest southern drawl she could affect. "I wasn't referring to you, sir, as a grunt. You're an infantry officer. That," she proclaimed as she pointed at Nathan, "is a grunt!"

While the battalion operations officer let out a loud howl, and Nathan Dixon gave Donovan the single-finger salute, Captain Pierpoint turned and walked away. "Thank God," the company commander muttered to himself as he made his way through the half-deserted mess tent, "I don't have to put up with Dixon all the time." Behind him, where he still sat, Nathan entertained the exact same sentiment as he watched Pierpoint leave.

3

It was still dark when Nathan, dressed to fight the damp cold of a Central European winter day, made his way into the mess tent. Unless otherwise arranged the day before, chow was served in two waves. The first, starting at 0430 hours, was meant to accommodate those personnel whose duties required them to leave Fort Apache on various patrols, missions, or administrative runs to brigade. The second seating, commencing at 0600 hours, took care of everyone who had no need to be up and about early. Nathan had hoped to link up with Second Lieutenant Gerald Reider in the mess tent at 0430. He had planned to introduce himself to the young officer and chat a bit. It would be important, Nathan thought, to put the new platoon leader at ease and assure him that he, a battalion staff officer, had no intention of interfering with how Reider ran his unit.

Whether or not Nathan believed this himself was unimportant. What was important was his initial intent and plan of action.

But the platoon leader of Pierpoint's 3rd Platoon was long gone before Nathan started to make his way through the food line. Not that this came as any great surprise to the blurry-eyed staff officer. He knew what it was like to be the new kid on the block, meeting your platoon for the first time and taking it out on your very first operation. Even now, the memory of the anticipation he had felt that first day ran through his mind. His father had warned him that he would have to contend with butterflies in his stomach. Butterflies, hell. As Nathan remembered it, he had found himself wrestling with something more akin to a flock of ravenous vultures determined to tear away at his innards. Looking down at his tray, bulging with anemic eggs, soggy pancakes, and limp bacon, Nathan wondered if Reider was having any better luck holding down his breakfast than he had had on his debut as a platoon leader.

With these and other scattered thoughts rattling about in his mind, Nathan made his way to an empty table. It was going to be a long, hard day slogging through the snows and the mud that lay just below it. Despite the vast changes in technologies and tactics, a few immutable truths have followed those soldiers who fought on foot through the ages. One was that an infantryman needed a good breakfast if he was going to be worth a damn. While it was true that he didn't have any responsibility, other than making sure Reider didn't start World War III, Nathan knew he had to carry his own weight. So the time he was taking here was far from an indulgence. It was a necessity.

Carefully, Gerald Reider inched his way down the ramp of the 3rd Squad's Bradley. Like the others, there was mud all over it, making entering and exiting the vehicle a challenge. It wouldn't do, a voice whispered to him from the back of his mind, to slip and fall on your ass in front of your new platoon.

When he stepped off the ramp and onto what passed for solid ground, Reider looked up at the soldiers of the squad who were assembled at the rear of the vehicle awaiting his verdict. In the darkness he could not see their faces, their expressions, their eyes. He couldn't tell what they were thinking or wondering. On the flip side, the new platoon leader thought, this was a blessing, for it meant that they could not see his face or the disgusted expression that mirrored the anger he felt.

Turning slightly, Reider brought his flashlight up and shined it back into the cluttered crew compartment of Bradley C-33. The appearance of this vehicle was little different than the others. It was a disaster, nothing at all like the ones he had trained on at Fort Benning. That he had never seen an infantry fighting vehicle belonging to a real combat infantry squad deployed in the field didn't seem to figure in Reider's calculations at that moment. Even if he had, the chances were that the young officer would have still been disturbed by what he had just seen.

Standards, after all, needed to be established and maintained. This was especially true in the Army. The highly regimented and structured manner in which a military unit does anything was more than slavishly following strict codes of order and discipline for appearance's sake. A rapid and effective response in combat required that nothing is wasted, whether it be time or motion. Successfully turning to meet and deal with an unexpected situation necessitated that there be no impediments to the smooth execution of established crew and squad battle drills. Gerald Reider knew this. And until that morning, he had assumed that adherence to proper load plans and commonsense organization prevailed. Obviously, his assumption on this matter had been erroneous. After seeing the random manner in which ammo cans, personal gear, tools, boxes of rations, and items that had no place in a combat vehicle were tossed about in the vehicles of his platoon, it was clear to him that load plans, if they existed, were being ignored. Drawing himself up in an effort to appear as large as he could, he again looked at the dark figures arranged in a semicircle at the foot of the ramp. How many other things that he had taken for granted, he wondered, were going to prove just as bogus.

Standing among the soldiers of the 3rd Squad was the platoon sergeant, SFC Eddy Taylor. He had escorted his new platoon leader from vehicle to vehicle and had stood by while Reider conducted his precombat inspections. While this practice wasn't a new wrinkle to an old soldier like Taylor, it was something that had, almost without notice, gone by the wayside. It wasn't that the twenty-five men who made up the 3rd Platoon were particularly lazy or careless. Each of them was proficient and qualified in his assigned duties. To a man, they understood what was expected of them. They had, after all, been doing those duties, almost on a daily basis, for the past six months. Perhaps it was their understanding of exactly what needed to be done and how best to do it that had led to the current state of affairs.

What is and isn't important, even in a combat unit, and especially in the American Army, can be subjective. It takes a forceful commander, utilizing his chain of command effectively, to keep a unit focused on its mission and the standards that he, the commander, feels are important, not what the soldiers decide on. This doesn't have to be done on a daily basis. For an American soldier, even having an officer come down on a regular basis, especially when the soldier feels it's not needed, would become annoying. But most soldiers understand "The Game." They know that officers have officer things that they are required to do and don't hold it against them. And because the soldiers of 2nd of the 13th saw themselves as professionals, they understood that such things as combat checks, inspections of personal equipment and weapons, and occasional retraining were all necessary evils.

By any measure, Captain Pierpoint was a good company commander. His unit performed all assigned tasks efficiently and in a timely manner. His soldiers were not particularly troublesome. If anything, his company was average when it came to such things as Article 15s, courts-martial, or serious incidents. But he was not a forceful commander. Like far too many of his fellow captains with his sights on the next grade and beyond, Pierpoint was merely "doing his time" as a company commander. Of all the assignments an officer has, those in which he actively commands a unit are the most important when it comes time to be promoted. So Pierpoint was anxious to succeed in command. To do so, he felt he needed to have the cooperation of the soldiers in his company, cooperation that might not be forthcoming if he "annoyed" them too much. To this end Pierpoint established a live and let live attitude. He closed his eyes to those things that his soldiers considered to be bothersome and unnecessary. In this way, he hoped to secure their support and assistance in seeing that his command time was both successful and uneventful. That he was being rewarded with their scorn behind his back didn't matter to him, so long as the company continued to perform.

Added to this attitude was the routine nature of the operations soldiers like those in the 3rd Platoon executed day in and day out. Without notice or comment by Pierpoint, little things, such as precombat inspections, simply went away. When the company first sergeant noticed that the platoons were rolling out on mounted patrols without performing required before-operations maintenance checks or conducting precombat inspections, he took Pierpoint off to the side for a chat. On this matter, as in many others, Pierpoint merely responded with a shrug. "There's no need to be a prick about everything," he told his top ranking noncommissioned officer. "Everyone's miserable enough without me or the other officers making life here at the end of the world any more difficult than they need to be." Not wanting to be the heavy, the first sergeant said or did nothing to arrest what he considered to be a decline in standards. The company commander, after all, sets the tone and attitude of his command. The first sergeant figured, if that's the sort of company Pierpoint wanted, then by God, that was the sort of company he would get.

All this had been going on long before anyone in the company had ever heard of Gerald Reider. And Gerald Reider, dropped into this unit without any sort of introduction as to how things were done, could only rely upon what he had been taught. After seeing the state of affairs in his new platoon, and knowing that his response that morning would set the tone for the rest of his time with them, the new platoon leader came to the conclusion that he needed to make a stand, right then and there. He told himself as he stood there in the predawn cold, now's as good a time as any to get started. "Sergeant Taylor," Reider barked as he stepped forward through a hole the members of 3rd Squad made for him. "A word, please."

Knowing what that tone meant, Taylor shook his head and grunted. Without saying a word, he followed Reider until the lieutenant judged they were far enough away from squad to where he wouldn't be overheard. Quickly pivoting about on his heels in the mud, Reider immediately launched into his little tirade. "What the hell is that all about? How in the world can you, or any of the NCOs in this platoon, allow that to happen?"

Though he had expected as much, he felt the sharpness of Reider's rebuke. "Excuse me, sir?" Taylor replied, biting his tongue in an effort to hold back his true feelings.

"Those tracks are pig sties, Sergeant Taylor, not infantry fighting vehicles. That anyone in a unit that's deployed in the forward zone should permit his soldiers to exist and operate in such conditions is unimaginable."

Recovering his calm, Taylor drew in a deep breath. "Sir, you're new here. You've got to understand . . ."

"I may be new, sergeant," Reider barked, "but I'm not stupid. I do not intend to simply roll over and allow things to go on simply because that's the way the soldiers in this platoon like them or feel that's the way they should be done. We're going to do things right, Sergeant Taylor, starting now."

Again, Taylor waited until he was sure he could respond in a calm, clear manner. As he did so, he looked at his watch. When he was ready, the platoon sergeant spoke slowly, taking care to hide the anger that was welling up in him. "Obviously, sir, you are displeased with your inspection. What do you propose we do? We're expected to cross the SP in twenty minutes. Given that it will take us ten minutes to mount up and pull out of our holes, and another five to reach the SP, we don't have a lot of time."

Though his top soldier was taking care to be proper and respectful, Reider knew what was going through Taylor's mind. He'd seen and heard this sort of thing before at West Point. He was in the process of sorting out, exactly, what his options were, when 1st Lieutenant Nathan Dixon, totally unaware of what was transpiring, ambled up to the platoon leader and his platoon sergeant.

"One of your squad leaders told me I'd find you over here, Lieutenant Reider." Then, innocently, Nathan thrust his hand out to the younger officer. "Hi, I'm Lieutenant Dixon, from the battalion's S-3 shop. I'm scheduled to go along with your platoon today."

Seeing a chance to escape, Taylor snapped to attention and saluted, something that was rather uncommon those days in the battalion. Nathan, finally realizing that he had managed to blunder into something, returned Taylor's salute. Then his eyes cut over to Reider. Even in the faint predawn light, Nathan could see that the younger officer was all but biting his lip. "I just came over to introduce myself before we move out," Nathan stated hesitantly. "But if you're in the middle of something . . ."

"I'm afraid," Reider stated sharply, responding to Nathan but looking at Taylor, "that our departure has to be delayed. This platoon isn't ready for the morning's mission."

Though both men had the same thought, Nathan was quicker on the draw. *"What?"*

Ignoring Nathan's incredulous tone, and still looking at Taylor as he spoke, Reider started to explain. "The platoon isn't ready for the mission. The tracks are a shambles. It's obvious that these men, and their squad leaders, don't seem to give a shit."

This time, Nathan and Taylor exchanged looks before either spoke. Without a word having to be said, it was decided that Nathan would break the bad news to the enraged platoon leader.

"Ah, Lieutenant Reider, could I have a word with you?" Nathan stated as diplomatically as he could.

With a snap of his head, Reider turned to face Nathan. "Yes, Lieutenant Dixon?"

Nervously, Nathan shuffled his feet while glancing over at Taylor. This, he thought as he prepared to speak, was shaping up to be a long, hard day. "Sergeant Taylor, why don't you go get the platoon ready to move out while your platoon leader and I chat?"

To Taylor, Nathan's statement came as a blessing, one that he intended to collect on as quickly as possible. "Yes, sir," the veteran sergeant first class gleefully snapped before turning and fleeing into the darkness.

With that taken care of, Nathan turned to face an enraged Reider.

"Look, Lieutenant Reider," Nathan started, using as conciliatory a tone as he could manage, "it was not my intent to come barging into your platoon and tell you how to do things, but . . ."

By now, Reider had stood for all he intended to stand for. *"Good!"* he growled, ignoring the fact that he was, technically, addressing a superior officer.

All thoughts of being gentle or putting forth his views as friendly advice were abandoned as Nathan struggled to contain his growing anger. He hadn't wanted to insert himself into the middle of another officer's operation. Nor did he relish the idea of having to dissuade a fellow officer from doing something that, in truth, probably needed to be done. But there were priorities, priorities over which neither officer had any say. While Reider, as a newbie, might have gotten away with missing his departure time with a mild admonishment, Nathan knew he'd lose a good portion of his own hindquarters if he stood by and let that happen.

Drawing himself up in a manner that would signal to an ordinary soldier that hellfire and damnation were hovering in the wings, Nathan began to explain the facts of life at Fort Apache to Reider. "Look, Lieutenant, you don't have much of a choice in this matter. The SP time set for your patrol has been dictated to us by Brigade. It's based upon an overall plan of operation that's drawn up at division. While it's true that a delay by your platoon would be nothing more than a hiccup here at battalion, the failure of your platoon to sweep its area by a set time could trash the G-2's collection plan. There's a good reason you were given specific times to hit your checkpoints."

Unbowed, Reider didn't let Nathan finish. "In my opinion, my platoon is not ready for this, or any other operation. I shudder to think what would happen if we ran into something out there."

Seeing that the appeal to logic and adherence to the higher mission wasn't working, Nathan switched tactics. "Well," he stated as he put his hands on his hips, "I *know* what's going to happen if you don't make your SP."

The new platoon leader was about to meet Nathan's challenge with one of his own when a figure came up to them. "Lieutenant Reider?"

Nathan immediately recognized the impatient tone of Captain Pierpoint's voice.

"Your platoon is supposed to be rolling through the gates in five minutes," Pierpoint yelled out while he was still closing on the two lieutenants. "What are they still doing in their holes?"

Reider dutifully turned to face his commanding officer and explain. "Sir, I was about to head off and explain to you . . ."

Stopping in front of Reider, Pierpoint shouted in his new platoon leader's face. "You're not going to explain a damned thing to me, mister. What you're going to do is get off your dead ass and get your platoon moving. This company has never missed an SP in the past, and it's not about to start. Is that clear?"

While Nathan knew that Pierpoint's comment about making all its SP was hooey, Reider didn't. Stunned, the second lieutenant hesitated. Turning to Nathan for help was not an option. And though Reider knew deep down inside that *he* was right, the young officer understood that any effort to appeal to logic, at a time like this, was akin to pissing in the wind. So, as Taylor had done before, Reider snapped to attention, gave his company commander a rousing "Yes, sir," and disappeared into the darkness.

Finished with his platoon leader, Pierpoint turned on Nathan. "I asked that you go along for the express purpose of keeping that boy out of trouble."

Unlike Reider, Nathan understood the lay of the land and what he could and couldn't get away with. "As I understood it," Nathan responded calmly as he folded his arms, "it was the battalion commander who kind of insisted that I go with your 3rd Platoon today. Of course, sir, I could be mistaken."

Pierpoint hated it when he was corrected, especially by a junior officer. "Look, Dixon," the company commander countered as he waved his index finger in front of Nathan's nose, "this patrol better go off without a hitch. I expect Reider to hit every checkpoint on time and make it back here with all his vehicles running under their own power. I expect nothing less than a one hundred percent successful, no incident mission. Is that clear?"

Though Nathan didn't expect this patrol to be anything but routine, he was angered by the manner in which Pierpoint was pinning the success or failure of the mission on him. This was way out of line, and he suspected that Pierpoint knew it. Still, Nathan appreciated the fact that this was neither the time nor place to debate either issue. So, as the others had done, Nathan came to attention, brought his right hand up in a sharp, snappy salute, and gave Pierpoint his own rousing "Yes, sir."

Satisfied by this response, Pierpoint returned Nathan's salute, then hurried off himself to his own track so that he could make his SP time.

When Pierpoint had disappeared into the darkness, Nathan shook his head. A day that had started out as nothing more than a ride in the country was turning into a nightmare, a real nightmare. What was worse about it all was that they hadn't even moved out. Well, Nathan thought as he made his way over to where Reider's track was being backed out of its pit, we'll have plenty of time to sort all this out once we're on our way.

4

The lead Bradley of Reider's 3rd Platoon did cross its assigned SP on time, sort of. An SP, or start point, was a well-defined location at the beginning of a route of march. This was not where a unit actually began to roll forward. Units in enclosed areas, such as Fort Apache, often begin their journey in a confined space. This was complicated by the need for the Bradleys of 3rd Platoon to back out of their fighting positions and slowly make their way through the narrow streets of Fort Apache to the gate from which they would exit. Because there was so much going on within Fort Apache, tracked vehicles and oversize trucks had to be ground guided, or led about by a dismounted trooper. Only when they reached the front gate that opened onto the road beyond could the ground guide mount up and the vehicle proceed on its own. This resulted in a slow, somewhat spastic start. Hence the need to establish a start point, or SP, somewhere out there, beyond the fort's gate. When a unit hit its SP, it was assumed that it would be moving at the speed designated by the operations order, with each Bradley properly dispersed, and all weapons and turrets oriented to cover their assigned sectors of responsibility along the route of march.

On this particular day, in order to hit its assigned SP, Reider's lead vehicle had to move out as soon as it reached the gate, take off without waiting for the rest of the platoon's Bradleys, and barrel down the road at top speed. This fudging of normal tactical procedures, combined with a standing policy that stated an SP missed by less than five minutes didn't need to be reported, saved Reider from having to ruin Captain Pierpoint's imaginary perfect record. In reality, by the time the last of the 3rd Platoon's M-2 Bradleys trundled across the small bridge that represented their SP that day, they were some twenty-five minutes behind schedule. Nathan, riding in that vehicle, was hanging out of the open gunner's station when they did so. Looking at his watch, and then up at the strung-out vehicles ahead of him, he chuckled. Growing up in an Army family, he had heard enough of his father's "war stories" to know that this sort of thing was not at all unusual. Even he, while serving as a platoon leader at Fort Bragg, had found it necessary to personally sprint three hundred meters, burdened down by full field equipment and weapons, in order to hit an SP. No doubt, Nathan imagined, young Lieutenant Reider, riding high in the track commander's hatch of the second vehicle, was sweating despite the cold air that was pelting all exposed personnel with icy winds from the northwest.

The squad leader of the Bradley Nathan was riding in, Staff Sergeant Angel Hernandes, noticed Nathan's smirk. Keying the intercom, he joined in the humor of the moment. "Our boy is getting off to a good start."

Looking over at Hernandes, Nathan's smile broadened as he reached up with his right hand and keyed the intercom switch that sat dangling out of the bottom of the right ear flap of his crewman's helmet. "There's nothing like a good ass chewing by the old man, followed by a mad dash to the SP, to get a platoon leader's blood stirring in the morning."

Throwing his head back, Hernandes let out a howl. A veteran who had spent his eight years in the Army almost exclusively in combat units, the leader of the second squad had watched half a dozen bright-eyed and newly minted second lieutenant platoon leaders come and go. So he was able to see the humor in a situation that was, in truth, harmless. Making the whole thing funnier for Nathan and the squad leader was the fact that Reider, with so much to learn, wouldn't understand this for a long, long time. Like everything else, until he had a few months of experience under his belt, everything he and his platoon did would be, in his eyes, super critical, mission essential, and a direct reflection on him personally. Time, and escaping a few minor screwups like this one, would moderate this fatalistic view of life and allow Reider to get on with the chore of maturing into an effective combat officer.

Settling down on the gunner's seat, with only his head and upper chest exposed, Nathan prepared to enjoy the ride. With no immediate responsibilities, Nathan intended to enjoy what he considered to be a one-day vacation. That day's little sortie with the 3rd Platoon was, for the battalion staff officer, a real gift. In truth, he had no real authority. He hadn't planned the operation, given any orders relating to it, and wouldn't have much to do during it. The closest thing that came to mind as a definition of his role was a chaperone at a junior high dance, there only to make sure the kiddies didn't get out of hand. Turning, he faced Sergeant Hernandes and affected a bored expression. "Wake me up," he barked into the intercom, "if something happens."

Again, Hernandes laughed. "You planning to go to sleep for the next six months, LT?"

"I wish," Nathan shot back.

Farther up along the line of march, Gerald Reider was just beginning to sort out the jumble of thoughts and feelings that all but made his head spin. Nothing had gone as he had envisioned. The elaborate plan he had concocted to guide himself through his first day with his platoon had evaporated like a dream exposed to the harsh glare of the morning sun. That he had formulated his grand design without taking into account the reality of Fort Apache did little to mollify his bruised ego. Between the precombat inspections, and the figurative slap across the face that his company commander had given him for doing what he thought was his duty, everything had gone to hell. To be saddled with another officer, sent along to keep an eye on him, was insufferable.

Standing upright, Reider turned and looked back, along his platoon's line of march. He could see past 2nd Squad's Bradley, which was trailing his by about fifty meters, to the last vehicle in the column. Though the turret of that vehicle was oriented to the rear, keeping an eye open for any unexpected trouble from that quarter, Reider imagined that he could see through the open hatch that stood between him and First Lieutenant Dixon. What were his instructions? Reider found himself wondering. Was that battalion staff officer going to report everything that he said and did? And to whom would he report it?

Shaking his head, Reider eased back down into his seat and tried to turn his full attention back to his assigned duties. But he couldn't. It was as if Dixon were right there, hovering over him, as the instructors had done to them at Fort Benning on the live-fire ranges, observing every move and listening to every command the student officers uttered. It had been unnerving then, and the prospect of having that happen again, here, was more so. This left Reider to wonder if every new platoon leader was treated like this or if he was just lucky.

The sight of a village up ahead momentarily replaced all thoughts of Dixon and his own woeful plight. Without thinking, Reider grabbed the global positioning system he had tucked away in its pouch on his web belt and punched up the button to find out what his latest location was. After the grid coordinates flashed across the screen, Reider looked over to the map he had securely fastened before him, and plotted the coordinates. Only after he had found the spot on the map where the coordinates had taken him did Reider glance up at the terrain and countryside that his platoon was rolling through.

When he was satisfied he knew exactly where they were, he looked back down at the map and made a few quick calculations. He figured that they had a little more than seven kilometers to go before they reached Modřany. At their current rate of march, that meant they would reach their designated dismount point to the east of Modřany in about fifteen minutes, maybe a little longer. There the platoon would be split. Easing himself back onto his seat, the new platoon leader thought about that for a moment. He had not been permitted a say in how this patrol would be run. He had not been given a voice in deciding where the dismounts would marry up with the tracks. He hadn't even had an opportunity to pick which of his soldiers would go with him on the dismounted leg of the patrol, and which ones would stay with the tracks. Like everything else so far, the whole plan had been dumped on him.

And as if that weren't bad enough, Reider thought as he twisted around and looked around the open hatch, he'd been saddled with a battalion staff officer. Peering through the driving snow that was becoming noticeably heavier, he noted that he was now having trouble seeing the last vehicle in the column even though it was little more than one hundred meters away. I am sure I can deal with him, Reider thought. He's only a first lieutenant. The fact that Nathan Dixon wasn't even in Reider's chain of command would make ignoring the tag-along easier. After all, no one had told him that Dixon was in charge or even had a say in how things were done during the patrol. In fact his CO had made a point of stressing that this was his, Reider's, patrol. He doubted that Dixon's orders and instructions were any more specific than his own. If that was so, Reider reasoned, then he could safely ignore the more senior officer and any advice he might be inclined to pass on.

Cheered by this thought, the first bright spot in what had up to then been a dismal morning, actually brought a smile to Gerald Reider's face as he turned toward the front. Up ahead, he could see his lead vehicle, the 1st Squad's, as it slowed before entering the town of Dolny Peter. Despite the heavy, wet snow that was pelting him with increasing ferocity, Reider decided things were finally starting to look up.

It took more than a subtle shifting of gears and reduction in speed to stir Nathan. It was only after the Bradley lurched as the driver suddenly tapped the brakes that Nathan belatedly shook his head, blinked twice, and looked around to see what was going on. The commander of the 3rd Squad's Bradley was standing on his seat, facing to the rear of the turret that was still pointed down the road they had just traveled. Hernandes was holding on to the open hatch so that he could see over it and forward, in the direction of their movement. Placing his hand over the boom mike that hung in front of his lips, Nathan yelled out to the track commander and squad leader. "We there yet?"

Though he didn't hear the question over the growl of the Bradley's engine, Hernandes pretty much guessed what the first lieutenant was asking. "Not yet," the young man shouted back, not bothering to cover the boom mike. "We're about to go through a village." He was about to add, "You can go back to sleep," but decided not to. Though the battalion staff officer riding along with them seemed an affable type, Hernandes knew that officers were a strange breed. More than once he had seen one smile one minute, then bite off a person's head the next. So he gave them the same wide, respectful berth one would give an unfamiliar pit bull.

Still groggy, Nathan shook his head and looked around, craning his neck about to the rear until he saw the first building of the village they were entering. He didn't need to look at a map. If this wasn't Modřany, their dismount point, he thought, it had to be the one before Modřany, the one with "Peter" as part of its name. Not that it made much of a difference to Nathan where they were. Had he been "The Man," assigned even the slightest shred of responsibility, he would have been on top of the situation, able to rattle off the six-digit grid of the platoon's exact location in the blink of an eye. Easing back into his seat, Nathan shook his head in an effort to rid himself of a few tenacious snowflakes that clung to his brows and reminded himself that he was still an officer in the United States Army. That alone was more than enough justification for staying alert.

Of course, Nathan's current status as a spectator wasn't entirely to blame for his inattentiveness. In his time with the 2nd of the 13th, Nathan had found that he needed some sort of additional stimuli to stay awake when traveling in a tracked vehicle. The steady drone of the 600 horsepower Cummins diesel, coupled with the vibration that no amount of dampening could cancel out, conspired to put Nathan to sleep while part of a road-bound convoy. The M-2 Bradley Fighting Vehicle was, he had explained to Christina Donovan, the perfect Z generator, meaning that it had the ability to put him to sleep. Some found this hard to believe, especially those who needed ideal conditions, such as a bed, quiet, and darkness in order to sleep. Nathan Dixon wasn't at all like that, which he had found in his short military career to be both a boon and a curse. While with the airborne, his ability to relax and check out of the net, even when enroute to a drop zone, crunched together with dozens of other paratroopers with tons of parachutes and equipment strapped to their bodies, was admired by those who found they could not nod off no matter how hard they tried. Once on the ground, and denied any artificial means of locomotion, Nathan had no problem at all staying awake. So in the beginning, this knack of dropping off into a deep sleep was not an issue.

This all changed when Nathan was reassigned to 2nd of the 13th, an infantry unit that was trained to fight both mounted and dismounted. The commander of his new battalion had some very definite ideas when it came to track commanders, especially when they were officers, sleeping while their vehicles were in motion. "An officer," he told Nathan during his first interview on reporting, "is always on duty. When we're in the field, I expect him to be on top of things, twenty-four hours a day, seven days a week. Period." That Nathan was, at best, a third-rung staff officer commanding little more than a chair and a two-by-two-foot desktop didn't matter. His oath of office was no different than any other officer's, and his duty as an example to soldiers junior to him in rank no less demanding.

With Hernandes watching to the front, ready to assist the driver if necessary as they navigated their way through the narrow streets of Dolny Peter, Nathan looked at the buildings and what few people who were out and about. Most of the pedestrians, more concerned with keeping their footing as they made their way along the slick sidewalks, paid the Bradleys no heed. Only one woman, clutching a wool scarf tightly under her chin in order to keep it around her head in the wind that whipped by, bothered to look up.

For a second, Nathan and the Slovakian woman locked eyes. Though no words passed between them, the expression on her face spoke volumes. She hates us, Nathan told himself. She hates seeing us here, roaming through her village with the swagger of a conqueror, imposing upon her and her people a political solution without the slightest regard for what they believed in or wanted. Like so many other members of the NATO force deployed to Slovakia as a result of the Munich Accords, Nathan had expected to be greeted with joy and relief. They were, after all, there to keep a handful of radicals from forcing their will on a troubled land.

Not everyone shared that dream. A man who stood on a corner, preaching radical ideas that no one listened to, was called a fool. But the moment someone stopped, listened, and then shook his head in agreement, a magical transformation took place. Instead of being a fool, the orator became an oracle. If more people stopped, and joined to listen to the words that their friend seemed to be in agreement with, they too were exposed to the thoughts and ideas of the new oracle. If the speaker was skilled enough in his art, and his argument crafted so as to resonate with the masses growing about him, the former fool could easily move on and become the leader of a cause, his cause. After that, if the people around him were still there, shaking their heads in agreement, it took but a word from the self-appointed leader to transform ideas into action.

As the Bradley carried Nathan along, and the woman who had been staring at him finally looked back down at the sidewalk before her, Nathan kept watching her until she disappeared around a corner. All the while, the young American wondered if she and her neighbors had been overcome by the seductive songs of fools.

*   *   *

The seduction to which Gerald Reider was succumbing at that moment was one of power. Perched high in the open hatch of his Bradley, Reider looked down at the faces of those Slovakians who took the time to stop and gaze at the foreign intruders. For the first time in his life, he was experiencing the rush that someone in command of a modern combat vehicle feels when ordinary folk cast their eyes on a weapon of war as awe inspiring as a Bradley Fighting Vehicle. While professional soldiers and politicians who fancy themselves experts in such matters can debate the merits of the M-2 Bradley, anyone who has stood close to one as it rumbled by cannot help but be impressed by the menacing potential that the M-2 represents.

Weighing 33 tons, combat loaded, the M-2 is powered by a 600 horsepower Cummins diesel engine. That gives it a power-to-weight ratio of a little over eighteen horsepower per ton. This allows the vehicle, measuring 11.8 by 21.5 feet, to move out at an impressive forty miles an hour on the road, and up to thirty miles an hour cross-country. It's also more than enough to shake the ground it's traveling over, sending out tremors that alert those on foot that something big is coming.

If physical size and mechanical performance didn't impress the villagers who were watching, then the combat potential of the Bradley should have. Its middle name, after all, was "Fighting." The most noticeable, and ominous, to a casual observer is the barrel of the M242 25mm chain gun. Though not as lethal, round for round, as the 120mm main gun mounted on the M-1A2 Abrams, the M242 Bushmaster can penetrate up to one and one point three inches of armor, angled on a sixty degree slant, at a range of one kilometer with its armor-piercing round. When firing, the Bushmaster has a rate of fire that ranges from 100 rounds per minute up to 500. That, alone, would be more than enough to cause anyone on the receiving end to take notice.

But there was more. Mounted to the right of the

25mm gun was an M240C 7.62mm coaxial machine gun. With a maximum effective range of 900 meters, this machine gun was meant to deal with any "small" threats, such as enemy infantry in the open, that the track commander didn't want to waste his precious 25mm ammunition on. As impressive as both these turret-mounted guns are, it was the rectangular armored box, hanging precariously on the left side of the turret, that packed the Bradley's main punch. In that box, which had to be raised into firing position in order to be used, were two BGM-7 TOW II missiles. Armed with a chemical energy warhead, popularly known as HEAT for high-explosive, anti-tank, these missiles were capable of taking on and dispatching the most sophisticated tanks in the world at ranges exceeding 3,700 meters, or well over two miles.

What was not self-evident to Reider was the simple fact that these weapons, as fearsome as they might be, were of little value to him. Had they been in the Gulf, the TOW missiles and the Bushmaster would have been the weapons of choice. The matter of where and how he deployed his four Bradleys, so that they could bring all their weapons to bear on the enemy, would have demanded much thought and careful consideration.

As wonderful as all this sort of thing was to technocrats who measured military might by the caliber and sophistication of the weaponry employed, the very lethality of the Bradley made it ineffective for the mission that Reider's platoon was on. There would be no tanks equipped with computer-driven fire-control systems that needed to be dealt with in or around Modřany. That day no one expected Reider's platoon to come across targets protected with 1.3 inches of rolled homogeneous armor plate slanted at a sixty-degree angle. Even if a member of one of the parties involved in the dispute was to defy logic and orders to the contrary and take a potshot at one of Reider's Bradleys, Reider or the commanders of his other Bradleys could not simply flick the safety off of their main gun and cut loose in response. They were bound by rules of engagement that required "measured and proportional response." The soldiers in his platoon had the right to defend themselves, but they could do so only, literally, round for round and in a manner that did not endanger the lives or property of innocent civilians.

One of those "innocent civilians," the owner of a butcher shop, stood in the open doorway of his business. This simple man understood matters far better than the platoon leader he was looking up at. As annoying as Reider's infantry fighting vehicles were, the butcher knew they were, for the moment, benign behemoths. While the people of Dolny Peter would have to do with a few less dishes that night due to breakage caused by the vibrations that shook structures built in another century, no one would suffer because of them. They would go away, the butcher thought, as they always did, headed off in this direction or that, seeking signs of trouble he knew they would never find.

After the last Bradley had passed his door, the butcher looked down the street in the direction they had come from and checked to see if any more were following. When he was satisfied that the four Bradleys he had counted were all there were, he wiped his hands on his bloody apron, and stepped back into the shop, closing the door behind him. As he made his way back behind the counter, the butcher took note of the time. He would need to include that bit of information, he reminded himself, when he phoned in his report to the commander of his militia unit. That man, the butcher thought, was insufferable. He hadn't quite gotten it through his thick Hungarian skull that the people he commanded were mostly kids and middle-aged men, such as the butcher himself, who had real jobs and families that demanded attention. "Professional soldiers," the butcher muttered to his assistant as he picked up the phone and dialed the number he had long ago committed to memory. "They're all a fucking pain in the ass, American and Hungarian alike."

The young man, who was of ethnic Hungarian stock, like the butcher, and a member of the same unit the butcher belonged to, stopped what he was doing. "But the Hungarian officers are here to help us. They are putting their lives at risk for our benefit."

As he listened to the phone ring and waited for someone to answer, the butcher placed his hand over the receiver. "The only thing those arseholes from across the Danube want to do is replace the Slovakian flag that flies in the town square with a Hungarian one."

"If you feel that way," the annoyed assistant asked, "why do you participate?"

Before he could answer, a cautious male voice answered the phone with a simple "Yes?"

The butcher removed his hand from the receiver for a second. "This is Janos, just a second." Then he placed his hand back over the receiver and faced his assistant. "All my life I butchered animals that have been too dumb to do anything but follow wherever the herdsman led them. I am not about to crawl up on my own table and let some bastard slit my throat whenever he has an appetite for fresh blood. I intend to fight back."

For a second, the boy looked at the butcher, who had already turned his back on his young assistant and begun to relay the information to the Hungarian captain on the other end of the line. "I suppose he has a point," the young man stated softly to the carcass he was working on. "I don't think I'd like to be in your place, not at all." With that, the lad lifted his right hand as high as he could over the bloody side of meat before bringing the cleaver it held down with all his might.

5

EAST OF MODŘANY
LATE MORNING, FEBRUARY 5

There was no great rush on the part of Gerald Reider's men to get on with the patrol once they reached the designated dismount point. There was nothing especially noteworthy at that location. It was a snow-covered farm field, no different than any of the many they had rumbled past that morning. The only reason that this particular patch of Slovakian earth was chosen over others was that it just happened to lie exactly one kilometer outside town. A small stand of trees blocked the line of sight from the village on one side, while a piece of dominant terrain lay on the other. It was a common practice to place dismount points far enough away from locations such as villages and such so that any yutz with a rifle and a mind to cause an international incident wouldn't be afforded a good hiding place to do it from. "If they're going to start something," the battalion S-3 explained to Nathan Dixon, "they're going to have to go out of their way to do it."

Like a line of ducks the Bradleys of 3rd Platoon followed the lead track as it made its way off the road and into the field. In the past, NATO troops had taken great pains to protect private property and limit the impact their operations had on the local populace. Had this been October of the previous year, a trooper in the lead Bradley would have dismounted, run to the front of the vehicle, and opened the gate that led from the road into the field that was to serve as the platoon's dismount point. Months of endless patrols and increasing hostility heaped upon the peacekeeping force, however, had numbed the soldiers of the 2nd of the 13th to such niceties. As it was, Staff Sergeant Kenny Slavobeck, commanding the lead track, thought he was a nice guy. Rather than simply plow into the gate and shatter it, Slavobeck ordered his driver to ease the nose of his track up against the gate leading to the field until the force of the Bradley popped the chain and caused the gate to fly open.

Once in the field the platoon executed standard battle drill. Slavobeck's lead Bradley continued to move forward in the direction in which it was pointed for about fifty meters before stopping. Reider, in the second track, followed Slavobeck's track into the field, but then cut sharply to the right after moving some twenty meters into the field. The 2nd Squad's track, behind Reider's, cut to the left at the same point where Reider's Bradley had made its turn, advanced a little farther on, and stopped. The last Bradley in the small column didn't advance into the field at all. Instead, as soon as it cleared the gate, Staff Sergeant Hernandes ordered the driver to stop and neutral steer. In this maneuver, the tracks of the Bradley spin in opposite directions, rotating the vehicle in place. When the nose of the Bradley was pointed in the direction from which they had just come, Hernandes ordered the driver to stop and shut the track down. The maneuver completed the circle of tracks, creating what is known as a laager.

Before dropping down into the turret, Hernandes looked about the snow-covered field, then turned his face up toward the gray sky. Squinting as the heavy, wet snowflakes pelted his face, the gunner shook his head. "Ordinarily I'd say let's get this show on the road." Then, he tilted his head down, shook the snowflakes off his brows, and looked Nathan in the eye, flashing a broad smile as he did so. "But today, even though my feet will be following our glorious leader, my heart will be here, in my nice, toasty warm Bradley Fighting Barn."

Nathan nodded. "Well, if it's any consolation to you, you're not the only one thinking along those lines."

Hernandes laughed. "And here I thought I was the only wimp in this platoon."

"Not by a long shot," Nathan replied. With that, the battalion staff officer pulled off his combat vehicle crewman's helmet, ducked down into the turret, and followed the leader of 3rd Squad through the small passage into the rear compartment, where the rest of the squad was starting to stir.

The mood was a bit different on the platoon leader's track. Eager to get on the ground and get started, Gerald Reider slipped down out of his position in the turret of his Bradley, grabbing his rifle and helmet as he stepped over the troopers who were still seated in the rear squad compartment. The rear ramp, which Reider had ordered the driver to drop before he had pulled his CVC helmet off, hit the ground with a thump just as Reider stepped onto it.

This was it, a voice in the back of his mind whispered as he made his way down the ramp in two quick hops. He was finally there, literally on the ground, ready and impatient to lead his platoon. It was only after he had moved into the center of the circle formed by the Bradleys of his platoon that he discovered that he was, at least for the moment, the only person on the ground. In his haste and excitement he hadn't taken note that the soldiers in the rear of his own track had been somewhat less than energetic. In fact, when he looked behind, into his own vehicle, Reider was taken aback when he saw that they were still there, pulling gear on, making adjustments to equipment, or checking the function of their weapons.

Pivoting about, he faced the men who made up his command section: a radioman, a Javelin antitank guided missile team, and a medic. "Come on, people. Let's get a move on," the young platoon leader shouted. "We haven't got all day." Only the radioman paused and looked up, as if to ask, Who? Me? Of course he didn't actually say that. He knew better. Reider was the second new platoon leader under whom the twenty-one-year-old radioman had served. That experience, together with the age-old second lieutenant jokes that were passed down from one generation of American soldier to the next, told the radioman that his platoon leader was serious, as serious as a heart attack. It would take time, he knew, for this hard-charging West Pointer to mellow out. Most of them did, after a while. And those that didn't, well, they were tolerated. One of the beautiful aspects of the Army was that sooner or later, everyone moved on.

From his track, Sergeant First Class Eddy Taylor watched his platoon leader. "Okay, folks," Taylor yelled down to the dismounts of the 2nd Squad that were in the rear of his track. "Let's get a move on. The LT is waiting."

"Oh, my. We're keeping the new platoon leader waiting," one of the more outspoken soldiers in the squad muttered as he rummaged around, searching for his parka. "We mustn't disappoint our new platoon leader."

Dropping down, Taylor peered into the rear of the vehicle at Specialist Four Keith Reisniack, the soldier who had been mouthing off. "Reisniack, how about shutting up and funneling that energy down your butt. The LT's doing his job, and it's about time that you start doing yours."

After picking up his 5.56mm squad automatic weapon, popularly known as a SAW, Reisniack gave Taylor a dirty look, but said nothing. It was one thing to mouth off to no one in particular; tangling with the platoon's top dog was quite another. "Okay, Sergeant Taylor," Reisniack replied as he prepared to follow his squadmates out the rear door. "I is movin', boss. I is movin'."

After the dismounts had filed out the small rear access door, Taylor crawled into the rear compartment, grabbed his Kevlar helmet, which he stored there, and plopped it on his head. Climbing over seats, gear, and ammo boxes, he struggled to squeeze his bulk, made wider by layers of cold weather gear, ammo pouches, and other such equipment, through the narrow opening in the rear ramp.

Despite the snow that was rapidly piling up, it felt good to Taylor to be out of the Bradley. At heart, Taylor was an infantryman. All the headaches, the long hours, the extended field duty, and aches and pains that multiplied with each passing year did little to dull the pride he felt in being one of the U.S. Army's forty thousand plus grunts. In an Army that numbered just under half a million, combat infantrymen made up less than 10 percent of the total. Within that total were all officers, whether or not they were in combat units, NCOs assigned to training or recruiting commands, and other such assignments that take them away from the fold. Yet, of all the branches within the Army, and there were quite a few, only the infantry had the ability to seize and hold terrain. Only men like Sergeant First Class Taylor and the men who belonged to him could pile into a trench and engage in hand-to-hand combat with a foe one day, and move on and clear a city, room by bloody room, the next. That the Army needed such men was all too often forgotten by a culture enamored with smart bombs launched from aircraft cloaked by stealth technology and nuclear-tipped missiles that could range the world. Such sentiment only served to enhance the allure that men like Taylor found in his duties and his skills. "Just remember," he always told his platoon. "We've got real job security, 'cause whenever the going gets tough, they always send in the poor, bloody infantry."

This was what it was all about, he told himself as he made his way to where his platoon leader was waiting. Doing jobs that no one else wanted, that no one else could do. Glancing to his left and right, Taylor made sure the squad leaders were getting their men out, onto the ground, deployed to either side of their track, and facing out into the vacant, snow-filled fields. "Squad leaders," he bellowed. "Let's spread those people out. Then fall in on me and the lieutenant. Pronto!"

Though he didn't know Reider yet, Taylor could tell by his new platoon leader's expression and posture that the lad was not happy. "Is this what passes for battle drill in this platoon?" Reider asked in a tone that confirmed Taylor's suspicions.

Taylor's shoulders drooped, as if someone had thrown a brick into his rucksack. "Here we go," Taylor muttered to himself as he continued to close the distance that still separated them.

With a sweeping gesture of his arm, Reider continued. "After taking their own sweet time climbing out of their tracks, the dismounts go wandering about the fields like so many cows looking for grass. And on top of that," Reider added as he pointed at a cluster of men standing in the lee of the 2nd Squad's track, "not a one of them has bothered to take up a decent fighting position."

Stopping, Taylor threw his arms out in frustration. "Sir, we're in the middle of an open field. There isn't anything resembling a fighting position around."

"They could at least drop down into the prone," Reider countered. "They do remember how to do that, don't they?"

Deciding that there was no point in pursuing this, Taylor gave up. "No sir. They have not forgotten how to do that. When we get back, I'll take care of that, as well as the load plan of the tracks."

"You bet you'll take care of it," Reider snapped. "You'll take care of it right this minute. Is that clear?"

For a moment Taylor stood before his platoon leader and stared at him. "What exactly, sir, do you want me to square away out here? The deployment of the squads, or the load plans?" he asked innocently.

Reider almost jumped up when he responded. "The deployment, sergeant! I want to get those men on the ground and acting like soldiers."

Out of the corner of his eye, Taylor saw the battalion staff officer standing in the field, watching and waiting, just out of earshot. Deciding that this was neither the time nor the place to engage his platoon leader in a "facts of life in the real world" discussion, Taylor gave Reider a halfhearted salute. "Yes, sir." With that he turned and walked to the three squad leaders who had come together but were wise enough to keep their distance. Like Taylor, they were fluent in body language.

Patiently, Nathan Dixon waited and watched as Reider and Taylor engaged in their one-sided discussion. The relationship between a platoon leader and his platoon sergeant is a very special one. There is nothing like it in the Army. It is a marriage between two people who not only come from different worlds, but who are destined to follow career paths that are equally foreign to each other. On the one hand, you have a young man, normally someone who is fired up with enthusiasm and ambition, ready and willing to take on the world, yet lacking any real experience. In theory, he has the potential to become the Chief of Staff of the Army, per-

haps even the Chairman of the Joint Chiefs. Yet even if
he does not reach that pinnacle, every assignment after
this one, his very first, will take him further and further
away from the soldiers who actually close with the enemy.

The other member of this odd couple is a soldier who
has spent his entire military career, usually ten to fifteen
years by the time he makes sergeant first class, dealing
with soldiers. With few exceptions, he has never been
more than a stone's throw away from the type of unit in
which he is currently the senior noncommissioned officer. He has occupied every position within that platoon,
including serving as platoon leader when no officers
were assigned. He has fired every weapon carried by the
members of his platoon. And more often than not, he
has personally experienced, at least once, just about
every sort of operation, mission, task, assignment, and
duty that a line platoon can be assigned. In short, even
if he's an average platoon sergeant, he has everything at
his fingertips that the platoon leader needs if that officer is to succeed there, and later on in his career. This
includes the respect of the soldiers in that platoon.

As Nathan watched, he thought about this. By the
time Taylor finally turned and walked away, Nathan
knew that the relationship between new blood and old
hand was going to be strained. Whether it would eventually mature into an effective one remained to be seen.

When he was sure that sufficient time had passed to
permit Reider to calm himself, Nathan advanced. He
already suspected, based on their brief encounter just
before moving out, that one, Reider was displeased with
Nathan's presence, and two, Reider imagined that since
the word *lieutenant* was used to describe their rank, they
were both equal. Though Nathan had no intention of
inserting himself into the affairs of the platoon, so long
as things stayed within bounds, he definitely wanted to
make sure that Reider understood which of them was
Tarzan and which was Jane. Using a trick he had seen

used by his superiors, Nathan snapped a crisp hand salute as he approached Reider. "I am sorry that we did
not have an opportunity to meet before we pulled pitch
this morning, lieutenant," Nathan boomed, "but we seldom have the time or opportunity to do everything in
the way the folks at the Infantry School would like."

Still angered by the half-assed and unprofessional
manner in which his platoon had deployed, Reider
waved the hand holding his M-16 at a group of dismounts who had still not taken up positions. "Does that
include taking your time to climb off tracks through the
ramp door instead of dropping the ramp, and then
standing around like a bunch of high school students
cruising the local mall?"

Nathan hesitated before responding. He looked
around, thinking about what he had seen and about
where this young platoon leader's mind was. It had
been, Nathan admitted to himself, a shitty deployment.
While the movement of the tracks into the field and
laager had been executed smartly, everything else after
that had been, by any measure, done badly. It mattered
little that there was, at that moment, no apparent threat
to them. Nor did it that the sheer wear and tear of day
in, day out operations had, over the long months in Slovakia, worn away the keen edge that had once been a
given in the 2nd of the 13th Infantry. Even so, Nathan
believed that the soldiers of the 3rd Platoon were being
too casual and lax in their ways.

Looking at Reider, the battalion staff officer nodded.
"There is, no doubt, room for improvement."

Like every second lieutenant of Infantry fresh from
the Fort Benning Infantry Officer's Basic Course, Gerald
Reider knew who Nathan Dixon was and what he had
done in Idaho during the crisis there. Expecting more
of a reaction to his platoon's pitiful performance, Reider
was somewhat taken aback by the casual manner in
which Nathan shrugged it off.

After a few very awkward seconds ticked by without a

word being exchanged, Nathan made a show of looking at his watch, then sweeping the area with his eyes, as if he were visually inspecting the activities of Reider's soldiers. "Well, I imagine I have a few minutes before the dismounted element forms up and moves out. I'm going to head back to the track I rode out here in, fetch my rucksack, and get myself ready. I wouldn't want to be the cause of a delay in your departure."

Taking Nathan's cue, Reider looked down at his watch, then over to Sergeant Taylor. His platoon sergeant was walking and talking to one of the squad leaders as they went from man to man, showing the dismounts belonging to that squad leader where to position themselves. Turning back to face Nathan, Reider swallowed and nodded. "Well, yes. I expect we'll be mounting up and moving out in another five minutes, ten at the most."

Nathan mustered a smile. "Good. I'll be over with the squad I rode out here with and I'll tag along with them when we move out. So don't worry about me."

The first thought that popped into Reider's mind was, Worry about you? Fat chance. Of course, like Nathan, Reider effected the appropriate expression, returned Nathan's crisp salute, and went about getting his platoon in hand and ready to move as the bothersome battalion staff officer wandered off.

6

From the corner of the field where they had dismounted, Gerald Reider watched Sergeant First
Class Taylor lead the four Bradleys out of the field
and back onto the road. On each of the Bradleys there
was now only the driver, the gunner, and a trooper serving as the track commander. Taylor, with Staff Sergeant
Kenny Slavobeck as his second in command, would conduct a mounted patrol along the roads while Reider,
with four dismounts from each squad and his small platoon headquarters section, would march north, through
the snow-covered hills. The two elements, after making
their appointed rounds, would marry up in another vacant field one kilometer south of the village of Pribeta.
Though the straight-line distance between there and
where Reider and the dismounts now stood was a bit

less than ten kilometers, it would be five hours before that link-up took place.

Reider was not at all sorry to see the Bradleys disappear into the swirling snow. In fact, the more he thought about it, the better he liked the idea that he was left with only a handful of dismounts and a long walk through the countryside. For the first time since departing the States, Reider felt as if he was in control. The trip out to this field, at a prescribed rate of march, along a designated route, and mounted in the second Bradley in the column, had demanded little from Reider. Like the soldiers who rode in the squad compartment down below, the young officer had been little more than a passenger.

Now, everything was different. Whatever happened from this point on, until they linked up with the Bradleys, hinged on him and his skills in exercising what the Army referred to as command and control. He would determine the order of march and give the word to move out. He would control his platoon by personal example, voice commands, and hand and arm signals. Everyone would move at the pace that he set along a route that he selected. This, Reider told himself as he turned to face his waiting soldiers, was what he had signed up for. This was where the rubber met the road.

That he would excel here, as he had done at West Point, was without question. Even the sight of Nathan Dixon, leaning against a post along the fence line, could not dampen Reider's growing excitement. They had come, he believed, to an understanding. The staff officer himself had admitted that he was just along for the ride. So long as Nathan Dixon kept out of his way and made no effort to inflict his opinion upon him, Reider felt he could live with the excess baggage he'd been saddled with.

*   *   *

Dealing with the men under his command was going to be different. There are two schools of thought concerning how a newly assigned second lieutenant should go about assuming his duties and responsibilities. One operates under the assumption that the young officer, even though he has completed the formal military education required to get him to the field, still has much to learn. Those who follow this philosophy view the platoon's noncommissioned officers as the people best qualified to finish the platoon leader's education. To accomplish this requires a cooperative effort, one that depends heavily upon mutual respect and, at times, an open and liberal dialogue between officer and NCO. The platoon leader must do more than trust his sergeants. He must be willing to actively seek their advice and opinion. For their part, the NCOs, particularly the platoon sergeant, need to take the new officer under their wing. Like mother birds, they guide and protect this hatchling until he's strong enough to take to wing on his own.

In contrast to this is the "take charge" school of military leadership. In the days before the Army discovered political correctness, officers who subscribed to this manner of doing business were referred to as "dictatorial." That term, unfortunately, sounds harsher than it actually is. George S. Patton could be listed as an adherent of this school of leadership. It is, in truth, the traditional approach to military leadership, one that is reinforced by the ease with which the males of our species dominate others.

In a nutshell, those who advocate taking charge emphasize that an officer simply step up to the front of his platoon and take on all aspects of commanding the platoon from day one. This "damn the torpedoes, full speed ahead" attitude has its advantages. Military units, after all, are not democratic institutions. Soldiers are expected to follow orders, often without question, and often in situations in which logic tells them that doing so can result in grievous bodily damage, or worse. If soldiers were given a say-so, precious few would have stormed Omaha Beach in June of '44, or stood by their regimental colors on Little Round Top as wave after wave of Rebels surged toward them. It is a cold, almost indisputable fact that the more difficult the situation, the more success in combat is determined by strong, confident leaders who are willing to give the necessary orders and, when necessary, personally set the example.

Which line of thinking an officer follows is pretty much determined by an officer's personality and experience. Like his classmates at West Point, Gerald Reider had experimented with different leadership styles and techniques. That is, after all, one of West Point's primary functions. It is a place where leadership is not only taught, but a setting in which aspiring leaders are provided an opportunity to practice those skills. By the time West Pointers shed cadet gray in exchange for Army green, most have settled on the style of leadership that they will, at least initially, use.

During his tenure as a cadet, Gerald Reider had discovered how much easier it was to achieve an end by giving orders rather than seeking consensus. Though he had dabbled with using more cooperative techniques, Reider found that he had neither the talent nor the patience to be a persuasive leader. As he explained to a fellow classmate, "If it is true that the shortest distance between two points is a straight line, then it must be equally true that the quickest way to get something done is to put someone who knows what he's doing in charge and let him have at it." To have sought the advice of his sergeants on how best to go about running this patrol would have been out of character. And if there is one thing that American soldiers resent more than bad chow, it is insincerity in their officers. Even the biggest bastard is preferred over a liar, provided that bastard knows what he's doing.

*   *   *

With the tracks gone, Reider turned to deal with the rump of a platoon that was gathered around him. Not counting himself or Nathan Dixon, Reider had fifteen troopers to work with. Each of the dismount sections, led by the squad leader in the case of 2nd and 3rd Squads, and the assistant squad leader for the 1st Squad, totaled four men. They were all armed pretty much the same. The squad leader had his M-16A2. The automatic weapon gunner toted an M249 5.56mm Squad Automatic Weapon, or SAW. The other two men carried an M-16A2 or an M203, which is an M-16 with a 40mm grenade launcher attached under its rifle barrel.

By way of augmentation of these standard weapons, Reider's platoon had been issued several sets of the Land Warrior automation system. The Land Warrior system is part of the United States Army's automation and force modernization effort, a step in transforming the American combat infantrymen from John Wayne into Buck Rogers. At the heart of it is a man-portable computer that is carried on the back of the individual soldier. Linked to this computer is an integrated sight mounted on the soldier's weapons, combining thermal imaging and laser range finding. The images and information gathered by this combination sight is passed to the computer, which, in turn, processes the raw data and sends it out to a heads-up digital display attached to the soldier's helmet. This not only gives the individual soldier an enhanced ability to see targets that would otherwise have escaped unaided visual detection, but it allows him to engage those threats with the same computer-aided pinpoint accuracy his brethren in the M-1 series tank had enjoyed for years.

Like all systems, this one was not without its disadvantages. To start with, unlike the tanker, the combat infantrymen had to carry every bit of the Land Warrior, including the weapon to which it was attached, either in his hands, on his back, or strapped to his helmet. Though each element, individually, was both compact and lightweight, the aggregate of the entire lash-up, combined with the normal combat load an infantryman carries, tended to be taxing. Since the time of ancient Rome, it has been a known fact that a combat soldier can carry a load equal to one third of his own body weight, for any length of time, and still maintain his ability to fight after he gets to where he's headed. It is therefore a given that the more you add to a soldier's load, the less combat capable he becomes. This presents the lucky few who are blessed with the Land Warrior system with some hard decisions. They must either discard other items, such as rations, extra water, body armor, or additional ammunition, or accept the fact that they will, eventually, buckle under the weight of their own load.

Within Reider's platoon, only the members of 2nd Squad were qualified on the system. This came about not because the soldiers in that squad were more technically proficient or bigger, but rather because their squad leader had less time in grade than the squad leader in the 1st Squad. When the word came out that one squad would be issued the Land Warrior, Staff Sergeant Slavobeck was wise enough to make it known that he didn't want any part of it. Understanding what taking the Land Warrior would mean, Slavobeck made sure Taylor knew how he felt about the Army's newest wonder weapon. "Let someone else sign for that shit and hump it from here to kingdom come."

This decision, on Sergeant Slavobeck's part, also had the effect of ensuring that his squad would never be the point, or lead squad when dismounted. Because the Warrior enhanced a soldier's acquisition and targeting abilities, it was a given that the squad equipped with it would be the point element. Staff Sergeant Dick Kittridge, who jokingly referred to himself as the number one for the number twos, led that squad.

At twenty-seven, Kittridge pretty much epitomized the professional NCO who was with the colors when the

United States Army stumbled into the twenty-first century. With the exception that he was serving as part of an expeditionary force whose mission had little to do with the actual defense of the United States of America, Kittridge had little in common with his counterpart who had led young American infantrymen across China, or through the jungles of the Philippines one hundred years before. Married, the father of two, Dick Kittridge had an education that included courses that, collectively, amounted to two years of college. But those courses weren't leading to anything specific. They had been endured for no other reason than to satisfy promotion requirements. Educated leaders, the party line went, make better leaders. And though Kittridge could rattle off the names of both officers and fellow NCOs where this truism fell flat on its face, he did what he needed to do to stay competitive.

Education aside, Kittridge more than met the marks set for being a squad leader. At six foot one, and one ninety-five pounds, the brown-eyed, sandy-haired sergeant had both the stature and the bearing that set him apart in a crowd. Born and raised in western Nebraska, Kittridge had played high school football. Though his skills as a linebacker were enough to ensure that his team always had a winning season, they weren't good enough to earn him a scholarship. Besides, the tall Nebraskan had, by his senior year, had enough of formal education. He was like many of his classmates, young men who had no clear idea of what, exactly, they wanted to do with the rest of their lives. The only things that were certain were that college was not for him and that whatever he did, he'd do it someplace other than Nebraska.

Soft-spoken, Kittridge seldom gave orders that sounded like orders. Instead, he used phrases like, "Well, how's 'bout we do this," or "What do you say we get this over with," to get the soldiers in his squad moving. Even under the most adverse, or harried conditions, Kittridge's voice seldom rose above his normal conversational tone. While this tended to make him appear lackadaisical when drilling a squad on the parade ground, both his superiors and subordinates appreciated his calm demeanor in a crisis.

Catching Kittridge's attention by waving his hand while staring at him, Gerald Reider gave the order to move out. With a nod, Kittridge acknowledged the order before turning to face the other three men in his diminutive squad. "Well, it's that time of day," he declared as he brought his own weapon up to the ready. "Let's switch 'em on and move out." "Switching 'em on" referred to activating the Land Warrior systems three of them carried. As with all computers, it took several seconds for the system to boot up and for the displays to focus. While this was happening, the soldier carrying the system brought his weapon up to a comfortable carry position and adjusted the small monitor that hung down in front of his right eye. Because the Warrior added weight to the soldier's weapon and needed to be stabilized, all of Kittridge's men so equipped had rigged their weapons slings in a manner that allowed them to support the weight of the combination weapon and sight on their shoulder. This took all stress and strain off the forearm and wrist as well as making for a steadier picture in the display.

After making sure that his unit was fully functional, Kittridge looked up and waited until his men signaled that they, too, were ready. With a motion of his left hand, Kittridge pointed in the direction in which they would move up and watched as first the rifleman, and then the SAW gunner climbed over the fence and took off across the adjoining field. When there was a separation of five meters, Kittridge looked behind at his last man to make sure he was ready, then followed. Of the four, only this last trooper, armed with the M-203 combination rifle and grenade launcher, was without a Warrior. The older NCOs had come to the conclusion that it was best to have at least one member of a Warrior-equipped squad go without. As with most gee-whiz technical devices, especially those that include monitors such as the ones that come with the Warrior, it was all too easy to concentrate solely on the Warrior's monitor and lose one's peripheral vision. By having one man unburdened by any whiz-bang high-tech gizmos hang back, it was generally believed that a Warrior-equipped squad could keep itself from being blindsided by a threat that was out there, in plain sight, but not quite right in front of them. A second reason was far more practical and dear to the heart of the sergeants who were accountable for the costly devices. If, in the course of a patrol, a man found he could not hold up under the additional load, the squad leader could rotate the Warrior to the unburdened trooper, giving the first man a break without having to go outside his own squad for assistance. Unit pride, after all, has to exist at all levels if it is to exist at all.

When Sergeant Kittridge and his three men moved into the next field, Reider turned to the 1st Squad's assistant squad leader, Sergeant Dubois. "Sergeant," Reider announced in an artificially deep voice that betrayed its pretentiousness, "move 'em out."

Specialist Four Henry Smith, the SAW gunner, had been squatting down next to Dubois when Reider gave his order. Using his weapon as a support while he stood, Smith leaned over once he was on his feet and whispered in his sergeant's ear. "Five bucks says he hasn't got the faintest idea what your name is."

Dubois glanced over at Smith and glared at him for a moment, but said nothing. Instead, the sergeant let his rifle sling slide down his arm. Just when it seemed that the weapon's butt plate was about to hit the ground, he snatched its upper handguard with his right hand and brought it across his chest to the position of port arms. Using the same motions that had become second nature during his tour with the Old Guard at Arlington, Dubois brought his weapon to the ready. "Okay, 1st Squad," the lean, African-American NCO stated without any undue ceremony or emphasis. "Move out."

With the squad leader of the 1st Squad, Staff Sergeant Slavobeck, accompanying the platoon sergeant as part of the mounted patrol, command of the 1st Squad's dismount fell to Sergeant Dubois. Like Kittridge of the 2nd Squad, Dubois preferred it this way. It was a break away from the rattle and roar that numbed one's mind and left those confined in the Bradleys rear squad compartment disoriented and claustrophobic. Nor did Robert Dubois miss Fort Apache. To him, the crowded and chaotic confines of that small base camp, where everything waist level and below was stained a dull mud color, was too much like the Chicago where he had spent his youth. This dismounted patrol, like his tour with the Old Guard, was an opportunity to escape a world in which grime and indifference to their fellow human beings blanketed the people who lived there with the same indiscriminate brushstroke.

With his two riflemen in front of him, and Smith, the SAW gunner, beside him, Dubois crossed the fence at the same place the 2nd Squad had. "Keep your distance from 2nd Squad," Reider shouted out to Dubois, "and don't let your people bunch up."

Without pausing, Dubois shouted over his shoulder. "Yes, sir."

Next to him, Smith sported a wide grin. "Whatever happened to 'Yessa, masta. Yessa. We's sure will, masta'?"

Looking back at Reider one more time, Dubois made sure there was enough distance between himself and his platoon leader before he turned on Smith. "When are you going to learn to keep your fat trap shut, you dumb cracker?"

"Dumb cracker?" Smith shot back. "Now I'm a dumb cracker. Hey, Hector," Smith called out to one of the riflemen in front of him. "Sergeant Smith is calling me a cracker. Is that harassment?"

Hector Santiago spun about, but continued to maintain his place in the loose formation by walking backward. "If I were you, white boy, I'd consider that a compliment."

Everett Cash, walking up front beside Santiago, threw his two cents in by calling back to Smith over his shoulder. "For you, that's a step up in the world. As I recall, yesterday you were a fucking dumb cracker." Like his assistant squad leader, Cash was black. Unlike Sergeant Dubois, he didn't let anyone forget it. "And, you'd best not forget, cracker, you're the minority in *this* outfit."

Before Smith could come back with his own comment, Dubois cut the banter between his energetic troopers short. "Okay, ladies. Let's cut the chatter and pay attention to what we're here for."

Unwilling to let that pass without comment, Smith continued. "What, exactly, oh powerful and all-seeing assistant squad leader of ours, *are* we here for?"

Dubois hesitated. He knew what he was there for. He was marking time, doing some field time, and earning a couple more ribbons for his blues. Even before he had received orders assigning him to Europe, he had been assured that there would be a slot waiting for him in the 3rd Infantry back in Arlington, Virginia, when he finished his tour with the 2nd of the 13th. All Dubois had to do was stay out of trouble and come back with a good record. Of course, he never told anyone in the 2nd of the 13th of this. The soldiers of that battalion were line doggies, field troopers who looked down their noses at the toy soldiers who spent their days guarding the tomb of the Unknown and planting dead veterans in Arlington Cemetery. Instead, Dubois gave his bothersome squadmate the stock reply. "We're here to protect the Hungarian minority of the region from ethnic cleansing."

Smith shook his head. "Oh, don't give me that line of

shit, sarge. From what I've seen, those Hunkies don't want to be protected. Fact is, I think they're just itching for the opportunity to have at the Slavs."

"He's right, you know," Santiago chimed in as he turned around again and joined the debate. "If you ask me, I say we give 'em our rifles, get out of the way, and let them have at each other. All we're doin' is postponing a major rumble."

"Maybe we are," Dubois responded, "and maybe we aren't." Then, after looking over his shoulder and seeing that Reider and his headquarters section was over the fence and coming on fast, Dubois quickly added, "One thing I do know for sure. That man back there is in charge, and he said move out. So, if you gentlemen don't mind, let's get our minds back on doing that."

The fence wasn't an obstacle. It was just a nuisance. But then, burdened with all his personal clothing and equipment as well as his weapon, doing anything was a chore for Gerald Reider. Besides his BDUs, the young officer wore a complete set of thermal underwear and a wool sweater. Over this he wore his cold-weather parka, which also served as his wet-weather gear. Equipment included a flak vest, a protective mask, and load-bearing equipment, called web gear. This loose harness was designed to distribute the weight of various pieces of equipment and gear that each soldier needed for both survival and combat.

Reider's load was common. On the belt, hanging over his left rear hip, was a canteen. Some infantrymen, especially those in light units, carried two. Since every Bradley carried a five-gallon water can from which a canteen could be refilled, mech infantrymen tended to have just one. On the front of the web belt, on either side of the buckle, were two ammo pouches. Each of these contained three thirty-round magazines. Loops on the side of these pouches permitted a soldier to carry hand grenades. As the situation did not warrant it, few carried fragmentation grenades. But Reider, a leader, was issued two smoke grenades, one yellow and one red. These he carried on the outside loops of his ammo pouches. On the left, hanging down at his side, was the pouch for the GPS. Reider had the only one that was with the dismounts. As a backup Gerald Reider also carried an ancient lensatic compass safely tucked away in its own little pouch sitting to the side of the right ammo pouch.

On the right hip, jutting out like an obscene growth on his leg, was Reider's protective, or gas mask. Though not attached to the web belt, the bulk of this piece of equipment prevented Reider, and just about everyone else, from hanging anything on his belt along that stretch. Further to the right, behind the protective mask, and riding on Reider's right rear cheek was an issued bayonet tucked away in its self sharpening sheath, Some of the old hands in the 2nd of the 13th kept their issued bayonets locked away and carried, instead, a more useful personally owned hunting knife. In time, Reider would come to learn that an infantryman's "coolness" was measured by the size and type of knife he carried.

Hanging from the left vertical strap was a first-aid pouch containing an individual dressing, and on the right one, a red-filtered flashlight. Some officers, who had access to them, used different-colored filters or non-issued flashlights. Nathan Dixon, for example, preferred a small Maglite with green filters. Like the knife, the flashlight was a measure of one's "coolness."

In addition to these items, Reider toted a map case that hung from a single strap riding on his right shoulder and cutting across his chest. In this pouch the young officer carried his map, safely enclosed in a plastic map case. Other useful items tucked away along with Reider's map, or tucked away in pockets in the map case, included his big notebook, a copy of the patrol order, pens, pencils, markers, a small pair of scissors, and a pamphlet issued to all soldiers in Slovakia that explained the local people and customs and included what the Army assumed to be useful phrases.

With a helmet and rifle thrown in, a leader has quite a load. But Reider carried more than what the Infantry School prescribed. With everything else going on, the second lieutenant never thought about the mud that stuck to his boots. The snow that was coming down was heavy and wet. Instead of being showered with light, delicate crystals that floated down from the heavens, Reider and his men were being pelted with wet globs of malformed flakes that almost made an audible noise, like a raindrop hitting a solid surface.

The ground covered by this heavy blanket of snow had begun to thaw after a warm front had swept the area the previous week. Together with a sun that had momentarily broken the long winter gloom, it had managed to soften the top few inches of mud, but that was all. Now mud from this layer, sandwiched between the still-frozen ground below and the wet snow on top, clung to the boots of Reider and his men as they made their way through the fields. Gerald Reider hadn't given the mud much thought until he went to climb over the fence. Though the weight it added wasn't overwhelming, it was still noticeable. In time, this uninvited burden would make itself felt.

Behind Reider came several men who did not belong to any of the squads. Collectively, these soldiers were referred to as the platoon headquarters section, a title that was more grandiose than the four troopers deserved. Reider's physical burden, in comparison to what these men carried, was nothing. First there was the radioman. At five foot five, Specialist Sam Pavlovski was tied with Angel Hernandes, squad leader of the 3rd Squad, for the dubious distinction of being the shortest man in the platoon. Yet Pavlovski carried the heaviest load. In addition to just about everything that his platoon leader had, the RTO, short for radio telephone operator, carried the platoon radio. Tucked in the rucksack with this radio were accessories, such as a longer antenna, a spare battery, and a small manual that no one actually read. As Pavlovski kept pace with his platoon leader, the RTO's sharp, sharp chin and beak-like nose were all that could be seen jutting out from the oversized hood he had drawn up over his helmet.

Two men who could argue with Pavlovski as to who was hauling the most came up to the fence on Pavlovski's heels. These men, Sergeant Zeke Fishburn and his assistant, Private First Class Jeff Jefferson, had the unenviable task of schlepping the platoon's Javelin anti-tank guided missile system. Fishburn, a big man who had grown up in the hill country of East Tennessee, was the gunner. As such, he carried the 9.9-pound command launch unit, or CLU, in a padded carrier that was slung across his left shoulder. In a modified frame on his back was one missile, snugly secured in the tube that also served as the launcher. Together, tube and missile weighted 32 pounds. Since the Javelin was an anti-tank weapon, and Jefferson carried only one additional round, both men were also armed with rifles. In the early days of the 2nd of the 13th's deployment to Slovakia, Fishburn's CLU and the missiles that went with it had all been safely secured back at Fort Apache when the platoon sallied out on a patrol. The growing hostility between the Slovakian government and its ethnic Hungarian populace, however, and the increasing use of armor by the Slovakian troops to keep their rebellious brethren in check, changed that. In order to maintain their credibility as a fighting force, orders had come down to issue out the Javelins.

The last man in Reider's small command group was Specialist Four Isaac Smollett. Technically, he did not belong to the platoon or even the company. As were all medics, Smollett was a member of the battalion's medical section. But since policy dictated that the same medic, when possible, be assigned to the same units, Smollett was, for all practical purposes, a part of 3rd Platoon. Like everyone else, he wore the same uniform, flak vest, and load-bearing equipment. Unlike the other members of the platoon, he carried two medical aid bags, one on his back and a smaller one slung over his shoulder.

After a pause of several seconds, Reider's last squad, the 3rd, came up to the fence. When the squad leader got there, he turned to his guest, Nathan Dixon. Gesturing with his right hand at the fence, Staff Sergeant Angel Hernandes bowed slightly. "After you, sir."

Nathan looked at the small, wiry Mexican-American. Though he had only seen him in passing, Nathan liked the staff sergeant. As the senior ranking Hispanic in Company C, Hernandes took it upon himself to keep the other Hispanics in the company in line. "And I was always taught," Nathan quipped as he made his way over the fence, "that age should precede beauty."

Hernandes looked up and smiled. "Sir, I hope you appreciate that decorum and the Uniform Code of Military Justice prevent me from responding to that as I would like."

When he was on the other side, Nathan paused and returned Hernandes's smile. "Sergeant, I was counting on that." Laughing, Hernandes pulled himself up and over the obstacle, while Nathan turned away and headed off after the bulk of the platoon. The snow showed no sign of letting up. Though he should have been able to see well past the point element, given the small size of Reider's dismounted element, Nathan had trouble seeing Reider himself, moving forward, alone, less than twenty meters away. Looking around, Nathan tried to spot some sort of terrain feature. That, of course, was impossible. On the left, he could barely make out a line of trees. With the snow it was impossible to tell whether it was a thin lot of trees or the edge of a major forest.

To the right, the battalion staff officer saw nothing but the snow.

Still, Nathan had a sense of terrain that had saved him from major embarrassment on numerous occasions. Pulling at the map case that hung around his left shoulder, Nathan flipped it open. After orienting the map so that it matched the lay of the unseen ground around him, Nathan pulled a marker out of his pocket, made a check where he thought they were along the route of march that he had neatly copied to the map before leaving Fort Apache, and studied it for a moment. Without missing a beat, he walked along, studying the map before him and memorizing the lay of the land that they would come across within the next kilometer. When he was sure he had it burned into his memory, Nathan closed the flap on his map case, let it drop to his side, and looked around again. It would be a long day, he thought as he watched Specialist Smollett in front of him trudge through the snow. And no doubt, Nathan thought as he lifted his own feet and looked down at the mud-snow mix that clung to his boots like glue, it would be an exhausting one. But, he sighed as he looked up and all about, it wouldn't be spent in the battalion tactical operations center. And a day spent out of the TOC, to Nathan, was a great day, no matter what the weather.

7

WITH 3 CHILDREN

NORTHEAST OF MODŘANY,
EARLY AFTERNOON, FEBRUARY 5

For the better part of an hour, no one spoke. Like Nathan, the soldiers reveled in the silence that engulfed them as they made their way through one snow-covered Slovakian farm field after another. To them this was a treat, for quiet and privacy were all but nonexistent at Fort Apache.

The living conditions simply didn't accommodate it. Quartered twenty men to a tent, with less than two feet separating cots, there was no escape from the prying eyes and curious ears of one's tent mates. Someone, it seemed, was always playing his music a bit too loud, or carrying on a conversation that never seemed to end. And even if, by some miracle, everyone in one tent fell quiet, the odds of all the people quartered in the tents on either side doing likewise at the same time were something less then nil.

The operational requirements of the battalion definitely didn't permit it either. Patrols, mounted and dismounted, were always coming and going. Facilities like the battalion tactical operations center, the mess hall, and the battalion aid station operated twenty-four hours a day, seven days a week. The battalion maintenance section labored away on tracks that were being run into the ground by continuous use under adverse conditions. It seemed that a night didn't pass when a Bradley wasn't towed in, flanked by its armed escort, after midnight. All these varied and essential activities required power, power supplied by generators that ran round the clock, contributing to the cacophony that hammered away at the soldiers who lived within the wire of that camp.

Things were different outside Fort Apache. Even with one's platoon mates staggered about him at a distance of five meters, a man could revel in the illusion of being alone. With only the crunching of snow underfoot disturbing the wonderful, blessed silence, a soldier could listen to his own sounds for a change. Some of these noises were unavoidable, such as labored breaths as the platoon trudged up a rolling slope, or the noise one's throat makes when swallowing excess saliva. Others were accidental, like the rubbing of the nylon webbing against the cold-weather parka, or the clink of the metal adjuster on a rifle's sling banging against the hard plastic of the weapon's upper hand guard. A few of these sounds could even be felt, such as the noise a helmet made when it rubbed against the inside of a parka hood that was drawn up over the wearer's head. Taken together they resonated in a way that was reassuring, almost comforting, to a soldier. To hear them, and nothing else, means all is well. Everything is as it should be.

Nathan was enjoying it all. After taking in the stunning beauty that surrounded him for a few minutes, he permitted his consciousness free reign, pursuing whatever thought his mind happened to stumble across. Some of them were professional, dealing indirectly with their tactical situation. One that kept recurring to him was the tiny size of the "platoon" he was accompanying. What young officers, such as Reider, saw as a platoon of dismounts seemed more like a reinforced squad to an officer like Nathan, who had served in an airborne division. One good firefight, Nathan told himself, against a determined foe of any size would pretty much use this "platoon" up. Until he actually saw the problem for himself, so well illustrated here in Slovakia, Nathan had always wondered why men like his father, who had made their reputations by advocating the use of firepower to win their wars, always seemed to be worried about the number of bayonet-wielding foot soldiers they could muster. This left Nathan hoping that the high-tech, hard-wired Army he found himself in performed in actual combat, as well as it did during briefings in the Pentagon. Otherwise, Nathan thought as he looked at the silent figures around him, they, with me along with them, would pay the price for backing a doctrine based on a small, high-tech Army.

Not all of Nathan's thoughts were so sanguine or professionally oriented. More and more, the lonely young infantry officer found himself thinking about a fellow officer. Though his father's views on relationships between service members, no matter what the circumstances, foolish at best, Nathan could not deny that he was infatuated with Christina Donovan. What had started out as nothing more than a friendship meant to fill what few idle hours they managed to steal was becoming something more. As Nathan arrived in the unit just as it was in the midst of its deployment to Slovakia, he had never been afforded the opportunity to be with Chris in a purely social setting. In fact, as he thought about it while his feet mechanically carried him along with the 3rd Squad, he had never seen Chris Donovan in anything except her baggy BDUs. Still, not even the motley camouflage pattern of the standard issue uniform could disguise a figure that was decidedly feminine. Everything about her, from the twinkle that she always had in her eyes when she spoke, to the shy smile that lit her face every time she caught him staring at her, intrigued Nathan.

Chris Donovan was not at all like Nancy Kozak, the only other female officer Nathan had ever worked with. Lieutenant Colonel Kozak presented a coldness to the world that almost radiated from her. While Nathan would not call her personality harsh, there was something about Nancy Kozak that made a man look at her differently than he would any other woman. That Nathan had watched her use her bayonet on a foe without blinking an eye, then wipe the blood off on the leg of her BDUs with the same casualness that a mechanic wiped his hands on his coveralls, didn't help. Even in the best of times, under ideal conditions, Nathan could not see that female officer as anything else but an officer.

Christina, on the other hand, was different. He was dying to be with her. Not as a fellow officer. Not as a highly trained and competent chemical warfare specialist. But as a woman, dressed to the nines and wearing young urban female camouflage paint. He found himself fantasizing more and more about this. What would she look like with her hair down and without the impressed ring that her helmet band always left behind. How would she act as he stared at her across a table lit by a single candle? Would he be able to feign indifference to the sensual and alluring manner in which she spoke when the two of them were alone? And, most important of all, would he be able to keep from saying or doing something foolish, something that would shatter the bonds of mutual affection that he sensed were growing between them?

*   *   *

These thoughts were still swirling about Nathan's head, evoking all sorts of involuntary physical reactions, when the platoon halted. Like a long train coming to a stop, with each car rolling forward until it smacked the stationary car before it, the distance between the soldiers closed until they were clustered together at the edge of a stand of trees. Gerald Reider, who was busy checking the GPS in order to verify their exact location, didn't notice this. But his acting platoon sergeant, Staff Sergeant Kittridge, jumped on his fellow squad leaders without hesitation. "Okay, people. You know the drill. Let's spread out and cover your sectors."

Caught off guard by this, Reider looked up and watched the soldiers who had already flopped down on the ground to rest. On cue, those prone to do so were already moaning and muttering, under their breath, as they pushed themselves up off the ground and shuffled off to where they were supposed to be. In 3rd Platoon, battle drill dictated that the lead squad cover the sector defined by ten o'clock to two o'clock, with twelve o'clock being the direction of travel. The next squad took up positions from two to six, and the trailing squad filled in between six and ten. The Javelin team, under the direction of the gunner and without having to be told, wedged themselves in where they could cover the most likely tank avenue of approach. Reider's RTO and the platoon medic hovered in the center, within arm's reach of their platoon leader.

As he watched the squad leaders reshuffle their men, Reider took note that Lieutenant Dixon and the 3rd Squad didn't stagger in until after Kittridge had made his comment. Perhaps, the young platoon leader thought as he watched the battalion staff officer settle down, his unwanted guest had not noticed the lapse in deployment that had been corrected by Kittridge.

Over with 3rd Squad, Nathan was also checking their

location. After taking a sip of water from his canteen, he pulled his map out of the faded canvas map case on which "Dixon" was labeled in handwritten block letters. On close inspection, one could detect that the block letters had been redone several times, with each retracing always being somewhat less than exact. Unlike Nathan's other equipment and clothing, all relatively new and made of high-tech fibers, the map case was old, faded, frayed, and one hundred percent cotton duck. It had been his father's. Scott Dixon had given it to his son when the younger Dixon was preparing to leave for his first assignment. "This is a loan," the old man told his son. "As soon as you manage to find one that suits you, I want it back, in exactly the same condition I gave it to you."

Nathan had understood the full meaning of what his father had said. Scott Dixon was like that, lacing every word he uttered with meanings, even emotions. In his three and a half years of active duty, Nathan had looked for a map case of his own. He had even contemplated buying one that was, technically, superior to the one his father had lent him. Still, the young staff officer hadn't. It wasn't that he was hoping that some of the luck his father had always seemed to have plenty of would rub off on him from his father's map case. Nathan was too familiar with the ways of war to know that luck in battle was fickle and random. Rather, his reasons were personal and, in truth, rather childish. As an Army brat, Nathan had never known the security of a hometown or community. He had lost his mother at an early age and watched his father walk out the door, time and again, for duty that could very well take him away as well. So the map case that had been his father's, a case marred with stains from years of use by Scott Dixon, was a security blanket of sorts to Nathan. In a profession where all is up for grabs twenty-four hours a day, even one's own life, the map case that had been passed on from father to son was the one thing that gave Nathan a sense of stability.

It took a moment to orient the map to the lay of the ground. Looking around, Nathan picked out terrain features. The snowfall, he noted, was lightening up. Pulling off a glove, he held his hand, palm up, and felt the flakes fall on his finger for a minute in an effort to see if the snow was actually changing to rain. That, he thought, would make things really miserable. Though he knew that the wonderful white blanket that covered everything in sight would eventually melt and turn the landscape into a bottomless morass of mud, Nathan hoped it would wait until at least they returned from this patrol.

Satisfied that the weather was cooperating, at least for the moment, Nathan went back to finding their location. A soldier in 3rd Squad, lying prone next to Nathan and tired of staring into the empty woods before him, turned and watched Nathan. While Private First Class Dave Tilton would have never dreamed of asking his platoon leader a question that he didn't need to, he felt no such restraint when it came to Nathan. Nathan, after all, wasn't in Tilton's chain of command. Though the first lieutenant was still an officer, there wasn't much he could, or probably would, do if Tilton came across as being too mouthy. So Tilton inched over, closer to Nathan. "How far've we gone?"

Looking up from his map, Nathan gave Tilton a look that he had learned from his father, the sort of stare that always warned Nathan that he had forgotten something, like please. In Tilton's case, he caught on instantly and quickly amended his question. "How far have we gone, sir?"

Satisfied that the soldier had sufficiently corrected his oversight, Nathan leaned over toward Tilton and flopped the map on the ground between them. "We're here," Nathan stated matter-of-factly as he pointed to the mark he had made on his map.

"And we started from where, sir?" Tilton quickly asked.

"We started here," Nathan indicated, "and we have to go here."

After looking at the map for a few moments, Tilton looked at his watch, then groaned. "Oh, man. That's all we did in an hour? Less than two kilometers?"

"This snow and mud isn't helping," Nathan explained. "I expect we'll have to tack an extra hour or so on to our time."

"That . . ." Tilton was about to say "sucks," but checked himself when he saw Nathan staring at him. He didn't know this officer well enough to curse like that. "It'll be sloppy seconds in the mess hall tonight for us?"

This caused Nathan to chuckle. "So what's so different between sloppy seconds and fresh slop?"

"At least when it's fresh," Tilton explained, "it's warm and it's soft. I hate it when the servers scrape the side of the warming pan and serve you stuff that's been drying out for hours."

In a world with few amenities, and where personal comforts were as scarce as privacy, mealtime and the food quality were, to most soldiers, critical issues not to be trifled with. Leaning closer to Tilton, Nathan winked. "Well, I hate that, too, which is why I always give them my nasty, 'you better not do that' first lieutenant look."

"No doubt it works for you, sir. But a shit for brains PFC, pardon the expression, can't get far with something like that."

Sitting up, Nathan started to put his map away. "Tell you what, private. If you can manage to follow me through the mess line tonight, I'll make sure you don't get screwed by the servers, pardon the expression."

Tilton nodded. "You're on, sir." Then a sly smile lit the soldier's face. "But, sir, if I follow you through the mess line, won't the battalion bugs and gas officer be jealous?"

Tilton's mention of Chris Donovan caught Nathan off

guard. His face must have shown his surprise, for Tilton's smile became a smirk. Recovering as quickly as possible, without making it seem as if it was any big deal, Nathan opted to play it cool. "I'm sure Lieutenant Donovan will understand."

The cold, measured manner in which the first lieutenant responded to his little aside was all the warning Tilton needed. "I imagine so," he muttered as he moved away from Nathan and resumed his former position, scanning into the vacant woods.

After confirming the location of his platoon, and comparing the map to what little he could see along the route they would be taking, Gerald Reider spent the bulk of his break scraping mud off his boots with a stick. In the two kilometers that they traveled, he had already begun to feel the effects of the added weight. This was made more noticeable by the fact that his travels from the States to Germany, and then on to Slovakia, had not permitted him much time for any physical training, or PT. Instead of arriving in top physical form, Reider was unprepared. Already his muscles were starting to let him know just what bad shape he was in. That the mud he was disposing of would be replaced by new mud, churned up from under the pristine layer of snow they would be moving through within five minutes, did not matter. Reider wasn't the type to throw his hands up and do nothing. Anything, even futile efforts, were preferable to meekly submitting.

By the time Reider was finished with both boots, ten minutes had passed from the time he had ordered the halt. When he stood up, the soldiers around him started to make their own preparations to move out. Squad leaders came to their feet and looked about to make sure that their men would be ready. Sergeant Dubois shouted over to Hector Santiago, a notorious candy fiend. "Hector, you make sure you police up all those candy wrappers."

With feigned innocence, Santiago turned and looked over to where Dubois was standing. "What candy wrappers?"

"Don't make me come over there and check on you, trooper. 'Cause if I do, you'll eat every wrapper I find on the ground."

Like an eight-year-old caught in a lie, Santiago bowed his head and mumbled "Okay, okay," as he brushed some snow away to recover two wrappers he had tried to hide.

"Hey, Hector," Henry Smith called out. "Sarge got you again."

Dubois had zero tolerance for horsing around, especially in the field. In a flash, he shifted his attention from Santiago to Smith. "Can it, trooper. Get your butt in gear, and get ready to move out."

Noting the growing look of concern on his platoon leader's face as this exchange took place between the members of the 1st Squad, Dick Kittridge jumped in. "All right, ladies. Let's cut the chatter and get moving. We don't want to keep the boys with the tracks waiting on us."

Without another word the 3rd Platoon gathered itself up, resumed its previous formation, and stepped off when the platoon leader gave the signal.

Still, not everyone permitted himself to be cowed into silence. From somewhere up ahead, Nathan heard one of the soldiers singing the TV theme song from the Western series *Bonanza.*

Hernandes, who was walking alongside of Nathan, couldn't resist. He let out a muffled chuckle and flashed a toothy grin as he shook his head. "I feel sorry for our new LT."

"Why do you say that?" Nathan asked as the words of the TV song drifted back along the sullen column of men.

Hernandes looked at Nathan for a moment.

"The man has a lot to learn, sir. I just think this is one hell of a place for an officer to learn to be, well, an officer."

Nathan thought about that for a moment, comparing it to his own experience as a new platoon leader.

Finally, Nathan looked at Hernandes, then at Reider. "Well, sergeant, he'll either do well, or he'll find out real quick that he made a bad career choice. Either way, there isn't much you or I can do except help him when we can."

Having forgotten the rest of the words, the anonymous singer kept the tune going, but substituted "dadah, dadah, dadah" in place of the words for the next line.

"Even so," Hernandes countered, "I'd hate to be in his shoes."

From somewhere near the front of the platoon, Nathan could hear Sergeant Kittridge's voice sing out loud and clear. "Foss! Shut the hell up and pay attention to what you're supposed to be doing." Instantly, the singing stopped. By this time, Sergeant Hernandes had moved away from Nathan, permitting silence to descend, once more, on the platoon as it made its way forward. Left alone again, Nathan, was free to conjure up the image of a woman he found himself slowly becoming obsessed with.

8

Complacency and monotony inevitably lead to inattentiveness. Inattentiveness inevitably leads to mistakes. And mistakes, in combat, create what after action reports sometimes wistfully refer to as "situations."

Reider's sixteen men, with First Lieutenant Nathan Dixon tagging along in the rear with 3rd Squad, continued their trek through empty fields and past abandoned farmhouses. In the lead, the 2nd Squad was following a tree line as it ascended a hill. Staff Sergeant Dick Kittridge watched as his two point men, David Foss and Lester Kim, reached the crest of the hill. Neither man stopped there, but continued on. As they were moving about thirty yards in front of Kittridge, it took a few moments for the squad leader to make it to the top of the hill, where he could look out at what lay beyond.

As was his habit, Kittridge paused a moment to scan the terrain to his front before starting the descent. The first thing he checked on was his own men, to see if their actions could cue him to anything unusual or un-expected. When the squad leader saw that Foss and Kim were continuing along the tree line that split the hill on the reserve side as it had on the front, Kittridge contin-ued to look about. To accomplish this, he needed only to traverse the muzzle of his rifle, slung over his shoul-der and parallel to the ground slowly as his right eye watched for any unusual heat signatures in the small helmet-mounted viewer that hung an inch before his right eye. While snow could reduce the effective range of the Warrior's thermal sight, the close nature of the terrain they were traveling through didn't make that a problem.

Just as Foss and Kim had done when they had reached this spot, Kittridge went about his visual sweep of the area in a more or less mechanical, almost disinterested manner. So much of what Kittridge did now was habit, created by training and repetition, rather than by con-scious thought. So it came as something of a shock to Kittridge when a cluster of bright images suddenly popped up in the center of his thermal viewer. As if kicked, Kittridge stopped traversing his rifle, gripped the handguards tighter to steady it, pulled his head back, and blinked. When he opened his eyes again, the dark images that all heat-producing objects generate in a thermal sight were still there. Mentally he switched focus in his eyes, going from electronically generated images before his right to normal vision in his left. He did this in the hope of identifying whom he was looking at. Thermal sights, after all, cannot differentiate be-tween a warm body in an American uniform and one draped in the camouflage pattern of another.

Though he had already suspected he knew the truth, Kittridge had hoped that the dozen or so figures clus-tered around a stationary truck were civilian. In an instant, when he saw the color of the truck and the uniforms the men wore, Kittridge realized he had a problem. Dropping to one knee, the squad leader jerked his head to the left, over to where he had last seen Foss and Kim. Bewildered, Kittridge watched as his two point men continued to move on down the hill, following the tree line, looking this way and that but never seeing the danger that lay just off to their right. Scanning back and forth between his men and the Slovakian soldiers, Kittridge looked to see if there was any chance that the curvature of the hill would block the line of sight between the two groups. Unfortunately, from where he was, that didn't seem likely. Only the fact that each of the opposing groups was equally inattentive kept one from spotting the other.

Kittridge's first reaction was to call out a warning to his wandering point element. That, however, was just as likely to alert the Slovakians. Instead, he turned about to see how far the 1st Squad was before deciding on his next move. Sergeant Bobby Dubois, who had been keeping an eye on what the squad before him was doing, didn't need anyone to tell him that something was wrong. By the time Kittridge looked back, Dubois had deployed his four men in a skirmish line. Each man was on the ground, either in the prone or on a knee, watching, waiting. Using his free hand, Kittridge signaled to Dubois what he had seen. When he was sure his fellow squad leader understood, Kittridge turned to his SAW gunner, who had automatically dropped to prone and taken up a good firing position. "Keith, stay here. I'm going to go after Foss and Kim and get them back here."

Without taking his eyes off the Slovakians, who were in the process of trying to dig their truck out of the mud it had stuck in, Reisniack nodded. "Roger that."

Carefully, Kittridge retreated a few feet behind the crest of the hill before he took off at a run, crouching as low as he could, into the woods a few feet, then back over the crest of the hill and down the other side after

Foss and Kim. As he went, his eyes kept shifting back and forth between his own two men and the Slovakians.

Though for different reasons, Gerald Reider had been equally distracted when the situation began to develop. Like all new second lieutenants, he was paranoid about getting lost. That fear, coupled with his unfamiliarity with the terrain, caused him to check his location frequently, using the GPS. In order not to slow down his headquarters section, or the 3rd Squad following it, Reider attempted to do this while continuing to maintain the pace. This, naturally, required something of a balancing act.

First, he had to sling his rifle over his shoulder. Then he needed to pull the GPS out of its pouch. After punching the button to active the device in order to obtain the current eight-digit grid coordinate displayed, Reider then had to read the grid coordinates, memorize them, replace the GPS back into its pouch, and pull out his map. Next he marked the spot on the map that corresponded to the eight digits he had memorized. Without pausing, the young platoon leader studied the map, quickly memorizing what he saw so that he could relate the map symbology to the actual ground. Only then did he look up to verify that what he saw on the map corresponded to the terrain that lay all about him.

It was only then that he saw the 1st Squad, deployed in line, double-timing up the hill to where a single trooper was intently aiming a SAW at an unseen threat that was on the reverse slope of the hill Reider was now climbing. Stunned by this sight, Reider's mind was immediately flooded with half a dozen questions. What had the point element run into? Where was the rest of the 2nd Squad? Why was that squad's leader maneuvering against the threat without waiting for him to assess the situation? And, most important of all, What was he to do?

Even as these questions were racing through his mind, Reider was busy stuffing his map back into his map case. Breaking into a run, he made for the crest of the hill. Behind him, the four men of his headquarters section, who had been watching their platoon leader fumble with his map on one hand, and the lead squads deploy, picked up their own pace to keep up with their officer.

From behind, Sergeant Dubois heard the huffing and puffing of his platoon leader as Reider came up to where he had deployed his squad. Knowing that his platoon leader was ignorant of the situation, and quite anxious to remedy that before the was inundated with the lieutenant's questions, Dubois whispered to his men to stand fast. Maintaining a low profile, he dropped back away from the crest of the hill and met Reider partway down the slope. "Sir," Dubois stated quickly, before Reider had a chance to bludgeon him with a thousand questions, "Sergeant Kittridge's squad spotted a Slovakian Army truck, stuck in the mud, about two hundred yards off in that direction on the other side of this hill."

Out of breath and gasping for air, Reider struggled to regain both his composure and his ability to speak. As he did so, Dubois continued to report. "We've counted fourteen Slovakians, armed with small arms. They look like regulars, but I can't be sure. They seem to be pretty occupied with digging their truck out and haven't seen us yet."

"How can you be sure?" Reider managed to gasp between breaths.

Without hesitation, and in an effort to demonstrate that he had both experience and confidence, Dubois straightened up a bit and calmly stated, "I'm sure." Then, as an afterthought, he added, "sir."

Realizing that he was embarrassing himself by standing there winded like a West Point plebe after his first unit run, Gerald Reider nodded and hid, as best he could, how much the short run up the hill had taken out of him. "Let's . . . go . . . and have a look."

Crouching low, the lieutenant and the squad leader made their way up to the crest of the hill. Crawling the last few meters, they settled in before Dubois pointed out the Slovakian truck. "Over there," the NCO whispered as he pointed.

While he stared intently at the truck, Reider fumbled about with his left hand, blindly searching for the binoculars from the case he was lying on. When his gloved hand fell on the case, Reider found he needed to roll over onto his side to get at them. As he did so, he looked around and counted heads. Besides himself and Dubois, there were only four other men on the crest of the hill, two of whom had SAWs. After pulling the binoculars free, and before using them to take a closer look at the Slovakians, Reider faced Dubois. "Why did Sergeant Kittridge and the rest of his squad continue on?"

Though Reisniack, Kittridge's SAW gunner, had told Dubois what had happened, the sergeant E-5 did not recount how the men belonging to a sergeant E-6, equipped with their high-tech acquisition and fire-control system, had wandered on, oblivious to the danger that lay right in front of them. Yet he didn't want to fabricate a lie to cover for his fellow NCO on the off chance that his story wouldn't match the one that Kittridge was sure to weave later. "Sir," Dubois finally responded flatly, "I'm not sure."

Though this strange maneuver, taken solely on Kittridge's own initiative, bothered Reider, the platoon leader didn't have time to dwell on it at the moment. "Right, okay," Reider mumbled as he rolled back onto his stomach and brought the binoculars up to his eyes. While the binos did make it easier to see what the Slovakians were doing, the real reason Reider had dug them out and was using them was to buy him some time to think over what he should do next, while creating the illusion that he was doing something intelligent and meaningful.

The orders that he had read over and over the night

before had specified that while this was a show of force, contact between NATO personnel and the Slovakian Army or armed rebels was to be avoided. To the young officer his instructions appeared to be contradictory. He had felt that way about them the night before, but had said nothing, lest his new company commander think him an idiot because he asked for clarification. Since that statement in the company order was a direct lift from the battalion order, and since the battalion commander who had signed it and the operations officer who had written it took the time to articulate this point, it had to have made sense. But at the moment, confronted with real people less than two hundred meters away, with the balance of one squad off doing God knew what, the glaring disparity between the two tasks at hand stood before Reider like a snake poised to jump up and bite him.

Just when Gerald Reider became aware that he would have to say something and, eventually, do something, Nathan Dixon, the man who had really written the battalion operations order for this patrol, came up and slithered his way up next to Reider. "So, what do we have, LT?"

Suddenly struck by the realization that he had not taken the time to deploy his 3rd Squad, Reider quickly pushed himself up a bit and turned to look behind to see what those people were doing.

Guessing what Reider was looking for, Nathan smiled, more to himself than anyone else. "Before I came up here," Nathan explained patiently, "I took the liberty to deploy the 3rd squad to watch our back door."

The visible relief that Reider was unable to check was short-lived as another wave of embarrassment swept over him, this time brought on by the realization that his unwanted guest had done what he, himself, should have done automatically. Regaining his balance, Reider acknowledged Nathan's comment with nothing more than a nod and a nonchalant "Good" before returning to stare at the Slovakians.

For several seconds, Nathan waited for Reider to bring him up to speed on what was happening and what he, Reider, intended to do. When the platoon leader didn't, but instead turned his head so as better to ignore the battalion staff officer, Nathan felt a surge of anger well up inside of him. While he knew Reider was preoccupied dealing with the situation at hand, Nathan did not appreciate what he took to be a snub. To be ignored by Major Jon Sergeant, or even the battalion operations sergeant, was one thing. Being snubbed by a shit for brains, still wet behind the ears second lieutenant who didn't know up from down was quite another.

"Lieutenant Reider," Nathan commanded in a voice that was just forceful enough to convey his displeasure, "What is going on here?"

Conditioned to respond more to that tone of voice, Reider finally turned his head toward Nathan. "We have a truckload of Slovakian soldiers over there, at about two hundred meters distance, working on extracting their vehicle from the mud. The squad leader of my point element is over there, on our left somewhere, further down the reverse slope of this hill."

It didn't occur to Nathan that Reider had intentionally neglected to add a "sir" at the end of his summation. Instead, Nathan's attention shifted over to the left. As he did so, he asked, quite innocently, "What are they doing?"

A silence followed as Nathan looked for and spotted Kittridge with his two wayward souls. Reider's hesitation in responding to Nathan's question more than answered it. Without meaning it to, Nathan had just added to the animosity that Reider felt toward the junior battalion staff officer.

On either side of these two officers, the soldiers of 3rd Platoon, minus Kittridge and his point men, alternated between watching the Slovakians as they went about freeing their truck and the two officers who had, so far, done nothing. Those closest to Nathan and Gerald Reider, like Sergeant Dubois, heard the exchange between them and all but felt the tension. The others, while concerned about their current situation, didn't much care what one officer thought of the other. They just wanted someone, anyone, to make a decision, preferably one that got them out of there, and quickly.

It was Zeke Fishburn, the Javelin gunner, who finally galvanized Reider to act. Though he understood that Nathan was the senior of the pair, Reider was Fishburn's immediate superior within the chain of command. Slowly making his way forward from where he and the rest of the headquarters section had been patiently waiting for instructions, Fishburn got close enough to Reider so that he could speak to him without raising his voice. "Lieutenant?" Fishburn whispered.

Instinctively, both Reider and Nathan turned to look. Ignoring Nathan's stare, Fishburn addressed his question to his platoon leader. "Do you want me to set up the Javelin?" he said, adding, almost as an aside, "just in case."

A decision! Reider realized that he was being called on to make a real-world decision for the first time in his life, one he would need to make on his own, working under orders that he was only now beginning to realize he didn't fully understand. It wasn't fair, the young officer thought. It was like a trick question, or a pop quiz handed out by an instructor to students who knew he knew they were unprepared. It was the proverbial rigged tactical problem, the sort where there is no right answer, no given school solution. Yet a decision was required, and he was being called on to make it.

"No," he snapped after a moment of hesitation. "There'll be no need to." Satisfied, and relieved, Fishburn nodded and backed away to where his assistant gunner was waiting.

Now that he had made one decision, the next seemed

to come quite easily. Turning his attention to Dubois, Reider began to issue his orders. "Have your men drop back to where the 3rd Squad is. I want you to cut over to the left into the tree line, like Sergeant Kittridge did, and make your way over the crest of the hill down to where Kittridge and his point element are. As you move down the hill on the far side, make sure your people aren't spotted by the Slovakians. I'll follow with the rest of the platoon once you're in the tree line. Is that clear?"

Dubois, who had been listening intently, nodded. "Yes, sir."

"Okay, sergeant," Reider ordered, "get moving."

Without any further ado, Dubois backed down the hill. When he was a good five yards below the crest of the hill, he issued his hushed orders to the three men. "Okay, 1st Squad. Slowly, back down off the crest and follow me. We're going to go slow. Keep quiet and stay alert. Now move it."

In unison, the members of Dubois's squad did as he ordered, took up positions around him, and then followed when he stepped off. Behind them, still on the crest of the hill, Gerald Reider watched them go while studiously avoiding any eye contact with Nathan Dixon. Maybe he had made a bad call here, Reider thought. Maybe he should have just had his men stand up and go brazenly tromping forth in order to create a "show of force." The new platoon leader, however, didn't feel that such a course was, at this particular moment, proper. So he opted to follow the caveat that had confused the issue and opted to "avoid contact." He had no doubt that if he had chosen wrong, he would hear about it later. But that wasn't important for him at the moment. What was important, and what gave him a surprising boost in spirits, was that he had made a decision, a real honest-to-goodness decision that was being acted on. While this little incident was, to the men in his platoon, all part of just another day "in the hood," to Second Lieutenant Gerald Reider it was a watershed. For the first time all day, he felt as if he were truly in charge.

With this thought in mind, Reider slithered down from the crest of the hill, followed by Reisniack and Nathan, and began to make his way toward the tree line that had already swallowed up Dubois's squad. Any further concern over the forlorn Slovakians and their truck disappeared with the same ease with which Reider had dismissed a course at West Point once final semester grades for it had been posted.

9

NORTHEAST OF MODŘANY, MIDAFTERNOON, FEBRUARY 5

What little banter there was within the four small groups that together made up the dismounted patrol now centered on the near run-in with the Slovakian regulars. Some of the soldiers felt the need to make their views on Reider's decision to slip by the Slovakians known. Others lamented the ridiculous position in which the rules of engagement they had to operate under kept putting them. These discussions were neither debates or, with few exceptions, two-way conversations. Rather, talking about what had just happened was little more than a means of releasing nervous tension.

In the course of these impromptu postmortems, the platoon was pretty much divided up evenly, with half the troopers doing all the talking and the other half doing all the listening. The talkers tended to be loud and quite animated. Some were so absorbed in their own oratory that they didn't notice that the person they were speaking to wasn't answering. Instead of adding their comments, or offering a contrary view, the listeners merely tilted their heads now and then in a cursory nod, or grunted when the speaker paused to catch his breath. All the while, these unwilling targets of pointless rhetoric continued forward without missing a beat. It wasn't that they were being rude or unsociable. Rather, those soldiers who were supposed to be listening were either sorting through their own feelings or had been jolted into a higher state of awareness as a result of the run-in with the Slovakians. With their weapons held at the ready, they ignored the banter of their companions in the same manner that one tunes out the incessant yipping of a small, annoying dog. Their focus was tight, almost myopic, centered solely on their own thoughts or the task at hand. To them the incident back on the hill was a reminder that the picturesque landscape they were moving through concealed a force whose intentions were suspect and threatening.

Being an officer does not make one immune to the stress or anxiety such an incident can generate. If anything, the rank and position an officer holds tend to magnify such feelings. Unlike a rifleman, an officer is expected by those who follow him to lead them through each and every incident safely. In and of itself, this is an awesome responsibility, one that few people care to take on, and even fewer are truly prepared for. Yet this is not the only burden that an officer must carry with him. By virtue of his office, a leader is also saddled with the responsibility of accomplishing tasks handed down to him by higher authorities. All too often, these two goals are in conflict. Back on the hill, for instance, each soldier had simple choices to make, and then only in response to orders. In a crisis each soldier, regardless of how professional or well trained he is, always has an option. Either he follows the orders that have been handed down to him and sallies forth, or he opts to place self-preservation over duty, honor, and country. Like the simple computer binary coding, this equation is little more than a yes-or-no proposition. What drives a man to risk life and limb is frequently determined by the trust that he has in the leader who is there, with him, issuing the order and sharing the risks. Even in the high-tech, computer-driven Army of the twenty-first century, Clausewitz's supposition that morale is to physical as three is to one still rang true.

Officers, on the other hand, are not only charged with doing the telling, they must generate the conditions that will motivate a soldier to execute that order. It has always been that way, and so long as nations place the flower of their youth in harms way, it always will be. Leaders will have to initiate action by issuing sound, coherent orders. They will need to motivate their soldiers to carry out those actions by using a combination of encouragement, threats, and personal example. Finally, the leader, be he officer or NCO, or simply the first guy to stand up and start something, will have to oversee the actions he put into motion. And, since each action can, and usually does, lead to a new, and sometimes unpredictable response by the opposition, the officer is faced with having to make new decisions, often before his previous one is carried through to completion. Thus, even the simple, rather straightforward situation that had faced Reider back on the hill was able to generate a level of stress that would unnerve an average person. Yet officers deployed on the cutting edge, like Reider, are expected to deal with these sorts of situations again, and again, and again. Day in and day out, they are required to push aside whatever personal fears they harbor or self-doubts that burden them, and lead. Needless to say, they must find a way of dealing with the stress and strain their decisions leave in their wake. How well Gerald Reider accomplished this would determine how long he would be able to maintain his sanity.

* * *

After worming its way through the tree line, picking up Sergeant Kittridge and his wayward point element along the way, the 3rd Platoon came across a road that the battalion operations order required them to follow. It wasn't much of a road. Even the line on the map was more impressive than the unpaved farm trail that alternately weaved through wooded lots and then, within a few short steps, ran straight as an arrow across open meadows. Fresh tire tracks indicated that this "road" was, on this day anyway, quite popular and therefore warranted following.

Given the dearth of civilian activity, other than in the towns they had rolled through that morning, it was obvious that the Slovakian truck they had come across had used the same road. This fact, and the dark woods they passed through, did little to lessen the anxiety that was already becoming quite palpable to Gerald Reider. Physically and psychologically, the leader of the 3rd Platoon was isolated between the 1st Squad, which he followed at a distance of twenty meters, and the men of his small headquarters section, who followed him at a respectful distance. While he trudged forward, keeping one eye on what lay ahead and another on the terrain to either side, Reider found himself wishing, for the first time that day, that he had someone he could talk to.

Though he tried not to let it, Reider found his mind straying. It had seemed that no matter how much of a badass he had been at West Point or the Infantry Officers Basic Course at Fort Benning during tactical training exercises, there had always been a fellow cadet, or another second lieutenant, who had been willing to cross the gulf that separated the leader du jour from those who followed. Back then, after all, they were more or less equal. Both knew that, in time, they would find themselves in the exact same position. While Reider did not vocally advocate the philosophy of "cooperate and graduate," he quietly enjoyed the benefits.

Slowing his pace, Reider turned his head and looked back, beyond his RTO, the Javelin crew, and Smollett, the medic. Through the falling snow he could see a man in the distance who, up to that moment, had been an unwanted guest, traveling in his own pocket of isolation. Maybe, Reider found himself thinking, just maybe, Lieutenant Dixon will find it in himself to discount the manner in which I've treated him up to this point. God, Reider thought as he faced front and let the weight of his helmet drag his head down till his chin almost touched his chest, I hope he's not as petty as . . .

Within the space of a single step, Gerald Reider was able to snap his head upright and, with equal agility, erase that cloud of self-doubt. Instead of owning up to his own frailties, the young officer reminded himself that a leader had to be strong, self-reliant, and confident. This was not the time, he told himself as he watched the soldiers in front of him fan out as the road passed from woods and back into open fields, to become weak-kneed. "I can do this," he mumbled out loud. To have thought otherwise, Reider reminded himself, would have been a betrayal of all he believed in and had worked for.

Back with the 3rd Squad, Nathan Dixon found himself equally trapped in an internal, very personal struggle that was every bit as contentious. The incident back on the hilltop had ended Nathan's idyllic romp though the Slovakian countryside and brought home to him, in a very real manner, the fact that he was little more than a fifth wheel on this patrol. When it had dawned on him what was happening, the urge to run forth and take charge had been quite compelling. His orders to the squad leader he was with only highlighted Nathan's habit of taking charge. He was, after all, the senior officer present. This alone carried an awkward responsibility that the battalion staff officer had yet to learn to deal with effectively and tactfully.

By nature Nathan was an aggressive leader. As the older of two sons, he had grown up wearing the mantle of leadership that is so often draped upon the shoulders of an older sibling. Though this led to an occasional punishment that he deemed to be undeserved, Nathan had found the role to his liking. A tour with the 17th Airborne Division, where he had learned the meaning of "lead, follow, or get out of the way," had refined his innate leadership skills and left him craving greater responsibility.

Unfortunately, the system to which both Nathan and Gerald Reider belonged did not allow an officer, no matter how gifted, to pursue a career track that took him or her from one successive command slot to another. Not only was there a limit to the command positions available, but the opportunity to command larger organizations became fewer and fewer as one climbed the military pyramid. Within the 2nd of the 13th, for example, there were three platoon leaders in each line company, but only one company commander. At the next level, there were but four line companies, led by only one battalion commander. That left an almost equal number of officers within that battalion in staff positions. Although each of these staff positions did carry with them a certain amount of unique and very real responsibilities, as well as a handful of subordinates to assist in the execution of those duties, to a true leader there is nothing like a troop command.

Coupled with this cruel fact of life was the Army's system of "up or out." This managerial system became institutionalized within the Armed Forces by a former chairman of the Ford Motor Company, Robert Strange McNamara, after he was appointed the Secretary of Defense under JFK. It was meant to cut away dead wood in the officers corps and allow those whom the system deemed to be the best and the brightest to rise to the top quickly. In the process the Old Army died. The tradition of the professional company commander, portrayed so well in John Ford's 1949 film *She Wore a Yellow Ribbon,* disappeared overnight. No longer could an officer settle into a rank and duty position that fit him and served the Army's needs to a T. Along with the drive to convert combat leaders into managers of violence, McNamara fostered a system that required officers to bounce back and forth from command slots to staff positions and, along the way, get promoted according to a schedule that was designed by experts to optimize the available workforce. While these changes did give the United States Army a more modern, efficient structure, those who studied war and the men who wage it worried that such practices would smother those who were little more than warriors and unduly reward those who knew best how to "play the game."

Few first lieutenants, fresh from commanding their first combat unit, of course, are able to view the problem from that sort of historical perspective. Like Nathan, they tend to regard their assignment to a headquarters as a second- or third-string staff officer as some form of punishment. As a reward for doing well as a platoon leader, Nathan had been shuffled off to Europe and dumped into a staff position where he wasn't even permitted to make the morning coffee until he had been "checked out" by one of the sergeants in the operations section. While there was no overt or intentional scorn or disrespect directed toward Nathan, the young officer learned the meaning of one of his father's favorite sayings: "He who has commanded, can never be commanded."

Intellectually Nathan understood that there was a time and place for all things. Growing up as the son of a soldier had taught Nathan to be patient. As a small lad, his real mother had insisted that they wait until his father came home to eat in the evening, so that they could spend some time as a family. At the dinner table,

Nathan learned that he needed to wait until his mother had conveyed her daily trials and tribulations to his father before he could have his say. Vacations and family outings were synchronized with a division training calendar, not planned according to family needs. These lessons, like those concerning leadership, were already deeply etched on Nathan's psyche before he passed through Jackson Arch at the Virginia Military Institute for the first time as a cadet. One must serve, Nathan was told, before one can command.

So Nathan accepted his time in staff purgatory with few reservations. Once this bitter pill was swallowed, it dawned upon him that he had much to learn, and he began to see his staff time as less of a punishment and more as an opportunity to learn about how the Army he belonged to really worked.

Still, despite this, habits and human nature are not easily shelved when one changes jobs. Back on the hill, where they had come across the Slovakians, Nathan had reacted instinctively. As soon as he saw the squad ahead of him break into a trot and deploy into line, Nathan had turned to Staff Sergeant Hernandes, the squad leader of 3rd Squad, and ordered him to deploy his men to cover the platoon's rear. There had been no real emergency that had required Nathan to step forward and assume control like that. Although he was well within his rights as defined by the Uniform Code of Military Justice, and in accordance with the traditions of the service to do so, injecting himself into a unit's chain of command like that was not done capriciously. It simply wasn't kosher to usurp a part of another man's command out from under him just because you were there and he wasn't.

Yet there had been no hesitation on the part of Sergeant Hernandes or his squad in carrying out Nathan's order. Not only was Nathan an officer, issuing a lawful order that made sense, this first lieutenant from the battalion staff enjoyed a high degree of respect, even from those who had never served with him. Few officers that were as junior as Nathan had amassed anything resembling a reputation in Army Inc. Normally the up-and-coming stars weren't singled out from the pack for special handling until they were at least captains. Were it not for his participation in a misbegotten military operation in Idaho, Nathan, too, would have been viewed by the soldiers of the 3rd Platoon as nothing more than a shit for brains first lieutenant.

Saying nothing, Nathan moved on. He was no longer gazing about, enjoying the countryside around him. Except for an occasional glance to check their progress, his eyes pretty much remained fixed on the boots of the man in front. They watched as soldiers pried each foot free of the snow and mechanically threw it forward a couple of feet. The soldiers' boots, covered with a fresh layer of churned-up mud, shed little of this unwanted burden before they plunged down, back into a patch of virgin snow, where they would sink down and pick up a fresh coating of mud.

Nathan gave little thought to this. Instead, his mind was turning over and over again what had just happened. Being more aggressive, Nathan thought the proper course of action would have been to establish a base of fire, just in case, and then to show themselves. By executing a show of force, even on this small a scale, the dismounted patrol would have fulfilled one of the battalion's enumerated tasks. The sudden appearance of an American patrol, in the middle of nowhere during a snowstorm, would surely have made its way up through the Slovakian chain of command. While the odds were that this one incident would do nothing to deter a determined Slovakian commander from carrying out his next operation, it would introduce an element of doubt that would cause him to look over his shoulder more often. Slovakian staff officers would not be able to brag to their commander that they had no need to fear American intervention. They, like their superiors, could never be sure when and where an American patrol would pop up, just over the next rise. That, at least, was the theory.

The option to sally out, into the open, back on the hill, however, had not been Nathan's. By the time the battalion staff officer had reached the crest of the hill where Gerald Reider was observing the Slovakians, Nathan had managed to remind himself that this was not his platoon. He was simply there to keep Reider from making big mistakes. Given that the decision to back off and slip around the Slovakians didn't even qualify as a mistake gave Nathan even less of a reason to say anything. The battalion operations order that was driving this patrol provided Reider two choices: avoid confrontation or conduct a show of force. Some would view Reider's decision as that of a new platoon leader, one who was still unsure of himself, or his troops, or the situation to have been the best. Either way, Nathan concluded, what's been done has been done. There was no point in second-guessing the new platoon leader. Nor would casting disparagement on him later do anyone any good. Already, Nathan had decided that when they returned to Fort Apache, he would say nothing. If pressed for an opinion, Nathan would do his best to sidestep the issue by supporting Reider's decision.

Abruptly, something in Nathan's subconscious brought him to a halt. With a blink of his eyes and a slight shake of his head, he dismissed the thoughts that had been occupying him and refocused his attention on what was going on around him. The first thing that came to Nathan's attention were the boots of the man in front of him. They had stopped moving. Instead, the boots, and the soldier they belonged to, had moved off to one side of the trail. There, the soldier lay in the snow, seeking cover behind a tree that was far too slim to provide either cover or concealment. Looking up ahead, beyond the man he had been following, Nathan could see that the forest they had been moving through opened into a field. Though he couldn't see all of the platoon, those that he did see were deployed, as they had been, back on the hill. After a quick check of his map showed that they were still a click or more from their next checkpoint, Nathan concluded that Reider's point element had come across something else.

Without hesitation, Nathan turned, as he had before, to Sergeant Hernandes. "Deploy your squad, sergeant," Nathan ordered in a low, calm voice that betrayed no alarm or concern. "I'm going on up to see what sort of speed bump we've hit this time."

Having taken a measure of this young staff officer and determined that he was okay, Hernandes smiled. "Roger that, sir. And, sir," the Hispanic NCO added just as Nathan was turning away, "if you happen to come across a kiosk along the way, I'll take a cup of coffee. Black, with one pack of sugar."

Though he was anxious to get up front and find out what was going on, this opportunity to show that he was one of the good guys was too much to pass up. With a hint of a smile, Nathan looked back at the rest of Hernandes's squad. "I assume that's four coffees?"

From his position off to one side of the trail, Alan Larkin, the 3rd Squad's SAW gunner, looked back at Nathan. "If you don't mind, sir, make mine a Coke. Regular, none of that diet shit." The expression on his face, and tone of his voice, told both Nathan and Hernandes that this young trooper took the banter between officer and NCO seriously.

As he rolled his eyes, Hernandes flashed Nathan an expression of disbelief, then turned toward Larkin. "If you don't start paying attention to your sector, trooper, the only thing you're going to get from the lieutenant and me is one of my diminutive size seven and a half boots planted squarely on your fourth point of contact."

Chuckling, Nathan headed up the trail, past the platoon headquarters section, and over to where he saw Gerald Reider. With the same ease that had allowed him to flip-flop from deep personal contemplation to immediate awareness of his surroundings, Nathan now shed the smile he wore on his face and replaced it with an expression he called his warrior's mask.

10

Watching Dick Kittridge using the Land Warrior sensors attached to his weapon to survey the farmhouse that lay little more than one hundred yards from them was, in a word, weird. Holding his weapon up high, above the pile of freshly cut logs along the side of the road, Kittridge moved the rifle slowly from left to right. While he was doing this, instead of looking up at the weapon his extended arms held, his head was tilted down, as if he were staring into the dirt at the base of the logs behind which he was hidden. Though that was where Kittridge's eyes were pointed, that's not what they were seeing. Rather, Kittridge was enjoying a clear and unobstructed view of the walled farmstead. With his full attention riveted on the green and black images that were being displayed in the heads-up display that hung from his helmet before his right eye, Kittridge searched the place for signs of activity. Other members of the squad, also equipped with the Land Warrior, and deployed to the left and right of Kittridge, were doing likewise when Nathan came up to Reider and the 2nd Squad.

Understanding what was going on, and not wanting to interfere, Nathan quietly settled into a position behind the logs next to Reider, but close enough so that when Kittridge finally gave his report, Nathan could hear it. At the moment Kittridge was saying nothing. Even if he could have seen the two officers, one behind the other, he would have ignored them, for the Warrior system demanded that the operator pay close attention to what he was doing.

Under ordinary circumstances, Kittridge's hands, like most other people's, functioned in conjunction with his sight. When reaching out with his hands to pick something up, Kittridge's eyes not only cued the brain when the hands were nearing the object, but aided in guiding the fingers on his hand as those digits wrapped themselves about the object. When using the Warrior, especially under the conditions in which Kittridge was doing so, the hands and the eyes are not operating in a familiar manner. Kittridge's eyes, in this case, were looking down and not in the general direction where his hands were. He did not have the advantage of seeing his hands in relationship to the farmhouse. All of this required a high degree of concentration and coordination.

From somewhere over to the left a soldier in Kittridge's squad where neither Nathan or Gerald Reider could see, relayed his observations in whispered tones. "I've got a hot house, but no activity."

"Ditto on that, sarge," another voice intoned.

Without pausing his own scan or altering his stance, Kittridge responded. "Roger that. Foss, keep an eye on the house. Reisniack, check out the sheds and yard to the left of the house. Kim, watch the road." After hearing a quick succession of "Wilcos" and muffled grunts in acknowledgment of his orders, Kittridge finally brought his weapon down and looked up at his platoon leader. To Nathan, who was looking over Reider's shoulder, Kittridge looked more like an alien being, half man and half machine, than a human. After blinking, which was necessary to moisten his eye as well as permit them to refocus after having viewed the world on the mini-video cam in front of his right eye, the leader of the 2nd Squad filled Reider in.

"The place is, or was very recently occupied," the NCO stated in a crisp, low voice. "Two vehicles are parked in front and the one on the side. All been run in the past two or three hours. Yet there doesn't seem to be any activity in either the house or the farmyard. But that doesn't mean," he quickly added before his platoon leader had the chance to formulate an improper conclusion, "that there isn't someone in there. That place is built like Fort Knox, with few windows and walls that are probably one foot thick. For all we know, everyone could be around back or in a room that we can't see into."

Though he was pretty sure that he understood everything he was being told, Reider paused before he said anything. Slowly, he looked away from Kittridge as he raised his head above the log pile. Looking over at the farm compound, he saw that the road they had been following passed right in front of the gate that served as both a front door and entrance into the farmyard. Just as he was told, there were two cars parked off to the side of the trail and a third just inside of the open gateway. Other than that, he could see nothing. Had he been in-country longer, Reider would have looked longer to see if he could detect any signs of animals. The Slovakians, professionals though they were, often took those animals that they didn't kill along with their masters.

After he had seen all he could from where he was,

Reider eased himself back down behind the log pile and pondered his options. The road where they were to link up with the Bradleys lay just a kilometer or more on the other side of the farm and up the trail that ran by it. It would have been so nice, Reider thought, to finish up this patrol without any complications or incidents. Looking around for a moment, Reider saw that they could slip past the farmhouse, using the woods they had just left. That would allow them to avoid contact, just as they had done before. After a short, brisk march to the main highway, they could link up with the Bradleys, mount up, and be on their way, back to Fort Apache. Though he would have achieved nothing of value for God and country, the young officer reasoned, this patrol would have given him one good mission under his belt. A small accomplishment like this would go a long way toward building some badly needed self-confidence as well as establishing him as a competent platoon leader.

Then, even though he didn't mean to, the new platoon leader found himself glancing over at Nathan, who was squatting down behind the same pile of logs as Reider and Kittridge. Reider couldn't help but note that the first lieutenant he had been saddled with was watching his every move. It was then that it occurred to Reider that if it wasn't for the fact that this battalion staff officer was with them, he would have been free to execute his plan.

But Lieutenant Dixon was there, watching and waiting for him to make a decision or to screw up. No doubt, Reider reminded himself, Dixon knew of the line in the operations order that required both the mounted and dismounted patrols to investigate all unusual occurrences and incidents along the patrol's route. Whether or not that included a farm that was apparently occupied, but showed no signs of activity, was up to debate and interpretation. Of course, Reider knew that he could have asked Dixon his opinion on the subject. Doing so would have been quite acceptable, given the circumstances. Dixon, after all, had been in Slovakia with 2nd of the 13th from the beginning whereas Reider was new to both the unit and his position as a platoon leader.

To reach out like that, however, and seek the advice that he yearned for would have required a leader who was far more secure in his position and confident that such an action would not reflect adversely upon him. Second Lieutenant Gerald Reider, unfortunately, found that he could not. Whether it was Reider's ego or his resentment that his commander hadn't trusted him to lead this patrol alone that caused the young officer to reject the idea of seeking advice didn't matter. Having made it this far, Reider was determined to see it through on his own.

Looking away from Nathan, Reider glanced around until he spotted Sergeant Dubois. His four men were deployed on either side of the trail they had been traveling on just as it emerged from the woods. Pointing to the leader of the 1st Squad, Reider signaled him to come up and join him behind the pile of logs. After telling his men to stand fast, Dubois pushed himself up off the ground, and took off to join his platoon leader, Sergeant Kittridge, and Nathan.

With Reider right next to Kittridge, Dubois found that he had no place to go but between the two officers. Nathan, seeing the hard-charging NCO eyeing the spot behind the pile of logs next to him, moved away from Reider to give the squad leader a bit more room. Once settled, Dubois turned to Reider. "Yes, sir," was all the former member of the Old Guard stated by way of signaling his platoon leader that he was set and ready to receive whatever orders came his way.

The short trot from the tree line had not fazed Dubois. That, and the fact that there didn't seem to be any sort of threat facing them, allowed the sergeant to speak in the same deep baritone that he always used. Reider's tone, on the other hand, seemed to be an octave or two deeper than he normally used. This left Nathan wondering if the new platoon leader was simply attempting to affect a more commanding voice or if he was, for some reason, nervous. Not that either was inexcusable. After all, he was new to a challenging position. It only made sense that Reider would try something new.

"Sergeant," Reider started, "I want you to take your men and check out the house over there and the farmyard. While we haven't seen signs of life in there yet, there's every reason to believe that the house is, or has recently been, occupied. Second Squad will hold where they are and provide cover, just in case."

Having done this sort of thing countless times, Dubois was tempted to ask, "in case of what?" But he, like Nathan, understood Reider's current plight. Instead, the squad leader nodded. "Roger that, sir. We're ready."

"Good," Reider snapped. "I'll be going forward with you. Move out."

As Dubois twisted about so that he could signal his squad, Nathan saw that the NCO wore an expression on his face that could have been read as either confusion or concern. Guessing that Dubois was no more worried about what he would find in the farmhouse than he was, Nathan assumed that the sergeant was wondering why Reider was going with them. Like Nathan, Dubois knew that if, God forbid, something did happen while they were advancing on the house, Reider would be pinned out there, along with the four men of the 1st Squad. A man who is pinned by fire is, by definition, deprived of his ability to move, shoot, or communicate. Sometimes, if the fire is heavy, or particularly effective, he is unable to perform any of the three aforementioned combat functions. In a situation like that, the poor bastards caught by such fire find that the only thing they can do is press their bodies into the ground as far as the unyielding soil will permit and pray that the people who are supposed to be covering their move are able to lay so much fire on the enemy that *they* have to abandon their efforts and go to ground themselves.

The concern that Nathan had, and assumed Dubois shared, was how Reider would control his platoon from out there if he was pinned by fire. While Nathan understood Reider's desire to "John Wayne" it just as the statue of Iron Mike in front of Infantry Hall at Fort Benning exhorts aspiring leaders to do, the older officer questioned his judgment. Nathan felt constrained by his ambiguous status with the platoon. He was neither Reider's company commander nor platoon sergeant, the people who traditionally teach young officers how to behave in the real world. Unlike before, Nathan found he was unable to let this go by without comment. A bad habit, once started, is often impossible to change unless something really big occurs that forces a change. And in a combat unit, "something really big" usually means that someone has died.

"Lieutenant Reider," Nathan stated while Sergeant Dubois was watching his men move forward. "Are you sure it's a good idea to go forward with the lead squad like that?"

Couched in terms that were in and of themselves harmless, Nathan's question nonetheless caused Reider to become flushed with anger. The idea that this straphanger would have the audacity to question his judgment in front of his men like that, while they were in the middle of executing a maneuver, angered him. Biting back the sharp response that popped into his head, Reider contented himself with giving Nathan a dirty look. Instead of explaining himself to Nathan, Reider turned on Dubois. "Get your men moving, sergeant. We're not going to a goddamn picnic."

Stung by the harsh words that he did not deserve, Dubois gave Nathan a hurt look, then shouted to his squad as he stood up and prepared to lead them forward. "Move it, people. Move it." Ignoring both officers, Dubois ran out from behind the logs just before his squad pulled up even with them and led it forward.

Without giving Nathan or his comment another thought, Reider stood up, made a quick adjustment to his equipment, and took off after the 1st Squad. Rising, Staff Sergeant Kittridge let out a yell, "Cover them!" In the same motion, the squad leader laid his weapon down on the top of the log pile, pulled his rifle butt into his shoulder, and prepared to fire. Subconsciously his thumb tickled the safety on his weapon as he watched the farmhouse and waited. Getting up himself, Nathan leaned against the wet logs and watched the 1st Squad and Reider move forward.

After several seconds passed, Nathan heard Kittridge's voice. "He'll learn." Looking over, Nathan saw that the squad leader, though he still had his eye glued to the Land Warrior sight, had relaxed his stance. "Give him time, Lieutenant Dixon. I'm sure you had some funny ideas when you were new."

Nathan chuckled. "You're right, sergeant. I guess it goes with the turf. After all, what would be the point of being a second lieutenant if you didn't make mistakes."

Without taking his eyes off his sector, Kittridge let a small smile light up his face. "That's right, sir. After all, anything that doesn't kill you only makes you stronger."

Turning away from the sergeant, Nathan found himself wishing he hadn't used that particular saying. Like his mother, he believed that there are some things, and sayings, best left unsaid. "They're in," Kittridge announced as he eased off both his weapon and sight some more. After making one more quick scan of the area after the last of the 1st Squad disappeared inside the house or through the open gate leading to the yard, Kittridge stood up and stretched for the first time since he had reached this point. Flipping his sight up, Kittridge smiled and was about to say something when Sergeant Dubois reappeared in the open door of the house. "Lieutenant Dixon!"

Lifting his hand to his ear while looking at him, Dixon indicated that he was listening. "You better come over here, Lieutenant Dixon. We've got one hell of a mess in here."

Having been in Slovakia for six months, both Nathan and Kittridge knew what that meant. "Well, sir," the squad leader of the 2nd squad stated sheepishly as he prepared to gather up his men and move forward. "I guess I spoke too soon, huh?"

He received no response from the young staff officer. Instead, Nathan moved around the pile of logs and slowly made his way forward. As he did so, he prepared himself, mentally and physically, for what he was about to see.

11

NORTHEAST OF MODŘANY
LATE AFTERNOON, FEBRUARY 5

The cold, both around him and the one that left his nose running, spared Nathan from the stench of death until he was a few yards from the house. Sergeant Dubois, with his weapon pointed down at the ground next to him, waited patiently just outside the door for the battalion staff officer. With a nod of his head, he steered Nathan to the partially open gate leading to the farmyard. "Most of them are out back, sir," he added before Nathan disappeared through the covered archway.

Nathan nodded and swerved toward the gate. Passing through it, he could hear someone throwing up. "Great," Nathan thought as he made his way into the enclosed space. Just what we need. A new scent added to the mix.

He didn't have long to wait before he got his first

good whiff of the stench. Long before he turned the corner, the smell of fresh blood and animal manure penetrated his clogged nostrils and gave his senses a jolt of reality. In many ways being a battalion staff officer had its advantages. Staff officers, particularly those who work operations, rub shoulders with the trigger pullers, or at least those who command them. This close association with the people who actually make things happen infects the staff officer with some of the same excitement and rush combat generates. Yet the staff officers are spared many of the unpleasantries of combat. Staff officers, after all, seldom see the fruits of their labors, which, in battle, are the dead and wounded, both friendly and enemy, with a sprinkling of civilians mixed in. On this day, Nathan would be spared none of that.

Rounding the corner, the young battalion staff officer was greeted by a scene that, at first glance, didn't seem all that out of place for this part of the world. Off to Nathan's right lay a barn with two doors, both of which were open. One side had been converted into a garage for the family car, while the other was used to protect an ancient tractor that was covered with more primer and rust than paint. The car, which was backed in, wasn't in much better shape. If it weren't for the fact that the door on the driver's side was open, Nathan wouldn't have given the car a second thought. He did, however, slow his pace long enough to take note of a cluster of fresh holes in the driver's-side door, made obvious by the brightness of the metal that had been left exposed after bullets had chipped away the paint. This sight invited a closer inspection of the family car. Very quickly a foot, protruding out of the driver's side of the car at an awkward angle, came into focus. Well, Nathan sighed, there's one.

Turning his head away, his eyes fell upon a row of open animal sheds that lined one side of the barn. In them were animals lying quietly on the ground, just below their feeding troughs. If one were not aware of what had happened here, one would have suspected they had settled down for a nap after eating their fill.

"In here, sir," a soldier standing in the open barn door stated in a voice that betrayed no emotion. Even though he knew it would turn his stomach, Nathan headed over.

As bad as the yard had been, the barn was worse. Nathan paused at the entrance next to the trooper who had called out to him. Hector Santiago stood there in silence, cradling his weapon and watching Nathan's every move as the battalion staffer allowed his eyes to adjust to the dark interior while, at the same time, he choked back the nausea he felt rising. "We counted nine in here," Santiago stated matter-of-factly. "Don't know how many there are in the house. The LT and Sergeant Dubois are still checking that out."

Nathan nodded as he looked around at the bodies strewn across the floor. A sudden spasm of vomiting by someone caused him to avert his eyes over to a corner where another member of the 1st Squad, PFC Everett Cash, was kneeling on the ground, spewing what little he had left to give. "Not a pretty sight," Nathan mumbled, more in an effort to say something rather than stand there like a dumbstruck newbie.

"And what sight would that be?" Santiago asked as innocently as he could. "Cash regurgitating his breakfast or the corpses?"

Nathan looked over at Santiago, who was smiling. At times like this, even Nathan was thankful for the graveyard humor that had become fashionable with 2nd of the 13th. It served to break the tension and jerk the mind, if only for a moment, off of the grimness the soldiers often faced. "Take your pick, specialist," Nathan responded. "Neither one is particularly appetizing."

Santiago's grin grew wider. Soldiers like to play "Gotcha" with officers. It was a secret sort of contest between enlisted men to see who could gross out an officer or catch them in an embarrassing situation. Some of the bolder EMs varied this theme by trying to see how far they could push an officer without actually becoming insubordinate. Either way, it was a means soldiers used both to test the nerve of those who were charged with leading them and, sometimes, get back at them for wrongs, real and imagined, the soldiers believed officers had visited upon them. When an officer responded with humor, the less vindictive types rewarded their superior with a smile, a slight nod of the head, and a knowing look that said, "Hey, you're okay."

Using this break as a good time to exit the barn, Nathan turned his back on the dead civilians. "Get your bud out of here into the open air," Nathan ordered as he stepped off. "And then poke around the barn some. See if you can find anything interesting in here."

"Like what, sir?"

Nathan looked over at the corpses once more before he answered. "They're all male and of military age." Then he looked into Santiago's eyes. "My guess is that they're militia. Could be the Slovaks caught them in the middle of something and offed 'em."

"You think that truckload of soldiers we saw a while ago did this, sir?"

There was no longer any hint of smugness or humor in Santiago's voice. His tone told Nathan that the man's question was as honest as it was serious. Though Nathan suspected that the Slovakian soldiers they had evaded back on the hill had been the very same ones who had brought death to this place, Nathan wasn't willing to commit himself. Instead, he passed the question back to Santiago. "What do you think?"

"I think," Santiago stated in a voice that was as cold as it was bitter, "we should have taken those shits on when we had the drop on them."

The look in Santiago's eyes told Nathan that this was no idle statement. Like so many Americans committed to a peacekeeping mission that wasn't keeping the peace, Santiago wanted to do something, anything, to justify their presence and bring an end to the slaughter. "Go help that man," Nathan ordered, "and see what you can find."

This time Santiago said nothing. Instead, he lowered his eyes, shook his head, and turned away from the staff officer.

Unable to go on, Gerald Reider stopped in mid-stride as he was about to enter a room on the second floor of the farmhouse. In the few moments it took him to search the ground floor, Reider had come to realize how different knowing about something was from being able to face it. It had taken the sight of a body, soaked in its own blood, to make him appreciate that he was not at all prepared for this. Hesitating, he stepped back from the doorway he had been standing in until he was stopped by the hall wall behind him. Leaning his head back, his helmet made a dull thump as it hit the wall. For a second he closed his eyes.

All the lectures on tactics and military history at West Point, as well as the countless maneuvers at Fort Benning, had failed to give him the wherewithal to greet the sights and smells that had assaulted him the second he stepped into this farmhouse. The corpse at the threshold, riddled by small-arms fire and left lying crumpled in a pool of its own blood, bore no resemblance to the abstract, two-dimensional image that flashed across the TV screens of America. War was hell. Reider knew this. Everyone knew that all of mankind's wonderful progress had done nothing to make warfare any less vicious or vile. Yet knowing something on an intellectual level had done nothing to lessen the visceral impact that now caused a dryness in Reider's mouth, set his knees to shaking, and created a dizziness that scrambled every thought in his head. For the first time in his life, this young officer understood what panic felt like.

"Lieutenant, I've found another one down here." The

voice of Sergeant Dubois came at Reider like a lifeline thrown to a drowning man.

And like those of a man feeling himself slipping away, Reider's body and mind struggled to grab on to it. With more effort than he could have imagined such simple acts could require, Gerald Reider opened his eyes, straightened himself up, and swallowed the bitter bile that lingered in his throat. "Right," Reider finally managed. "Keep checking."

"I'm done down here," the NCO replied quickly. "Do you need some help up there?"

At that moment Reider couldn't tell, for sure, whether the assistant squad leader of the 1st Squad was simply trying to be helpful or if the NCO had detected something in Reider's voice that told him his platoon leader was experiencing a problem. Either way, Reider swore, he wasn't going to allow his men to see him like this if he could help it. "No. I'll finish up here. Go out back and see how the rest of the squad is doing."

After a pause, Reider heard Dubois shuffle off without another word.

Left alone, Gerald Reider stared at the doorway he had attempted to go through before. It was a meter away, maybe less. One or two steps would be more than enough to carry him through. That's all he needed to take, Reider told himself. One or two steps. Simple. One step was nothing, twenty-eight or thirty inches for him. With his eyes still fixed on the door before him, Reider's mind attacked this problem. Given my pace, Reider told himself, I've already taken something like twelve or thirteen thousand steps today. Thirteen thousand steps have brought me here, he mused, and now I can't find the strength to make one more. Just one more, his mind repeated.

What sort of strength was he lacking? Reider found himself wondering. Surely it wasn't physical. At Fort Benning he had finished a twenty-five-mile forced march in the afternoon and played racquetball that evening.

Physically, Reider knew he wasn't lacking. So that meant only one thing. If it wasn't a question of physical strength, then it could only mean that he lacked the moral strength to go through that door. Angered by his own weakness, Reider drew himself erect and prepared to go forth.

Manfully, the determined young infantry officer barged into the room with more force and vigor than the situation called for. Still, for Reider, this was a victory. He knew this and, for the briefest of moments, as his eyes scanned the room he now stood in, Gerald Reider felt a surge of triumph. Only slowly did this exhilaration begin to ebb as he took in the room and the reality of his situation reasserted itself.

Though simple, there was a decidedly feminine decor to the room. The small bed and the stuffed animals neatly lined up on it reminded Reider of his sister's room. This particular comparison struck Reider as disturbing. How would he feel, he suddenly found himself wondering, if a foreign soldier came barging into her room? As this thought swirled around in his mind, his hands tightened on the weapon he held. That, he decided, was why he had defied his parents' wishes and entered this profession. No one is going to do this in my country, the young officer told himself.

This latest thought was still building into a rage that was rapidly superseding the queasiness he had felt just moments before, when his eyes saw her in the corner of the room. From where he stood, only a tuft of blonde hair was visible. It required him to take yet one more step before he could see all of the girl. Even before his left foot hit the floor, Gerald Reider was sorry that he had.

The girl was curled up in a tight little ball. Her knees were drawn into her chest, held there with clasped hands. Her head was bowed down, resting on those knees, causing her hair to cascade down about her. The off-white nightgown, with ruffles on the sleeves, draped her in a protective tent from which only the toes of her bare feet, hands, and head emerged. Were it not for the dark red streams of dried blood that stained the front of that nightgown, the young officer would have been tempted to reach out and wake her up.

Sharply, his emotions turned about yet again, and the nausea that he had so recently mastered renewed its effort to overcome Gerald Reider. That his sister was not a natural blonde did not matter. This sight, more than anything else he had seen up to now, struck home. Even as this comparison worked its way into his consciousness, Gerald Reider's fertile and analytical mind quickly deduced that whoever had murdered this girl had done so at close range, while she huddled in panic in the corner, looking up at her executioner.

"No matter how many times I've seen something like that," Nathan Dixon stated slowly in a low voice, "I still become, well, sick."

Not having heard Dixon enter the room behind him, the first lieutenant's words caught Reider off guard. It took everything he could to keep from literally jumping right off the floor. That he was not able to completely restrain the start that shook him was obvious when he turned to face Dixon. When he saw the platoon leader's reaction, Nathan quickly added, "I'm sorry. I didn't mean to sneak up on you like that."

Though he tried to shrug off his reaction, all Reider managed to get out was "Well, no, I . . ." before he found himself looking back at the dead girl. With his emotions in a knot, Reider dropped the guard that he had erected between himself and the interloper from the battalion staff. "Why the girl?"

"That's easy," Nathan stated as he pulled the thick comforter from the bed and stepped forward to cover the small corpse. "The Slovaks mean to end it, once and for all. Rather than leave even the tiniest sliver behind to fester and reinfect their community, they intend to root out every vestige of the Hungarian minority that exists within their borders and eradicate it."

"But she's a child!" Reider protested. "Just an innocent child!"

Finished, Dixon stepped back before answering. Slowly, he shook his head. "She's more than just a child in the eyes of the Slovak majority. She's the mother of the next generation, a generation that, if allowed to come into this world, would be taught to avenge the horrors that were visited on their people here, during this civil war." Then, turning to face Reider, Dixon added, "These people are not Americans. To them their history, religion, race, land, and family are bound together to create a culture that is very real to them, something that is almost tangible. Who they are as a people," he stated as his voice slowly trailed away, "is almost as important as life itself."

"That's a pretty damned cold way of looking at murder," Reider snapped.

Unfazed by the anger in the platoon leader's voice, Nathan looked into Reider's eyes. "This isn't murder. It's genocide." Then, feeling that he was about to lose his own composure, Nathan stepped out of the room and made his way toward the stairs. As he did so, he quickly wiped away the tears that he had mercifully been able to hold back until after he had left the presence of his fellow officer.

12

When Gerald Reider finally made his way back down to the ground floor, the scattered members of Sergeant Dubois's squad had come together in the kitchen. In the center of the room PFC Everett Cash was sitting at the table. His helmet lay upside down next to his left elbow. His right elbow was resting on the table. Between his hands he propped up a face that was tinged with subtle hues of gray and green. The expression that contorted Cash's face reminded Reider of one his roommate at West Point wore after one of his world-famous weekend drinking binges.

Immediately behind Cash was Specialist Smith. Like Cash, he had shed his helmet. Unlike his mess buddy, Smith was on his feet and moving about the kitchen, opening cabinets and pulling out drawers, searching for something while nibbling on a chunk of cheese that he held in his hand. Reider watched Smith for a moment, unsure whether he should reprimand the man for what he took to be the theft of food, or remain silent.

The sound of someone clearing his throat, off in a corner, caught Reider's attention and spared him having to make that particular decision. Turning toward the direction from which the noise had come, Reider saw the other members of the squad, Sergeant Dubois and Specialist Santiago. Between them stood 1st Lieutenant Dixon. Smith, who had heard Reider enter the room, was staring back at his platoon leader. Dubois and Nathan, speaking in hushed tones, paid Reider no heed. Guessing what was on Reider's mind, Santiago's face quickly lost the look of concern it had been wearing. It was replaced with a sheepish expression, like one a child sported when caught by a parent doing something wrong. In a hushed tone, which could have been meant either as an alert to Lieutenant Dixon or a greeting to Reider, Santiago gave a crisp "Lieutenant Reider."

Looking over at Reider, Nathan Dixon neither greeted his fellow officer nor even acknowledged his presence. Instead Dixon returned to the hushed conversation he had been holding with Dubois. The squad leader, for his part, found himself in an awkward position. At the mention of Reider's name, Dubois had tensed up, looking away from Dixon, over to Reider, and then back to Dixon. The tone of his voice, which also shifted, was what finally tipped Nathan off that the NCO had suddenly become very self-conscious and withdrawn.

With as much finesse and diplomacy as he could, Nathan ended his discussion with Reider's subordinates. "Your people have been kind enough," Nathan stated innocently to Reider, "to update me on what they found while you were finishing upstairs. Unless you found another one after I left you, the body count seems to be fourteen. One in the garage, ten in the barn, two on the ground floor, and one up there." His eyes quickly glanced up at the ceiling as he uttered the words *up there*. "From what the sergeant and his men saw, there was no struggle, no resistance."

The speed with which Nathan spewed out this information didn't leave any time for Gerald Reider to build up his righteous indignation at what he took to be Nathan's interference with his platoon. Instead, Reider found that he had no choice now but to deal with the tactical situation and wait, perhaps until later, to reprimand his squad leader.

"Sergeant Dubois," Reider asked in an effort to assert his rightful authority and ease Dixon out of the picture. "Did your people find any weapons or military equipment?"

Santiago, seeing that his assistant squad leader was still unsure of what was going on between the two officers, answered instead. "No, sir. No weapons. But we did find some empty boxes, empty plastic bags, packing material, and freshly dug holes in the corner of the barnyard near the dung heap. My guess is that the Slovakian Army found this militia Kommando just as they were getting ready to go out and raise some hell."

While he was not sure how Santiago could be so certain that those odds and ends equaled proof positive that this had been an ethnic Hungarian Kommando, Reider took the man at his word. After all, neither Dixon nor Dubois, soldiers who had been doing this for some time, challenged his assertion. "Okay," the platoon leader sighed, not knowing what else to say. After a quick peek at his watch, Reider announced in a commanding voice, "We'd best get moving. We're running late and we still have a click to go to the linkup point."

Only Smith offered up a challenge. "Don't we have enough time to make some tea?" Surprised at this question, Gerald Reider looked over to Specialist Smith, who had continued rifling the cabinets while the officers had been engaged in a bout of psychological sparring. Having found what he had been looking for, the squad's

SAW gunner was holding a tea bag, dangling by a thin string, in one hand and a bright red teapot in another. "It's for Cash, sir. He kind of lost it out back when we found the militiamen in the barn. The tea will help settle his stomach."

Incensed at being challenged like this over such a trivial matter, Reider drew in a deep breath. "A brisk pace in the cool afternoon air will do even more for him. Now gather up your gear and get moving. All of you." When he ended this order, Reider was staring right at Nathan with a look of disgust in his eyes. To him, the battalion staff officer now represented not only a threat to his authority, but had shown poor leadership by standing idly by while one of his men ransacked civilian property.

It wasn't until Cash tried to comply with the order and stand up that Gerald Reider realized that, perhaps, he had been a bit hasty. Pushing up off the tabletop with his hands, Cash started to move the chair he had been seated on away with the back of his legs and stand up. Instead, he went crashing back down into it when his knees buckled. Had Smith not jumped behind the chair and arrested its backward motion, Cash's dead weight would have shoved the chair out of the way, leaving him free to sprawl on the floor.

Seeing that Cash was safe, all eyes turned to Reider. Going from one man to the next, the platoon leader saw expressions that ranged from anger to restrained disgust. Only Nathan Dixon's eyes said nothing, though deep down inside, the staff officer yearned to.

It took several minutes to form up the platoon before Gerald Reider nodded to Kittridge to lead off, down the trail. Now more than ever, Reider looked forward to seeing this day end. Looking down at the ground before him as he followed along, the young officer tried to ignore the aching leg muscles that had tightened up during their search of the farmhouse. Rather then dwelling on the exhaustion that was starting to become overwhelming, the physical discomfort he was now beginning to experience, and the images of death that were as new as they were horrific, Reider concentrated on sorting out what he would say when he reported in to his CO.

Reider pondered this as he struggled to lift one heavy, mud-covered foot up out of the muck and throw it forward. Was finding civilians butchered like that actually as routine as Dubois and his men made it appear? Was it really permissible simply to walk away from something like that without so much as covering the dead? It had to be, Reider told himself, otherwise Dixon would have said something. Why else would Dixon say nothing when he, Reider, had given the order to move out? Surely, Reider reasoned, Lieutenant Dixon would have intervened had it been necessary. That was, after all, why that officer was there, to make sure the new platoon leader didn't get into trouble. Of course, Reider reasoned, Dixon could be letting him screw up in an effort to embarrass him for the way he, Reider, had been treating Dixon. Even at West Point, Gerald Reider had seen classmates exact a cruel revenge on a fellow cadet by letting the unsuspecting soul mess all over himself in public without lifting a finger to prevent it.

No, no, Reider told himself as one of his leg muscles sent a wave of pain through him. West Point was different. This, he tried to convince himself, was the real world, the real Army. He firmly believed that officers didn't do that sort of thing. They were not only professionals, but they were officers and gentlemen, even if people like Dixon hadn't graduated from the Academy. Hadn't they all taken the same oath of office? Reider reasoned as the painful charley horse in his right leg finally began to subside. Weren't they all there in pursuit of the same goal?

Looking up, Reider scanned what he could see of the

snow-covered countryside that they were traveling through. This certainly is one hell of a conversation to be having with oneself, he told himself, especially at a time like this. Embarrassed by these thoughts, as well as the numerous aches and pains that simply defied his efforts to ignore, Reider now began to wonder if things would, over time, get better. Would he ever manage to master the pettiness with which he had treated others he considered a threat to him, like Lieutenant Dixon? Would he be able to look at the corpse of a young child without feeling a thing like that staff officer had? And, even more important to Reider at that particular moment, would he be able to find the discipline and willpower that would allow him to ignore the physical discomforts that threatened to overwhelm him?

Trudging along in silence, the soldiers of 3rd Platoon made their way forward, toward the main road and the linkup point where, in less than half an hour, they were to marry up with their Bradleys and bring this patrol to an end.

The fact that the Bradleys were not in the field waiting for them when they arrived did not bother Nathan Dixon. Emerging from the last patch of woods they would have to navigate through that day, Nathan took a quick glance about looking for the terrain features he had been expecting to see. The trail they had been moving along since leaving the farmhouse ran straight down a gentle, concave slope. The point at which the trail intersected the road that the 3rd Platoon's Bradleys had been patrolling all afternoon was at the foot of that slope. Just ahead, twenty meters or so shy of that intersection he saw Gerald Reider standing in the center of the trail. The platoon leader was, as best as Nathan could determine, checking his GPS and map to make sure that he, and his platoon, were in the right place. The soldiers of the 2nd and 1st Squads were haphazardly deployed to either side of the trail between Reider and the paved road.

Stepping aside as the members of 3rd Squad filed past him, Dixon checked his watch, then reached for his canteen. It was light, which meant he had very little water left. Not that he would need much more. If he was still thirsty when the tracks arrived, he could always refill it from the five-gallon water cans each of them carried. And even if they were empty, which sometimes happened due to laxness or oversight, Nathan knew he could survive until they reached Fort Apache. Chris Donovan, no doubt, would be waiting there to buy him a soda at the small PX set up every night in the corner of the mess tent.

The thought of her brought a smile to Nathan's face. He'd have to be careful tonight, he told himself. If he played the role of the weary warrior, back from the long grueling foot patrol just right, she'd be putty in his hands. But if he overdid it, he'd be on her shit list for a week. Nathan recalled that his own mother had been like that. "Women," he mused. "They're either heaven or hell."

Tobias, who was the last man in the 3rd Squad, had just come up even with Nathan when he had mumbled that last bit about heaven and hell. An easygoing young soldier, Tobias smiled as he turned to face Nathan. "And sometimes, sir, they're a little of both."

With a broad grin, Nathan raised his canteen to toast Tobias. "I'll drink to that."

He was finishing up the last of his canteen when Nathan heard the faint squeak that a track makes as it's being pulled through the metal teeth of a drive sprocket. Slipping his canteen back into its pouch, Nathan decided to stand fast for the moment. He'd be out of the way where he was, of both Reider and the Bradleys as they left the road and deployed in the field. He hadn't been needed all day so far and was quite confident that he wouldn't be needed now that the patrol was but a few minutes from wrapping up.

Only slowly, as he stood there, thinking of Chris Donovan, did Nathan become aware of the fact that the engine noise making its way to where he stood wasn't quite right. Even before his conscious mind began working on this discrepancy, Nathan instinctively turned his head to the right, slightly, so that he could hear better. Though his library of memorized sounds identified the oncoming vehicle as a tank, his logical mind rebelled against that notion. There were no American tanks operating in this area, he told himself. The platoon he was with was the only U.S. unit that he knew of that was supposed to be there. And the Slovakian Army, as bold as it had been of late, the battalion staff officer told himself, wouldn't dare violate the NATO prohibition against deploying any of its tanks, even if the weather was grounding NATO aircraft.

It had to be the snow, the terrain, and perhaps even the surrounding woods that were distorting the roar of the 3rd Platoon's Bradleys, Nathan convinced himself. Had to be.

Still, as the noise grew louder, Nathan continued to look over, to his right, where the paved road disappeared behind a curve and another stand of trees. While the sound grew louder and more distinct, Nathan's apprehension increased, so much so that he felt himself taking an involuntary step back, toward the tree line they had just emerged from. "You're being foolish," he started to mumble. "You're tired and being foolish."

That thought, as well as the last vestige of doubt, disappeared the instant he saw a long, oversized 125mm barrel poke around the corner and come into view. Instinctively, Nathan took another step backward and crouched. Farther down the slope the soldiers of the 3rd Platoon were reacting according to their particular experience and curiosity. While most remained in their positions, either prone or kneeling, a couple actually stood up, as if to greet what they thought was their ride home. Even when the protruding barrel grew in length and the front edge of the Slovakian T-72 tank came into view, these soldiers, including Gerald Reider, continued to stand and watch the foreign tank roll forward, toward them.

For his part, the tank commander of the T-72 paid Reider and his bewildered soldiers no heed. Snuggled tightly in the open hatch of his tank, like a cork in a bottle, the black-clad tanker craned his neck around the front opening hatch and peered down the road ahead. Only when the fast-moving tank came up to the point where the trail met the road it was traveling on did something cause the Slovakian tank commander to look over to his left. As surprised as Nathan and Reider's men were to see the Slovakian tank, the appearance of armed men deployed in a field mere meters from him was even more stunning to the Slovakian commander. Wide-eyed and mouth agape, the tank commander found that all he could do, for the moment, was stare at the soldiers. Were it not for the forward moment of the vehicle, which carried the flabbergasted Slovakian away, he would have been rooted in place by the shock.

Before the first tank disappeared behind the next curve in the road, a second T-72 rolled into view. This one had its main gun traversed off to its right flank, so that Nathan could see only the back of the tank commander's shoulders and head. Like all armies, the Slovakians employed standard battle drills and formation. And like the U.S. Army, theirs stipulated that combat vehicles moving in a column stagger the orientation of their gun tubes. Unfortunately, as the current case in hand amply demonstrated, the threat you come across may not necessarily be in the area you are facing. Whether it was the scrambling of Reider's men to seek whatever meager cover they could find in the open field they were in, or a call from the lead tank, the commander of the second tank abruptly spun about, looked at Reider's men, then started to scream out orders.

By now Nathan was lying flat on the ground, hugging it and the most substantial tree he could find with all the enthusiasm of a radical environmentalist. He watched as the gunner of the T-72 slew the turret of his tank about over the frontal arc of the tank and then, with agonizing deliberateness, elevated and aimed it at Reider's men. Were it not for the fact that the window of opportunity in which the speeding tank could engage was small, Nathan was convinced that this second tank would have taken them under fire. Whether the tank's wild shooting from the hip would have caused any casualties on Reider's men, if indeed the tank commander did intend to fire, didn't matter to Nathan. The Slovakian's actions were hostile and, without doubt, placed American soldiers in danger. Bringing his rifle up to his shoulder, Nathan yelled down the hill to Reider. "Get your men down and deploy the Javelin, Lieutenant!"

The turn of events that had put a serious wrinkle in his successful afternoon patrol left an already exhausted Gerald Reider momentarily befuddled. It took the image of a 125mm smooth-bore cannon pointed at him and Dixon's shouted orders to pierce this mental haze. In a flash, he emptied his hands and threw himself forward into a shallow ditch that ran alongside the downward-sloping trail. The snow and the soft layer of mud that lay beneath it cushioned his fall.

Only after the fact did Reider come to appreciate that his actions might have been a bit too precipitous. With a jerk, he lifted his head, blowing whatever breath he still had in his lungs out through his nostrils in an effort to expel the liquid mud that had rushed down them. Though only marginally successful, it did permit him to move quickly on to the next order of business, which was to wipe the muck from his eyes and look around. By the time he had cleared enough of the rich brown goo from his face, the tank was gone. It, and the gigantic cannon that had sent him sprawling, was nowhere to be seen. No doubt, Reider quickly summarized, it had continued on, unimpeded, down the road just as the first tank had. The relief that this reevaluation brought was horribly short lived. From somewhere behind him, Reider heard Specialist Zeke Fishburn, the Javelin gunner, yelling to his assistant gunner. "Shit! Here comes another!"

With a snap, Reider turned his head to face the spot on the road where the other two tanks had made their appearance. This third tank, unlike its brethren, had been afforded sufficient time to bring its gun about to meet the threat that the first two hadn't been able to engage. With its main gun already oriented on their general direction, it took just a second for the gunner of this third tank to lay his sights in the center of where Reider's platoon was and cut loose with the tank's coaxial machine gun.

The rattle of machine-gun fire caused Reider instinctively to drop his head yet again. This time, however, he had the forethought to turn his head sideways. Still, this move did not keep the cold liquid mud from finding his right ear and filling it.

As annoying and unpleasant as this was, Gerald Reider's physical discomfort didn't come close to matching the mental anguish he was experiencing. Around him the screams of his sergeants as they implored their men to stay down mixed in with the chatter of the T-72's machine gun. Against all of this, the *pop-pop-pop* of an M-16 firing back seemed pitiful and quite lame. At least, Reider thought as he tried to gauge if the tank's machine gun was having any effect, someone was shooting back. That had to be good, he told himself. That had to make a difference. It *had* to.

Slowly, the vibration that shook the earth he lay upon became less and less pronounced, just as the sound of the tank's machine gun diminished. Unable to resist the

need to find out what was going on around him, Reider
lifted his head and looked about. He did so just in time
to see the third, and what he hoped to be, last Slovakian
tank disappear, around the corner, just as the other two
had before. Only after it had passed from sight did Reider, and every other man in his platoon, look over to
the point in the road where all of the tanks had appeared. For several seconds, everyone held their breath
as they watched and waited to see if there would be a
fourth.

Even though he had not emptied the magazine that was
in his weapon, Nathan Dixon pressed the magazine release button on the side of his smoking weapon and let
the partially expended magazine fall away. This he managed to do while pushing himself up off the ground and
lurching forward down the hill, to where the Javelin
crew was. As psychologically therapeutic as shooting
5.56mm ball ammunition at a tank might have been for
Nathan, he knew it would take something decidedly
more substantial, like a Javelin anti-tank guided missile,
to send a telling message to the next Slovakian tank. To
this end, he was determined to go down to where the
crew was struggling to bring their weapon into play and
do whatever he could to ensure that they were ready,
next time. That this would prove to be unnecessary only
became apparent as Nathan made his way forward.
Their crisis was, for the moment, past. In place of the
shock that had rocked each and every one of them came
the sickening realization that their trials for the day were
just beginning.

13

NORTHEAST OF MODŘANY,
EARLY EVENING, FEBRUARY 5

Except for the fading sound of drive sprockets rapidly pulling tank tracks along the road, silence descended on the snow-covered field where the 3rd Platoon lay scattered. Even before he was sure that they had seen the last of the Slovakian tanks, Nathan Dixon was up off the ground and running as fast as the snow and the mud let him down to where Fishburn was struggling with his ATGM's command launch unit. Throwing himself down on the ground next to the Javelin gunner and his wide-eyed assistant, Nathan watched the pair. "What the hell is taking you so long?" the battalion staff officer finally shouted.

Without looking away, Fishburn responded, half in anger due to his own ineptitude and half apologetically. "We only take the CLU out of the carrier for inspections and to clean it. Hell, I can't remember the last time was when we did any serious training with this piece of . . ."

"Okay, okay," Nathan snapped. Then, he softened his tone. "Do the best you can and let me know when your system is up and ready."

With a click, Fishburn snapped one more catch into place, then turned to face Nathan. "We're ready now, sir."

With a weak smile and nod, Nathan acknowledged Fishburn's announcement before turning and looking around. The first person he laid his eyes on was Staff Sergeant Kittridge. As well as the squad leader for the 2nd Squad, he was also the senior NCO with the dismounted element. As such, he had been playing the role of platoon sergeant during the afternoon when it had been necessary to do so. After checking his own four men and making sure they were safe and ready for whatever came next, Kittridge had gotten to his feet to sort out the platoon. Like Nathan, he had been wondering what was with the Javelin crew. By the time he found where the Javelin crew was hunkered down, Nathan was with them and Fishburn was hoisting the missile tube onto his shoulder. It was then that he and Nathan locked eyes. "Have you seen Lieutenant Reider?"

Nathan got up onto his knees. "No." Then he shouted back, "Any casualties?"

Not having finished checking the other squads, the NCO looked about. "Squad leaders! Check your men and sound off."

It took a moment for Gerald Reider to appreciate that the immediate danger had passed. Slowly, the shock of being under fire for the first time gave way to a feeling of embarrassment, then anger. The embarrassment stemmed from the cold, wet mud that coated his face and was, at that moment, relentlessly penetrating every gap and opening in his clothing. The anger that accompanied it was at his failure to execute his duties as a platoon leader. Even now, listening to the shouts of Nathan and his NCOs sorting things out, Reider imagined that he had failed. The young officer came to the inescapable conclusion that by throwing himself into this muddy ditch, he had tossed away both his dignity and his moral authority to lead. For the first time that day, the idea of simply rolling over and giving up joined the jumble of thoughts that whirled about in his befuddled mind.

To do that, however, was not an option. He was a West Pointer, Reider told himself. He was the inheritor of a proud tradition and, as such, was charged with the responsibility of upholding it. Though his cynical peers who had attended other colleges and were at that moment pursuing their own careers in law and business considered the words *duty, honor,* and *country* out of place in their modern, sophisticated world, to Reider and his classmates they had power, real power. It took more than mere words, after all, to motivate men to put up with the sacrifices that a peacetime Army heaps on its members while the country they are charged to defend enjoys unparalleled prosperity. And it takes more than a simple turn of phrase to motivate men and women to place their lives on the line, day in and day out, to hold a line that so few even knew existed.

With that minor crisis settled, he began the torturous task of extracting himself from the ditch in which he had sought shelter. His efforts to pick himself up out of the mud, forced him to make a number of compromises, none of which were particularly thrilling. This included such actions as placing his gloved hands down, under his chest, into the mud, and pushing up. The weight of his body and the softness of the mud meant that his hands, gloves and all, sank deeper into the mud, permitting it to flow freely into the thin gaps, filling his gloves and spreading up his arm. Even after he had managed to get himself up onto his knees, Reider could still feel new streams of dampness radiate their way up his pant legs and down into his boots. The thought of what he looked like, as he pulled a glove off and used a finger to scoop mud out of his right ear, only added to a feeling of discomfort that overwhelmed every square inch of his body.

Lieutenant Dixon's voice, a voice that had been a source of annoyance all day, called out his name and brought to him the attention of the entire platoon before he was ready. "Are you all right, Lieutenant Reider?"

Looking over to where Dixon stood, towering over the vigilant Javelin gunners, Reider imagined he saw Dixon sporting a smile. Though he had no way of knowing for sure if his deplorable predicament was the reason for the grin the battalion staff officer was sporting, Reider didn't like it. Even if they had survived the unexpected confrontation with the Slovakian tanks without any apparent harm to them, this was neither the time nor place to be smiling. "I'm fine," Reider said. He was about to add that he was a little shaken, but such an admission, he realized, would be wrong, even though he was. He was both an officer and the leader of this platoon. As long as those two things were true, Reider told himself, he'd do his best to maintain his dignity and his authority. Standing up, Reider stepped out of the ditch, shook each arm, leg, and foot in turn, then started to make his way to Dixon. "A word with you, Lieutenant," Reider intoned as he grew near.

Still concerned with their situation, Nathan looked around before responding. "Before we do that, Lieutenant Reider," the senior officer stated in a calm, firm tone as his eyes darted, "I suggest that we pull the platoon back, up the hill, and into those trees."

Reider stopped in his tracks. He stared at Nathan for the longest time, fuming that he had not thought of doing that very thing first. "Yes, of course," the bedraggled officer finally mumbled. "Sergeant Kittridge," he shouted. "Redeploy the platoon up there."

Kittridge didn't need to look over and see where Reider's mud-covered glove was pointed. For that matter, he hadn't even needed to hear Reider's order. By the time it had been given, Kittridge was already signaling the other squad leaders with his hands to pack up and move out based on what Nathan Dixon suggested.

Taking his cue from Dixon, Gerald Reider waited until the squads finished pulling back into the tree line where Dixon had sought cover during the spat with the tanks. Even as they were doing so, the more outspoken members of the platoon managed to shed their fears and began making light of their current plight. From his position, Tobias of the 3rd Squad called out to no one in particular. "Man, isn't it just my luck. I leave the 'hood to get away from drive-by shootings and *bam!* Look what happens."

Taking up that theme, Everett Cash, another African-American in the 1st Squad, looked up at Sergeant Kittridge, who was walking near him, overseeing the platoon's redeployment. "Hey, that's right, Kitt. Can I file with the Justice Department and have those assholes arrested for committing a hate crime?"

Stopping in front of Cash, Kittridge looked down at him. "Keep shooting your mouth off, soldier, and I'll show you what a real hate crime looks like."

Wide-eyed, Cash looked about in mock bewilderment. "Help!" he called out. "I'm being oppressed."

From a distance Nathan watched in amusement while Gerald Reider looked upon the same scene with growing confusion. Not far from the two officers, tucked away a bit deeper in the woods, Specialist Four Sam Pavlovski squatted on the ground with his radio nestled between his legs. He was in the process of switching antennas from the short whip to a longer one in the hope that the greater range of the second antenna was all that was necessary to contact Taylor and the Bradleys. After a quick glance at Pavlovski to check his progress, Nathan turned toward Reider. "When was the last time you made contact with the Bradleys?"

Reider, covered with mud and still smarting from his clumsy performance in the field, didn't look at Nathan when he answered. With his head bowed slightly, he looked past the battalion staff officer using the short brim of his helmet to hide his mud-covered face. "Uh, just before we came across the farmhouse, I attempted to make contact. And then again, before leaving, I had the RTO try again."

The words *attempted* and *tried* pricked Nathan's ears. In his efforts to stay out of Reider's hair, Nathan had intentionally hung back. "You attempted to make contact?" Nathan asked with a note of surprise in his voice.

"We didn't make contact." Looking up into Nathan's eyes, Reider realized for the first time that he had really screwed up. "I didn't think anything of it. The CO had warned me that there would be times when the two elements of my platoon would be out of contact."

Now it was Nathan's turn to look away. Lifting his eyes, he stared up at the branches of the heavily burdened trees, bent to the breaking point by the wet snow that clung to them. That he had missed seeing the RTO or Reider make those radio checks did not surprise him. What struck Nathan was the fact that Reider had failed both times and had not even bothered to inform him.

Dropping his chin, Nathan stared at Reider, who hadn't moved. "I think we have a problem here, Lieutenant Reider."

Not sure if the battalion staff officer was talking about their tactical situation or the animosity that he felt toward the senior lieutenant, Reider played it safe. With a nod, he acknowledged Dixon's comment, then waited for him to continue.

"The last roving checkpoint that Sergeant Taylor was scheduled to establish is less than five clicks from here. Even if you take into account the lay of the land, we should have been able to contact him at least once."

Reider's mind snatched onto Dixon's use of the word *we* instead of *you.* He wondered if Dixon was simply trying to be kind to him and not blame him, or if Dixon was being pompous and considered himself a part of the platoon. Either way, the second lieutenant said nothing as he stood there waiting for Dixon to go on.

"What kind of shape are your men in, lieutenant?" Nathan asked.

Not sure of what sort of answer the battalion staff officer was looking for, Gerald Reider looked over his shoulder to where his men were deployed. A few of them, including Sergeant Kittridge, returned his stare. Reider didn't know these men. He didn't know how to read their expressions yet, or judge how they felt, physically or emotionally, by their carriage and actions. They were strangers to him, in every way. This wasn't like a tactical exercise at West Point or Benning, where you could use your own mental and physical status as a means of gauging those around you. Back then Reider had been among peers, cadets and newly commissioned officers who were of the same age, general background, and outlook. The men in his platoon, he realized, had little in common with him other than the fact that they all wore the same uniform, were gathered together in the same unit, and at the moment, faced the same ambiguous situation. So Dixon's question concerning the status of his platoon was, for Reider, far more difficult to answer than he could ever have imagined.

Turning back to face the waiting officer, Reider shook his head. "I'm not sure," he finally admitted.

While the members of 3rd Platoon were, individually, just as much strangers to Nathan as they were to Reider, Nathan had the one thing that Reider lacked, experience with troops. "I expect your men are beginning to wear a bit thin," Nathan ventured, trying to put the best face on his assessment. "I know I am. This snow and mud takes a lot out of a person."

Reider replied with an unsolicited response. "Yes, it does, doesn't it."

Now it was Nathan's turn to reply with a simple nod as he looked over to Pavlovski as he sat in the snow, speaking into the radio's hand mike. "Tango seven five Yankee, this is Tango seven five mike, over."

Hearing the call signs, Reider turned to watch in silence, perking his ears up in the hope that he would hear a response to Pavlovski's call.

"Tango seven five Yankee, this is Tango seven five mike, over," the RTO repeated. Again, there was silence. Looking up at his platoon leader, Pavlovski articulated what both officers already knew. "Sir, negative contact."

For a moment Nathan said nothing. "Switch to your company frequency and see if you can contact him, your CO, or anyone else. If you can't contact anyone on that net," Nathan added after a moment's hesitation, "try battalion command net."

Reider looked at the battalion staff officer. "That radio doesn't have the range to reach the base camp."

"I know," Nathan replied. "But, if there's something going on that we don't know about, there's a good chance Colonel Miller might send someone out after us or . . ."

"Or?" Reider asked when Nathan didn't finish his last sentence.

"Or, Lieutenant Reider," he finally continued, "find out what happened. Either way, I have no doubt that as long as the Old Man has a breath left in him, he'll do whatever it takes to pull our collective chestnuts out of the fire that we seem to have landed in."

Too tired and confused by the events of the day to maintain his aloofness, Reider gave in to his compelling need for straight answers. "What's going on? I mean, what do you suppose has happened?"

"Do you want the short version or a Fort Leavenworth–style assessment?"

Gerald Reider didn't much care for Dixon's witty response to what he felt was a sincere request for information. He hadn't been around in a unit long enough to develop a taste for either the cynicism or dark humor that Nathan enjoyed so much. "Look," Reider snapped. "Cut me some slack. I know I'm new to this and the unit. And I know I have a lot to learn. But as far as I'm concerned, this is neither the time or place to be playing silly-ass games with the new kid or sharpening your wit. So if you don't mind, Lieutenant Dixon, let's dispense with the bullshit. Now what in the hell is going on?"

Nathan's hand instinctively tightened its grip around the upper handguard of his rifle as he struggled to hold his tongue in check. At that moment he was of two minds. His gut instinct yelled at him to jack the little shit-faced second lieutenant standing in front of him and read him the riot act. While some contended that seniority between lieutenants was like virtue among whores, Nathan Dixon, who happened to be a senior first lieutenant, didn't see things that way. As far as he was concerned, Reider had crossed the line and needed to be slapped down.

Yet his instincts as a leader checked Nathan's more visceral response. Like Reider, he too was tired, and hungry as well. Falling behind in their schedule because of the slow going in the snow, the platoon had not stopped long enough to eat the one MRE they had been issued for their noon meal. Like his father, Nathan was not at his best when he was tired and hungry. Still, Nathan restrained himself and his response, though he did his best to make it as clear that he was not at all pleased with the manner in which his fellow officer was carrying on. Taking one step forward, Nathan straightened up as much as he could and locked eyes with Reider. "Look, as best I can tell, *lieutenant,* we're in deep shit. Like you, I have no idea how deep it is, or even what color that shit is. One thing is certain. The situation out there has changed. Now," Nathan continued, toning down the harshness in his voice a bit, "what we, you and I, need to do is sort out just what has happened without putting those soldiers over there in harm's way."

Nathan paused, as much to catch his own breath as well as to judge the effect his little tirade had on Reider. When he was sure that his measured effect had hit the mark, he continued. "I suggest you leave a couple of men here as an outpost, just in case Sergeant Taylor manages to make it here with the tracks. Then, provided we don't luck out and make contact with someone real soon, you should take the rest of your platoon back to that farmhouse to rest." Looking up, Nathan noticed that the sky was now beginning to darken as the afternoon slipped away. "There's no point in keeping your people out here." Then, looking back down at Reider, Nathan added, "Your troopers aren't prepared for this. I'll bet there isn't even a single shovel in this whole platoon."

This caused Reider to take a quick glance over his shoulder at the lightly equipped soldiers of his platoon. He imagined that Dixon was right. Except for the rucksack on Nathan's back, Reider didn't recall seeing anything other than web gear, canteens, and ammo pouches on his men. "I suppose you're right," he finally replied, looking back at Nathan. "Then what?"

"For you and the bulk of your men, nothing. You stand fast, keep a low profile, get as much rest as you can, and wait till I get back. If you don't object," Nathan continued, "I'm going to take one of your men and make my way to where Sergeant Taylor's last checkpoint was to have been set. Perhaps," Nathan went on, "they're still there."

For the moment Reider didn't mind having the battalion staff officer issue his guidance to him like this. Not only did it make sense, but it was comforting, given his own uncertainty, to have someone else make the decisions. "Fine, fine," Reider finally acknowledged. "And if they're not, or if we fail to make contact? Then what?"

Adjusting his gear in preparation for what he expected to be a fast-paced march, Nathan managed a grin. "Let's not generate any more problems or concerns than we have to. Get your men under cover where they can dry off and rest, see if there's anything to eat at the farmhouse, and see what develops."

"My orders," Reider stated firmly, "stated clearly that we were not to pillage or loot. We each have one MRE. I'll have my men eat that."

Annoyed at this, Nathan shook his head. "In the first place, Lieutenant Reider," Nathan patiently began to explain, doing little to hide his frustration, "you have no need to tell me what's in the orders. I drafted those orders for the battalion commander. In the second place, we don't know how long we're going to be out here. So I suggest you hold on to that one MRE meal as long as you can. And last," he concluded as his voice rose ever so slightly, "I shouldn't have to remind you that it was those bastards who fired at us first. All bets, as far as the rules of engagement and conduct, as far as I am concerned, are off. From here on in, until someone with more horsepower than I have comes along, we make up our own rules of engagement and conduct. Do you understand?"

Having no desire to continue this debate, which he was obviously losing, Gerald Reider acquiesced. "Fine, fine," he stated warily. "Pick your man. I'll get things moving here."

Without another word, Nathan stepped past Reider. "Sergeant Kittridge, I need a man to go with me."

Though irked by the fact that Dixon had given that order rather than letting him notify his NCO, Reider said nothing. To have gotten into it again would have prolonged the battalion staff officer's departure. At that moment there wasn't anything Gerald Reider wanted more than to be rid of 1st Lieutenant Nathan Dixon.

14

Darkness came quickly, leaving Nathan Dixon little choice but to follow the road rather than move through the fields parallel to it. "Don't wait for me to tell you to get off the roadway if something comes our way," Nathan told Evens Tobias before moving out.

Tobias was always ready with a response, whether it was appropriate or not. "You don't need to worry about that, lieutenant. My mama didn't raise no fool. You're gonna have to be quick if you want to beat me into the ditch."

Satisfied with the choice Sergeant Kittridge had made, Nathan gave one more look in the direction of where Reider stood, surrounded by his squad leaders. As fraught with danger as splitting up the platoon was, Nathan saw no good alternatives. To hold everyone there throughout the night, at the pickup point, especially after being hosed by Slovakian tanks, was a nonstarter. Yet if Sergeant Taylor and the Bradleys did show up, Nathan expected that they would go to where they were supposed to meet Reider and the dismounts. So someone needed to be there. Nor did merely waiting around, hoping that someone would call or come to them, strike Nathan as being a particularly attractive choice. As tired as Nathan was, his need to find out what had happened, if that was possible, was proving to be more compelling than his sore muscles.

Besides, Nathan found that he needed a break from Lieutenant Reider, even if it was for just a few hours. The battalion staff officer really didn't expect he'd find any answers by going to where the Bradleys had set up a roadblock. Yet even negative results provide some intelligence. Either way, good or bad, Nathan would be able to use the time to come up with a plan of action if dawn came without a major change to their predicament.

With darkness to hide them, and ears pricked, Nathan moved at a brisk pace. Movement along the road, despite the snow that no one had bothered to plow all day, was quick and almost enjoyable after slogging cross-country all afternoon. There was no layer of mud beneath it that gave way under weight and then caused one to slip about when the foot was used to push off.

Even in a digitized Army, where high-tech gadgets are heralded as the solutions for everything from reconnaissance to managing logistics, the senses that each and every soldier is issued at birth are still an infantryman's most valuable assets. Nathan Dixon had been lucky in his first assignment, going to an airborne unit where a soldier is still considered to be the ultimate weapons platform and not just part of a system's software. Like generations of paratroopers before him, he had been taught to develop his natural skills and trust his instincts to deal with situations that not even the most gifted writ-

ers of fiction could dream up. So when Nathan's nose
began to twitch, his body tensed, he slowed his pace,
and he brought his rifle up to the ready even before his
conscious mind flashed its warning to him.

Behind him Tobias heard the rattle of the metal on
Nathan's sling as it clicked against the hard plastic handguard of his rifle and saw the dark shadow he was following slow to a crawl. Following suit, Tobias brought
his own weapon up, laid his thumb against the safety,
and closed the distance between himself and Nathan
until he was close enough to where he felt it was safe to
whisper. "What's up?"

Nathan didn't look back as he continued to creep forward. "Can't you smell it?"

Lifting his chin, Tobias sniffed the air. "Burnt
rubber," he announced. "And . . ."

The second odor, far more pungent than the pervasive scent of burning rubber, was impossible to mistake.
"Stay loose," Nathan ordered as he continued on, toward the next bend in the road. "And hang back some,"
he added with a slight wave of his left hand.

More than happy to comply, Tobias stood fast while
Nathan continued forward. Crouching down, the soldier
watched the battalion staff officer go around the point
in the road where it made a sharp turn to the right. A
glow, which neither man had noticed before, reflected
off Nathan's figure just before he disappeared. Standing
up, Tobias made his way forward, subconsciously tilting
his head over to the left in an effort to see around the
corner as soon as he could. The faint glow became
brighter as he drew near until, just before he, too,
rounded the bend, the glow lit up the road before him.
All the while, just as the light grew brighter, the stench
of burnt rubber and flesh became stronger. What he saw
when he took those final few steps was therefore no surprise.

Tobias walked up next to Nathan, who stood in the
middle of the road with his rifle held down at his side.

Like Nathan, he stared at the burning hulk for a moment before either man said a word. Speaking first, Nathan asked Tobias if he could tell whose track it was. With a grunt, something resembling more of a moan, Tobias shook his head. "Sir, I can't even tell if it's a Bradley."

Drawing in a deep breath, despite the nauseating odor of death that went along with it, Nathan stated flatly, "Well, it is."

"Those tanks, the ones that tried to hose us. You suppose they were the ones that, well, did this, sir?"

"Maybe," Nathan answered as he brought his rifle up and cradled it in his arms. "Judging by the way the turrets were pointed, and the speed at which they zipped by, no doubt they were looking for the others when they stumbled on us."

Encouraged by this, Tobias looked around, out into the dark field to their left. "Then Sergeant Taylor's still running around out there!"

This caused Nathan to look in that direction also. "Well, let's see." Bending over, Nathan began to move around the smoldering remains of the Bradley in the road. Using the light from the small flames that still flickered up through openings in the derelict hulk, Nathan searched the side of the road until he found what he was looking for. Straightening up, he stopped and pointed to the ground. "That's where the other Bradleys left the road and took off," he concluded as he looked out into the darkness. Then, looking back at the ground, he continued forward for a while. When he stopped again, both men were well beyond the burning Bradley and the faint light that it gave off. Staring down the dark road that continued to meander through the fields and woods, Nathan pondered his next move.

"How many sets of tracks did you see leading off the road into the field?" he asked Tobias.

Standing just behind the staff officer, Tobias looked

back for a moment, then up the road, just like Nathan. "Two, sir."

"Same here," Nathan announced. "Since it's unlikely that we both missed a set of tracks in this snow, and I doubt if two Bradleys would beat feet one behind the other while trying to get out of a kill zone, that means there's a track missing."

"You're not thinking of going out and looking for it, are you, sir?"

Nathan turned and looked at the dark figure next to him. "The point where Sergeant Taylor was to set up his roving roadblock is less than two clicks up the road. I'm going at least that far."

"Begging your pardon, sir, but what's the point?" Tobias responded, making no effort to disguise his exasperation with Nathan's decision. "We know the Slovaks whacked one of the Bradleys and that two took off. For all we know, they've already doubled back to the linkup point and are there right now, waiting to pick us up and tell us what happened."

"Maybe," Nathan admitted. "Maybe not. Either way, we're going on. I need to be sure. Besides," he added as he stepped off, "those Slovak tanks are just as likely to turn around and head back looking to finish us. After all, this is their country."

Shaking his head, Tobias looked back at the shattered Bradley. "Yeah," he mumbled. "Everyone keeps tellin' me that. I just wish someone would tell those assholes in Washington."

From down the road, out of the darkness, Tobias heard Nathan call. "Let's move it."

Without a word the soldier picked up a quick pace and took off after Nathan.

Just before midnight Kittridge, followed by one of his men and a soldier from the 1st Squad, stumbled into the farmhouse and made his way toward the kitchen. As they did so, the trio had to be careful where they stepped, lest they stumble over someone who was already curled up and fast asleep on the floor. Like most farms in that part of the world, furniture big enough for a grown man to sleep on was sparse, forcing Reider's men to settle for the floor and whatever blankets they could scrounge up.

On entering the kitchen, Kittridge noted that neither the RTO, sitting at the table and calling on the radio, nor his platoon leader, off in one corner, had moved since he had last seen them. Stepping up behind Sam Pavlovski, the RTO, Kittridge listened for a moment before he spoke. "Any luck?"

Without bothering to face the leader of the 2nd Squad and his acting platoon sergeant, Pavlovski wearily shook his head. "I ain't heard shit, Kitt. And I doubt if anyone's hearing us."

Placing a hand on Pavlovski's shoulder, he gave the tired RTO a reassuring squeeze. "Take a break, trooper. I'll listen for a while."

Awakened by the exchange between Pavlovski and Kittridge, Gerald Reider looked up from the corner where he was huddled. "Has Lieutenant Dixon returned yet?" he asked.

Looking over in the direction from which the slurred question had come, Kittridge shook his head. "No, sir." Then, since his platoon leader was awake, he rendered his report. "I set the next watch at the linkup point. The last relief had nothing to report. There's been no movement of any kind since we had that run-in with those tanks."

Squinting his eyes as he looked up into the subdued light of the room, Reider yawned. "What time is it?"

"Just after midnight, sir."

Struggling, Reider stood up. "I've had a few hours' sleep, sergeant. Why don't you try and get some. I'll take radio watch till oh two hundred."

Kittridge offered no resistance to his platoon leader's

suggestion. He was dead on his feet after their long day as well as two trips, back and forth, between the farmhouse and the linkup point. "Yes, sir," he replied and with that, disappeared into the front room behind the two men he had just relieved.

For the longest time Gerald Reider sat slumped down in his chair, hands shoved deep into the pockets of his BDU pants, staring at the radio sitting on the table. Next to the radio sat an old lamp whose single low-wattage bulb burned, providing the only light in the room, or for that matter, the entire house. The short nap that he had taken had done little to refresh him. If anything, it added a few more cobwebs to an already befuddled mind.

Somehow, he had never imagined it would be like this. As all of his classmates came to realize during their four-year struggle to survive the Point, being an officer in an under-strength peacetime Army was going to involve performing duties and participating in missions that were anything but glamorous or challenging. That was why he had opted for an assignment in Germany on his dream sheet. While peacekeeping was not what a good infantry officer aspired to, serving in a troop unit in Slovakia was, in Reider's opinion, one hell of a lot better than doing time in a half-strength Stateside unit with next to nothing when it came to training funds. At least, he had been told by a Tac officer who had served in Bosnia, they had an opportunity to spend time with their troops and equipment. "You'll develop more leadership skills and greater technical proficiencies in the first three months in Slovakia than your counterpart in the States will during his entire tour," another officer at Fort Benning told him before he had left the Infantry School.

Slowly he pulled his right hand out of his pocket and rubbed his face. God, he thought. I'd have given anything for those three months, or even just one of them, before being thrown into this. Item by item, he took stock of his plight as he continued to stare at the silent radio and rub the stubble on his chin with his right hand. He didn't know his men. If it weren't for the fact that the NCOs were a bit older and wore their rank on their helmets and collars, he wouldn't even have known who the squad leaders were. He barely understood his mission. Yes, he knew they were to keep the peace, but how, exactly, did one accomplish that laudable goal when none of the people involved in the conflict were the least bit interested in being peaceful? And as far as the politics of the region, he had only the sketchiest comprehension of the dispute that was causing one group of Slovakians to slaughter their fellow countrymen. Whether it was his frustration over the day's events, exhaustion, or, for the first time, a full appreciation of the situation he faced, Gerald Reider finally admitted to himself that he was in over his head.

Appreciating one's situation, while a good start, did little to solve the problems that needed to be dealt with. Gerald Reider was trying to sort through that process as best as his impaired mental faculties permitted, when he felt a rush of cold air sweep into the kitchen. In the other room, he heard someone enter the house in the front, stomping his boots on the floor as he made his way in. Glancing at his watch, he noted that it wasn't time, yet, to send out the next relief for the men at the linkup point. Looking up at the door leading into the front rooms, Reider listened to the sound of men dropping boxes on the floor and shuffling about in the darkness just beyond the faint light of the kitchen. He was debating with himself as to whether he should get up and check when Nathan Dixon stepped into the doorway and stopped.

The light sitting on the table in the middle of the kitchen couldn't have been much more than twenty-five watts, barely enough to illuminate the tabletop under it, the radio, and parts of the figure siting before it. Yet it was more than enough momentarily to blind someone who had been in near total darkness for the last five hours. Stopping as soon as he hit the doorway, Nathan blinked and held up his free hand, waving it vaguely between his face and the lamp in an effort to shield his eyes. "Where's Lieutenant Reider?" Nathan asked, not realizing that the man he was addressing and the one he sought were one and the same.

"Right here, Lieutenant Dixon," Reider responded warily. "I take it you didn't find Sergeant Taylor."

Lowering his hand, Nathan moved toward the table, still squinting. Grabbing the back of a chair that sat across the table from Reider, Nathan pulled it out, moved around till he was in front of it, then collapsed into it. Believing that Nathan's refusal to respond to his statement in any fashion was all the answer that he needed, Reider wasn't quite ready for the volley of bad news that the battalion staff officer unleashed on him. "As best I can determine, someone ambushed Sergeant Taylor and your Bradleys while they were manning their last roving checkpoint."

A blow to his body could not have been more devastating. Reider all but leaped forward, out of his chair. "They *what?*"

Leaning back in his seat, Nathan Dixon, his face showing no expression, other than that of total exhaustion, reached behind him and opened the door of the small refrigerator that sat behind him. "My guess is the Slovakian Army," he replied as he fished about in the small refrigerator. After pulling out a half-finished bottle of milk Reider's men had left, Nathan continued. "The Bradley we found at the checkpoint had been nailed, as best I could determine, by an RPG. One shot, through the driver's compartment and into the engine. We found a lot of blood there, some discarded first-aid packaging and such, but no body. Whoever was hit was, apparently, still alive when they pulled out of there."

While Nathan, who had had the time to absorb the shock of his discoveries and their meaning, was able to speak of them in a rather bland, matter-of-fact manner, Gerald Reider was beside himself. "Jesus Christ! Are we at war?"

Waiting until after he had finished chugging down some milk, Nathan looked at Reider and shook his head. "I don't think it's war, at least not a full-blown, knockdown, drag-out fight sort of war. I think they're just trying to test us. NATO, I mean."

"A test?" Reider shrieked, unable to overcome the dual curse of being exhausted and excited at the same time. "What kind of fucking test is that? I lost one of my tracks!"

"Two," Nathan intoned after taking another swig of milk. "I think those tanks that rolled past us were waiting in ambush just up the road from the checkpoint where Taylor was with the Bradleys. The way I see it, Taylor was hit, he sorted things out there, started up the road to the linkup point, and . . ." Nathan paused as he slammed the empty milk bottle on the table. "Wham! The Slovs took out another Bradley."

Slowly, as Reider stared dumbfounded at the milk bottle, as if it had some importance to what he was being told, Nathan let go of the bottle, brought his two hands together in his lap, and stared down at them. "That one wasn't near as lucky as their first. A 'K' kill, catastrophic. Neither Specialist Tobias nor I could tell which track it was." Then, with eyes that betrayed, for the first time, a sense of grief, Nathan looked up at Reider. "I think the whole crew went with it. But I can't be sure of that," he quickly added. "It was still burning when we passed it, both coming and going."

For the longest time the two officers sat in silence, each staring off in the distance. Finally, Reider broke the silence. This time he had better control of his voice, though the manner in which his words were uttered betrayed his shock. "The other tracks? Any sign of what happened to them?"

The question reminded Nathan of his own frayed mental and physical condition. He looked over at Reider, studying that officer's face for a moment in an effort to see if he could imagine what his state of mind was. The news he brought, Nathan told himself, heaped on this poor soul in the lackadaisical and haphazard manner that it had been, had to be devastating. Still, Nathan decided, he seemed to be holding together and functioning. That was a plus, a big plus.

"We found two sets of tracks leading off the roads into the fields beyond at the site of the tank ambush. I'm guessing that the survivors of Taylor's element, hit twice by the Slovaks and with wounded on board, took off for Fort Apache. I doubt," Nathan concluded, "if, after all that, they'd hang around and try for the linkup point. Odds are, whoever was still in command assumed that the same thing, or worse, happened to us."

The next question Reider hit Nathan with was one that the more senior officer had pondered as he had made his way back along the dark Slovak road. "What do we do now?"

Nathan didn't answer right off. Instead, he sat up right in his chair, taking his helmet off as he did so. After running his fingers through his matted hair, he unbuckled his web belt and let the harness slide off his shoulders. Slowly he peeled off his parka. Reaching over, he retrieved his map case, fished out his small scale map, and plopped it down on the table between himself and Reider, who was waiting patiently for a response.

"There's been speculation," Nathan stated as he looked down at the map before him, "that the Slovakian government was looking to see just how committed NATO, and in particular the United States, was to this mission." Nathan looked up at Reider. "They've studied their history and keep an eye on the news networks. They know the American public can be a fickle lot, especially when it comes time to support military intervention into conflicts they, our fellow Americans, feel is none of our business. I'm sure you heard the political rhetoric, from all sides, before you left."

Reider, listening with rapt attention, nodded.

"Well, the Slovakians have too," Nathan continued, looking back down at his map. "For the past month they've renewed their operations, especially here," Nathan pointed, "in the U.S. sector. They started pushing, trying to see just how far they could go. Well, when they were assailed with little more than harsh words and unfulfilled threats, they began to step up both the intensity and frequency of their attacks on the ethnic Hungarian minority in the region. All the points marked with circled Xs on my map," Nathan stated as he pointed them out to Reider, "have been sites of 'cleansing' operations in the past month. As you can see, Fort Apache is right in the center."

"An apt name," Reider replied glumly.

Nathan sat back in his seat. "Its official name is still Freedom Forward. But no one, at least not anyone in country, calls it that anymore."

"Go on," Reider directed.

"Well, the Hungarian government, from the start, has been equally suspicious of the resolve of their NATO partners and the ability of this mission to protect their ethnic brethren north of the Danube. Even before we arrived, there were rumors that Hungarian Army officers were being slipped into Slovakia to organize and arm the Hungarian minority in this country. Though never admitting it officially, the government in Budapest has made it clear on numerous occasions that if we, NATO, could not protect their people, they would. When they stopped making those threats, shortly after the Slovakians began their latest round of attacks, the intelligence community in Brussels began to become alarmed."

"This farm," Reider interrupted. "This was a base of

operations for one of the Hungarian militia units."

"Officially," Nathan corrected the young officer, "they are called Kommandos. A Brit coined the name. A throwback to the Boer War. Since the Slovakian Army has been relying on a goodly number of militia units in its ranks, the distinction helps keep everyone straight as to which side we're discussing."

Again, Gerald Reider responded to this with little more than a nod. "So where does that leave us?"

Pointing to the spot on the map where the farmhouse they occupied sat, Nathan sighed. "Right in the middle of a bloody civil war." The more senior of the pair pulled his hand away from the map and shoved it into his pants pocket. In the early morning quiet of the dimly lit kitchen, both Nathan and Reider stared at the little dot for the longest time as if, by studying the two-dimensional representation of this foreign land long enough, they would divine an answer to their dilemma. Finally, without shifting his posture or making any sort of motion, Nathan broke the silence.

"Two weeks ago Division published a series of contingency plans to cover a situation like this," he stated slowly after weighing the consequences of revealing something that had, up to that point, been most secret. That he himself knew about it was pure chance. An insatiable reader of anything and everything that passed through the battalion's ops center, Nathan had come across it one morning while rifling through the task force operations officer's desk. "One plan called for all NATO forces to hunker down, in place, while air strikes hammered Slovakian forces in sector."

"What are the odds of that happening," Reider interjected, "given the shitty weather we're experiencing?"

Nathan looked over toward the window to see if the snow, which had been trailing off when he had returned, had finally ended. "While the Air Force does boast of its all-weather capability, the likelihood of collateral damage to civilian targets in conditions like this is, for the folks back in Brussels and Washington, too high." Nathan looked back at Reider. "That's why Division came up with another option, affectionately referred to as 'circling the wagons.' That little gem calls for the battalions to abandon their separate base camps and fall back upon their respective brigade base camps and hold fast until the weather clears or the politicians can sort out some sort of cease-fire."

Again, there was a protracted silence. This time it was Reider who ended it. "In a nutshell," he stated by way of summarizing what he understood, "if, in fact, the Slovakians have decided to have it out, once and for all—"

"Given all the evidence," Nathan cut in, "I'd say there's no 'if' about it."

Reider sighed and nodded. "Well, so it seems. As I was saying," he picked up again, "regardless of what everyone else is doing, it seems we're stuck out here on our own with only two choices, which are stand fast, or . . ."

"Make our way back to Fort Apache, as quickly as we can," Nathan concluded as he leaned forward over the map, following with his eyes the route they would need to take. Pulling his right hand from his pants pocket, he used his fingers to measure the approximate distance. Reider, bending over, watched and made his own mental calculations. "I make it to be approximately twenty to twenty-five kilometers, straight-line distance, back to Fort Apache," Nathan stated without looking up from the map.

Reider looked up at his fellow officer. "I assume we'll be traveling cross-country."

With a nod Nathan replied. "But of course. We have no way of knowing who the good guys are, provided there *are* any good guys out there."

"That means a march of at least twelve hours, probably more."

As before, Nathan nodded without looking up. "I'd plan on more."

"Great," Reider announced suddenly as he sat upright. "When do we leave?"

Surprised by this sudden announcement, as well as the manner in which the young platoon leader had announced his deference to Nathan's authority, Nathan looked up at Reider and, for the first time that evening, he smiled. "An hour before dawn." Lifting his right arm in an exaggerated manner, Nathan looked at his watch to determine just how much sleep that would give him. "Your men are settled in and need the rest. I know I do and," Nathan stated confidently as he stood up and looked down at Reider, "no doubt you do, too."

Still studying the map sitting before him, Gerald Reider simply shook his head. "It's been a hell of a first day."

This caused Nathan to chuckle. "It could be worse, you know."

Looking up at the battalion staff officer in surprise, Reider blinked. "Oh?"

"My father always told me," Nathan explained, "that as long as you can utter the statement, 'It could be worse,' it can be."

Too tired to engage his de facto superior in a war of wits, Reider simply agreed. "I guess so."

"Get someone to take over radio watch, and get some sleep yourself," Nathan commanded.

"I will," Reider announced. "First, however, I'd like to study the map a bit." Then, he looked up just as Nathan was in the process of gathering up his gear. "Sergeant Kittridge saved one of the beds upstairs for you, Lieutenant Dixon."

This statement gave Nathan pause. Looking back at the platoon leader Nathan asked, "Which one?"

"They took the girl's body out back, into the barn, along with the others who were, ah, in the house," Reider replied.

For a moment Nathan's eyes looked up at the ceiling, as he pondered whether he would be able to sleep in that room. Then, with a shake of his head, he dismissed all apprehensions and went about policing up his rifle and equipment. "Specialist Tobias and I brought back two cases of MREs we found in the track at the checkpoint. They're in the front hall. Have Kittridge distribute two per man as long as they last. I brought two of my own with me," he added as he shook his rucksack, "so don't hold any back for me."

"Roger that," Reider acknowledged before turning back to study the map.

With nothing more to discuss at that moment, and overwhelmed by exhaustion that was compounded by the plight that they were in, Nathan left the kitchen and made his way toward the stairs.

15

NORTHEAST OF MODŘANY,
DAWN, FEBRUARY 6

The smell of cooking and the hushed voices from downstairs woke Nathan just as one of Reider's men stuck his head through the door to announce it was time to get up. "We found some eggs and bread, sir," the soldier stated. "Kitt is saving some for you."

Sitting up, Nathan looked over at the dark form in the doorway. "Thank Sergeant Kittridge for me and tell him I'll be down in a minute."

With a muffled "Yes, sir," the figure disappeared, leaving Nathan alone to gather up his gear, straighten himself out, and prepare for a long day. This would be the last time he'd have to himself. By now, Nathan figured, every man in the platoon knew the score. If he guessed right, Reider had already explained to them what the two officers had discussed a few short hours before. So

Nathan knew that as soon as he went downstairs, all eyes would be on him. They would watch him like a hawk, attempting to discern his mood and attitude in an effort to gauge the severity of their position. It was critical, therefore, that he mask his own concerns and apprehensions. As a good officer in a tight spot is expected to, Nathan needed to make as good a show of it as he could.

He was so conscious of what he said and did when he entered the kitchen that it took some time for Nathan to catch on that the men of the 3rd Platoon were putting up a front of their own. Naturally he expected them to be somewhat subdued. So it didn't surprise him when no one said much of anything as he was served a plate of eggs, some sort of fried meat, and a chunk of two-day-old bread. It wasn't until he was halfway through his meal that Nathan began to realize that the silence of the troops about him was motivated by more than just their precarious situation.

Leaning back in his seat, Nathan took a good look around the room for the first time. "Has Lieutenant Reider been awakened?"

The few men who were still in the kitchen looked at each other with long, sheepish stares before all eyes finally fell on Staff Sergeant Kittridge, the acting platoon sergeant. In return Kittridge looked to his left, then to his right, before finally looking over to where Nathan sat waiting patiently for a response.

In the United States Army, a platoon sergeant is an important position. He is more than the most senior noncommissioned officer within the platoon. Unlike an officer platoon leader, the platoon sergeant is one of them, an enlisted soldier. Yet, like the officer, he is above them, removed from them by his assigned duties and responsibilities. Taskmaster and buffer, the platoon sergeant is the number-one protector of those soldiers entrusted to his care. This was especially true when it came to the officer appointed to lead that platoon. If

NCOs are the foundation of an officer's career, then his first platoon sergeant is the cornerstone. It is a difficult position to fill, one that takes much seasoning and a great many skills.

As the senior squad leader, Sergeant Kittridge found himself catapulted by the circumstances of the moment into a position that he was not quite ready to fill. Unlike Sergeant First Class Taylor, the actual platoon sergeant, Kittridge, or Kitt, wasn't comfortable yet when it came to covering one officer's errors from another. This resulted in a long silence between Nathan's question and his response, a silence that alerted Nathan that there was something afoot. "Lieutenant Reider, sir," Kittridge finally stated with little conviction in the delivery of his response, "is awake."

Sure that there was more going on than the simple misplacement of their platoon leader, Nathan stared at Kittridge as he continued to eat, trying hard to imagine what it was he was missing. For his part Kittridge tried to look away from Nathan and finish his own meal. As is the tradition, senior NCOs and officers didn't eat until all the personnel entrusted to their care have eaten first.

Finally unable to take it anymore, Nathan laid his fork down, placed his elbows on the table, clasped his hands, and asked the question he was not quite sure he wanted to hear the answer to. "Where, Sergeant Kittridge, is Lieutenant Reider?"

Swallowing his last mouthful of food with more force than normal, Kittridge looked up at Nathan with large, sheepish eyes. "Well, sir, it's like this."

In three years of service Nathan had never heard a good answer from anyone when the response was prefaced with those words. Drawing in a deep breath, he prepared himself for the worst.

"It seems that when we were hit by those Slovakian tanks," Kittridge explained, "Lieutenant Reider was in the middle of checking his GPS. In all the excitement he dropped it."

Though he waited for more of the story, which Sergeant Kittridge seemed reluctant to continue, Nathan didn't need to hear anything else. "How long ago did he leave?"

Kittridge looked up at Sergeant Dubois, who was standing off to one side. "He left just before I woke you, sir," Dubois volunteered.

No one moved or said a word as Nathan figured out, in his head, how long ago that had been and then, how much longer Reider could be expected to be gone. Finally, with an exaggerated motion, Nathan looked at his watch. "Well, there's little we can do to speed that along. We'll miss our SP. But that doesn't mean," Nathan stated as he looked up from his plate at Kittridge and forced himself to smile, "that we should waste this wonderful meal. How about we finish it up, Sergeant Kittridge?"

Relieved, Kittridge's shoulders slumped as a smile flashed across his face. "Yes, sir." After that, the normal conversation of men collected together under such circumstances picked up where it had been before Nathan had appeared. There would be time later, Nathan told himself as he looked around, ate, and listened in on the chatter, to deal with Gerald Reider.

When he had walked out of the farmhouse and headed off to recover his lost GPS, it had seemed like an easy task. All he had to do was walk to the field to where he had been, kick about in the snow till the toe of his boot whacked it. Of course Gerald Reider had yet to learn that nothing, especially when it's done in the dark, is ever as easy as it sounds. Within minutes of arriving at the field where they had been waiting to link up with the tracks, Reider quickly became painfully aware of the fact that he had no idea where, exactly, he had been standing when he had dropped his GPS. While he was pretty sure he had been midway between the tree line and the road, judging that distance now was more difficult than he thought. As a result, he quickly gave up all hope of simply bending over and picking up the GPS and started a systematic search of the trail he had been standing on when he dropped the damned thing.

He was in the process of making another sweep, up the trail, back toward the tree line, stomping his feet as he went, when he heard the sound of a truck. Immediately, he stopped pounding the ground with his boots, pricked up his ears, and turned around to look. Believing that the truck was still a good distance off, he remained where he had been standing, listening in an effort to judge how far it was, and if it was alone. Unfortunately the snow and the trees that lined the road off to his left muffled the sound of the truck to such an extent that by the time he caught sight of its headlights down on the road, it was too late. Like a wild animal caught in the open and exposed, Gerald Reider dropped into the prone position and watched as the nose of the truck inched its way around the bend and along the road, just as the three tanks had done the day before.

Now fully aware of his danger, Reider unslung his rifle from his shoulder. Though his heart was beating as fast as it could, the young platoon leader kept his cool, watching the truck as it lumbered along. Everything would be okay, he reassured himself as he lay there. All he needed to do was wait until the truck had disappeared down the road before he continued his search for the missing GPS.

The truck, unfortunately, did not cooperate with Gerald Reider's plan. It refused to keep going until it had disappeared, out of sight just as the tanks had. Instead it came to a stop at the point where the road it was on met the trail that Gerald Reider was on. In the gathering light of early morning, Reider watched as the driver threw open his door and climbed out onto the truck's running board. Pausing, he turned and leaned back into the cab to retrieve his rifle. Then, with the greatest of care, the driver lowered first one foot to the ground, then the other.

The driver was still in the process of sorting himself out when a second figure came around the front of the truck from the passenger side. Seeing his driver standing there, this new figure shouted. Though it was impossible to see a badge of rank, the well-practiced harshness of the man's voice made it obvious that this new man was an NCO. Moving slowly, the driver waved his free arm as he muttered something in return before making his way to the rear of the truck. As he did so, the NCO remained in front of the truck, where he fished a map out of a case hanging down at his side, and a flashlight from his web gear. Unconcerned with light discipline, the NCO flicked on the flashlight and used it to assist in reading the map.

Two things quickly became clear to Gerald Reider. The first was that the Slovakian soldiers down on the road were out there looking for something. Chances were, Reider guessed, they were looking for his platoon. The second thought that popped into this mind, as he watched the driver undo the latches of the truck's tailgate, was that if he was going to get out of this spot, now was the time to do it, before the Slovakians in the rear of the truck were on the ground and formed up.

Having reached this conclusion, Reider slowly lifted himself off the ground. As he did so, his eyes darted from the driver, now shouting to the men in the rear of the truck, back to their leader, who was at the other end of the truck studying his map. Once he was on his feet, the young officer began to back up, slowly, never taking his eyes off the truck and its occupants. All thoughts of finding the GPS vanished. Salvation, and getting away undetected, was all that mattered.

Step by step, Reider eased one foot back at a time, setting the toe of his boot down, through the snow, in search of firm footing. When his toe hit solid ground,

Reider rocked back on that foot, from toe to heel. The only noise he made as he backed up was the sound of crunching snow. All the while he kept his eyes on the Slovakians. Eventually, he knew he'd have to turn his back on the Slovakians. Reider hoped he could make it to the tree line before that happened. But hope, like one's footing when walking backward, is an iffy thing. One cannot rely too heavily on either.

This suddenly became painfully obvious to Gerald Reider as his rear foot settled upon an object in the trail that slid out from under him. His mind, occupied with keeping tabs on the Slovakians, perceived the danger but was unable to respond to it in time. In an instant, Reider's slow, stealthy retreat was transformed into a wild and uncontrolled flailing as he lost his footing and flipped over backward. First his mind screamed *Oh, shit!*, and then his lips did, just before his butt slammed onto the trail. In the process, Reider lost both his rifle and the protection of what little darkness remained.

On the road below, the Slovakian NCO stopped what he was doing and turned to peer into the field above him. The men who had been dismounting from the truck, oblivious to what was happening, continued banging their equipment around, stomping their feet inside the truck or on the road, and muttering to each other in the process. Unable to sort out this racket from the sound that he had just heard on the hillside before him, the Slovakian leader snapped an order. Immediately his men went silent.

Up on the trail Gerald Reider was in the process of sorting himself out when all fell quiet. Pausing, the young officer realized that the Slovakians hadn't pinpointed his position yet. But that, Reider quickly realized as he looked down at half a dozen upturned faces on the road, wouldn't last long. Pushing his hands down into the snow, he began searching for his rifle. When he didn't find it right off, he became desperate, reaching out this way and that. For once fortune favored him.

As he moved his hands around in the snow, both hands latched onto something. While one was his rifle, he had no idea what the other object was. Lifting his left hand, he was surprised to see that he had found his GPS. Whatever joy this discovery brought was short lived as it struck him that it was this wonder of modern technology that he had tripped on.

Glancing back at the road, he saw that the Slovakians were as still as they had been, motionless and scanning. Everything, the platoon leader told himself, now depended upon a matter of luck and keeping his cool. Unfortunately, first one ran out, then the other gave out.

On the road, one of the Slovakian soldiers shouted and pointed right to where Reider still sat. This immediately sent Reider into a frenzy as the sound of weapons being unslung, safeties clicking off, and rifle bolts being jerked back shattered the quiet. Abandoning all caution, Reider finished retrieving his lost prizes, scrambled to his feet, and headed up the trail, for the tree line, as quickly as his feet and the snow he plowed through permitted.

Behind him he heard more shouting. At first he didn't know what it meant. He assumed they were calling for him to stop. He had a few more seconds, he thought as he continued to drive on, slipping backward on the slick trail one step for every two he took forward. Somewhere in the back of his mind, he half expected the Slovakians to yell "Halt!" three times before shooting, just like American sentries were instructed to do. The Slovakians, of course, didn't subscribe to such niceties. Theirs was a policy of shoot first, and don't bother asking questions.

He was about to reach the tree line when a new sound cut through his own huffing and puffing. From out of no where, a noise that vaguely reminded Gerald Reider of something from a video game was added to the mix. Though he didn't want to, and knew that he shouldn't,

Reider found himself looking over his shoulder, back at the Slovakians. A quick peek, and a glimpse of flashes emanating from the kneeling and prone figures that lined the side of the road, told Reider all he needed to know. He was under fire.

In the absence of Gerald Reider, neither Staff Sergeant Kittridge nor Nathan Dixon were idle. Much needed to be done before the 3rd Platoon began its trek home. This included a briefing, given by Nathan, to the assembled members of the platoon. Grim faced, Reider's men listened to the young staff officer explain the situation, as he saw it, and what he proposed to do. As he was doing so, Nathan watched and listened to their reactions. With the exception of a few well-placed grunts and expletives, the riflemen assembled in the small living room listened attentively. When he was finished, Kittridge oversaw the distribution of the MREs Nathan and Tobias had brought back the night before. This, together with the filling of canteens, adjustment of personal gear, and checking the function of their weapons, took time, time Nathan hadn't expected to have but was determined to put to good use.

When Kittridge and the other squad leaders reported that all was ready, Nathan had the acting platoon sergeant fall the men out for a precombat inspection. Having had but one command, and that one being an Airborne platoon, Nathan knew only one way of doing things, the Airborne way. At a minimum everything in an Airborne unit was checked twice. Not only did a paratrooper's life depend on the proper function of his parachute, he knew that once he had hit the ground, whether it be from a high-flying transport or a helicopter, what he and his mates carried off that aircraft with them was all they would have for some time. So they took the prodding and tugging and pulling of gear by officers and NCOs in their chain of command in stride.

The soldiers of the 3rd Platoon, C Company, on the other hand, weren't used to having a conscientious officer in their midst. Some of the men didn't much care for the way the battalion staff officer who had been hoisted upon them was treating them. There was more than the usual mumbling between them as the men stumbled out of the warm farmhouse and lined up in the frigid morning air that cut through them like knives. More than once Kittridge ordered them to settle down in a low, almost plaintive tone of voice. It wasn't until Nathan had decided that he had let this go on for too long that he finally stepped in. "The man said fall in and shut up," the first lieutenant snapped.

At once the disgruntled chatter ceased and all eyes turned toward Nathan. "Listen up and listen up well," Nathan started as soon as he knew he had their complete and undivided attention. "We're in deep shit. You all know what happened to Taylor and the tracks. And you've all seen what the Slovakians did to the people who lived here and the Hungarian militiamen out back. If we don't get our act together, and execute our assigned duties as we all were trained to, we're next."

Pausing to let his points sink in, Nathan waited until he was sure Reider's men were ready. "Each and every one of you knows that neither side in this dispute has any love for us," he continued. "Both the Slovak Army and the ethnic Hungarian militia are more than willing to gun us down where we stand in order to get at each other. We cannot afford to ignore what happened yesterday or assume that it was an isolated incident. It was too well executed and far too brutal to be the act of one seriously deranged Slovak commander. So, until we have evidence to the contrary, we are at war."

Again Nathan paused to give each member of the 3rd Platoon time to consider what this meant to him. "We are soldiers," Nathan began again in a firm, yet more reassuring voice. "We have the training, the weapons, and the ability to see this through. I know the way back to Fort Apache and, if need be, all the way back to the brigade base. All we need now is discipline and determination, both of which I can demand, but neither of which I can pry out of you if you refuse to face up to your duties as a soldier and your responsibilities to the other people in this platoon. I didn't ask to come out here with you, and you didn't ask me to come. But we're stuck with one another, just like we're stuck with the situation we find ourselves in. Given that, so long as I am the senior officer on deck, we're going to do things my way. Is that clear?"

At first there was silence, a silence that was as cold and still as the early morning air.

Taking one step forward from behind Nathan, Staff Sergeant Kittridge snapped in his best drill-sergeant voice, "I didn't hear you people!"

A few of the troopers straightened up, lifted their chins, and responded with a mournful "Yes, sir."

"Shit, people," Kittridge groaned as he put his hands on his hips and bent over forward at the waist. "You can do better than that."

This time the platoon roared as one. "Yes, sir."

Coming to attention, Kittridge pivoted about as best he could in the snow and saluted Nathan. "Sir, 3rd Platoon is ready for inspection."

The battalion staff officer and acting platoon sergeant were better than halfway through this inspection when the sound of gunfire reached them. At once both the officer and the NCO realized what this meant. In unison they turned and faced each other, ignoring the stares from the rest of the platoon. "Sergeant Kittridge," Nathan commanded without hesitation, "I'll take the 3rd Squad and see what I can do to help your platoon leader. You stay here, form up the rest of the men, and be prepared to take off in the direction we discussed as soon as I return. Clear?"

With a crisp "Roger that," Kittridge spun about to where Staff Sergeant Hernandes stood. "Third Squad, follow the lieutenant. Everyone else, form up on me, *now!*"

This time, there was no need to give an order twice, or explain what was expected. The men of Gerald Reider's platoon responded and moved with a purpose.

The distance from the field by the road to the farmhouse was just over one click, or, almost seven tenths of a mile. At West Point, and again at Fort Benning, Gerald Reider had run the two miles in under thirteen minutes, maxing that portion of his PT test with ease. But those runs had always been made on flat, dry tracks while he was wearing sneakers and, at the most, a sweat suit. Yet not one of the two dozen well-armed soldiers chasing him could manage to catch up to Gerald Reider, despite the physical handicaps that combat boots, field equipment, and a winding snow-covered trail through the woods conferred upon him. Still, to Reider, it felt as if he were getting nowhere fast. A distance that he had been able to cover in less than five minutes when being tested by the Army was now, seemingly, taking him forever.

With his heart pounding as he had never felt it pound before, and sweat dripping down his face, Gerald Reider pumped his arms for all they were worth in an effort to put as much distance as he could between himself and his pursuers. The fact that he still held his rifle in his right hand and the recovered GPS in the other didn't help matters. At some point Reider came to appreciate this. Yet he was unwilling to slow down, even a bit, to sling his rifle or return the GPS to its carrying case, which was flopping wildly against his thigh. All he could think of, and do, was run like hell.

Not everything was stacked against him. Once he had reached the tree line above the field, there was a clear path that his men had beaten down during the night, as one relief after another had trudged from the farm-

house to the tree line to wait for Sergeant Taylor and
the Bradleys that never came. The meandering nature
of the trail itself also helped Reider. After disappearing
in the woods, he had enough of a head start so that the
line of sight between him and the Slovakian soldiers was
lost. Even with the growing light of dawn, Reider was
able to stay one bend in the trail ahead of his pursuers.

With the immediate danger past, for the moment,
Reider began to wonder if it would be to his advantage
to turn on the Slovakians chasing him and fire a few
rounds their way. Perhaps that might give them pause,
he reasoned. It would certainly slow them down some,
maybe even enough to buy him the time he needed to
reach his platoon and get it deployed. A pause would
also permit him an opportunity to collect himself, rest
a bit, and put away the damned GPS he was still carrying.
It would also provide him an opportunity to redeem
himself. Without the need for any more justification,
Reider now began to seriously look for the right spot
from which he could make his stand.

Rounding another bend in the trail, Reider came
upon a stretch that was relatively straight. At the next
turn the trail made a sharp, ninety-degree turn. Up
there, Reider told himself, would be a perfect place to
ambush the Slovaks. It was a textbook site, tailor-made
for a classic "L" ambush. Lowering his head, Reider
fixed his eyes on the position he would occupy and
made for the scrub and undergrowth that now lay dead
ahead. "Just a little further," he mumbled out loud. "Just
a few more . . ."

The image of a rifle barrel, protruding through the
very bush where he was planning to go, brought Reider
to a dead halt, right in the middle of the trail. How in
the hell, his racing mind asked, did they get ahead of
him?

From somewhere off to his right, a voice snapped out
an order, in English. "Get the fuck out of the way!"

From up ahead, another voice shouted out additional

commands, "Keep going! Stay on the trail and keep going." Though he didn't know who the voice belonged to or what was going on, Reider complied.

With Reider out of the way, Nathan Dixon settled back into the prone position he had been in before the young officer had appeared. As he did so, he called out to the men of the 3rd Squad. "Stand by. Hold your fire until I give the order."

His choice of the 3rd Squad, though a snap decision, was a good one. He had, after all, spent most of the previous day with them. Not only did he now know them by name, he had, by listening to their casual banter, acquired an idea of what sort of soldier each of them was. Such knowledge, in a tight situation, can make all the difference.

Once he was settled again, Nathan leaned over next to Alan Larkin, the squad's SAW gunner. "You'll be the first to fire," Nathan whispered. "Aim center of mass and cut loose with a good, long killing burst."

Too keyed up, Larkin didn't respond. Instead he just tightened his grip on his weapon, pulled the stock of his SAW deeper into his shoulder, and stared down the trail. Like his squadmates, Larkin had trained for this moment for years yet had never heard the word *kill* muttered as part of an order given in earnest. The fact that he was about to actually kill someone, a real live person, contributed to the tension that gripped him as tightly as he held his weapon. "Easy," he muttered to himself as he rested his thumb against the safety of the SAW. "Easy."

A hand came to rest on his shoulder. It was the lieutenant's hand, he told himself. His layers of clothing and the officer's glove did little to muffle the warmth of the reassurance he felt from that simple act, an act that did much to calm nerves hovering on the verge of snapping.

Then, like a scene in the movies, Larkin saw them. Led by a big man holding an assault rifle at the ready, the Slovakians came barreling down the trail. Flipping the safety off, Larkin sighted along the barrel of his SAW, pointing it right into the midsection of the lead Slovakian.

"Steady," Nathan whispered to the SAW gunner as he brought his own weapon up and took aim. "Steady."

Only when he was sure that all the members of 3rd Squad, those deployed with him at the head of the trail as well as those off to its right, could bring their weapons to bear did Nathan give the order. "Now!"

With surprising ease Larkin and the others in 3rd Squad commenced their bloody execution. Hit from the front and side, the Slovakian squad leader was literally thrown back into the man who had been following him. That man, startled by this, didn't have enough time to react for he, too, was quickly bowled over by the devastating gunfire that raked the length of the trail.

Above the rattle of Larkin's SAW, and the sharp *pop-pop-pop* that is so characteristic of an M-16's report, Nathan could hear those Slovakians still alive scream as the shock, horror, pain, and dismay of what was happening to them struck home. Lowering his own rifle, the battalion staff officer studied the pandemonium that was unfolding before him. The front three Slovakians had gone down in the first volley without ever being fully aware what was happening to them. Those who had been following, after a split second of confusion, either froze when they came to realize that they were in peril, or turned without a second thought and started to run as fast as they could. This effort, however, was hampered by men who weren't moving quickly enough or by those of their comrades who were still running forward, trying to catch up with their leader. There would be no meaningful response, Nathan concluded, from their foe.

Larkin, after easing off his trigger for a moment to let his weapon cool and settle, laid his sight squarely into the center of this tangled confusion of flailing arms and legs before cutting loose with a second, long, and equally devastating burst. Any hesitation or second thoughts he had previously entertained about slaying a fellow human being were forgotten as the smell of cordite filled his nostrils and the rapid kicks of his SAW fell in sync with the rabbit-like beating of his own heart. Only after he heard Nathan shout "Cease fire" for the third time did Larkin let up on the trigger.

When the SAW gunner finally complied, he was seized, in an instant, by a strange feeling that was a mix of satisfaction and horror. No one, as best he could see, who had come into his field of vision during the ambush was left standing. In the stunning silence that followed their mad and fearful execution, only the moans of men freshly laid low and recoiling from the shock of being hit could be heard.

Standing up, Nathan yelled out to the concealed members of the 3rd Squad. "Get 'em moving, Sergeant Hernandes! On the double."

Having anticipated the order to move out, Angel Hernandes was on his feet and relaying Nathan's command almost before that officer had finished issuing it. "Okay, people. Move, move, move."

Only Specialist Larkin, still reeling from the adrenaline rush that intoxicates a man during combat, hesitated. Seeing one of the stricken Slovakians out on the trail flap an arm about as he screamed out in pain, the SAW gunner turned to Nathan. "There's wounded out there, sir!"

Nathan knew what Larkin was saying, asking. Such considerations, however, like caring for the enemy's wounded weren't part of Nathan's plan. His first and only concern was getting the men of the 3rd Platoon out of harm's way and back to Fort Apache as quickly as he could. With an expression that was as cold as the snow underfoot, Nathan looked into Larkin's eyes. "Move it, soldier."

After throwing a quick glance back at the devastation he had helped create, Larkin bowed his head, hoisted his weapon up into his arms, and took off after his squad.

That left Nathan standing there, alone. In the quiet punctured only by a single, low moan, Nathan took one more look down the trail. He felt no pride in what he saw. There was no feeling of exhilaration or joy from the one-sided victory he had engineered. In fact, at that moment he felt nothing. That would come later, just as it did with his father.

If fortune saw him through this crisis, he would carry the sights, the sounds, and the smells that were now being committed to his memory with him for the remainder of his life. They would come back and visit him, all of them, night after night, with a force and a power that he could not, at that moment, imagine. Though he had lost not a drop of blood, First Lieutenant Nathan Dixon was wounded in a way that only one who has been there understands.

16

When Gerald Reider caught up with the 3rd Platoon, they were already moving along the route that Nathan hoped would lead them to Fort Apache and safety. There was no need to explain what had happened. Those of the 3rd Platoon who had not been part of the ambush on the trail had heard the gunfire. The squad that was taking up the rear of the small column, before the 3rd Squad resumed that duty, saw the expression of the members of that squad when it did. Whatever was happening elsewhere in Slovakia didn't matter. As far as 3rd Platoon were concerned, they were at war.

When they were finally able to slow their pace, Sergeant Hernandes threw up his right hand as a signal for his men to settle down. Like them, he was short of breath after the breakneck pace that Nathan had set during their drive to catch up with the rest of the platoon. The young staff officer, however, didn't let up once they had rejoined the 3rd Platoon. Whereas he had been content to hang back with the 3rd Squad the previous day and say nothing about what the platoon was doing, the events of the last twelve hours had changed everything.

Quickly he made his way up the column. Though he didn't hesitate long enough to return their stares, each man he passed looked off to his side as Nathan came up even with him. They were, just as Nathan had expected them to, measuring him using every conceivable gauge. From the expression he wore, to his gait, the soldiers whom the Fates had bequeathed to him were anxious to learn as much about him as they could.

The inspection of this officer from the battalion staff, executed with more subtlety by some than others, was a two-way exchange. Men who had been little more than company the previous day had become his responsibility. From a military standpoint they were his to lead and command. Yet there was more to this new relationship. At that moment, these men he was now leading meant more to Nathan than any other living soul on the face of the earth. On a more personal level, a very selfish, yet wholly human one, the soldiers of the 3rd Platoon were now the instrument of his delivery. Whether he lived or died, continued on to a successful career, or sank into obscurity and dishonor, depended entirely on how well these soldiers obeyed his commands, performed their duties, and weathered the tempest they had been tossed into.

In this way, without a word being said, a contract between leader and led was forged. Nathan knew that these men who were eyeing him did so with a mix of curiosity and concern. For the moment, he was satisfied that they would follow and obey. That they would continue to do so, however, was not a given. Nathan understood that isolated from all visible support and assistance, unsure of what was happening around them, the soldiers of the 3rd Platoon would follow only as long as he led well, cared for them, inspired hope, and succeeded. This, at the small-unit level, is the burden of command. It is something that is often discussed but seldom understood.

Soaked with sweat, shaken by his experience, and unsure where, exactly, he fit into the scheme of things at the moment, Second Lieutenant Gerald Reider had, like Nathan, kept going when he had bumped into the rear of his platoon. Unlike Nathan, however, Reider ignored the stares of his men. He made no effort to return the expressions that betrayed their concerns. Instead, like a beaten dog, Reider hung his head low, turning away from anyone who dared look his way too long.

Within that young officer, a terrible struggle was being waged, one for which there was no school solution. Thoughts that concerned what to do next with his platoon were mixed and muddled by the shame of having run away from the enemy. To this was added a growing feeling of guilt. Reider could not escape the conclusion that it had been his stupidity that had put his platoon in danger. Efforts to focus on important matters, issues that needed to be addressed, were stymied by his physical and psychological response to what had just happened. In addition to being overheated and winded by his physical exertions, Gerald Reider was experiencing that washed-out feeling that is the aftermath of a massive adrenaline rush. Even worse, the shock of combat was hitting the young man with the same impact a physical trauma would have inflicted. Crowning all of this, the words "I've failed" kept swimming in and out of his conscious mind.

With little thought as to what he needed to do and where he should go, Gerald Reider continued forward past his own command group without a word. When the

RTO, Specialist Sam Pavlovski, saw Reider continue on up the column without sliding into the slot he had filled the day before, Pavlovski turned to Isaac Smollett, the medic. "Do you think I should follow him?" Pavlovski asked.

Having seen their platoon leader's expression as he went by, Smollett shook his head. "No, don't bother. Wait till that Lieutenant Dixon comes up, then latch on to him. I sort of think he's in charge now."

Taking one more look at Reider, who was still pushing on, Pavlovski nodded. "I guess you're right. Dixon *has* sort of taken command. Not that I'm doing either of them any good," the RTO added. "I haven't heard squat outta this," he stated, waving the hand mike he habitually held to his ear, "since yesterday afternoon."

Ever trying to be helpful, Smollett asked Pavlovski if his battery was good. In response to this the RTO grunted. "I switched the batteries back and forth so much last night I can't tell anymore which one was in the radio yesterday when we started out and which one was the spare. I sort of lost track."

Walking behind Smollett, Zeke Fishburn whistled. "That doesn't sound good, not one bit. I thought you guys were supposed to mark your batteries when you installed them, to prevent this sort of thing from happening?"

Now it was Pavlovski's turn to show his disgust. "If things had happened the way they were supposed to, we'd be back at Fort Apache, kicking back and enjoying a day off instead of . . . well, you know."

Pavlovski's voice trailed off as he finished this last comment. Reminded of their isolation and precarious situation, no one picked up the discussion. Instead, they bowed their heads, withdrew into their own thoughts, and trudged on in silence.

* * *

Nathan was no psychologist. He was an infantry officer, trained to lead foot soldiers across the deadliest place on earth, the last few hundred yards that separate American forces from their enemy. Out in that patch of ground, whether it be a strip of sand in the Persian Gulf, or a snow-covered field in Central Europe, there is little room for illusions or fantasies. Nor is there time to indulge in fuzzy, feel-good leadership plied by officers who are concerned with everything but what they were trained to do. In that piece of real estate, more than anywhere else, God judged the quick and the dead. So it should not have been surprising that Nathan Dixon, fresh from an action that was as close and personal as it could get, did not bother to take Gerald Reider's bruised ego and feelings of confusion into account.

Because Nathan was suffering from his own physical exertions, as well as the psychological impact of what had just taken place, it took him a good while to catch up to Gerald Reider. That the young platoon leader was not with his small command group, where he had been the previous day, angered Nathan because that meant that he had that much farther to go, up the column, to find Reider. When he was finally close enough to hail him, Reider was closing up on the 2nd Squad, the point element.

Making no effort whatsoever to hide his shortness of breath or frustration from having to chase him, Nathan called out to Reider. "Hold up, lieutenant. We need to talk."

Still lost in his own thoughts, Reider did not immediately respond to Nathan's order. "I said stop, Lieutenant Reider. Now stop," Nathan commanded with a sharpness that cut through Reider's mental haze.

Mechanically Reider halted and turned to face his pursuer. Saying nothing, the younger officer watched and waited while Nathan covered the last few yards that separated them.

"Did you find it?" Nathan asked when he stopped with less than a yard between them.

"Find it?" Reider repeated.

Unable to pick up that the younger officer was somewhat befuddled, Nathan took a step closer. "The fucking GPS!" the battalion staff officer snapped. "The goddamn piece of crap that you went back to find. The one that nearly cost you your life, not to mention the lives of every man in this platoon."

This irate and unexpected assault cut Reider to the quick and brought forth the anger he had been harboring since he had first met Nathan. "Just who in the hell do you think you are, mister? This is my platoon. Mine!" the young platoon leader shrieked, thumping his clenched fist on his chest every time he said the word *mine.* "Where do you get off giving my men orders and treating me like a plebe?"

Nathan didn't flinch. Still feeling the animalistic charge that the smell of gunfire and the sight of blood and torn bodies can elicit, his response overrode clear thinking. With his left hand, Nathan took hold of the flap on his coldweather parka where the single black bar, the symbol of his rank, was attached. Reaching across, he thrust his right hand into the opening of Reider's parka, grabbed the right collar flap of that officer's BDU shirt, and pulled it out, exposing the dulled gold bar of a second lieutenant that was sewed to it. With a jerk Nathan lifted Reider's shirt collar up and before that officer's eyes. "You see this?" Nathan hissed as he shook his own rank. "This trumps your gold bar." Not content simply to let go of Reider's collar, Nathan added a shove that was sufficient to rock the junior officer back onto his heels. "Let there be no doubt in your military mind, *lieutenant,* I am in command here," Nathan continued as he straightened himself up. "Is that clear?"

Pausing only long enough to collect himself, Reider prepared to take a step closer to Nathan and go, literally, toe to toe with the son of a bitch who was facing him. Only his West Point training and conditioning, and the look in Nathan's eyes, kept Reider in check. Pulling back from the edge, for the first time, and making as clear an assessment of the situation as his emotions permitted him, Reider realized instantly that his position was not only untenable but, in light of the situation, foolish. With great difficulty Gerald Reider forced himself to choke down what little pride he had left and come to attention. The words "Yes, sir" were uttered through clenched teeth.

Satisfied that he had achieved target effect, Nathan took a moment to compose himself before returning to his initial point. "The GPS, Lieutenant Reider. Do you have it?"

Without a word, Reider flipped open the carrying pouch, pulled the damnable device out, and handed it to Nathan.

Quickly the battalion staff officer pushed the button to activate the current location readout, memorized the grid coordinates that were displayed, and then handed the GPS back to Reider. As the platoon leader put the GPS away, Nathan took his map out, found the spot on it corresponding to the grid from the GPS, then looked around. "Okay, we're headed in the right direction," he muttered, more to himself than to Reider.

Only after he had studied the map a few more seconds and replaced it did he look back at the rumpled platoon leader before him. In the intervening time, Nathan's own emotional outburst had receded. As Reider had been moments before, Nathan was overcome by a spasm of common sense. "Lieutenant Reider," Nathan stated flatly. "We're in deep shit. You, me, and the men of your platoon. How this situation turns out depends entirely on how we react and respond."

Finding it hard to believe that these words were being spoken by the same officer who had just manhandled him, Reider said nothing. Taking his silence to mean that the younger officer agreed, Nathan was about to go on when Sergeant Dubois came up next to him. "Is something wrong?" the assistant squad leader asked innocently.

Turning, Nathan looked at Dubois, then back at the rest of the platoon, which was closing up on the spot where he stood. Quickly, Nathan realized that this was neither the time nor place to carry on his "discussion" with Reider. "No, we're doing fine, sergeant. Just keep your men moving."

With a nod Dubois left, giving Nathan, and then Reider, a once-over as he did so.

Turning back to Reider, Nathan saw that the young officer was still standing there, glaring at him. "It might be a good idea," Nathan said, offering no explanation, "for you to go up forward, with the point element."

To this Reider said nothing. Slowly, the platoon leader turned away and made his way forward, keeping his bitter thoughts locked away, for now.

Alone, Nathan stood fast as the other members of Dubois's squad filed past him. Each man, having witnessed the confrontation between the two officers from afar, looked into Nathan's eyes as they moved on. Whatever doubt they had concerning who was in command had been, for them at least, erased.

For Gerald Reider, of course, it was another matter.

17

In much the same way as it had the day before, the
3rd Platoon made its way across the Slovakian countryside in silence. While the two officers mulled over
the twin issues of the tactical situation they faced and
the heated exchange that had taken place between
them, the individual soldiers of the lost platoon pondered their plight.

To say that they were lost was misleading. Between
Nathan's map-reading skills, a commodity that was becoming more of an oddity in the Army of the twenty-
first century, and Reider's GPS, the two officers knew
exactly where they were. Using data transmitted by sat-
ellites, the GPS not only provided them with their location, it had the ability to tell Reider and Nathan how
far Fort Apache was. Unfortunately the GPS could not
tell either officer what was going on there. What lay just

beyond the crest of the hill they were ascending, or around the next bend in the road, was a mystery. Even the platoon's state-of-the-art tactical radio, capable of secure communications and randomly hopping from one frequency to another so as to prevent jamming, was, for the moment, all but useless. It had a limited range. Without Bradleys and their more powerful, vehicular mounted radios, there was no one to talk to until they got closer to Fort Apache or, if fortune smiled on them, someone came out looking for them.

When the men thought of themselves as lost, they were taking into account the big picture. All of them had been in uniform long enough to understand that the Army is a vast, complex machine with many moving parts. They appreciated the fact that they were, individually and collectively, but a tiny part of this vast behemoth. That, of course, meant that they were the most expendable. Soldiers, after all, are the currency that buys and pays for ground in war.

Within 2nd of the 13th, the 3rd Platoon was only one of nine infantry platoons. They, the dismounts of that platoon, accounted for less than point zero two percent of the total personnel assigned to that battalion. Such statistics went far to explain why many of Reider's men felt that they were, in the larger scheme of things, for the moment, lost. Before moving out that morning, Sergeant Kittridge summed up their plight by stating that they had merely been "misplaced," by battalion. "It's like when my wife gets in a hurry," he explained after Nathan had presented them with the facts of their situation. "She always seems to misplace her car keys." While being compared to misplaced car keys might seem degrading, infantrymen, low men in the military food chain, understood Kitt's analogy and accepted his premise. Given that, they were both ready and willing to follow Nathan Dixon, an officer who both had a plan and appeared to possess the wherewithal to make it work.

After the one-sided firefight with the Slovakians, Nathan drove the platoon at a good pace for better than two hours. Though the snow was deep, the mud that had been such a nuisance the day before was less of a problem. Temperatures had dropped well below freezing during the night and turned the mud rock hard. Nathan took advantage of the men's freshness and motivation to put as much distance between themselves and the site where 3rd Squad had decimated the Slovakian squad. Only after he was sure there was no immediate danger to them did he raise his hand and pass the word along the column to halt in place for ten minutes.

Even when the last man around him had settled down into a position that was as comfortable as the circumstances permitted, Nathan did not rest. After telling Sam Pavlovski, the man he now considered to be "his" RTO, that he was going up front to talk to Kittridge, Nathan signaled to the leader of the 3rd Squad. "If someone comes up behind us," he directed an attentive Staff Sergeant Hernandes, "take off and roll up the platoon as you go. Don't wait for me to tell you." Only after Hernandes gave him a thumbs-up did Nathan make his way toward the front of the column.

As before, Nathan eyed each man he passed, checking them in an effort to gauge how well they were holding up to his pace. Unlike before, few gave the officer going by a second thought. The earlier excitement and imminent danger that had piqued their curiosity had been dulled somewhat by the labors of their march. Now they were more concerned with getting as much rest as Nathan would permit them.

At the head of the column, Nathan found both Reider and Kittridge squatting off to one side of the trail they were on, looking at a map Reider had spread on the ground. The two men stopped talking as Nathan drew near. "I was telling the lieutenant here," Kittridge stated hastily as Nathan settled down on his haunches and looked at the map, "that we have a decision to make here real soon."

Kittridge's quick, defensive tone told Nathan that the senior NCO with the platoon was a bit uncomfortable with his current chain of command. Reider, after all, was his platoon leader, now and for a long time once they rejoined the battalion. Someday, Kittridge knew, Reider would rate him. He would write an evaluation in which loyalty was one of several traits that a superior used to judge his subordinates. While such considerations were out of place given their current plight, some people take a bit longer to change gears from a peacetime, business as usual mentality to the requirements of war.

Nathan looked at Reider without expression, then back at Kittridge. "Yes, I know. The main road, just west of here," Nathan stated flatly.

"It really shouldn't be much of a problem," Kittridge stated without much conviction.

"It would seem so," Nathan came back. "Of course, we can't totally discount the fact that the Slovaks are aware of our presence. The troops we faced earlier were no doubt dispatched to find us after our run-in with the tanks yesterday evening. It would not be unreasonable to expect them to pursue us, attempt to intercept us, or . . ."

"Both," Gerald Reider added.

Nathan nodded. "Yes, or both. Probably both."

"While all that's true," Kittridge stated with a tinge of hope in his voice, "there's a lot of road to cover, sir. What are the odds that they'll be at the point where we cross?"

Nathan rocked back on his heels, using his rifle, held butt down in front of him, to help balance himself. He looked down for a moment as he considered how best to respond. The man was searching for a ray of sunshine, something positive to look forward to.

Questions like this place a leader in an awkward position. On the one hand, he can lay out the unvarnished truth as he sees it in an effort to prepare his men for what he, the leader, believes will actually happen. On the other, he could conceal the facts, as he understands them, and the impact those facts may have on his men in the very near future. Between the two black or white choices lies a middle ground, where the facts are fudged. Looking up at Kittridge, Nathan fashioned the best smile he could manage as he began to trot down the middle road.

"You're quite right, Sergeant Kittridge," he started. "It would be quite a stretch for the Slovaks to cover every inch of the road, especially if they're taking on all of NATO."

"So you don't think our problems are isolated?" Reider interrupted.

Nathan's smile disappeared as he looked up at the low-hanging clouds. "That's the only thing that seems to make sense," he explained. "If this had been some sort of local affair, directed at this platoon alone, the battalion's ready reaction force would have been dispatched to extract us. That force would have included aviation assets."

"What are the chances they'd send choppers out in this?" Reider asked.

Lowering his head, Nathan looked over at Reider. "We're out on the edge here. Normal safety restrictions are routinely ignored, Sergeant Kittridge."

Demoralized by the impact of what Nathan was saying, Kittridge sighed. "Yeah, I imagine that's right." He also looked over at Reider. "I can't tell you how many times in the past we've been sent out in a Bradley that, by all rights, should have been deadlined but were circle Xed, sent out even though they have no business being on the road due to operational requirements."

"So what you're saying," Reider continued, "is that not only are we on our own, but that you expect trouble ahead."

There was no point mincing words now, Nathan decided. "That about sums it up. We're open to attack anywhere along our line of march. The Slovaks are not stupid," he explained. "They know where we were. And I imagine they have already guessed where we're headed. If they have the time and resources available to get us, that road looks to be about the best place to do it. All they have to do is draw a straight line between where we sprung that ambush and Fort Apache to figure out where we'll be crossing."

"Then we simply don't go there," Reider responded.

Before he replied, Nathan eased himself back onto his bottom in order to relieve the aches and pains he felt in his legs. The previous day's march, and this morning's exertions, were taking their toll on muscles that had become soft after months of routine staff work. "I don't know about you and your men, sergeant," he stated as he settled in and stretched his legs, "but I'm sore all over."

The acting platoon sergeant looked over his shoulder at his men, who were taking full advantage of this break. "I'm afraid I have to admit that we're not in as good a condition as we should be in. Our six months at Fort Apache has taken the edge off the men."

"Exactly," Nathan added. "Any detour has to be weighed against the added distance that such a deviation would entail as well as the time it would take," he explained patiently to Reider. "And don't forget, each of your men have only two MREs each and not a single blanket between them. We can't expect to find a well-stocked, abandoned farmhouse where we can spend the night like we did last night."

"So," Kittridge picked up, "we have to go for it, the risk be damned."

The senior lieutenant shook his head. "We have to be willing to take prudent risks. When we come up to the road, we'll take our time and do it right. That's why I came up here. We need to go over where we're going to do this and how. Lieutenant Reider," Nathan directed as he shifted around onto his knees so that he could better see the map laying on the ground. "You'll stay with Sergeant Kittridge and his point element. The best place I think we can cross is here," he stated as he pointed to a spot on the map. "It provides us with the most cover and concealment, on both sides of the road, without requiring us to go out of our way."

Both Gerald Reider and Staff Sergeant Kittridge took a moment to study the location Nathan had indicated. When they were finished, they looked up to him and waited for him to continue. "Lieutenant Reider, you'll wait until I close up with the main body and deploy them before you go across."

"Okay," Reider replied mechanically as it slowly dawned on him that the battalion staff officer was drawing him back into the tactical operations of his platoon.

"When I give the word," Nathan went on, "you'll take your point element across and secure the far side. When you're sure all is clear, deploy your people to cover the crossing of the rest of the platoon."

"I expect you'll keep the Javelin," Reider stated in an effort to clarify that point.

"Yes. I want it set and ready before you go."

"Then if you don't mind," Reider ventured, "I'd like to have all the LAWs passed forward to Sergeant Kittridge's squad. That'd give me something to cover your move in case tanks show up again."

"Good idea. I'll see that it's done. Now," Nathan turned back to the map, "once we're all together again, Lieutenant Reider, you'll strike out for Fort Apache with an eye toward terrain that provides us the best covered and concealed route possible. As we get closer to home, the likelihood of running into Slovakians will increase."

"How will we make the final run?" Kittridge asked. "It'll be dark and I expect everyone will be trigger happy if, as you say, the Slovaks have gone on the warpath."

Struggling to stand up, Nathan didn't answer until he was on his feet. Looking down, he smiled. "That will be easy. We don't go in. Instead, as soon as we're close, we hunker down someplace nice and safe, make radio contact, and let them come out to us. Like you, I'm not thrilled about going all this way back only to be nailed by friendly fire." Then, he looked back and forth between the two upturned faces. "Any more questions?"

Before they answered, both Gerald Reider and Staff Sergeant Kittridge looked at each other as if they were trying to pool their thoughts. After a moment, they began the painful process of standing up. Only then did Gerald Reider respond. "No, no questions."

"Good," Nathan chirped. "Then let's get moving." With that, he turned to head back.

As he watched the first lieutenant walk away, the thought of thanking him crossed Reider's mind. Just as quickly, however, the new platoon leader discarded that notion. What in the hell would he be thanking him for? Letting him participate in the functions of his own platoon? No! Reider thought to himself. I don't owe that son of a bitch a damned thing. With that, Reider gathered himself up, turned, and gave Staff Sergeant Kittridge the signal to move out.

18

With the 2nd Squad deployed on either side of them, Nathan Dixon and Gerald Reider eyed the open ground they would soon be crossing. To their immediate front there were fifty or so meters of farm fields. The texture of the ground was masked by a thick blanket of snow. If the field had been plowed before the snow fell, or was broken up by old furrows, the going would be slow.

At the far end of this field, which was pretty much level with the tree line where the 3rd Platoon lay concealed, was the road. There was neither a fence nor a ditch on either side of it, a fact that Nathan viewed as a mixed blessing. The lack of a fence meant they would be able to make the crossing faster. On the other hand, no ditch meant that once they were out there, there was no place to hide until after they had finished crossing the road and made it to the clump of trees where the platoon would rally.

"How far is it to those trees?" Nathan called out to Staff Sergeant Kittridge.

Using the laser range finder on his Land Warrior, Kittridge zapped the far tree line, read the range displayed in his heads-up display, and called it out. "Three hundred ninety-five meters, sir."

"A quarter mile, more or less," Nathan mused aloud as he continued to survey the fields.

Reider picked up the thought. "At best, we can cover that distance in two minutes."

"But we won't be able to do it at a run," Kittridge countered. "Between the loads our people are hauling, and the condition of the ground, we'll need more like four to five."

"Once you're out there," Nathan stated, "there should be no reason to stop until you reach cover over there."

Kittridge nodded as he listened to Nathan. "Five minutes for my squad to cross, another two to three minutes to set up, and five minutes for you to close up on us."

"Sounds like a plan," Nathan announced as he pushed himself up onto his haunches. Looking down at Reider and Kittridge, who continued to stare intently at the far tree line for another minute or two, Nathan waited till they, too, rose up off the ground. When neither man said a word, Nathan slapped his hand on his thigh. "Unless you have any further questions or observations, Lieutenant Reider, it's time to move out."

With his mind focused on what lay before him, Gerald Reider responded to Nathan's directive instinctively. "Roger that."

As Reider and Kittridge stood up and turned to rouse the 2nd Squad, Nathan looked over at Zeke Fishburn. "Get your Javelin up here," Nathan ordered with a sweeping motion of his arm, "and set it up over here. This time I want you to be up and ready."

Their newly self-appointed platoon leader didn't need to say anything more. With no desire to repeat their fumbling of the night before, both gunner and assistant gunner leaped to their feet, trotted over to where Nathan had pointed, and went about preparing missile and sight. All this was executed smoothly and without a word being exchanged between the pair. The thoughts that fluttered through each man's head, however, were more or less the same. In part neither Sergeant Fishburn nor Specialist Jeff Jefferson cared to be confronted with a situation that would require them to use the antitank guided missiles that they had been humping around for the balance of two days. Like Nathan, they simply wanted to get on with their march as quickly as possible and return to the relative safety of Fort Apache.

Yet, like all professionals, both Fishburn and Jefferson longed to use their specialized skills and fire their sophisticated missile. That they had botched their opportunity to do so the night before irked each of them and left them with a desire to redeem themselves to their comrades and friends. By the time Fishburn settled himself down, behind the sight of his Javelin, these conflicting desires created a tension within the sergeant E-5 that surpassed any concerns that he had held concerning the platoon's plight.

When Reider and the 2nd Squad were ready to go, he turned to face Nathan Dixon. With a simple wave of his hand, he motioned on.

With no need to say anything else, he brought his weapons to the ready and took a deep breath. Knowing that he would be setting the pace, Reider stepped out with a brisk and purposeful stride. Even before his left foot hit the ground, all concerns he had about Slovakians and tanks were replaced in a flash by a fear that he would stumble over something hidden by the snow and fall flat on his face, just as he had earlier that morning. To anyone who has never been in a leadership position like this, such thoughts may seem out of place. Yet most soldiers put almost as much importance upon how their leader looks and conducts himself as they do on his knowledge and skills. It is a very human trait, much akin to the one that leads a man to pursue a female who is pretty long before it even crosses his mind to hand out whether or not that woman has a brain.

Unlike their platoon leader, the soldiers of the 2nd Squad weren't concerned about how they looked as they moved from the tree line that had been concealing them. Leaving the tree line, to them, was akin to stripping oneself naked before going out on a January morning. They were exposed to anyone who was out there, lying in wait for them. Except for a quick glance over to Reider every now and then, just to make sure that the man leading them was still moving forward, each member of the 2nd Squad was busily searching patches of terrain that seemed like a good spot for a Slovakian to hide in.

The members of 2nd Squad deployed as they normally did. Specialist David Foss was in the front and to the right of Gerald Reider. As there were two Davids in the 3rd Platoon, he was nicknamed D2, since he was the 2nd Squad David. From Maine, Foss had joined the Army after leaving high school with no other goal in life but to escape the small town in which he had spent his entire life. Like those of a cat moving across unfamiliar ground, Foss's eyes darted between the road that disappeared in the hazy, grayish white distance to his right, and the tree line they were advancing on.

Lester Kim, on the other hand, gave the appearance of being totally oblivious to the danger that everyone else in the platoon was so keenly aware of. Having grown up in the streets of New York City, the son of parents who left Korea before he was born, Kim was unfazed by the hazards the platoon faced. As he reminded his squad leader on many occasions, duty in Slovakia, where he could carry a semiautomatic rifle with a grenade launcher attached to it, was a cinch. "After all," he told

Kittridge, "I made it through puberty and walking to school in the city, every day, without all this firepower."

Behind Foss, Reider, and Kim, hanging back ten meters or so, were Kittridge, on the right, and Keith Reisniack, toting the fully automatic squad automatic weapon. Using the same 5.56mm ammunition that the M-16A2 did, the SAW had replaced the Vietnam-era M-60 machine gun. Though it didn't have the range or the hitting power of its 7.62mm predecessor, the SAW was decidedly lighter, more compact, and easier to handle, something that Reisniack and every SAW gunner came to appreciate at a time like this. In a firefight, he would provide the base of fire for the squad, which was why Kittridge kept him back and near at hand.

When springing an ambush, the most critical decision the attacker has to make is when to fire. The drill, in most armies, when hit by an ambush, is to turn into the assailants and counterattack, with all weapons blazing and at a dead run. Given this, the people lying in wait don't want to allow their prey to be too close when the shooting starts. On the other hand, an attacker doesn't want to spring the trap too soon, before all the intended victims are in the kill zone. Ideally the killing doesn't start until there's no chance that the poor bastards to be hammered are too far away from cover to run from their assailants, yet not so close that the ambush party is in danger itself.

Like all good infantry officers, Nathan knew this. From his concealed position back in the tree line, he watched the 2nd Squad as they moved across the open field. Here the ideal spot to hit Reider and the four men with him was the road. It could very well be a trigger point, a well-defined terrain feature that the leader of a unit in ambush could use to initiate, or trigger, an ambush. The enemy leader simply had to brief his people that they were to hold their fire until the first, second, or maybe third enemy soldier crossed the road before firing. His men, if he had briefed them well and trusted them to do so, could open fire on their own based on the criteria established by their commander. While it was not always wise to judge your opponent's actions based on what you would do, oftentimes such comparative assessments are all a combat leader has to work with.

So it was not surprising that a feeling of relief swept over Nathan when both Kittridge and Reisniack stepped off of the road and into the farm field on the far side without incident. If they had made it that far, Nathan had already determined, they would be good to go. Of course the mere fact that the point element reaches safety doesn't mean that the rest of the platoon is out of danger. In his readings on small-unit actions in Vietnam, Nathan often came across accounts of VC and NVA ambushes that allowed the lead element to pass safely before springing their ambush on the main body. Though he didn't expect the Slovakians to use such a sophisticated ploy, Nathan reminded himself to warn the rest of the platoon to be alert.

With Kittridge over in the other tree line, Nathan turned to Staff Sergeant Hernandes, the next-ranking NCO present. "Okay, let's mount 'em up and move 'em out. And remind your people to stay alert."

Understanding the battalion staff officer's caution, Hernandes nodded. "Roger that, sir." Rising to his feet, the leader of the 3rd Squad shouted to his left, then his right, "You heard the man. Put your butt in gear and keep your eyes and ears open. We aren't out of the woods yet."

Unable to resist the opening, Evens Tobias tapped the butt of his rifle on the tree he had been lying next to. "Was that suppose to be a joke, sarge?" As the rest of the platoon hooted and chuckled, Hernandes scowled at Tobias. "Don't make me come over there and wipe that smile off your face, trooper."

Throwing up his hands in mock surrender, Tobias moved into the open field before his pursuing squad leader could reach him. "I's movin', masta. I's movin' along like a good little darkie."

Embarrassed by this ill-timed display of irreverence, Hernandes looked over to Nathan sheepishly. Though he was tempted to join the laughter that echoed all around him, Nathan maintained his "mask of command." "Get 'em formed up and moving, sergeant," Nathan ordered as he prepared to do so himself.

From his position Sergeant Fishburn took his eye away from the sight of his Javelin and looked up at Nathan. "You want us to move now, with you, or hang back some and cover your move, sir?"

Nathan thought about this for a moment before he shook his head. "No. Just keep a missile at the ready as we make the crossing."

"Will do," Fishburn replied without another thought as he and his assistant gathered up their weapon.

From his new position, Gerald Reider watched as the bulk of his platoon broke cover and moved into the open ground he had already traversed. Tucked away in the relative safety of the tree line, the men who had accompanied him were snatching what little rest they could. Guessing that the quiet staff officer who had taken over command of the platoon would keep moving once he hit these woods, Kittridge was busy orienting himself on the ground that now lay ahead of them. His squad would need to sprint out in front once the rest of the platoon closed up. Out in the field, few of the men with Nathan and Hernandes were paying much attention to what was going on around them either. They were simply coming on, struggling through the deep snow and broken field.

As he watched, the young platoon leader had a chance to see a good part of his own platoon, the one he was supposed to be in command of, perform a simple maneuver for the first time without being involved in it himself. For him it was quite an enlightening experience. Though the range was still too great to differentiate which squad was which, he could clearly see that the one Lieutenant Dixon had deployed to the right was far too bunched up. While they were not exactly shoulder to shoulder, the clump they were moving along in was of no tactical value whatsoever. On the other side, the second squad of dismounts coming on had just the opposite problem. They were so spread out that it took Reider several seconds to account for all four members of that unit. Only in the middle, where Reider assumed Dixon had placed himself, was there any semblance of a sound formation. Reider told himself to make a note of this.

That officer was still watching his own platoon when the throb of a diesel engine from somewhere off to his left cut through the still winter air. With a jerk he cocked his head and pricked up his ears. The clattering of tracks, and the growing sound of an engine being run full open, could mean either trouble or salvation. Looking back across the field, he saw that the squads with Dixon had also heard the ominous rattling of a tracked vehicle.

Nathan had no difficulty in identifying the sound. He stopped so suddenly that Pavlovski had to make a quick sidestep to avoid bumping into the staff officer from behind. Even before the RTO regained his balance, he was looking about as he took note of the approaching vehicle. "What is it?" the RTO asked without thinking.

"A BMP," Nathan blurted out even as his head pivoted, first to his left, then right, and finally straight ahead to the road they needed to cross. He had a second, maybe two, in which to make a quick assessment of their situation. The BMP was still out of sight, to their right, just around the bend. But it would soon be there, long before the overburdened infantry with Nathan would reach the spot on the road where they had to cross. That would leave them up and exposed to whatever weapon the commander of the BMP chose to use on them. So a run for the road was out of the question. Simply dropping down where they stood, and becoming one with the earth, was Nathan's next choice. While it was inviting, Nathan didn't feel comfortable trusting his life, and the lives of his men, to the hope that the commander of the BMP was so nearsighted or oblivious that he would not notice thirteen clumps, dressed in woodland green camouflage uniforms, strewn about a snow-covered field.

So the battalion staff officer made the only decision that made sense at that particular moment. "Back to the tree line, on the double!"

No one needed to be told twice or have the reason for the order spelled out for him. By now all had heard the engine of the approaching BMP. Some had even begun their own retrograde, slowly backing up while Nathan pondered their fates.

While fear and danger are perhaps the greatest motivators that a commander has at his disposal, they cannot overcome the problems of time, distance, and chance. In their haste to regain the cover of the tree line they had just left, two men, Henry Smith of the 1st Squad, and Isaac Smollett, the medic, lost their footing and fell flat on their faces. Smith was lucky. Sergeant Dubois, his squad leader, was right behind him. While barely slowing his own pace, Dubois reached down, grabbed Smith by the flak jacket, and jerked the man back up onto his feet.

Smollett, on the other hand, did not belong to a coherent unit. Like all the people who belonged to the platoon's small headquarters section, he simply followed the platoon's leader wherever he went. He, like the members of the Javelin team and the RTO, knew that the platoon leader had little time to play squad leader, so it was often up to them to anticipate where they were supposed to be and move with a purpose without having to be told. When the medic went down, no one noticed. Pavlovski, the RTO, was right on Nathan's heels, watching the back of the man he was dedicated to serve. Fishburn, hauling his missile launcher guidance system, had his eyes fixed on the spot he planned to set up, while Jefferson, his assistant, struggled to keep pace with him while hauling the missiles. It wasn't until Nathan reached the tree line himself and spun about to take one quick glance behind him that he saw Smollett still out there, a good fifty meters from the tree line, struggling to get to his feet. Without hesitation, the young staff officer took one step and began to rush back, out into the open, to render whatever aid he could to the platoon's aid man. The appearance of the BMP that had sent them scurrying, however, prevented Nathan from taking another. "Get down," Nathan yelled as loud as he dared, "and stay down."

With a panicked look on his face, Smollett stared at Nathan as he stepped back into the shadows of the tree line he had gained. "Get down," Nathan repeated as he glanced back and forth between Smollett and the BMP. "Lie low and don't move." Only after the man turned his head and pressed it into the snow did Nathan step back and slowly ease down into a crouched position.

On the road the BMP trundled along with its turret and 30mm main gun pointed straight ahead. The commander of that vehicle, bundled up against the cold and squatting as low as he could, neither moved his head nor gave any order for his gunner to scan the open fields to either side. Both men, bored as mounted troopers often become after spending hours of rolling along without a break, were content to cover their assigned sector of responsibility and no more.

It wasn't until a second BMP, following a good fifty meters behind the first, appeared that Nathan became anxious. While its turret was pointed to the right, and away from the tree line that he was in, Nathan knew that the Slovakian BMP had to be looking straight at the spot where Lieutenant Reider and the 2nd Squad were.

Looking to his right, Nathan tried to locate the Javelin team. Although he could not see them, Nathan knew they were over there, somewhere. "Fishburn. Are you set?"

A voice filtered back through the undergrowth along the tree line. "We're set."

"Lay on the second BMP," Nathan commanded.

Fishburn's "Roger that" had barely reached Nathan's ears when a third BMP made its way around the bend. This one, following standard tactical practices, had its turret and main gun turned to cover the side of the road that the second could not. Without a shred of evidence to support the fact, Nathan's overactive imagination told him that both the gunner and the commander of that BMP were looking directly at him. The odds of this being so were, of course, quite small. Still, the feeling gripped Nathan like a cold hand.

Only after the third BMP was well on its way down the road without making any hostile moves was Nathan able to shake his unfounded fear. This relief was short lived. Following the third BMP was a truck. The canvas that normally covers the bed of the truck was absent, exposing the soldiers seated in the rear to the elements. Like the commanders of the preceding BMPs, these miserable wretches were bent over and bundled up as tightly as they could, in an effort to keep what little warmth their bodies were generating from escaping. Only one man, an air guard, standing behind the cab of the truck and holding on to a machine gun, showed any sign of life. Nathan watched from his concealed position as the air guard in the lead truck stomped his feet in an effort to keep warm.

Air guards are responsible for keeping an eye open for hostile aircraft. Vigilance against an attack from that quarter, however, was all but meaningless when low-hanging clouds hid the tops of the tallest trees. Whether

it was for lack of a viable threat or simply a chance oc-
currence, the Slovakian air guard in the first truck
turned his head in Nathan's direction just as his vehicle
came even with the spot where Specialist Smollett lay
hunkered down in the snow, in plain view.

Nathan didn't notice this. With the passing of each
vehicle, the young officer had become less apprehensive
and more confident that the Slovakian column would
bypass them without incident. From the tree line he
hardly gave the air guard, who pressed himself up
against the cab of the truck in an effort to protect himself from the cold wind that whipped past him, a second
thought. Nathan had already turned his head away from
the first truck to see if another vehicle would appear
from around the bend before the air guard caught sight
of the motley green mound that Specialist Smollett appeared as. Only when the air guard started banging on
the top of the truck's cab and shouting did Nathan realize that something was amiss.

On both sides of the road, all eyes, except Smollett's,
were drawn to the lone air guard. From his side of the
road, Gerald Reider could see a Slovakian NCO stick his
head out of the passenger window and look up at the
air guard. Shouting so as to be heard above the drone
of the truck's engine, the air guard told his sergeant
what he saw even as he pointed toward Smollett, though
the Slovakian in the cab of the truck could not see it.
Alarmed, both Nathan and Reider watched as the truck
pulled over, off to the side of the road, and came to a
stop. By the time this had happened, the air guard had
managed to shift his machine gun over to cover the field
where Smollett lay. The men riding in the bed of the
truck, who had been roused by the unexpected stop,
had shaken off the stupor induced by the cold and bore-
dom of the ride and, too, were looking over at the field.

On either side of him, Nathan could hear the movement of the soldiers with him as they slowly brought
their weapons up to the ready. When he heard the click

of safeties being flicked off, he whispered the order to hold fire. "No shooting unless I order it," he passed on to his right. Then, turning his head, he repeated the same words to those who were off to his left. "No shooting unless I order it." Having done so, Nathan returned to watch what the Slovakians would do next.

On the road, the Slovakians began to dismount. Farther up the road were the three BMPs that had continued moving on after the truck had stopped. When they finally noticed that there was a break in the column and came to a halt, there was a wide gap between them and the trucks they had been escorting. At first confused, one at a time, they sat where they had stopped until the NCO from the truck, now on the ground, shouted and waved to the commander of the last of the BMPs, pointing at Smollett as he did so. It started to become obvious to Nathan that trouble was unavoidable.

Quickly, Nathan assessed the threats that faced them and determined how best to handle them. The appearance of a second, and then a third truck, all loaded with troops, made it crystal clear that the tiny two squads with him would not be able to survive in a firefight against the force they faced. The only option that made sense to Nathan, as he watched the Slovakians deploy, was to lay down covering fire so Smollett could get up and start running, then turn tail themselves before the Slovakians could overwhelm them with numbers and firepower.

Without hesitation, Nathan ordered Fishburn to lay his sights on the third BMP. It was closest to them and the one that had its gun laid on them. The lead BMP wisely kept its attention on the road ahead, while the second maintained its turret oriented on the woods where Reider and his men were. They did this as a precaution against an ambush, one in which the attacker could just as easily be on the other side of the road as well.

After Fishburn had acknowledged his order, Nathan instructed the squad leaders to divide their fires between the two groups of Slovakians now forming up on the road. Sergeant Dubois and his 1st Squad would fire on the soldiers who had been in the lead truck and were now preparing to strike off across the field to investigate the object that their air guard had spotted. Hernandes and his people had the task of suppressing the second group of Slovakians deployed in a skirmish line along the side of the road.

From out in the field, Nathan heard Smollett calling out, "What the fuck do I do?"

In the calmest voice that he could manage, Nathan told the medic to lie still and wait for him to give the order. "After the shooting starts, make the tree line and keep going. We'll be right behind you."

Specialist Pavlovski, who was next to Nathan, looked over at the officer. "You mean we're not going to stand here and take them out, sir?"

Surprised at the question, Nathan looked at Pavlovski. "Hell, no. We're going to drop back some, shift to the left, and cross the road further south."

"What about the 2nd Squad and the new platoon leader, what's his name?" Pavlovski shot back. "We gonna leave them over there on their own?"

"Sergeant Kittridge and Lieutenant Reider will figure it out. They know where Fort Apache is and how to get there."

Unconvinced, Pavlovski persisted. "And what if the battalion's not there anymore?"

Though tempted to tell the RTO to shut up, Nathan held his tongue. "We simply have to sort that out when we get to it." With that, he turned his head away and focused on the situation that was unfolding before him.

Timing was everything. Unlike an ambush, where you wanted your foes to be well committed to the point where they could go neither forward nor backward without being punished, Nathan wanted to keep the Slovakians at arm's distance. All he wanted to do was to create momentary confusion, and perhaps pin his foes down.

He just needed to buy enough time for Smollett to get up and reach the woods, then allow the squads there the opportunity to pull back before the Slovakians recovered and were able to bring their superior firepower to bear on them. Such was Nathan's plan.

Watching the Slovakians from the first truck, he decided to count to ten after they had started forward before giving the order to fire. The click of another safety being flipped off caused Nathan to repeat his previous order. "Hold fire until I say so." When he heard it being passed on, Nathan closed his eyes, took a deep breath, and steadied himself. Opening them, he caught sight of a Slovakian NCO waving his men forward.

As that man's lead foot hit the ground, Nathan started to count out loud. "One thousand, two thousand." Slowly Nathan brought his own rifle up to his shoulder. "Three thousand four thousand." With great care, he pulled the stock of his weapon back into his shoulder. "Five thousand, six thousand." Laying his cheek against the butt of his rifle, he took aim at a Slovakian advancing on them who held his machine gun, supported by its sling, at the ready. "Seven thousand eight thousand." With a minute motion of his thumb, Nathan moved the rifle's safety from "Safe" to "Fire." "Nine thousand . . ."

A flash from somewhere on the other side of the road, followed by an explosion that rocked the second BMP, started Nathan. Instinctively, he paused his count, lifted his head, and looked up to see what had happened. As a secondary explosion shook the stricken BMP, a volley of small arms erupted from the tree line where Gerald Reider and the 2nd Squad were. It only took a moment to figure out what had happened. Noting that the Slovakians to his front, and those still on the road, were caught off guard and were oriented on this new danger, Nathan didn't hesitate any longer. *"FIRE!"*

The chatter of small-arms fire, and the crack and *whooosssh* of the Javelin's motor cutting in shattered the silence. Without giving any thought to the friendly bullets that were flying past him, Smollett leaped to his feet and took off at a dead run. After dispatching the Slovakian machine gunner he had been lined up on before Reider had opened fire, Nathan pushed himself up off the ground, got into a crouched position behind the tree he had been using for cover, and watched the short flight of the Javelin.

For those who think in conventional terms, the Javelin is a strange weapon. It is propelled by two stages. The first motor has relatively low power. The purpose of this is to "kick" the missile out of the tube. After gliding a short distance, the second, more powerful rocket motor ignites and sends the missile on to its target. Here's where things really get a bit weird. Rather than make a beeline for the target that the gunner has in his sight, the missile leaps up, at a steep angle, into the air. Depending on the launcher-to-target range, the missile can climb anywhere from one to two hundred meters. After passing its apogee, or high point, the missile drives toward the designated target at an angle of forty-five degrees. The top attack aspect means that the Javelin missile attacks the lightly armored top of the target.

But that's not all. Just in case the target is protected by reactive armor, a form of antitank missile protection popular in vehicles designed by the former Soviet Union, the Javelin has a tandem warhead. The first, or lead, charge has the task of detonating the reactive armor at the point of impact, clearing a path for the second warhead, which is the real killer. Only then does the Javelin behave in a conventional manner. The shaped charge warhead detonates, forming a jet stream of molten metal. Contrary to popular belief, this jet stream does not "burn" its way through the target's armor plate. Rather, the speeding metal molecules of the jet stream literally displace, or push out of the way, the molecules of the armor. This stream of molten material, from both the missile's warhead and the armor plate itself, continues on, cutting through anything in its path such as hydraulics, electronics, ammunition, fuel, and, of course, crewmen. Items that are inflammable or explosive tend to respond to this according to their nature, adding to the mayhem caused by the jet stream itself. With luck, for the Javelin crew that is, enough of this sort of material inside the target will react to cause a catastrophic kill. And even if it doesn't, the effect of having a Javelin reach out and touch you is more than enough to mess up a crew, not to mention its equipment and weapons, which are all crammed tightly into the small, confined spaces of an armored fighting vehicle.

When he heard the Javelin's first rocket engine kick in, Nathan couldn't help but cease fire and watch. In his three years of active duty, he had never seen a real live Javelin launched, either in anger or in training. Apparently he was not alone. Like the fans at a ball game watching a kicker as he tried for the winning field goal, soldiers on both sides of the firing line paused to watch the Javelin as it went through its wild gyrations. The crews of the three BMPs, who knew in their hearts that one of them was the intended recipient, paid particular attention to the missile's flight. Two of the BMPs' commanders had the presence of mind to attempt evasive maneuvers. But the distance from the launcher was too short, and the speed of the missile too quick, for their belated efforts to have any influence on the final outcome. With unerring accuracy Sergeant Fishburn maintained his sight on the target Nathan had designated and watched, with great satisfaction, as the BMP he had targeted was hit, and began the spectacular process of tearing itself apart from within.

It was during this interim that Specialist Smollett reached the tree line. Motivated by fear and an overpowering sense of self-preservation, he had not interrupted his own flight to watch the flight of the Javelin. Those few Slovakians who also ignored the one-sided missile/BMP duel turned their attention on Smollett, but to no effect. Their fire was so wide of the mark that it was doubtful if the platoon medic, given his state of mind, even took note of the *zing* of near misses.

Seizing upon this opportunity to break and run, Nathan shouted his orders. "First Squad, lay down cover. Third Squad and Javelin, pull back and rally one hundred to the rear." While he waited for the squad leaders to acknowledge his orders, he surveyed the Slovakian positions and the actions of the surviving BMP. This one, which had been the lead BMP, after slewing its turret to the right to engage Reider's people, was hastily traversing back to the left, now that it was clear that the major threat to it was on the other side of the road. Even before he had a definite target, the gunner of the BMP was firing his coax machine gun. Though his aim was no better than that of the accompanying infantry, the volume of fire being directed against Nathan and the two squads with him was building. Anxious to get out of there before that fire began to have a telling effect, Nathan, using all the lung power he possessed, repeated his orders. "First Squad, lay down cover. Third Squad and Javelin, pull back and rally one hundred to the rear."

This time, after hearing Nathan's shrilled orders, the squad leaders replied. First came Hernandes. Off to his right, Nathan caught a glimpse of figures moving away from the tree line as Hernandes called out, "We're moving, we're moving." Dubois's deep baritone rang out above the chatter of small-arms fire. "Roger, sir. First Squad, pick up your fire." Satisfied, Nathan was about to drop back and move over to the left behind the 1st Squad when he heard the distinctive, low pitch *pow-pow-pow* of a BMP's 30mm main gun. In an instant the woods where the Javelin crew had been erupted in a shower of small explosions and splinters as the mix of high-explosive and armor-piercing rounds plowed up ground and shattered trees. Instinctively, Nathan drew away. Only when he heard the terrified shriek of "Medic!" did he pause.

Unsure exactly what to do, Nathan hesitated, looking first in the direction from where he had heard the call, then over at the BMP, which was continuing to pump 30mm rounds into the wood line. The young officer hoped the BMP would pause, that it would cease its firing or something so that he could dash over there and see who was hit and if there was something he could do. Yet in the back of his mind, Nathan also came to the realization that even if the BMP did check fire, it would be just that, a pause, a momentary cessation of fire in order to assess the effectiveness of its initial volley before opening up again. Any effort by Nathan to go over there and aid whoever had been hit would surely carry him into the field of vision of the BMP's gunner, prompting that man to squeeze off his rounds directly at him.

Doing nothing to help one of his own, however, wasn't an option. What sort of leader would do that? And who would follow such a leader? While he could very easily spell out to the soldiers of the 1st and 3rd Squads later that the situation didn't permit a recovery of their stricken comrade, Nathan knew in his heart and soul that those men would never again fully trust him, no matter how logical his decision had been.

In combat, luck and the element of chance are something that no leader worth a damn depends on. Yet successful commanders, to a man, cannot ignore the roles that these unpredictable elements play. For Nathan, the unsolicited and unexpected assistance of the 2nd Squad, acting totally independently of him and the rest of the platoon, once more made a difference. This time the 2nd Squad's intervention came in the form of an AT-4 light antitank rocket fired at the last BMP. Only peripherally did Nathan take note of this action as he made his way to where the cries of pain were tapering off into moans. Putting his head down, Nathan tried to force himself to ignore what was going on out on the road. Now that he had committed himself to such a risky course of action, there was no turning back, no stopping. For better or worse, he was going to find the wounded man.

Being very much a human being, however, Nathan could not totally block out the rest of the world around him, especially those elements that could very well have an immediate and deadly impact on him. So when the sound of the 30mm cannon firing again reached his ears, Nathan turned his head and looked. Even before he saw the BMP, the change in pitch of that weapon's reports told him that the BMP gunner was firing on a new target. When he saw the aspect of the BMP's turret, he knew it was the 2nd Squad, his twice-over savior, that was being hammered. A wisp of grayish smoke, tinged with black, could be seen issuing from the rear of the BMP, it was clear that the 2nd Squad's AT-4 had hit, but not killed, the BMP.

With his attention riveted on the BMP, Nathan almost bypassed the stricken soldier he had set out to rescue. Only the pitiful cry of "Help me" stopped him from doing so. Looking away from the BMP, Nathan turned his attention to the issue at hand. In an instant, he saw that the BMP had extracted its own cruel revenge. The wounded man, sitting on the ground and covered in blood, was Jeff Jefferson, the assistant Javelin gunner. With his palms up and arms outstretched, Jefferson reached up toward Nathan. "Help me!" After looking the man over a second, the young officer saw that the source of all the blood, as best as he could tell, were numerous slashes and cuts that covered Jefferson from head to toe. Only that portion of his body that had been protected by Jefferson's flak vest survived unscathed. Quickly Nathan made the decision that Jefferson, though in pain, was not in mortal danger. "Where's the gunner?" Nathan asked, guessing that Fishburn would never run off and leave his assistant behind like this.

Through his sobs, Jefferson stammered, "I don't know. I don't know. Help me."

Glancing about, Nathan's eyes darted over the shattered patch of woods until they fell on Fishburn's body, lying in a heap, just inside the tree line. Taking a step or two in that direction, Nathan quickly saw all he needed to see. The corpse was badly chewed up. Fishburn's helmet was gone, blown off by the 30mm HE round that had taken half of the Javelin gunner's head. The sight of that wound, as well as one that left a bloody hole ripped out of the middle of Fishburn's flak vest, was all Nathan took time to look for. Turning away from the dead gunner, he made his way back to Jefferson. "On your feet," the battalion staff officer yelled as he heard the snap and *zing* of near misses past his head. "Get up and get moving."

"I'm wounded," Jefferson screamed, not making any effort to help himself. "I can't."

When he reached the stricken man, Nathan didn't hesitate or argue. Bending over, the officer stuck his hands into the armholes of Jefferson's flak vest. With all the strength of a man running on pure adrenaline, Nathan yanked the man up and onto his feet. "I said move! Now move, or stay here and die."

The officer's sudden action brought howls of pain and a shower of curses from the wounded man. But the swiftness of Nathan's action and Jefferson's own lethargy were sufficient to get the man up, off the ground, and on his feet. *"MOVE!"* Nathan yelled as he held on with one hand, and pulled the man behind him. Though Jefferson issued a nonstop babble that consisted of screams of pain, sobs, and vicious curses, his feet managed to respond and keep pace with Nathan as the pair disappeared into the woods. Behind them, on the road, the confused and bloodied Slovakians continued to fire blindly into the woods that flanked them.

19

For the second time in less than twelve hours, Gerald Reider was running for his life. His painfully slow progress, the sweat that streamed from his brow and burned his eyes, and the desperate gasping for breath as his lungs cried out for air were all too familiar to the young platoon leader. Yet this time it was different. Above all the physical sensations that assaulted Reider, he was experiencing a sort of euphoria, a lightness of heart and spirit. His running was not the panicked flight of a lone 'cruit officer who had been caught by the enemy as he stumbled blindly around on his own. This retreat was part of a plan, the concluding segment of a successful engagement. This time, the hasty withdrawal away from an agitated foe had been his decision, one that was both sound and correct. And that, to Gerald Reider, made all the difference in the world.

* * *

The decision to engage the Slovakians back at the road had been Reider's. He had watched the Slovakians as they had paused, then dismounted, leaving little doubt as to what they were up to. The manner in which the truck-mounted Slovakians went about deploying, with their backs to him, told Reider that they were not aware of the 2nd Squad. Only the commander of the second BMP in the line of march had the presence of mind to continue covering his assigned sector of responsibility, which was the tree line where Reider and Kittridge's squad lay hidden. So it was a no-brainer for Reider when it came time to pick a target on which to use one of the 2nd Squad's two AT-4 light antitank rockets.

The honor of firing this shot fell to Kittridge. The choice was not based upon the fact that he was the most senior enlisted man there. If rank had entered the equation, Reider would have taken the shot. Rather the decision was based solely on practical wisdom. Of the five professional soldiers on Reider's side of the road, Kittridge was the only man present who had ever actually fired an AT-4. While everyone else, to include Reider, had undergone extensive and repetitive training on the AT-4 that involved dozens of engagements on simulators, the difference between an engagement simulator and the real thing is pretty much akin to what the average American would experience if he were to compare a video game with the sensation of actually driving a car in the Indy 500. The most expensive state-of-the-art simulator cannot replicate every detail, whether it be the sound and vibrations that the rocket motor makes as it ignites and slides down the fiberglass tube that the gunner holds against the side of his head, or the shower of snow crystals and wave of heat that pelts his face as the rocket leaves the tube right in front of him. Even the anticipation of these alien sensations has been known to cause soldiers to flinch at the last moment, either spoiling their aim or jerking the launcher in a manner that ruins the flight of the unguided rocket.

So Kitt took the shot. An option to use the second AT-4 against another BMP at the same time was never seriously considered. Unlike the Javelin, which boasts a more potent warhead, the AT-4 is classified as a light antitank weapon, or LAW. The physical classification that earns it this title comes with a price. The warhead of the AT-4's projectile, or rocket, is smaller, simpler, and less lethal. In a game of averages, it would be less likely to cause a catastrophic kill. So the technique of engaging, or being ready to engage each target with a volley of LAWs, one pioneered in Vietnam, was adopted by the United States Army. While Staff Sergeant Kittridge was taking the first shot, a second trooper stood ready with the squad's second AT-4. Private Les Kim, a man who had demonstrated a high degree of proficiency in handling the AT-4 during training, was tagged for this. If Kitt failed to achieve the desired target effect, Kim would fire his LAW at the same BMP. If the squad leader's rocket did find its mark, then Kim would hold fire and save his AT-4 for another target to be designated by Reider as the situation developed. As the engagement unraveled, this is what occurred, though Kim's rocket did not have quite the same effectiveness that Kitt's had.

Unlike macho action thrillers produced in Hollywood, both sides in war usually pay a price when they come to grips. There are exceptions, such as that very morning, when Nathan managed to orchestrate a hasty, though well-executed ambush on an unsuspecting and unprepared foe. But the foes that Reider took on, while initially caught off balance and punished accordingly, were able to regain a degree of control and lash out at their assailants. In the case of the 2nd Squad, the commander of the lead BMP maintained his composure, making sound assessments and turning to engage the threat that appeared to be most threatening to him. At first this had been the Javelin. The flight characteristics of the missile, and the utter devastation that the Javelin had wrought, all but dictated this. Yet when Kim's AT-4 rocket smacked into the rear of the lead BMP, causing serious internal damage but not enough to force the crew to bail out, the commander of the BMP reassessed the threat and turned on 2nd Squad.

The choice of weapons was also an easy one for the commander of that BMP to make. While his 7.62mm coax put out far more rounds than the 30mm cannon, the physical, visual, and psychological effect of cannon fire, especially when spewing out rounds tipped with high-explosive projectiles, can be quite intimidating. A volley of large caliber rounds, even when fired with little regard for aim or accuracy, is often effective when the goal is to drive the opponent to ground or cause him to break off his attack. This is called suppressive fire, fire that is meant to deny an opponent his ability to move, shoot, or communicate. Of course, if luck is with you, and the gunner is skilled, then death to your foe results, which is, after all, the ultimate form of suppression.

The rapid response of the BMP, and the realization that they no longer had the ability to do damage to the surviving BMP, left Gerald Reider no choice but to order the members of the 2nd Squad to fall back. Like many other military terms, "fall back" was adopted to make the act of fleeing from the enemy so much more palatable to both the commander in the field and historians charged with sorting out the chaotic and messy details of combat. The response of the soldiers of the 2nd Squad to Reider's order to break contact and pull back depended on how close they were to the beaten zone being plowed up by 30mm high-explosive rounds. Reider and Kittridge, who were situated some thirty meters to the left of the targeted area, were able to ease back a bit before they rose up, turned, and began their flight. Keith Reisniack, the SAW gunner, had taken up a position in the center of the squad, which placed him closer to the chaos created by the 30mm cannon, but far enough away so that rational thoughts and decisions were pretty much unimpaired.

Les Kim and David Foss, on the far right of the squad, were less fortunate. Since it had been Kim who had fired the offending LAW, the telltale signs generated by the backblast of the rocket served to cue the BMP commander as to where best to direct his fire. Though both were professional soldiers, neither Kim nor Foss had ever been under fire. Their reaction to this new experience came not from the training they had participated in over the years, but rather from their instinct to flee from danger. Surrounded by the concussion of explosions caused by near misses, the cacophony of noise, and a shower of splinters flying from shattered trees and the shells themselves, both Kim and Foss surrendered all semblance of discipline and logic as they took flight. Not even Kittridge's order to pull back, bellowed out by a man as eager to depart the area as any of his squad, was heard by men overwhelmed by panic.

Their efforts to save their lives served only to draw attention to themselves. The sight of forms moving away from his aim point gave the BMP gunner a more definitive target on which he could adjust his fire. After pausing, the gunner randomly selected the target he thought he had the best chance to hit. With an ease honed by long hours of repetitive drills, the gunner manipulated his sight and the weapon slaved to it until he had the sight picture that he was comfortable with. Anxious to resume their fire, the commander of the BMP repeated his order to fire. The gunner, however, would not be hurried. Seeing an opportunity to exact a modicum of revenge, the gunner took his time to ensure that his aim was as perfect as he could humanly make it.

In the tree line, the renewal of fire and the piercing screams of a man in pain caused both Kittridge and Gerald Reider to slow their pace and turn to see who had been hit. Through the trees Reider watched as one of his men, surrounded by flashes and explosions, flailed his arms about madly, then dropped to the ground. Pausing, Reider was about to turn about and head over to where the man had fallen when Staff Sergeant Kittridge came up alongside Reider, grabbed his lieutenant by the arm, and yelled as he pulled the officer, "He's dead! Keep going!"

Caught off guard, and conditioned to respond to crisp orders like the one Kittridge had just barked in his ear, the young second lieutenant complied without hesitation. Even though he felt the urge to look back, just to be sure, Gerald Reider gave in to his own instinct for survival and continued his flight.

In the end, the decision to slow the flight of the 2nd Squad and regroup was not the result of a careful weighing of their tactical situation or based on predetermined criteria established by either Reider or Kittridge. Rather, it was the realization both of these men reached independently that they, themselves, could not keep up the pace.

Kittridge, trailing Reider by a few meters as they wound their way through the light woods, was the first to speak. Gasping, he managed to shout out a statement what was half plea, half command. "Lieutenant! We've got to slow down. The men, we'll lose them. Can't keep up."

Whether the statement "Can't keep up" applied to Kittridge or the men he seemed to be concerned about didn't even occur to Reider. He was at the end of his own rope. The only thing that had kept him going was his pride. As foolish as it may seem, given the circumstances, Reider imagined that the surviving members of the 2nd Squad would have looked down on him with disdain if he had brought their headlong flight to an end, too soon, simply because he didn't have the stam-

ina to keep up with them. So he had ignored the pain
that racked his body. With all his might, he blocked the
sharp pains that shot up his legs from muscles that had
been pushed beyond their limits. Instead, he concentrated on his labored breathing, which had become a
desperate struggle to capture enough air to fill his lungs.
The plea for a halt came none too soon for Reider.

Like a runner who had reached the end of his course,
Reider let his entire body relax. So intense had his efforts been that for a moment the young man continued
to stumble forward, forcing him to grab a nearby tree
lest he fall over on his face or trip over feet that had
now, inexplicably, lost all ability to function in a coor-
dinated manner.

Still gasping for breath, Reider looked around to see
if the men who were following him had seen him lurch
forward and almost fall. To his relief, Reider saw that all
of the members of the 2nd Squad were endeavoring to
maintain their own balance or bent over, grasping their
knees with their hands as they gulped in air by the
mouthful.

During this pause, Reider gave himself a pat on the
back for having survived this trial by fire with flying colors. Staff Sergeant Kittridge, on the other hand, drew
himself up, looked around, and counted heads. A few
meters off to his left was Keith Reisniack. The SAW gunner had matched Kittridge, step for step, during their
flight on a parallel track.

Looking beyond Reisniack, it took Kittridge a second
or two to catch sight of Les Kim. This was as much due
to the beads of sweat that flowed down his brow into his
eyes as from the trees that blocked his line of sight. Kim
was bent over, gulping down air between dry heaves that
racked his body. The sight of Kim was the first confir-
mation that it had been Foss who had been cut down.
"Kim," Kittridge called out in a voice that betrayed that
he, too, was still suffering from their precipitous flight.
"You okay?"

Without lifting his head, Kim raised a hand and waved it awkwardly. "Can you keep up?" the squad leader inquired.

After pausing, the second-generation Korean-American stood upright, looked over to where Kittridge stood, and waved again. "Yeah," Kim managed. "Good to go."

Having used the time to gather his own strength, Kittridge turned to face Reider, who had been watching and listening without saying a word. "Sir," Kittridge announced without ceremony, "we're ready anytime you are."

Reider took this as a challenge, one he could not ignore. Throwing out his chest and standing as erect as his burden of flak vest and gear allowed, Reider replied with more bravado than he felt, "Okay. Form up, move out." Without telling the three soldiers who were making their way over to line up behind him where they were going, Reider turned and stepped off, doing his best to conceal wobbly legs that still cried out for rest.

It was a good ten minutes before curiosity got the better of the West Pointer and he slowed his pace until he was even with Kittridge. The squad leader, who had been paying little attention to what his platoon leader was doing, was genuinely surprised when he looked up and saw Reider walking next to him. "Oh, excuse me. My mind was on . . ."

Though Reider waited for Kittridge to finish, the NCO didn't. Instead, he shook his head as if he were erasing whatever thoughts he had been brooding over. "Is there something I can do for you, lieutenant?"

The cold formality of the squad leader's question caused Reider to hesitate for a moment, wondering if this was a good time to ask his question. But having set out to find out the answer to what was troubling him, Reider plunged ahead. "How did you know," Reider asked hesitantly, "that the man who went down back there was, well, dead?"

Kittridge didn't look at Reider. Instead, he walked on for several steps, staring down at the ground without saying a word. When he spoke, it was in a whisper. "I didn't."

Had Kittridge raised his hand and slapped him, Reider could not have been more shocked. Stunned, Reider stopped in his tracks. Only his head, his mouth agape and his eyes as big as saucers, moved as he continued to follow Kittridge as he plodded along a few more feet. "You what?" Reider shrieked.

After stopping, Kittridge turned and looked back at Reider. "You heard me," he replied bitterly. "I didn't know. There was no way of knowing." Then, with a hushed, almost plaintive tone, the NCO added, "Not without going over there."

Staggered, Gerald Reider could do nothing but stare at the man. Turning and leaving one of your own behind was against everything that had been pounded into his young skull at West Point. Tales of great feats of heroism and self-sacrifice by leaders struggling to save the life of one of their men filled the histories of units and battles that he had been exposed to during his military training. So the shock of finding out that he had been party to turning his back on one of his own stunned Gerald Reider as nothing else could have.

Reider closed the distance between himself and Kittridge in two easy steps. "Why did you lie to me?" Reider demanded. "Why did you insist that he was dead?"

Kittridge didn't answer his platoon leader, at least not right away. He avoided the man in his face. Rather, the squad leader cast his eyes over toward the remaining two members of his squad who had been listening to the exchange between their leaders. Both men wore dispassionate expressions that neither betrayed their feelings nor expressed their thoughts. If they had something to say to a man whom they had followed so long, they would wait until later, under more private circumstances.

Reider, however, would not be denied. He demanded an answer. He needed an answer.

"How could you turn your back on one of your own without even bothering to check?"

Finally, Kittridge looked into the face of his platoon leader. "Because if I had '*bothered*' to check, *sir*, I'd still be there, lying right beside him, dead or damned near it. Either way, I wouldn't have been any use to the rest of the squad, men who still had a chance."

"You're a coward!" Reider snapped before he had time to ponder the ramifications of such an accusation.

The sergeant's response was quick and unequivocal. "In your eyes that may be so, sir." Stepping even closer than he was, Kittridge drew a deep breath before he continued. "But let me tell you this. We ain't at West Point anymore. This," he exclaimed as he jabbed his finger down, pointing at the ground he stood on, "is the real world. Every man in this squad, in your platoon, has lived in the shadow of death for the past six months. We've counted the dead, sorted the dead, loaded the dead on trucks, hell, we've even had to dig up the dead to find out who they were. All the while, every time we had one of those nasty, real world missions, ones that they don't train you for at Benning or list as part of the mission of the infantry, each and every one of us has wondered, will *we* be next?"

Easing back some, perhaps because he realized how close he was to crossing the line of insubordination, or because he had vented his anger, Kittridge's tone softened, but only a bit. "Foss was the man's name, sir. David L. Foss. He and his wife live in the same housing complex back in Germany as my family. His wife visits mine at least once a day. They exchange gossip and news. They share everything we tell them in our letters. When we get back there, I'm going to have to face that woman. I'm going to have to look into her eyes and explain to her what happened to the only man she loved. Then I'm going to have to live the rest of my life wondering if there wasn't something I could have done to save him. That man, and the knowledge that I turned my back on him, will be with me till the day I die."

For a moment, Kittridge tried to say something else. But the words didn't come. Only a tear that he couldn't hold back, broke free. Unable to continue, the NCO turned his back on his platoon leader and continued his trek toward a place of safety that none of them believed existed any longer.

It was not physical exhaustion that brought an end to Nathan Dixon's flight. Rather, it was PFC Jefferson's moans and sobs that finally caused the staff officer to call for a halt. With the same thoroughness he had become accustomed to while serving with the Airborne, Nathan rallied his troops about him, established sectors of responsibilities for each of the squads, and watched as the squad leaders went about deploying their men. Only when Nathan was sure that each and every man had assumed his place in their tiny perimeter did he, himself, flop down into the snow, next to a tree, to rest.

Slowly, almost belatedly, he allowed himself to relax. Like a doll whose string had been cut, Nathan's head flopped backwards until the top of his rucksack arrested its fall. Only now did Nathan come to realize how spent he really was. Automatically, his right hand fumbled about as his gloved fingers searched for his canteen. As he did so, his mind took stock of the various body parts and their condition. He was soaked from the inside out as a result of his exertions. Not only had he had to push himself on, Nathan had been forced to pull, shove, and all but drag Jefferson the whole way.

The young officer, as young officers are prone to do, had made a snap judgment concerning Jefferson's wounds. Before they had even left the shattered tree line where Jefferson's comrade still lay, Nathan judged the assistant Javelin gunner's wounds to be nothing more than cuts caused by shrapnel and splinters. This opinion had, of course, been based more on guesswork than careful examination. But the choice to keep the man on his feet, despite his protests, cursing, and screams of agony was a wise one, if not self-serving. It not only took the rump of the 3rd Platoon well away from the Slovakians back on the road, it proved, unwittingly, to Jefferson himself and those who were concerned about their buddy's welfare, that his injuries were far from mortal.

With great effort, Nathan lifted his head up off the rucksack he carried and looked around. In the center of the little circle was Jefferson. Propped up against a tree, he continued to sob as Specialist Four Isaac Smollett knelt beside him, carefully inspecting each wound and tending to it. The platoon RTO, Sam Pavlovski, sat across from Smollett, watching the medic go about his task.

"Ah, now," Smollett would say as he peeled back torn fragments of uniform to expose a fresh wound. "This one isn't so bad. Barely broke the skin." As Nathan watched, he was reminded of how his stepmother would tell him the same thing. No matter how bad the cut, or how bloody the wound, she would tell him in a calm, almost soothing voice that he had nothing to worry about. That his injury looked far worse than it really was. Even when he lay in the street in front of their quarters at Fort Hood, in a pool of blood with a shattered bone sticking out of his leg after falling off a skateboard, Nathan's stepmother was able to retain her cool demeanor and almost convince him that all was well.

For his part Jefferson watched everything the medic did, complaining when he thought Smollett was being too rough or bewailing his fate when he had nothing else to complain about. "Did you see what those fuckers did to Zeke?" he groaned to Pavlovski without ever taking his eyes off of the nimble fingers of the medic working on him. "They cut him in half. In half, man, like he was a piece of meat."

"Hold still, Jeff," Smollett cooed, as much to end the man's rantings as to keep his agitated patient from thrashing about. "Sergeant Fishburn is gone, and there's nothing we can do to help him. He's with God."

From across their blood-soaked comrade, Pavlovski snickered. "Jeez, Isaac. I thought you were studying to be a doctor when you joined the Army, not a rabbi."

Without looking up, Smollett smiled. "Either one would have pleased my mother. Fact is, any path I had gone down, other than the one I chose, would have pleased her." Looking up, his smiled broadened. "After all, in America, good little Jewish boys grow up to become doctors, or lawyers, or bankers. Every now and then, one even becomes a rabbi. But none willingly join the Army, especially as an enlisted man."

"Shit, man," Jefferson shrieked as he jerked away from Smollett. "What the fuck're you doing?"

"Oh, now," Smollett replied, never raising his voice as he glanced down again at the cut he was cleaning. "That didn't hurt."

"Bullshit! It's my fucking arm! I can feel it."

Looking into the injured man's wild eyes, Smollett stared at him. "Who's the medic?"

"You are," Jefferson snapped.

"Which of us has had two years of medical schooling?"

Though agitated, Jefferson hesitated before he replied this time. "You."

"And who's been taping up the cuts and wiping the runny noses in this platoon for the past six months?" Smollett continued.

Though he was far from mollified, Jefferson's anger was visibly subsiding. "You."

"Well then," Smollett concluded. "That means I'm the better judge of what hurts and what doesn't. *Nichts zu?*"

Though he was nearly beaten into submission by

Smollett's manner and illogical logic, Jefferson didn't give up without a fight. "Smollett," the wounded man stated by way of surrender, "has anyone ever told you that you can be a real asshole?"

Going back to cleaning the cuts on Jefferson's arm, Smollett smiled. "Yeah, you guys. At least every other day."

In the course of watching the medic work and listening to the banter between him and his wounded companion, Nathan was reminded of how much the men he was leading were strangers to him. The only thing that had compelled them to follow his orders and believe in him was the single black bar attached to the camo cover of his helmet and a trust and confidence in the experience that bar represented. Until they had reached the road, Nathan had found little need to flex his authority or exercise his skills as a leader.

Now, however, that could very easily change. A decision of his had cost the platoon one man and chewed up another. Looking away from the medic and Jefferson, Nathan eyed the soldiers who manned the loose perimeter around him. Most were, like him, leaning against trees, more concerned with resting than maintaining their vigilance. A few shot an occasional glance back behind them to see what Smollett was doing and to stare at Nathan. When the young officer's eyes fell on a soldier who had been watching him, he would quickly twist his head about and look outward, as he should have been, in a response that reminded Nathan of a child caught entertaining evil thoughts.

In the middle of this casual inspection of the two squads with him, a shiver caused Nathan to shake. The cold that had been a welcome relief after his exertions was now becoming uncomfortable. The damp uniform and thermal underwear he wore no longer provided the protection they were designed to. The only solution to this was either a change of clothes, which Nathan didn't have, or activity. Without needing to look down at his watch, Nathan knew it was time to move out.

Shifting about so that he could reach his map case, Nathan pulled it out, unfolded it to the section that exposed the section of Slovakia that they were traveling through, and studied it. Both squad leaders, Staff Sergeant Hernandes and Sergeant Dubois, took this as a cue to gather around their leader. The men in each of their squads, in turn, roused themselves from their rest and prepared themselves for the continuation of their trek by either readjusting gear that had shifted during their flight or checking the function of their individual weapons.

Dropping to one knee in front of the staff officer, Hernandes remained silent until Nathan looked up at him. "What's the plan now, sir?"

Nathan didn't answer right away. Neither the tone of the sergeant's voice nor the expression he wore betrayed the man's thoughts. Nathan sighed. "We go for the other spot along the road we had looked at crossing," Nathan finally stated. "After that, we head for the rally point just short of Fort Apache, just as we had planned. I am assuming that Lieutenant Reider will do likewise."

With a nod, Hernandes acknowledged Nathan's pronouncement and accepted his order. Dubois, however, wasn't so quick. "Sir?" he ask in a crisp voice. "Are we going to cross the road as we did before, in two groups, or go across together this time?"

Nathan knew what lay at the heart of this challenge. Dubois, without being disrespectful, was questioning Nathan's wisdom. So it starts, Nathan told himself as he stared at the assistant squad leader.

Surprisingly, it was Hernandes who took the greater offense at his fellow NCO's inquiry. Making no effort to conceal his anger, Hernandes turned on Dubois. "There was nothing wrong with what the lieutenant did back at the road," he barked in his fellow squad leader's face in a voice loud enough for all to hear. "Lieutenant Dixon did exactly what any sane and intelligent combat infan-

tryman would have done. To have done otherwise would
have been dumb. That the Slovaks came along when
they did is nothing more than a matter of bad luck."

Enraged by Hernandes's tone and public admonishment, Dubois glared at the Hispanic NCO. Hernandes,
however, would not be cowed. Leaning closer to Dubois,
Hernandes lowered his voice. "This ain't the Old Guard,
trooper. This is the real Army. Out here we listen to our
officers, do our duties, and hope that God sees fit to see
us through. You pop off one more time like that
and . . ."

"He gets the point, sergeant," Nathan finally announced before the excited NCO could finish. "We've
been here too long. Gather up the men and prepare to
move out."

Though he heard Nathan's commands, Hernandes
did not respond, not right away. Rather, he continued
to stare at Dubois, and Dubois returned the glare. Not
until the more junior of the pair broke, looking down
and turning his head away, did Hernandes make a move
to get up and carry out his orders.

With the two NCOs gone, Nathan pushed himself up
off the ground, straightened out his own equipment,
and made his way over to where Smollett was finishing
up. "Any reason that Jefferson can't keep up?" Nathan
asked as he looked down and watched.

Smollett replied without looking up at Nathan. "He'll
do fine, sir. His injuries will smart some, but none are
anywhere near life threatening, thank God."

Hearing this, Jefferson snapped. "What the hell you
thankin' him for? If you're to be believed, he put us in
this mess."

Unshaken by this assault on his beliefs, Smollett
smiled as he stuffed his unused medical supplies back
into his aid bag. "God will see us through, all of us. After
all, we're his children."

"Says who?" Jefferson sneered as he inspected the
medic's handiwork.

"The Bible, of course. It states clear as day, 'Blessed be the peacekeepers, for they will be called God's children.' Since we're a peacekeeping force, that makes us his." Turning, the bright-faced medic looked up at Nathan. "Isn't that so, sir?"

Before Nathan could answer, Jefferson cut in. "Well, if we're his children, I say the old man needs to be arrested for child abuse. Look what he did to me!"

Nathan shook his head. "On your feet, soldier."

Upset that he wasn't receiving the sympathy he thought he deserved, Jefferson staggered to his feet, with the assistance of Smollett and Pavlovski, and took his place in the line of march. Without another word, Nathan stepped off and took the lead. Behind him the soldiers of the 1st and 3rd Squads followed as they began the next leg of their journey.

20

EAST OF FORT APACHE,
EVENING, FEBRUARY 6

Looking up, Gerald Reider studied the sky for a moment in order to determine if it was actually getting darker or if his mood was simply becoming more somber. Unable to read the prevailing gray skies that hung over them, he thrust out his arm and peeled back the glove that covered his watch. It was well after 1600 hours, but that meant little to him. Belatedly, he realized that he had been in the country for such a short time that he had yet to learn how to judge the time of day by the location of the sun or the cycle of the day. Frustrated, Reider dropped his arm, intertwined it with the other, and pulled them both tightly up against his chest as he leaned his head back against the old stone wall he was sitting behind. It *was* actually getting darker, he told himself. Of course, the premises of this conclusion were based solely on the fact that, in his mind, their prospects or current situation couldn't possibly get any dimmer. Never having been in a troop unit before this, let alone in combat, Gerald Reider didn't know how wrong he could be.

The wall Reider was snuggled up to separated a farm field from the tree line the young officer was facing. It was made up of an odd assortment of irregularly shaped stones that the owners of the field, over the centuries, had run across as they had gone about tending crops and pursuing a livelihood. If those stones could have told their stories, they would have revealed a history that was marked by political unrest and conflicts older than the nation that had fostered Reider and the three soldiers of the 2nd Squad who sat huddled together, a little apart from their officer. Five millennia before the birth of Christ, farmers had gone about their chores in that field, ignoring, as best they could, the political tides that swept over them. Over the centuries, many people had come to this field, often with warlike intentions. The Slavs were the first intruders of any importance, migrating into this land from the east. From the South, Magyars, later called Hungarians, cast their shadows over the countryside. Poles swept in from the north, and then receded back to their own homelands as others vanquished them. And there were the Germans, making their way over the mountains in the west and flowing over the land Gerald Reider and his men had been traversing.

Of course, such matters were of no interest to these wandering American soldiers. Their concerns were more down-to-earth, more immediate. At that particular moment, Reider could imagine that he and the pitifully small force he was supposed to be leading were barely hanging on to the lower rung of Maslow's ladder of needs, the one labeled "food, shelter, and warmth." Like so many other things he had learned in the classroom, Reider had blown the concept of a hierarchy of needs off as soon as the exam covering that portion of the course was over. Like his fellow cadets, Reider had had his eye on other disciplines. The precise application of firepower, the thorough integration of technologies into all branches of the service and their endeavors, and the dissemination of information vertically and horizontally were the proper concerns of the twenty-first-century warrior. Unraveling the secrets of the microprocessor and how they influenced his chosen profession had been the focus of Reider's years at West Point, not understanding the psychological intricacies of the men he would one day lead. That Napoleon's quote, which stated that morale is to numbers, as three is to one, could still be true this day had never occurred to Reider. The distance that lay between him and his soldiers could not be measured in feet or meters. They were strangers to one another. Strangers in a strange land caught in a strange conflict that demanded solutions and measures none of them had answers for.

From where he sat with the two remaining members of his squad, Staff Sergeant Kittridge looked over at his platoon leader. Beside him sat Reisniack, holding his head in his hands, staring down at the ground with a forlorn look on his face. Next to him was Les Kim, who wore an expression that betrayed the bewilderment he felt. The veteran NCO could see that his platoon leader was doing little to hide the dejection that he had slumped into. Not that Kittridge could blame the man. He, himself, had felt the last of his energies drain away when they had reached the rally point and then, cautiously, approached Fort Apache, which lay just beyond the field and over a slight rise. The sight of smoke billowing up from the 2nd of the 13th's base camp and a Slovakian flag fluttering over what had been their home for the past six months was more than enough to convince even the most optimistic of them that Fort Apache could no longer provide refuge or safety.

In the wake of this sad discovery, what had happened to their battalion, while important, was not nearly as crucial to Kittridge and his squad as what would become of them now. None of them had concerned themselves with the "big picture" beyond counting down the days that were left before they redeployed back to Germany. As the little teeth on a great cog, they didn't bother to match the names of towns associated with other battalions in the brigade with real, geographic locations. While company commanders had been made aware of the contingency plans brigade had generated and passed onto the battalions under its control, the world in which their squad leaders existed centered around their assigned Bradley and the men who manned it. Keeping that vehicle combat ready, and their soldiers healthy, fit, and out of trouble in the adverse conditions in which they existed were, for NCOs like Kittridge, a full-time job that demanded their undivided attention. What little they knew outside that microcosm came from casual conversation, well-laced with rumors, shared by the NCOs in the mess tent. Had Reider been with the battalion a week, perhaps as little as a few more days, maybe he would have been apprised of the battalion's contingency plans. Only now, as Kittridge thought of this, did the reason for sending a battalion staff officer along with them begin to make sense. Nathan Dixon had been their insurance policy, a policy that the Fates and circumstances had arbitrarily canceled on them back at the road.

When it became clear that his platoon leader was as befuddled and demoralized as his men, not to mention himself, Kittridge concluded that it was up to him to initiate the next step. Like Reider, he understood that the basics needed to be dealt with before greater, more ambitious efforts could be undertaken.

The effort required to push himself up, off the ground, and onto his feet was quite telling for Kittridge. While their days at Fort Apache had been anything but sedentary, the exertions of the past two days had been over and above anything Kittridge had been forced to endure in a long, long time. It took the staff sergeant a minute or two to overcome the aches and pains that racked his body before he was able to walk. Even when he did, the stiffness of his muscles and joints caused him to stagger a bit.

This served both to warn Gerald Reider and to permit him an opportunity to shrug off his own despondency before Kittridge reached him. "Sir," Kittridge started hesitantly as he looked down at his platoon leader, "I understand why we came here. Like you, I expect that when the others finally do make it over that road they will come here, since this was the rally point. But," he went on, "I need to get the men in, out of the elements, where they can dry out their clothing and find some warmth."

Reider didn't take note of the fact that Kittridge had used the word "I" and not we. That he still considered the members of the squad his and not this young officer's responsibility was natural. Reider was new. He had yet to have an opportunity to weave himself into the fabric of the platoon, to show that he was really a leader worthy of the title. The rank and office Reider held mandated only obedience. Respect and consideration were still commodities that had to be earned.

Muscles are not the only thing that lock up and fail to respond properly when they have been exercised beyond their normal limits. In fact, when the human body is pushed, it is the mind and its ability to reason and solve problems that gives way long before the body does. Looking up, Reider wondered if the NCO towering over him was presenting a problem that he, Reider, had to solve or if the man was merely stating an obvious fact as a preamble to an issue to which he already held the answer. Cautiously, Reider nodded and answered in a manner that would not betray his confusion. "Yes, you are correct, sergeant."

After a long, awkward silence, in which neither man spoke, Kittridge renewed his efforts to initiate action.

"There's a place near here, sir. An abandoned hunting shack that lies about two clicks outside of Fort Apache's perimeter."

Reider's challenge was immediate and to the point. "What are the chances, Sergeant, that the Slovaks aren't there, or will go there?"

There was confidence in the NCO's voice when he replied. "Oh, sir. No one goes there. It's been left unused, at least by the locals, for a long, long time. Probably since before the troubles broke out. And definitely since we've been in Slovakia."

With his curiosity stirred, Reider continued his inquiry. "How can you be sure?

Now Kittridge hesitated. "Well, sir, you see, the troops call the place the Sugar Shack. They use it to, well . . ."

"I'm listening, Sergeant Kittridge."

"Well, sir. The officers don't know about it," Kittridge blurted. "It's someplace private, away from Fort Apache where male and female enlisted personnel can, well, be alone."

Reider stared at his NCO as he continued to question the man. "How sure are you that those other people haven't been there, or will go there?"

Now that the cat was out of the bag, Kittridge told all. "Well, sir, some of the soldiers, none of mine, of course, have outfitted the place with some basic creature comforts."

"Such as?"

Fidgeting, Kittridge looked over at his two men before answering. "Cots, lanterns, some blankets, rations . . ."

"Rations?" Reider blurted.

"Well, sir. Some of the troops manage to slip away right after duty, skip the evening meal, and spend the night there. Someone, and I don't know who, always makes sure there's at least a case of rations, sometimes more. And of course, there's always a pile of those entrées that no one eats piled up in the corner."

Though pleased that he had been thrown a life preserver, Gerald Reider hesitated before blindly reaching out and grabbing it. "And what happens if we're there and Lieutenant Dixon and the rest of the platoon come here?"

Having already addressed that question in his own mind, Kittridge presented his lieutenant with the solution. "We're going to have to split up, sir. While two men go to the shack to warm up and rest, two of us need to stay here. If Angel, I mean Staff Sergeant Hernandes, leads his group to the shack, those folks in the shack will come back here and retrieve the two men on duty. If, instead, they come here, then we can lead them to there. Either way, we're covered."

As inviting as the thought of curling up where it was warm and dry was, Reider hesitated. His tiny platoon was already splintered and scattered. To back up what was left yet again bothered him. It was against everything he had been taught. Still, as he pondered this, his body was shaken by a shiver that ran up his spine and fanned out along every limb. Reider's immediate response, as uncontrollable as the events that had led him to this spot had been, was to squeeze his arms tighter against his chest. After the spasm passed, leaving behind a greater awareness of the cold that had caused it, he knew he had no choice.

Glancing up, Reider looked into Kittridge's tired eyes, then over at his other two men huddled together. "Okay. Leave me one man here who knows the way to the shack in the dark and take whoever's left over to it. Come back in four hours to relieve us."

The expression on Kittridge's face did not change as he gave his platoon leader a nod, which in the field, came as close to a salute as you could get. "Yes, sir." With that, he moved away to spread the word and get things moving.

✕

The gust of cold air hit the two men in the small hunting shack before their exhausted minds could alert them to the sound of boots stomping upon the wooden porch. Even then, only Reider bothered to turn his head toward the door to see who was there. Keith Reisniack's only response was to curl up into a tighter ball.

Once in the doorway, Nathan Dixon stepped to the side in order to allow the men behind him to enter as his eyes adjusted to the light. While it was true that the small fire, now mostly glowing embers, wasn't throwing off much in the way of illumination, to a man who had been stumbling about in forests and across snow-covered fields in a darkness that was blacker than black, the dying fire was blinding.

One of the last men to enter the room, just in front of Kittridge, was Staff Sergeant Hernandes. Even before his eyes became accustomed to the light, he was giving orders. "Make sure your weapon is on safe. Then find yourself a spot. I want you people to strip off your parkas, boots, and socks. No one eats or goes to sleep until the medic, Sergeant Dubois, or I check your feet." There were no complaints, not even a murmur. His men knew the drill, and despite their overwhelming desire simply to flop down on the floor and rest, they understood the need.

Having done his part by leading them first to the linkup point, and then to the hunting lodge, Nathan relinquished his authority for the moment, and basked in the glory of this small, but important, success. Both parts of the platoon were together again. This, and the fact that they had covered the ground that he had established as their goal for the day was, even to him, surprising. And on top of that, they had managed, despite the fact that Fort Apache was no longer theirs, to find a safe haven that offered both food and shelter. To men who had been fighting the elements for two days, as well as their fears and an uncertain future, such small victories were important. The rest would permit them to recharge their emotional and physical batteries, while the achievement of something, even if it was simple survival, would serve to encourage them to continue on.

After his eyes had become accustomed to the dim light the small fire cast over the room, Nathan looked around. He found himself thankful that he had never taken Chris Donovan here. Though sorely tempted, on a number of occasions, Nathan had shelved his urges and had, instead, held to his plan to whisk the bright young Chemical Corps officer to Paris or Berchtesgarden. So entrenched had this fantasy weekend with the red-haired second lieutenant become that he had turned down an opportunity to go to Prague with her for a two-day planning session at NATO's forward headquarters. There would have been far too many eyes following them for the two to enjoy themselves.

This place was, Nathan concluded, little better than a roof over their heads. Even with a clogged nose, the battalion staff officer could tell that the place reeked. Off in one corner was a sizable accumulation of MRE pouches that had not been disposed of by soldiers from the battalion who frequented the Sugar Shack. Laced with the smells of mold and mildew common to wooden structures built by men to be used by men when enjoying manly pursuits was the pungent odor of urine. No doubt it was emanating from one of the corners where people uninterested in braving the elements had relieved themselves. No, Nathan told himself, this would never have done.

The image of Chris Donovan's pale blue eyes, peering into his, suddenly evaporated as the sound of someone's voice, calling out his name, penetrated Nathan's warm daydream.

"Lieutenant Dixon," Staff Sergeant Kittridge repeated. "There are some rations over here, if you'd like."

Blinking, Nathan cleared his thoughts and refocused them on the here and now. "Yeah, sure, thank you." Then, catching himself just before he took his first step, the young officer hesitated. "Have the men had theirs yet?"

Confused by the question, Kittridge shook his head. "No, sir, they haven't. We, uh, just got here, sir. They're still in the process of dropping their loads, shedding some of their outer layers, and waiting to have their feet checked."

Looking around, Nathan tried to hide the embarrassment he felt at being caught in the middle of an erotic fantasy. Though he knew that Kittridge had no idea what he had been thinking, the incident reminded Nathan to keep his attention focused on the matter at hand. "Well, in that case, sergeant, I'll wait until the troops have finished and have theirs. Besides," he added, "I need to check my own feet. It's been awhile since these puppies have been worked this hard."

In an age of stealth technologies, computer-driven fire controls, ballistic missiles, and surveillance from space, when even riflemen go into battle carrying weapons that are capable of firing precision-guided munitions, the need to check a soldier's feet seems almost silly. It could even be argued that the custom of foot inspections by officers and NCOs in the age of modern, professional armies is degrading. But while weapons, as well as the motivation that compels a man to become an infantryman have changed, human nature hasn't. Soldiers, even in the twenty-first century, are still very human. Along with their weapons and high-tech gear, they carry the same frailties and habits that have bedeviled soldiers and armies throughout the ages. In fact, it could be argued that American soldiers in the twenty-first century are more susceptible to blisters, frostbite, and other such ailments than were their Revolutionary War or Civil War counterparts. Those men, whether they were following Washington to Valley Forge, or marching through Georgia, were walkers. They came from a society of walkers. They walked everywhere, often barefoot. Both body and foot sole were conditioned to do so, whether in the service of their nation or simply going about their daily lives.

Modern American infantrymen, on the other hand, do not have a background that prepares and conditions them for the rigors of dismounted combat. This is especially true for those assigned to mechanized infantry units, where they are trained to fight mounted or, if necessary, leave the safety of their Bradley only when it is necessary to secure an objective after being carried to it. So when long marches are called for, it is not at all unusual for a fair number of soldiers to develop problems with their feet.

When their efforts and the weather of the past two days were taken into account, it became critical that the NCOs of the 3rd Platoon ensure that the men entrusted to their care took care of their feet. In cold weather, blisters are but one problem infantrymen have to deal with. Like the rest of the body, feet sweat. If they are not dried properly, and on a regular basis, a man can quickly fall prey to immersion foot, renamed trench foot in World War I. It is a condition that causes skin that has been wet for a protracted period of time simply to peel away. Modern combat gear, which keeps water out and wicks moisture away from the skin, helps, but cannot totally solve the problem. Dry socks remain the best solution. The other cold-weather problem of concern is frostbite. Frostbite can put a soldier out of action just as effectively as a bullet.

While the 3rd Platoon was far from being the best in the battalion, the NCOs knew what was important. Even without having to be told by Nathan Dixon, they knew that their ordeal, far from being over, was probably just beginning. With Fort Apache gone, and no contact with battalion or brigade, survival, individually and collectively, would depend on how long they could last. So before the men were allowed to become comfortable, before anyone ate, and before any thoughts were given to sleep, Hernandes, Dubois, and Kittridge made sure that the primary weapons system of their men, the M-1A1 standard issue foot, was cared for and in working order.

While this was going on, Nathan made his way to where Gerald Reider lay. Awakened from a sound sleep, the young platoon leader's blurry eyes and confused expression told Nathan that any effort at holding an intelligent conversation with him would be an exercise in futility. So he didn't even try. "I pulled in the people who had been at the linkup point, and have directed Sergeant Kittridge to post a two-man watch," Nathan informed Reider, who sat swaying to and fro before the battalion staff officer. "We'll talk in the morning. For now, get some rest."

Unable to raise any objections, Reider respond with a faint "Okay," before toppling over asleep.

From across the room, where he was struggling to pull his boots off, Evens Tobias murmured. "Man, I see the LT has the right idea. Sleep, that's what I'm talking about."

Sitting off to one side, where he was looking at his own sore feet, Angel Hernandes looked up at Tobias. "All in good time, soldier. All in good time. Remember the Old Man's motto."

Three soldiers groaned in unison. "I know, I know," Tobias muttered. "First the horse, then the saddle, then the man."

Tobias, egged on by this response, continued. "Well, I say fuck the horse, sarge. It's up and left us high and dry."

Hernandes wasn't fazed by Tobias's response. "Today, and until further notice, your feet are your horses."

Lifting his foot with one hand, Tobias pointed to his heel with the index finger of his other. "Hey, if that's true, does that make this part of my foot the horse's ass?"

Though he shook his head while the other members of the platoon chuckled, Hernandes was pleased to see that Tobias, the class clown, was still able to joke about their plight. So was Nathan. The men still had spirit. They could still find humor in a situation that would have reduced many of their countrymen to tears long ago. Even before discussing their situation with Reider, Nathan knew what had to be done. Their efforts to date, while demanding, would pale in comparison to what he would ask of them in the morning.

21

It was as if someone had flipped a switch. One moment Nathan was sound asleep, the next, he was wide awake. What had stirred him from his slumber remained, for a second, a mystery. Then it all hit him at once. The pounding of feet on the floor he was laying on, the babble of voices, the rattle of weapons being grabbed from where they had been left, and, somewhere off in the distance, the sound of muffled explosions. Looking around the dark, crowded room, Nathan could see a flurry of activity as the soldiers pulled on cold-weather parkas, slipped into flak vests, and rummaged about in search of their gear.

Even before he could ask the most obvious question, one of the two soldiers who had been posted outside threw open the door. He didn't enter. Rather, he stood there in the doorway, silhouetted against the dark sky. "They're attacking Fort Apache."

From among the soldiers who had been shaken out of their sleep by this attack, a voice called out. "Who's attacking?"

Before the man at the door could reply, another voice sneered, "The fucking Zulu, you fucking moron."

"All right people," Staff Sergeant Kittridge announced in a deep, commanding voice. "Let's settle down and saddle up." Then he looked around until he spotted Nathan still on the floor fumbling with his parka, looking for the appropriate hole into which to shove his arm. "How do you want the platoon deployed, lieutenant?"

From behind, Nathan heard Reider's voice. "In a three-sixty perimeter around the building."

Having expected a response from Nathan, Kittridge stopped what he was doing, and looked over to where the other voice had come from. Confused, he muttered an "Uh . . ." followed by a "Well, yes," ending it all by tacking on a belated "sir."

For the first time since being awakened, Nathan paused a moment and thought. Outside, the only noise he could hear was a new spattering of small, closely timed explosions. Cluster bombs, Nathan thought. Since Fort Apache was built to protect its occupants from a direct ground attack, the Air Force was working Fort Apache over with bombs that released hundreds of small bomblets, or submunitions, the size of softballs. Whether they were intended to kill the current occupants or destroy property and equipment left behind didn't matter. Whatever was going on was happening out there, far from where he, and the 3rd Platoon, were sitting.

Fully recovered from his initial panic, Nathan relaxed. "You, trooper! In the doorway!" he bellowed above the sounds and excited voices in the room. "Did you or your buddy see or hear anyone approaching your position?"

The soldier in the open doorway shook his head as

the room went silent and listened for the response. "No, sir. No one. There was just the sudden sound of aircraft overhead and then the attack began and . . ."

"So we're not under attack?" Nathan asked quickly.

"No, sir. Not that I am aware of."

Easing up, Nathan waited for the rest of the platoon to absorb this revelation. "Okay, soldier," Nathan continued. "Go back out to your post, and keep your eyes and ears open. I'll be out there in a minute." As the man backed out of the lodge and shut the door, Nathan turned to Kittridge. "Sergeant, send two men, when they're ready, out to set up a second OP further down the trail leading to this lodge. Let the rest of the men take their time getting their shit together. Pass out the rations and water that's scattered around this rat trap, and get the platoon ready." Looking down at his watch, Nathan calculated how much time there was before dawn. "We move out in forty-five minutes. While you're doing that, I'm going to go up to the hill behind us and see what I can see." Then, as an afterthought, he added, "Relieve the people out at the first OP as soon as possible so they can get something to eat before we go. When we leave, we're going to be moving fast."

The last part of his orders brought a smattering of grumbles. Kittridge cut this short. "Okay, people, you heard the man. Pull up your socks and jocks and get ready to roll."

From the corner where he had been sleeping, Evans Tobias grunted. "Sarge. In case you haven't noticed, we've got nothing to roll in. We be ridin' our leather personnel carriers these days."

"Another crack out of you, trooper," Kittridge snapped, "and I'll personally roll your sorry ass down this hill and all the way back to Germany."

Tobias stopped what he had been doing and made a show of bowing in Kittridge's direction. "Yes sir, boss. I's movin', boss. I's movin'."

*   *   *

Outside the shack, Nathan paused on the wooden porch
and stared into the darkness. After having been confined in a small enclosed space with men who hadn't
washed or shaved in days, warmed by a wood fire that
threw more smoke into the room than up the chimney,
the clear, sharp morning air felt refreshing. Whatever
cobwebs still cluttered his mind were swept away as he
drew in a deep breath. When he exhaled, a thick cloud
of moisture, like the smoke from a fine cigar, gathered
before him. Standing there, Nathan reveled in this moment of wondrous silence until the door opened and
two men, sent by Kittridge to establish the new OP,
emerged. Rather than have them go around him, Nathan stepped down onto the ground and began to make
his way to the rear of the lodge.

The lodge was located on a hillside deep in the woods.
It sat on a shelf created by an ancient rock slide that
had swept down the precipitous incline behind the
lodge. This made access to the place all but impossible
except along the trail that only hunters and young lovers
had seen a need to use. Nathan was just starting to pick
his way up the face of the hill when he heard the sound
of someone coming up behind him. "Will you tell me,
Lieutenant Dixon, what the hell that was all about back
there in the cabin?"

Turning, Nathan looked down at Gerald Reider's
dark form below him, standing there with his feet spread
apart and his hands on his hips. Both the agitated tone
of Reider's voice, and the manner in which he had
enunciated *Lieutenant Dixon,* annoyed Nathan. His first
inclination was to blow the man off and get on with what
he was doing. Time was a valuable commodity that he
didn't much care to waste any of at that particular moment. Still, the young platoon leader was challenging
him, in a most direct manner.

Without bothering to retrace his steps, Nathan talked

down to Reider. "I'll make this short and sweet, lieutenant. I am the senior officer here. I always have been. When we were on patrol, before the shit hit the proverbial fan, I said nothing. There was no need to. I was sent along to observe and to be there just in case something happened. Well, in case you haven't been keeping track of current events, something did happen. My special instructions, as well as Army regulations and custom, mandate that I take charge. And until a competent authority, with more rank and horsepower than you, changes that, I am in command here. Is that clear?"

Unbowed, and still smarting from the manner in which Nathan had overridden him back in the lodge, Reider continued. "I don't see it that way. This is my platoon, mister. I have no intention of stepping aside and letting you run it. I've worked too damned hard to get here."

At that moment Nathan felt the urge to reach out and touch his fellow officer as he had never touched another officer before. Only the fact that it took time to descend the hillside, time that allowed a modicum of self-restraint to intervene, prevented Nathan from violating the Uniform Code of Military Justice. That didn't mean that his rage was totally dissipated when he finally came face-to-face with Reider. "You are this close, mister," Nathan hissed as he held the index finger and thumb of his right hand an inch apart in front of Reider's face, "from setting the record for the shortest military career in history. One more word from you, lieutenant, just one more fucking word," Nathan shouted, spewing tiny droplets of spittle in Reider's face, "and I'll bring court-martial charges against you the second we make it back to battalion."

Though the anger that had propelled him to this point was far from being squelched by Nathan's response, a cautionary voice from the back Gerald Reider's mind broke through his rage and frustration. It warned Reider that the man standing before him was not an upperclassman out to flex his ego or score brownie points. Nathan was a combat arms officer, in a combat situation. And as much as it galled Reider, Dixon, and not he, was the more senior of the two. Reider knew Dixon was right. Just as he knew that the enraged man before him would not hesitate to bring his career to a screeching end if he persisted.

It wasn't the threat of being court-martialed that finally tipped the scales and forced Reider to swallow his pride and step back, lowering his head as he did so in an unconscious show of submission. It was the sudden image of having to face his father, a man who had all but disowned him when he picked West Point over Harvard. Liberal New York lawyers, after all, don't raise their sons to be cannon fodder.

Nathan knew nothing of these and the other thoughts that raced through Reider's mind. And while time and the need to get moving were pressing, Nathan was just as human as Reider was. The battalion staff officer, too, was susceptible to feelings that were, given the circumstances, inappropriate. It had been a long time since he had had an opportunity to exert his authority over a subordinate in this manner. As a third-echelon staff flunky, Nathan seldom commanded more than the chair he sat in, and then it was only his until someone with more rank, or a greater need, came along. Like the first breath of cold air he had inhaled that morning, the dressing down he had just administered, as well as the capitulation that followed, were exhilarating to him. Had it not been critical for him to maintain his mask of command so as to capitalize on the effects of his tirade, he would have been gloating.

"I hope we're clear now on the chain of command, Lieutenant Reider," Nathan finally announced. "It's not essential that we get along. As far as I'm concerned, you can curse me and my family name till the day I die. All that matters is that you, and everyone else in this platoon, know who's in charge. Understood?"

Reider hesitated, bit his lower lip, and struggled to control a resurgence of his anger.

"Understood?" Nathan growled as he leaned forward into Reider's face until the brim of his helmet tapped Reider's.

"Understood," the second lieutenant finally murmured as his head jerked back in response to Nathan's assault on his space.

"Good!" Nathan announced. "I'm going up there to see if there's anything to be seen. In the meantime, go back and supervise the redistribution of rations, water, and ammo. I want the platoon to be ready to move out as soon as I come back."

Taking a step back, Gerald Reider gave Nathan the safest response any subordinate can after having been mauled as he had. The young platoon leader snapped to attention, raised his hand in a salute, and gave a crisp "Yes, sir."

Although the young officer's voice still betrayed his animosity, Nathan was satisfied with the simple acceptance of his authority. Love and admiration of one's leaders, Nathan knew, seldom won battles. Discipline and adherence to orders did.

From their OP on the far side of the clearing, at the head of the trail, Santiago sat, with his back against the tree, watching the two officers go at each other. "You'd think the platoon leader would have more common sense then to tangle with an hombre like Dixon."

Everett Cash, who was lying on the ground on the other side of the trail, facing the opposite direction, sighed. "You've been in the Army long enough," Cash responded without taking his eyes off the trail, "to know that the term 'common sense' can't be used in the same sentence as 'second lieutenant.' "

"I know. But you'd think they'd learn somethin' of value at West Point," Santiago insisted. "What do they do to 'em there? Beat them every day with an idiot stick?"

Cash chuckled. "They teach all those fine young boys and girls to be officers. It's up to the NCOs, like Taylor and Kitt, to teach a platoon leader the sort of stuff they need to know to survive."

Santiago shook his head. "Man, I didn't join this fucking Army to be a training aid."

"Why did you join?" Cash asked, anxious to get off a topic that concerned him just as much as it bothered Santiago.

"To get out of the barrio, man," Santiago replied without hesitation. "A tough hombre like me just don't hang up his colors one day and say, 'Man, I'm gettin' a job, or I'm goin' to school' and keep his respect."

"So you joined the Army just to get away from your gang?"

This time, when he answered, Santiago did little to hide the sorrowful tone in his voice. "One day I woke up to the fact that the only people who had left the gang had been planted in the ground or were doin' hard time. And the worst of it was, I couldn't remember half their names. The fuckers I had hung with, who were supposed to be my brothers, meant nothing to me the second they were gone."

Cash let out a loud guffaw. "You mean to tell me you left the streets to get away from death and mayhem by joining an organization that specializes in death and mayhem?"

"Hey, how the hell was I supposed to know I was goin' to wind up the middle of someone else's fuckin' war?" Santiago protested.

From the porch of the lodge, a low, ominous voice interrupted the lively chatter between Santiago and Cash. "The L in LP/OP stands for listening, trooper. That means you listen for the enemy, not the other way around." In silence Santiago watched as Sergeant Dubois, his squad leader, approached. "You call that a fighting position, soldier?" Dubois demanded when he reached Santiago and looked down at him.

Unintimidated by the buck sergeant towering over him, Santiago stared back with an innocent expression. "I'm listenin', honest. Ev, over there, is lookin' that way, and I'm coverin' the rear."

"Yeah," Dubois replied. "And I'm the tooth fairy."

Santiago smiled. "Hey, sarge, if you say so. But remember, I didn't ask, and you didn't have to tell."

Unlike Kittridge and Angel Hernandes, Bobby Dubois was not liked by the men in his squad. As the assistant squad leader, he often found himself in charge of all the nasty little duties and details the squad was stuck with. And since this assignment was, for him, little more than a stepping-stone to staff sergeant and reassignment back to the Old Guard, Dubois carried out his orders efficiently and without protest. While all soldiers know that they must, in the end, obey orders and do all sorts of unpleasant things, the lower-ranking enlisted in the United States Army expect their sergeants to stand up for them on occasion, when they feel that a particular duty is unreasonable or if they have been tasked out of sequence.

Dubois, however, refused to do this. He took every assignment without question and drove his men to complete them as quickly and as efficiently as they could. This habit of blind and unquestioning obedience resulted in Dubois and the soldiers of the 1st Squad drawing more than their fair share of additional duties. For this, the straight-arrow NCO was resented and despised.

Though angered by Santiago's remark, Dubois said nothing. Instead, he dumped the four MREs, sealed in thick brown plastic bags, at Santiago's feet. "Take two and give Cash two. They're going to have to last us two days."

The smirk on Santiago's face disappeared. "Two days? Where in the hell is that officer goin' to take us? Back to Germany, on foot?"

"If we have to, yes," Dubois replied in a low, serious tone. "It's either that or walk into the nearest town and surrender to the people we shot up yesterday." Then he added, with a hint of glee in his voice. "Can you spell 'hostage'?"

Having been on too many patrols that had come across the handiwork of the Slovakian Army in the past few months, Santiago knew that the Geneva Convention meant nothing to a people involved in a racially motivated war. When he was sure that Santiago had been silenced, Dubois turned around and headed back for the lodge.

When Cash heard his assistant squad leader's feet hit the wooden steps of the lodge, the young African-American soldier looked over his shoulder at him. "Fuckin' Oreo cookie. It's brothers like him that give us a bad name."

Santiago, still dwelling on what Dubois had said, ignored Cash's comments. "Do you think he's serious? I mean about marching all the way back to Germany?"

Shifting his body in the snow, Cash looked over to Santiago. "Hey, how the hell am I supposed to know? I'm a grunt. Nobody tells me nothing unless they want me to do something. And I don't bother no one unless I want something. All I want right now," Cash continued as he settled down and resumed his watch over the trail, "is to get up off this cold-ass ground and get moving."

Concerned with what lay ahead, Santiago didn't bother to reply. Instead he sat there, staring off into the predawn darkness, wondering how long they could keep going. Like everyone else in the small platoon under Nathan's command, Santiago was beginning to feel the effects of two days of marching through deep snow, two nights of sleep on hard, wooden floors without benefit of blankets or bedroll, and insufficient rations to sustain them. As terrifying as their encounters with the Slovaks had been, in Santiago's mind, they paled in comparison to the idea that their trek through this land, ravaged by civil war, was just beginning.

Even in the twenty-first century, fear of the unknown can be deadlier than the enemy.

22

They had been on the move for better than an hour before the eastern sky began to glow with the soft, faint light of a new dawn. Though still very much in evidence, the low-hanging clouds that had shrouded western Slovakia were breaking up. Had anyone bothered to take notice, they would have seen the signs that the weather was improving. The members of the 3rd Platoon, however, didn't. Instead of celebrating the promise of decent weather, they riveted their attention to more earthbound concerns.

After the previous day's run-in, the loss of two of their own, and a wake-up call courtesy of the U.S. Air Force, every man in the platoon was keyed up and on edge. This pervasive tension ran through the file of haggard men like a taut, steel cable. It was accentuated by the total absence of any living thing, human or animal, in the countryside they traversed. Only the sound of a flight of combat aircraft, knifing its way through the high, puffy clouds above, or the rumble of detonations, far off in the distance, interrupted the steady, monotonous crunch of combat boots plowing through virgin snow.

In the past the soldiers of the 2nd of the 13th had enjoyed patrols that resulted in little or no contact with the Slovakians. Run-ins with the civilian population, even when they had had not resulted in any sort of exchange, had always been fraught with apprehension. This was especially true for a generation raised on Vietnam War movies. To them, there was no such thing as a Slovakian who could be trusted. Every one of them, save Gerald Reider, had come across far too many scenes not unlike the one they had found at the farmhouse during the first day of the patrol. They had watched as members of the teams assigned to investigate these atrocities were given blank stares and mumbled excuses by neighboring farmers about how they had seen or heard nothing. To young Americans, who came from a country where racial lines were neatly drawn, it was baffling to understand how people who had the same skin color, names that sounded alike, and even prayed to the same God, could hate each other with such unbridled passion.

The truth of the matter was that few occupants of this region had remained on their farms or in the smaller, more isolated villages. On the one hand, there had been the Slovakian Army and its associated militia units. Even with the NATO peacekeepers in place, the Slovakians had persisted in pursuing a policy of unrestricted and thorough ethnic cleansing. These operations increased in both regularity and severity the farther away one got from a NATO base. While not as overt as it had been before the NATO troops intervened, the results were, nonetheless, just as telling. In direct and open opposition to this effort stood the Hungarian-Slovak militias.

Though sadly outnumbered and poorly equipped, they had sprung up in response to the Slovakian aggression. Yet rather than attempt to protect their own by throwing themselves against their better-armed foes, they opted to wage a cruel, covert war of retribution against the Slovakian population in the face of superior government forces and NATO troops. As in all civil wars, so long as there were targets to prey on and combatants willing to go after them, the spiral of escalating violence spun on and on.

Not everyone fled. In the face of these growing horrors, there had always been those who refused to abandon their homes and flee to either the Czech Republic, which didn't want them, or Hungry, where they were confined in wretched refugee camps along the southern bank of the fabled blue Danube. To some of the officers in 2nd of the 13th, these stalwart individuals were fools, people who didn't have the common sense to get out of the way of a runaway tractor trailer. Others saw them as stubborn patriots, men and women who refused to give in to tyranny and oppression. A few, such as Nathan, saw them for what they were, victims of a political struggle that they did not understand and who had no good alternatives but to hold on to the only life and home they had ever known.

The greatest concentrations of these diehards, as they were called, were in the areas between the brigade headquarters and its subordinate battalion base camp. During the six months the NATO forces had been in Slovakia, this zone had become a sort of haven for them. Frequent trips between the American camps by columns of supply and service units, as well as liaison trips by officers such as Nathan back and forth to brigade, had necessitated round-the-clock patrols of the roads and villages. Even those militia leaders who had become renegades by refusing to bow to either their own government's controls or NATO restraints shied away from operating within this zone. Farmers and villagers, though keenly aware that they lived under a persistent shadow even with NATO forces so close at hand, had managed to go about their lives.

In plotting the route he would follow, Nathan had taken this into account. Frequent trips to Brigade for meetings or to carry or pick up documents had permitted him to become familiar with the terrain, the routes, and even the rhythms of the populace. As is common when a people are forced to live in close proximity to an occupying army, some of their local merchants and the more industrious individuals managed to capitalize on the presence of soldiers who never seemed to lack for cash or the desire to part with it. Like all staff officers who traveled throughout the zone, Nathan knew the locations of the best bakeries, what time various kiosks were open, and which of the butcher shops were owned by people who liked Americans, spoke English, and didn't charge inflated prices.

So as the morning wore on, and Nathan took note that even this last vestige of an indigenous population seemed finally to have been cowed by the turn of events of the past two days, his anxiety began to mount. He had hoped that the security zone that had radiated out from Fort Apache to the east and southeast had been reestablished in the area between where Brigade was and the base camp of 2nd of the 13th that now stood abandoned. That this was not the case quickly became obvious as dawn revealed pillars of smoke dotting the horizon from farms and villages that had, until then, been spared. At first Nathan had hoped these harbingers of destruction and desolation were emanating from Slovakian military targets that had been taken out by the Air Force or attack helicopters attached to the Brigade. This faint hope, however, grew fainter with each freshly ransacked and torched house they passed. By the time Nathan called for a long halt just before noon, he had given up all hope of stumbling into the open arms of an American outpost short of the Brigade base camp.

*   *   *

While Nathan found himself a spot off a bit from the rest of the platoon and settled down to study his map, the soldiers of the 3rd Platoon threw themselves onto the ground. Nathan had driven them hard that morning, stopping only twice in six hours. Even then, each of the pauses was less than ten minutes in duration. The cumulative effects of two and a half days of hard marching, little sleep snatched on stiff furniture or hard wooden floors, scant rations, and the stress associated with their plight were beginning to take their toll. Even the squad leaders let themselves go, slumping down without thinking of security or checking the condition of their men. Having fared little better over the course of the past few days, Nathan, too, felt himself slipping. His fatigued mind, unable to grasp more than one or two thoughts at any given time, did not take note of the haphazard manner in which the men of the 3rd Platoon were scattered, or that no one was doing anything except tending to whatever personal need was most pressing.

For some of the men this was sleep. Smith and Tobias shut their eyes and drifted off as soon as they hit the ground. Others shifted equipment and gear that had been biting into their shoulders during the march. A few, who had not had an opportunity to eat anything that morning before they formed up and moved out, pulled one of their two rations from whatever pocket they had jammed it into and began to rip into the thick, brown plastic pouch. Those who had none watched with longing eyes as their companions prepared to feast upon that culinary delight known as Meals, Ready to Eat.

Neither veterans of World War II nor grunts who had done time in Vietnam could, in their wildest dreams, have imagined that the Army could come up with field rations that were less palatable, and more despicable, than those that they had been issued. How a society that had gone to the moon and had given mankind duct tape could conceive of something like the MRE is baffling. Yet the United States Army had managed to trump its past gastronomic achievements by developing a ration that was almost as inedible as the plastic pouch it came in. Chock-full of all sorts of dehydrated goodies that required copious amounts of fresh water that soldiers were always short of, the MREs were the most despised item the Army issued, aside from the flak vest. Were it not for the prospect of starvation, and the habit of eating a meal three times a day, few soldiers would willingly submit themselves to these provisions of modern cooking.

With the same care that a member of a bomb squad goes about his duties, the men with MREs methodically pulled each item from the MRE pouch, inspecting and sorting it before going on. Like a cluster bomb, an MRE contains many lethal submunitions, each wrapped in a foil package colored in a shade selected to extinguish even the most ravenous appetite. As the soldier picked his way through the pouch as gingerly as he would a minefield, he found himself forced to make snap decisions as to the disposition of each item. Some he laid on the ground next to him or in his lap, to be consumed before he moved from the spot he was currently occupying. Other MRE components were stuffed into a pocket, to be saved until later when he needed a boost in energy or he had mustered the courage necessary to put that particular food product in his mouth. A few, due to their reputation, were immediately thrown over the shoulder without a second thought if it was deemed to be a threat to physical well-being if consumed. This sorting stopped when a soldier stumbled across those parts of the meal he wanted to eat immediately.

Since the MREs had been passed out randomly, not everyone got his favorite meal or, more correctly, a meal that he could consume without fear of rejection. Even in their advanced state of exhaustion, a lively round of trading between those who were rummaging through their MREs broke out. Sometimes these trades were a direct exchange, one entrée for another. Other deals needed to be sweetened, by including a pouch of dehydrated fruit in addition to the main course. Some items, such as peanut butter and crackers, were never offered up. To have done so would have cast serious doubts on one's sanity. Of course, if any of the men in the 3rd Platoon had looked at their decisions to join the Army voluntarily, and allow themselves to be subjected to a life such as this, the sanity question would never have been raised.

From where he sat at the tail end of the diminished 2nd Squad, Gerald Reider spent the first few minutes of his break doing nothing but enjoying the fact that he was off his feet. With his legs stretched out before him and his back against a skinny tree, Reider let his head fall backward until his helmet thumped up against the tree. Closing his eyes, he concentrated on nothing else but drawing in deep, unlabored breaths of air that filled his lungs. Toward the end of this leg of their march, he had found himself panting, almost gasping for breath. By ordinary measures they had not been moving that fast. But heavily laden men, especially men who are already tired, climbing and descending rolling, snow-covered hills, do far more work than scantily clad runners jogging on a level track at twice the rate. Everything, Reider thought as he sat there, feeling the muscles in his legs as they twitched and spasmed, was running on reserve. What had started as a simple operation had turned into a marathon that had no discernible end, no limit. There was only more marching ahead, more miles to cover. There was nothing ahead to be gained. Behind them, nothing of value had been accomplished. The only object in this exercise seemed to be to keep going, keep moving, keep running.

He was tired, Reider told himself. Mentally and physically wrung out. Without moving his head, or opening his eyes, Reider pulled his gloves off, deposited them in his lap, one at a time, and lifted his dirty hands up to his face. As he rubbed his eyes and face with the tips of his fingers, he could feel the sweat on his brow, the stubble on his cheeks, and accumulation of three days of grime on his skin. With everything else going on, and his mind pinging about like a pinball that never dropped out of play, Gerald Reider realized that he hadn't washed his face since they had left Fort Apache on the first day.

Moving his hands away from his face, he tilted his head forward, opened his eyes, and looked at them. Learning to ignore one's own filfth was a hard lesson that Reider had had to master during his plebe field training. In all his years, he could not recollect ever seeing his father with dirty hands. Even when playing sports in the private schools he attended before going to the Military Academy, what little mud he picked up was wiped away without much effort. The hands he looked at, however, would need far more than a quick splash of soap and a second or two under running water. The grime was so ground into the skin that it looked as if it had been injected between the individual cells and left to set for years. These hands, Reider decided, would never come clean again.

After dropping them down onto his lap, the young officer looked around for the first time since they had reached this place. By now the men had settled into whatever activity that had been chosen to occupy their time. The sleepers had quickly slipped away and were enjoying their impromptu nap as only a soldier can. Those who were eating sat stuffing food into their mouths, anxious to finish their meal before someone decided to give the order to mount up and move out. Men who couldn't sleep, or had nothing to eat, just sat where they had fallen out of the formation, staring blankly at their own feet or up at the treetops. No one, Reider noted, was talking. There were no sounds, other than the crinkle of aluminum food wrappers and the sound of a man snoring.

There was nothing more to say. No one had any new information to exchange or jokes to share that hadn't been heard a hundred times before. They were all in the same relative condition, and had endured, up to now, the same experiences. Besides, to talk about what they were doing, how they felt, and what their immediate prospects were would serve no good purpose. If anything, to do so would only accelerate the decline of their already diminishing morale. Among the sixteen men lining the trail that meandered through a forest, only one man had anything of value to say. Just one individual's words, thoughts, and opinions mattered to them all, Nathan Dixon's, the senior officer present.

Turning his attention toward that officer, Reider watched him as he scrutinized the map that covered his lap like a throw. In a straight-legged infantry unit, you can march all day, and well into the night, without ever coming across terrain that is not covered by a single map sheet. Mechanized units, however, have the ability to range far and wide. In some operations a single mech platoon can find itself responsible for defending a position that would require the best part of a parachute infantry company, or moving over more ground in an hour than their footborne comrades could cover in a day. The requirement to traverse great distance is accentuated when a single battalion is given the mission to conduct security operations in a zone that would require three times the manpower, if it were to be done properly. Never knowing when they would be required to go anywhere within their zone, or over into an adjacent battalion's area to conduct liaison, staff officers such as Nathan Dixon carried dozens of map sheets, taped together and neatly stuffed into oversize map cases. As Reider watched Nathan, head bowed and finger moving along the surface of his map, the wisdom and outright necessity of doing this became crystal clear.

With nothing but his GPS and a map that covered a mission that had come to an unexpected end two days ago, the young platoon leader swore that he would never be caught short like this again.

Reider was mulling this over in his mind when a buzzing, off in the distance, intruded on his thoughts. At first he paid no attention to it. He thought it was nothing but his imagination. Only when Nathan Dixon lifted his head and cocked an ear skyward, in the direction of the buzzing, did Reider take it seriously.

Perking up, he listened with greater interest. Immediately he dismissed the idea that it was a helicopter. Choppers, no matter what kind they are or who they belong to, always sound as if they are beating the air with their rotors. It wasn't a jet aircraft either. They make either a whining or whooshing noise. It was a prop-driven aircraft of some sort. Yet, as the sound grew louder and more distinct, it didn't seem to have enough oomph to it. Even small prop engines tend to drone. This engine, even as it grew nearer, continued to buzz, like a remote-controlled model aircraft.

Like a thunderclap, Gerald Reider realized that the noise he was listening to was exactly that, or at least the military version of those toys. Having come to this conclusion a second or two before Reider, Nathan Dixon was already on his feet, making for where Reider sat. "Your smoke grenade, Reider," the battalion staff officer shouted as he dashed toward him. "Toss me your smoke grenade."

Not only had the platoon leader forgotten, over the course of the past few days, that he was carrying a red smoke grenade, he had even forgotten where it was attached. Animated, Reider sat bolt upright, looked down at his chest, and brought both hands up to assist in finding the grenade.

Though he had managed to locate it by the time Nathan reached him, he hadn't had the time to slip off the thick, blank rubber band that secured it and kept it from flopping around. Nathan, animated and glancing back and forth between the sky and Reider, didn't wait for Reider to undo the grenade. With more force than was needed, Nathan placed a hand on Reider's chest, to steady him, and grabbed the grenade with the other. With one quick motion, almost without stopping, Nathan jerked the smoke grenade up and free of both the strap it hung from and the restraining band. With the grenade in hand, Nathan continued to make his way to the edge of the tree line.

There he was joined by Kittridge, who had also jumped to his feet when he had heard Nathan's call for a smoke grenade. Like Nathan, Kittridge knew Reider had the grenade. All patrols carried at least one for use in emergencies. Even with all sorts of high-tech communications gear and navigation aids, there's nothing like colored smoke when it comes to marking a landing zone and giving an inbound pilot an idea of wind direction and speed. When he saw Nathan grab the grenade, Kittridge had followed the staff officer.

For a moment both men searched the sky, hoping to catch a glimpse of the RPV. Though the weather had improved, the clouds were still quite thick, rolling around in great, gray, puffy masses. "Too bad the uplink for our Land Warriors isn't functional," Kittridge mumbled as he fingered the control unit for the computerized system. Though they had been issued to the troops in the field, those parts of the system that would have permitted the soldier on the front line to transmit data and images of what he was seeing back to headquarters hadn't been sent to Slovakia. The limited size of the force deployed didn't include enough slots for the personnel needed to operate this component of the Land Warrior. So just the units used by infantrymen had been sent.

Nathan grunted as he slowly scanned the heavens. "Even if it was, the odds of them being on the same frequency as your unit after three days is pretty much nil."

Without bothering to pursue the matter, Kittridge moved on to the next item that he was concerned about. "Sir, do you think it's a smart idea to pop smoke?"

"Only way I know of drawing their attention," Nathan quipped.

Kittridge wasn't too sure. "True. But what about the other people?"

With a blink of his eyes, Nathan's chin dropped and, for the first time, he scanned the horizon and terrain that lay across the field from where they stood. When he saw nothing, he looked over to Kittridge. "Seems like we're damned if we do, and damned if we don't. Right now, I think we've no choice but to roll the dice."

Drawing in a deep breath, Kittridge looked into Nathan's eyes. Both men knew the soldiers of 3rd Platoon were beginning to suffer from their efforts. Both also knew that the declining morale and growing fear of their subordinates was, at this point, a greater issue than their lack of rations and inability to make contact with friendly forces. Something positive had to be done. Something that gave the men hope, even if it was a bit hollow, needed to be found. If, by chance, the RPV operator, sitting in a warm, secure van miles from where they stood, saw the smoke and identified them for what they were, there was a chance that this nightmare could be brought to an end. Nodding, Kittridge gave his approval. "I guess you're right, sir."

Nathan returned the nod. "I'm not concerned about right or wrong at this moment. It's luck I'm hoping for." With that, the two men resumed their search for the RPV that continued to drone on overhead.

It was Kittridge who spotted the RPV, darting in and out of clouds. "Over there," the NCO exclaimed as he thrust his finger upward. "At two o'clock, in those clouds."

At the last moment, from where they stood Nathan

caught sight of the slick, black, remote aircraft moving from left to right. "I see it."

Dropping his hand to his side, Kittridge mused. "But will it see us?"

Without hesitation, Nathan pulled the pin from the grenade, let the arming spoon flip up and off. Holding the grenade at arm's length as the hammer smacked into the primer with a loud snap, Nathan waited until he heard the grenade fizz and saw the beginnings of smoke pour from it before throwing it. By the time it had come to rest in the snow covered field, billows of bright red smoke were spewing from it. "Well," Nathan finally responded to the NCO's last question, "We'll soon find out."

For several moments the RPV continued to fly along, more concerned with dodging the next blanket of clouds than looking at anything on the ground. Then, like a bird of prey that has spotted something out of the corner of its eye, the right wing of the RPV dipped, taking it off its previous course, and it started a slow, cautious turn.

"He's seen us," Nathan announced.

"He's seen the smoke," Kittridge stated dryly as he corrected the staff officer.

Understanding his senior sergeant's concern, Nathan looked at Kittridge, made a quick sweep of the surrounding countryside, and then stepped out, away from the cover of the tree line where he had been standing. Saving his breath, Nathan unslung his rifle and held it in his right hand. With his face turned up toward the RPV, he began to wave his arms as he approached the spot where the grenade was still burning.

With a smoothness that would have put an eagle to shame, the operator of the RPV brought his turn to an end as soon as the nose of his tiny aircraft aligned with the source of the smoke. Slowing, the RPV overflew the smoke and Nathan. On the ground, Nathan followed the RPV as it passed above him, then disappeared from sight as soon as the trees that had hidden him blocked his line of sight. He remained unsure if he had been successful until he heard the diminishing drone of the RPV's engine change pitch, then begin to grow louder again. By the time he caught sight of it, looping around to make a second pass, Kittridge was standing next to Nathan. "Well, he's seen us. Now what?"

Still waving, Nathan shook his head. "Sergeant Kittridge, I have no idea."

23

By noon it had become obvious that the marginal improvement in the weather was a mixed blessing. While warmer temperatures were welcome, the sloppy, wet conditions they fostered slowed the 3rd Platoon's already painful progress. Not all of this, of course, could be blamed on the goo that clung to the soldiers' boots as they plodded along. In order to support and maintain the demands they place on their bodies, combat infantrymen engaged in protracted physical activities require up to twice the normal daily caloric intake than that recommended for their more sedentary countrymen. Cold weather, which requires the body to generate greater body heat, exacerbates this need. To meet both requirements would have necessitated that each soldier consume five or six complete MRE meals. Yet the cold hard fact was that since leaving Fort Apache three days earlier, the soldiers had consumed the equivalent of three meals apiece, total. With only one MRE left per man, and little hope of finding anything of substance along the route they were taking, hunger was fast becoming another burden that had to be carried by the fourteen men who marched west in search of safety and security.

Not everyone's thoughts were consumed by this dearth of food, shelter, and security. In the hours after they had spotted the RPV, Gerald Reider found he could not shake his growing hatred of the arrogant young staff officer who had usurped his role as a platoon leader. Though he had said nothing at the time, the manner in which Nathan Dixon had snatched the smoke grenade off his flak vest had rekindled Reider's feelings of anger and resentment toward the staff officer. Now, despite their situation, the young West Pointer found he could not set aside his scorn for this man. Reider convinced himself that if he did not say something now, the dark thoughts that clouded his judgment would grow, rather than diminish, as the platoon made its way through the barren Slovakian countryside. Taking to heart one of the many pearls of wisdom his father had dropped on him, Reider decided to face this issue head on, consequences be damned.

An opportunity to do so presented itself when Staff Sergeant Kittridge and his two men, who were still in the lead, rounded the corner of a tree line they had been moving along. Reider glanced over his shoulder. Spotting Dixon, Reider looked back at Kittridge, who was following the remaining members of his squad. With the heads-up displays of their Land Warrior systems in place, they were concentrating on what lay ahead, as well as to their immediate left and right, and not on what Reider was doing.

Pausing, the young officer waited at the point of the woods. The next squad in the line of march was Sergeant Dubois's men. Always alert, Dubois saw Reider stop. Immediately the leader of the 1st Squad tensed up as he raised his right arm as a signal for the other members of his squad to halt. It took a second for Reider to realize the misunderstanding. Shaking his head, Reider waved Dubois on past him.

Of Dubois's three men, only one bothered to look at Reider, face-to-face, as they filed by. Everett Cash, an outspoken soldier who bitched and moaned about everything regardless of who was listening, stared into Reider's eyes as he went by. Reider was familiar with the expression Cash wore. The young officer had been the object of the same burning, almost accusatory glare from many a black youth as they rubbed shoulders in the streets of New York City. Whether Reider had been traveling back and forth from the private school he attended in the city, or in the company of classmates from West Point who were there with him to spend a weekend at his father's apartment in Manhattan, the expression worn by a man who was a fellow New Yorker in name only was the same. Reider often wondered what was going on in the minds of those young men, hardened by life in a city that showed little mercy to people who were not born into wealth or who had not been fortunate enough to secure it for themselves. Of all the concerns Reider had regarding his abilities to lead a combat unit, Cash's casual glance reminded Reider that the most challenging one he faced was finding a way to relate to people with whom he had little in common and whom he had seldom given a second thought.

Following the 1st Squad, and trailed by the RTO, medic, and surviving Javelin gunner, came Nathan Dixon. Uncharacteristically Nathan was bent forward, looking down at the ground as he marched along. It was obvious that he was deep in thought. Reider had no way of knowing what the first lieutenant was thinking about. He might have been considering the next leg of their journey, an odyssey that seemed to grow in length with each passing hour. Or, Reider thought, the staff officer could have been pondering what to do about the rapid approach of hunger and the diminished capacity that would soon rob his platoon of both their ability and their resolve to go on. Though he, as an officer, felt that he should have been above such petty concerns, Reider could not deny the fact that he, himself, was beginning to be affected by their lack of subsistence.

Well, Reider thought as he drew himself up and prepared for the confrontation he had decided to bring on, regardless of what Dixon was thinking, the time had come to clear the air between them, once and for all.

There were no weighty matters rummaging about in Nathan's tired mind. Rather, he was entertaining an image that danced merrily before his mind's eye. The vision that was leading the commander of Reider's bedraggled platoon astray was that of Christina Donovan. It was blurry and unreal because, as he often did, Nathan was trying to picture what she looked like in something other than the baggy BDUs. At this particular moment, Nathan's fantasy had her in a print dress of off-white, made of a fine silk that was almost transparent. She was leaning against the deck railing of his father's house in Colorado Springs. It had been the last family home Nathan had known, so it had become, in his subconscious mind, a place of safety, security, and all that was good and warm. Behind Chris Donovan stood the Rocky Mountains, distant and silent. A gentle breeze, which Nathan's fertile mind could almost feel, sweeping down from the mountains, caught Donovan's long, flowing hair, causing it, and the hem of her skirt, to flutter in a lazy, almost whimsical manner.

Despite the plight of his platoon, and the aches and pains that could no longer be ignored, Nathan found that he was becoming quite aroused by this self-generated daydream. The response to this mental stimulation was both strong and obvious. In fact, it was becoming so much so that Nathan concluded that if he didn't turn his thoughts from the woman he longed for soon, he would have to reach down into his pocket and shift himself so that his fullness spread upward, instead of being bent over and pointed down his pants leg at a painful angle. Faintly aware of where he was, Nathan looked up to see if there was anything more pressing that needed his immediate attention, as well as to make sure that no one was looking at him.

The sight of Gerald Reider, waiting astride the trail they were following, caught Nathan completely off guard. Stopping short, the staff officer looked frantically to his right, across the field they were paralleling, and then left into the woods. All thoughts of Chris Donovan, and the physical discomfort that had accompanied them, shriveled up in an instant as Nathan assessed his surroundings and struggled to compose himself.

Nathan was still attempting to regain his psychological balance when Gerald Reider launched into his rehearsed spiel. "What have you got against me, Dixon?"

Still not fully recovered from being caught asleep at the switch by Reider's question and by the obvious sincerity with which it was put forth, Nathan was thrown into greater confusion. He literally had to step backward in order to recover both his poise and the clarity of mind that would be required to respond to a question that had come to him like a bolt of lightning. This action, unfortunately, almost brought Nathan into a collision with Specialist Pavlovski, the RTO, who had been following Nathan with the same absentmindedness Nathan had been lost in. This near miss did nothing to help Nathan. "Keep going," he snapped, when Pavlovski looked up at him, bewildered. Then, to forestall similar run-ins, the staff officer stepped out of the line of march, looked back to where Hernandes was, and motioned the leader of the 3rd Squad to move on by him. Nathan used the time it took Hernandes's people to pass to collect himself and formulate an answer. Only when he was sure that the last of the platoon, Evens Tobias, was out of earshot, did Nathan step up and present Reider with a reply. "I've got nothing against you," Nathan stated flatly. "I neither hate you nor like you. Hell, fact is, I don't even know you."

Whether it was because of the words themselves or the unenthusiastic manner in which they were delivered, Reider became animated. "Bullshit!" Committed now, Reider clenched his fists and charged ahead. "You've been hovering over me since we left the battalion base camp. You've gotten on my case every chance you could. And you've embarrassed me in front of my platoon. I demand an explanation."

Rather than become angered by this unexpected and totally inappropriate explosion of ego and emotion, Nathan sighed. With his right arm hanging down along his side, holding his rifle, and his left hand on his hip, Nathan looked down at the ground, shook his head, and chuckled. "Mister," Nathan began, "you've picked one hell of a time and place to play 'Me Tarzan, you Jane.' In case you haven't noticed," Nathan continued as he looked into Reider's eyes, "that platoon you're so anxious to lead is wading through some awfully deep shit. And not only is there no end in sight to this walking nightmare we're floundering around in, but I haven't got even the foggiest idea how in the hell I'm going to feed those people once the last of our rations run out tonight, let alone keep them moving tomorrow. So unless you've got something constructive to say in regard to solving those two issues, I recommend you shut the fuck up and do as you're told."

"But this is my platoon. Mine!" Reider roared back. "The least you could do is show me a little respect, ask me for my opinion, or include me in on the decisions. Is that too damned much to ask?"

Feeling his own blood warming to this challenge, Nathan mentally pulled back again to compose himself before he went on. "In a perfect world, Lieutenant Reider," he stated as soon as he felt he could do so without anger, "one in which the vehicles were parked in hard-stand motor pools overnight and everyone went home to the wife and kids once the training day was over, you'd have had the time and opportunity to grow into your position as a platoon leader. Your platoon sergeant, ably assisted by the squad leaders, would have helped you overcome your initial awkwardness and weaned you through your first couple of field training exercises, where casualties don't bleed or die."

Pausing, Nathan looked at Reider and tried to discern if any of this was sinking in. "Unfortunately," he continued, "we don't live in a perfect world. Not only were you thrown into a situation that none of us truly understand or know how to deal with, you got here just in time to be part of a sorry mission turned bad. And while it might be true that I have no idea who got a wild hair up their backside and decided to shout 'fuck it' and start shooting everyone in sight, I do have three advantages that you do not have."

Taking his hand off his hip, Nathan held his fist up in Reider's face. Each time he enumerated a topic, a finger went up as Nathan lit into Reider. "In the first place, I have experience leading troops. I did my platoon time in an Airborne unit and was top blocked all the way. Two," he continued as another finger popped up, "I have been part of this unit since we got here. I have an appreciation of both the people and the terrain of this wretched country. And three," he stated sharply as he dropped his hand and leaned forward, "like I said this morning, I'm the senior officer present. You may not like me. You may not care for how I treat you or do things. But I'm in charge. Even in today's touchy-feely Army, when the stuff hits the spinning blades, that's all that counts."

Without giving Reider a chance to formulate a response, Nathan continued. "This is the second time, Lieutenant Reider, we've had this discussion. That's twice too many times. One more time, mister, and I swear to God I'll not wait for a court-martial. I'll butt stroke you where you stand."

Unlike that morning, Nathan's threat had no visible effect on Reider. The angry young officer was unmoved by this new threat. For his part, Nathan was finished. He no longer cared if what he said registered with Reider. The man, Nathan decided right then and there, was a waste of his time and effort. He was fast becoming more than another burden that had to be shouldered. He was becoming an obstacle to the platoon's survival. Nathan now viewed Reider as an impediment that had to be ignored, if possible, or overcome, if necessary, if he was going to make it back to the brigade base camp and Chris Donovan.

Still, Nathan could not walk away without making one final point. "Those men you're so anxious to lead know what's going on," he stated firmly, trying to hide his anger and frustration. "While they haven't heard every word that's passed between us, they don't need to. Whatever chance you had of gaining their respect is gone. That's over, kaput, fini. Even if we survive this, they'll never look upon you as anything but a careerist doing his time with the troops in order to get his ticket punched. Given a chance, they'll walk right over you if necessary, to get through this, just like I'm about to do."

With that, Nathan stepped forward and began to go around Reider. The young officer stood rooted to the spot of ground he had chosen to make a stand on. Having gone this far, Gerald Reider was determined to get satisfaction. Reaching up, he made a grab for Nathan's arm. He wanted to pull the foul-mouthed battalion staff officer back. He wanted some sort of satisfaction, a resolution to the conflict that existed between two determined officers barely separated by rank and age. Reider had to finish what he had started in order to salvage some of his tattered pride and self-worth. At this point that was all he felt he had left.

But Nathan was too quick, and his strides too long. Gerald Reider's grasping hand seized only empty air. Nathan, like Reider's opportunity to make his mark on the Army, seemed to be gone, out of reach and fading fast in the distance.

Trudging along behind his two troopers, Dick Kittridge was trying hard not to think. A headache that felt as if someone had driven a wedge down the center of his skull was making everything he did, physically and mentally, a painful experience for the senior squad leader. The aspirin that he had procured from the medic earlier in the day had done little to reduce the dull, rhythmic throbbing. All Kittridge could do was what most of the men in the 3rd Platoon were doing— keep his mouth shut, try not to think about his individual and their collective plight, and soldier on as best he could.

They were moving along a stretch of road running through one of the many wood lots they had been dodging in and out of all day when a familiar sound penetrated the mental funk that Kittridge had slipped into. Starting somewhere deep in his subconscious mind, the noise connected with a memory. In turn, this audio cue conjured up an image. Even as the distant sound grew in intensity, Kittridge was slowing his pace without being fully cognitive of why he was doing so. Sometimes called a sixth sense, this involuntary response to outside stimuli is what often keeps combat veterans alive.

Lifting his drooping chin, Kittridge began to look around. Within him a trickle of adrenaline, initiated in response to apprehension that was building up in another part of his subconscious mind, was canceling out the painful throbbing that had, until now, dominated his every thought. This freed him to concentrate on his surroundings and his squad's tactical situation. Scanning his immediate front, the acting platoon sergeant had assessed that the danger he sensed was not imminent or local. This, of course, brought no relief, for now he focused his attention on determining the source and location of the sound that was, even then, finally beginning to breach the conscious mind.

It took another second or two before the image and sound that had already been formulated began to percolate up into Kitt's consciousness. He was not alone. By the time the reverberation of beating of blades and the high-pitched whine of a turbine engine echoed across snow-covered fields that lay somewhere off to their left, Keith Reisniack, the SAW gunner, had the answer Kittridge was searching for. "Ya hear it?" Reisniack asked, looking first at Kittridge, then in the direction from which the sound seemed to be coming. "Apaches," he continued. "Skimming along, hunting."

While Kittridge was pretty sure that his SAW gunner was only guessing about what the helicopter was doing, he had no doubt that the sound was, in fact, coming from a helicopter, maybe two. Forcing himself to refocus his vision, Kittridge peered through the small sight that hung off the lip of his helmet in front of him. Carefully, he scanned the area that lay off in the direction that the sound was coming from.

As good as the thermal imaging system of the Land Warrior was, it did not allow Kittridge to see through the trees, even ones that had lost their leaves many months before. Abandoning this effort, he continued to pivot in place until he was looking back down the platoon file. Gerald Reider, who was still some thirty meters back, was standing still, watching Kittridge and waiting, anxiously, to hear what the leader of the point element said. Using a conversational tone, and pointing in the direction from which the audio cue was originating, Kittridge said only one word. "Helicopters."

* * *

This announcement, though welcome, caused Reider to hesitate. Looking back along the file of soldiers who were now coming to a halt, just as he had, Reider wondered if he should pass the word on to Dixon, or go forward and investigate the report in person. Though he still smarted from Nathan's last rebuke, the young platoon leader was not yet ready to roll over and accept a position of diminished importance within an organization he was supposed to be in charge of. With a motion of his hand, Reider signaled Dubois to stand fast. Without waiting for the leader of the 1st Squad to acknowledge his visual command, Reider took off at a trot to where Kittridge stood.

Even before he came to a stop, Kittridge brought his arm up and pointed over in the direction of the sound. "A pair of helicopters, somewhere over there."

"Ours?" Reider asked excitedly.

"Apaches," Reisniack volunteered.

Glancing first at his SAW gunner, then back to Reider, Kittridge skeptically added, "Maybe." Then, after drawing a deep breath, he added, "Either way we need to go over and have a look-see. They could, after all," he concluded in a guarded manner that hid his optimism, "be out here looking for us."

Without hesitation Reider announced, "Stay here. I'll go look." Before Kittridge could reply, Reider was gone.

The excited young officer had no sooner disappeared at a trot, headed for the edge of the forest they were in, when Nathan Dixon came up to Kittridge. Pavloski, the RTO, was on his heels. By then, the sound of the nearby helicopters was so pronounced that Nathan didn't need to ask what had brought their forward movement to a halt. Instead, he looked at the senior NCO. "Why are you still standing here, in the middle of the woods? They won't be able to see us in here."

Expecting that his answer would evoke the anger of the battalion staff officer, Kittridge braced himself as he prepared to respond. "Lieutenant Reider ordered us to stand fast while he went to check it out."

To Kittridge's surprise, the first words out of Nathan's mouth were neither oaths directed at Reider nor admonishments for the acting platoon sergeant's judgment. Instead, he directed Kittridge to follow him with his squad. "Spread out, left and right," Nathan ordered as they bobbed and weaved their way between the trees that lay between the trail and the edge of the woods. "Deploy your people along the tree line, and don't break cover."

Without breaking stride or repeating Nathan's commands, Kittridge looked behind. "You heard the man," he shouted to the two men who were struggling to keep up with him. Pointing to each man in turn, Kittridge motioned in the direction he wanted them to move. "Reisniack, go the left. Kim, keep to the right. Eyes and ears, people," he admonished. "Eyes and ears open and mouths shut."

When Nathan reached the tree line, where Reider lay prone, the young staff officer came up, alongside Reider's right, and squatted down, next to a tree. "Have you seen them yet?" Nathan asked as he labored to catch his breath.

Lifting his arm, Reider pointed off to the front left. "They're somewhere over there, just behind that wooded hill, I think. Haven't seen them since I've been here."

Tilting his helmet over to the right in order to expose his left ear, Nathan turned his head sideways and listened for a moment. The mass of the hill by which the unseen helicopters were masked, as well as the motion of the aircraft, prevented Nathan from determining if they were going away, coming closer, or moving perpendicular from their position. Still, he continued to listen as the other four soldiers of his tiny command either watched him or peered off into the distance.

Finally, both his vigilance and that of the others paid off. Nathan had just determined that the helicopters were coming around the hill, to the right of it as they faced that terrain feature, when Les Kim sang out. "Apache, two o'clock low." All heads snapped to face that direction. Keith Reisniack, who could not yet see the chopper because of his position on the far left, called out to Kittridge. "Where? I don't see any . . ."

The acting platoon sergeant snapped, "Silence!" Then, in a calmer voice, he added, "Watch your sector. We may not be the only people waiting and watching."

Though meant for the 2nd Squad's SAW gunner, Kittridge's response stirred a concern that the excitement of the moment had stilled. As anxious as he was to determine which way the attack helicopter was going to go next, the idea that hostiles might be in the area, and drawn to the appearance of the American aircraft, caused Nathan to look away from the Apache and scan the open ground in front of him. As he did, he spoke to Reider. "Have you seen anything since you've been here?"

Having focused his entire attention on the search for, then identification of, the helicopters, Reider looked at Nathan, blinked, and then thought for a second before responding. "No," he stated flatly. Then he added, "But then, I wasn't really looking."

Nathan continued searching the various terrain features before him in an effort to detect anything out of the ordinary. "Well, you'd better start looking."

Though tempted to join the officers, Kittridge decided someone needed to keep an eye on the Apache. After rounding the hill, hugging the contours of the ground and staying just above the trees that covered the gentle slopes and the ground surrounding it, the attack helicopter leveled out for a second before it zoomed out into the field that lay between the hill it had been behind and the wood line where Nathan and the others lay hidden.

Just when it seemed that the Apache was going to continue toward the trees that concealed them and overfly them to the right, the Apache pilot began a series of radical maneuvers. First, the nose of the chopper pitched up, dropping the tail boom so fast that Kittridge thought that it would strike the snow-covered field under it. Then, even as the pilot of the attack helicopter applied more power and strained to gain as much speed and altitude as quickly as possible, he banked to his left, throwing his aircraft over onto its side and exposing its underside to everyone who was watching from the tree line.

This last maneuver, taken for reasons that Nathan could not imagine, was a mistake. Before the staff officer could utter a single word of concern or exclamation, a streak of yellowish-red flames, trailed by billows of white smoke, erupted from the tree line somewhere off to his right and into his peripheral vision.

Nathan didn't need to hear the *whoosh* of the surface-to-air missile's rocket motor to know what was happening. Like so many other events that he had happened on or been witness to during this ill-fated patrol, all Nathan could do was watch in horror and pray that somehow, things would sort themselves out in his favor.

24

Collectively Nathan and the men with him held their breath as they watched the Apache's frantic maneuvers. Flares, designed to spoof surface-to-air missiles by presenting a heat-seeking missile with targets that were hotter than the Apache itself, were launched. Streaming from pods built into the frame of the helicopter, the flares shot out and away from the Apache. Their appearance momentarily raised Nathan's hopes. "It has a chance," he whispered to himself.

Yet it didn't. The distance between the surface-to-air missile gunner and his intended target was too short, the response of the Apache pilot flawed, and the firing of the flares too late. The guidance unit of the inbound missile had insufficient time to identify the flares, generate a course correction to intercept them, and translate that data into changes in the flight surfaces of the missile itself. As if drawn to the Apache, the missile slammed into the underside of the helicopter, ripping through the thin skin of the aircraft before erupting into a ball of flame.

As devastating as this spectacle was to Nathan's hope for salvation, his response was somewhat unexpected, almost detached. To him, the whole scene unfolding before him did not make sense. While part of his mind remained focused on the Apache's last seconds of erratic and uncontrolled flight, a more analytical portion of his brain pondered why the missile hadn't exploded before hitting the helicopter. The warheads of surface-to-air missiles, according to Nathan's understanding, detonated before they made contact, releasing a maelstrom of shrapnel. It was this shrapnel, and not the explosion, that tore into the delicately balanced turbine engines of its intended target and inflicted mortal wounds to the aircraft. Perhaps, Nathan thought as he watched the stricken Apache plow into the ground, the missile's warhead didn't have time to arm.

This idle, academic curiosity was quickly tossed aside when a second Apache, hovering just above the tree line on the side of the hill where the first had appeared, unleashed a salvo of rockets. *"Jesus Christ!"* Kittridge screamed. "The bastard is firing on us."

In shock, Nathan turned away from the wreckage of the first aircraft and shifted his attention to the bright orange fireballs that were bearing down on them. As they loomed larger by the second, Nathan barely had enough time to shout, "Take cover!" and dive behind a half-rotted tree before the first of a half-dozen rockets exploded.

Fired in haste in an effort to suppress their foe, and while his pilot was still moving, the gunner of the second Apache had not taken time to make a precise lay. As a result, two of the rockets struck in the field to their front. These short rounds showered the 2nd Squad with a spray of dirt, shrapnel, and stones. Three of the rockets passed overhead. One came in so low that Nathan, who was pressing his face into the snow until the lip of his helmet hit the ground beneath it, felt the heat of the rocket's flaming tail on the back of his neck. Though the point of impact of these were far closer, the momentum of their forward movement carried the majority of their lethal debris away from them.

Only one rocket impacted in a manner that seriously endangered Nathan and the soldiers deployed to his left and right. This one, as fate would have it, hit a tree that stood in the center of their thin skirmish line. Instead of being pelted with dirt, rocks, and shrapnel, the soldiers of 2nd squad found themselves subjected to a shower of splinters and hot metal. The explosion of this one round was so close that Nathan felt the concussion and heat and heard the ear-splitting report simultaneously.

In the middle of this riot of noise and confusion, he also felt a sharp, stinging sensation across the back of his neck. It was a sensation akin to being clawed by an animal. In response, Nathan attempted to push his face down farther, even though the ground before him refused to yield. He didn't need to analyze what this was. He knew, even before the full impact of the wound was felt, that he had been hit. Whether it was shrapnel or bits of the tree that were impaling him as he lay there helpless didn't matter. All that he was concerned with now was the extent of the damage, the severity of his injuries.

In the silence that followed, Gerald Reider lay motionless for several seconds. He was not sure if he had survived a near brush with death or if he was mortally wounded and the pain simply hadn't registered yet. Slowly, and without moving a muscle, the young officer struggled to take stock of his physical condition. This was not easy. Though his helmet had sheltered his brain-housing group from external, physical damage, Reider's head was swimming. What thoughts passed through his conscious mind were a scattering of sensations and images that could not be corralled or organized into a coherent train of logic. Like a child blindly bobbing for apples, Reider grasped at whatever image or feeling passed before him.

The flak vest he wore, he quickly discovered, had protected his upper torso. His arms as well had escaped injury. Though he didn't remember doing so, somehow he had managed to tuck them in, under his chest, before the impact. It was his lower extremities, his buttocks and legs, that he was most unsure of. These had been exposed to the full flurry of the near miss. Nothing below his waist, for the moment, seemed to be registering. His legs were numb. They were two dead weights that neither passed sensations of pain up to his brain, nor responded to commands it sent down to them.

Unable to do much of anything until his head stopped spinning and logical thinking was restored, Reider lay still, centering whatever mental powers he could muster on sorting out the problem he was having with his legs. What feelings he was able to register weren't anything like the numbness that one associates with cold, something that had become quite familiar to him over the past three days. Rather, it was a stunned numbness very much like what one experiences after someone delivers a sharp blow to the upper arm. Along with the concern for his legs, Gerald Reider became aware of the fact that he hadn't heard anything since the explosion. This worry, however, was more easily dismissed as the sounds of someone yelling made their way into his stunned consciousness. The words were, at first, little more than faint, barely audible reverberations. They were muffled gibberish, sounding as if someone at the bottom of a deep hole was shouting up to him. With his inability to concentrate on more than one thing at a time, he ignored those cries for the moment and went back to sorting himself out.

The blast had swept over Staff Sergeant Kittridge without causing any serious harm. The ringing in his left ear was not much worse than what he always seemed to experience after firing a pistol without using earplugs. It was neither serious nor permanent. Their situation, however, was. Lifting his head, he looked across the field, past the smoldering pile of scrap that had, moments before, been a sophisticated attack helicopter, in the direction from which the friendly fire had come. He saw nothing. Scanning the far horizon, Kittridge searched it to see if the second Apache had simply moved to a new firing position, or if it had broken contact and fled. After a single sweep with negative results, the acting platoon sergeant threw caution to the wind. Standing up, Kittridge called out to his men. "Second Squad, sound off!"

From off to his right, he heard Les Kim come back with a crisp, "A-okay." He glanced over to where the Korean-American rifleman had gone and caught a glimpse of him, propping himself up on his elbows to face his squad leader. Though Kittridge could see that there was a look of concern in Kim's expression, Kittridge didn't have the time to reassure him. Pivoting about, Kittridge called out to his other trooper, "Reisniack!"

Off in the distance, through the lingering smoke created by the near miss, Kittridge saw a hand waving. The relief he felt was short-lived when he neither saw nor heard anything from the two officers, both of whom were somewhere between him and his SAW gunner. "You two," he shouted with his head cocked over one shoulder, "Keep down and stay alert." Then, realizing for the first time that the Apache had fired on them

as a result of missile fire that had come from somewhere off to their right, Kittridge turned in that direction again. "Kim, watch your three o'clock!"

Again, the young Korean-American's reply was quick
and to the point. "Roger."

Having tended to those concerns that were, for a
squad leader, the most pressing, Kittridge made his way
to where Nathan Dixon and his platoon leader were.
While he was moving along the tree line, and just inside
of it, Kittridge kept one eye on the hill that the two
attack helicopters had appeared from. He half expected
the bird that had attacked them to come back, if for no
other reason than to check to see if any of their buddies
in the first Apache had survived. He knew he would.
Taking care of your own, after all, was an article of faith
to a soldier.

Slowly, Nathan pushed himself off the ground with his
hands. The snow that managed to work its way into his
gloves was of no concern to him. All attention was focused on the hot, searing pain that radiated from the
back of his neck. To keep the stiff, heavy collar of his
flak vest from coming into contact with his injury, Nathan bowed his head low and slowly stretched his neck
out as far as he could while he attempted to get up. The
angle of his head caused a trickle of warm blood to ooze
down into his close-cropped hair and around along his
jawline until it spread over the side of his face and onto
his parted lips.

In the midst of these struggles, the first drops of blood
fell away. The thick, red globs landed in the snow right
before his eyes. Whether it was the sight of his own
blood, the taste of it on the tip of his tongue, or shock
setting in, Nathan was suddenly overcome by nausea.
Pausing in midstride, he hovered above the ground on
all fours, the young staff officer felt acid and the con-
tents of his stomach begin to force their way up his
esophagus. He was barely conscious of the dizziness that
caused his head to swim and his arms and legs to be-

come wobbly. Like a disinterested spectator, Nathan could only watch as steam rose up from the growing pool of red that gathered in the white snow before him.

Slowly, Nathan's field of vision began to narrow. His sight, which a moment before had been unhindered, was now reduced to a single pinprick of light surrounded by a gathering of darkness that was rapidly collapsing inward. Only at the last second, before that small circle of light disappeared, did Nathan realize that all pain was gone, that his feeling of nausea had suddenly passed, and that there was no longer the bitter taste of blood in his mouth. Only warmth, and a gentle falling motion, registered in his mind as he slipped into unconsciousness and toppled over.

Somehow, Staff Sergeant Kittridge knew what he would find even before he saw the two officers lying motionless in the snow. If anything, he was surprised that there was so little blood, considering that the rocket had detonated right above them.

Still, this dearth of gore was little comfort to the senior NCO. In a glance Kittridge assessed the situation and took action. Though both officers lay motionless, the fresh blood that liberally coated Nathan Dixon's collar and face left little doubt in the NCO's mind as to who needed his attention first.

Bounding over to where Dixon was, Kittridge dropped to his knees in front of Nathan but did not touch him, not right away. Movement of an injured person, particularly when there was a neck or head wound, can just as easily deliver a coup de grâce. Though anxious to get on with what needed to be done, the squad leader did nothing till he was ready. Even then, his actions were deliberately slow and tentative.

Like many infantrymen, Nathan wore the pouch containing his personal compression bandage on a ring high on his chest. This freed the attachments at his waist for other, bulkier items as well as making the bandage more conspicuous and readily accessible to would-be saviors. When he was sure that he could do so safely, Kittridge pulled the bandage out of the pouch, ripped open the plastic cover, and exposed a sterile cotton and fabric pad. With the bandage ready in one hand, Kittridge reached under Nathan's neck with his free hand. Slowly, he lifted the officer's neck up, toward him, exposing the wound. This broadened the gap between the collar of the flak vest and the rim of Nathan's helmet, giving Kittridge a clear picture of the wound as well as providing additional space in which to work. It also caused edges of the gash to separate farther and let the blood flow freer and faster.

Though this last action was unintended, it actually gave Kittridge an opportunity to see that the wound was neither deep nor fatal. Starting little more than an inch from the rear centerline of Nathan's neck, where his brain stem met his backbone, the gash ran at an upward angle until it ended just below Nathan's right ear. Only skin and a few minor blood vessels appeared to have been ripped apart by the scrap of shrapnel that, as far as Kittridge could tell, had continued on without lodging in Nathan's neck. Reassured, the squad leader unsnapped Nathan's helmet and let it drop to the ground. With this obstacle out of the way, he gingerly laid the compression bandage upon the wound, slowly applying pressure with one hand while continuing to support Nathan's neck in his other.

Kittridge was in the process of using the finger of one hand to unfurl the long tie flaps that were an integral part of the compression bandage when Keith Reisniack came up to where his squad leader and the two officers were. Stopping next to Reider, the SAW gunner looked down at his platoon leader of three days, then over to Kittridge. "Is he dead?" Reisniack asked, more out of curiosity than concern.

"Don't know" was all Kittridge said as he continued

to work on Nathan. "How 'bout getting your ass over here and helping me out."

Stepping over Reider, the SAW gunner made his way to Nathan's side, opposite his squad leader.

The shadow of something passing over him caused Gerald Reider to shudder. This last involuntary response to perceived danger provided a new squirt of adrenaline, which in turn swept away the cobwebs that had been befuddling his mind. With a start, Reider jerked his head up, twisting it this way, then that, in an effort to assess clearly, for the first time, his situation. The sight of two men, both on their knees just a few feet away, caught his attention. "What's happening?"

Though clear as a bell in Reider's mind, the question came out slurred and barely audible. Without turning his head to look over his shoulder, Reisniack glanced up at Kittridge, who was busy wrapping the wings of the compression bandage around Nathan's neck. "I guess the other LT is still with us."

While his fingers worked, Kittridge peered over Reisniack's shoulder at Reider. His platoon leader, wearing an expression that reminded Kittridge of someone stirred from a nap prematurely, heaved a sigh of relief. "It would seem so." Then, without so much as another word, he finished binding Nathan's wound. Only when he was satisfied with his efforts did Kittridge instruct Reisniack to stay with the unconscious staff officer while he went over to check Reider out.

By the time Kittridge made his way over to him and knelt down, Reider had managed to get himself up into a sitting position. Removing his helmet, he shook his head, blinked, and refocused his eyes before talking. "What's going on? What's our situation?" Then, taking note of Reisniack hovering over Nathan, he quickly added, "How bad is he?"

Kittridge took the questions in the order that he thought was important. "The Apache that cut loose with a salvo of rockets seems to have taken off. Haven't seen or heard from him after that. Nor," Kittridge added, "have I seen anything of the bastards that brought that one down," pointing to the smoldering wreckage in the field. "Of course," he continued, "I haven't taken the time to check that out yet."

For the first time, Reider realized that four of the five men who had been along the tree line were clustered together within arm's reach. What alarmed him the most was that none of them was paying any attention to either the field in front of them or the direction from which the missile had been launched. "Who's watching for . . ."

Before he could finish, Kittridge, guessing at the cause of his platoon leader's sudden anxiety, filled in the blank. "Kim's over there, on the left, sir. He's keeping watch."

Though still concerned that only one man was executing this vital duty, Reider continued to pursue his original questions. "And him?" he asked, pointing at Nathan.

"The lieutenant took a piece of shrapnel to the neck," Kittridge replied. "He lost some blood, but not much. There doesn't seem to be any serious damage. But," he added cautiously, "we won't know that for sure till he comes round."

Far from feeling all together, Gerald Reider knew he couldn't simply sit there. He felt he needed to do something. Carefully lowering his helmet back onto his head, he looked at Kittridge. "If he's out of immediate danger, then let's go see about our friends."

While his platoon leader stood up, Kittridge hesitated. "Sir, we are going to bring up the rest of the platoon before we move on the Slovaks, aren't we?"

When he was on his feet, Reider realized just how badly he had been shaken up. Were it not for the fact that he had his rifle to lean on for support, he would have toppled down, face first, right on top of Kittridge.

The acting platoon sergeant, seeing this, prepared to leap out of the way. Then just as quickly, he checked his desperate dive for safety at the last moment when it became obvious that the wavering officer towering above him would remain standing.

Somewhat recovered, Reider looked down at Kittridge. "No time," he blurted. "You and the SAW gunner follow me. Have your other rifleman, the one on the right, move deeper into the woods to cover our right after we pass his position."

For the second time that day, Dick Kittridge felt himself being ground between two rocks. The first instant had been that morning, back at the lodge, when the battalion staff officer had overridden his platoon leader's instructions. At that time, Kittridge had been able to ignore his platoon leader simply by doing what regulations and military law required of him, which was to follow the orders of the most senior officer present.

This time, however, Kittridge was on his own. The more experienced hand of Nathan Dixon wasn't available to reach in and save him, and his squad, from a course of action that he thought was, at best, questionable. He was still pondering his plight when Reider, now recovered from his bout with instability and dizziness, leaned over. "Well, sergeant. Are you going to just sit there?"

Kittridge looked up. He stared into Reider's eyes. Then, without saying anything, he stood, turned, and faced Reisniack. "Grab your SAW, Keith."

Reisniack, who had been listening, looked into his squad leader's eyes. Even before he asked the question, the SAW gunner suspected that he knew what the answer would be. Still, he felt compelled to try. "And him?" Reisniack asked, nodding toward Dixon.

"I don't think he's going anywhere anytime soon," Kittridge replied. "The bandage will hold his bleeding in check. He'll be okay."

Picking up on his squad leader's reluctance, Reisniack was slow to respond, moving with the same deliberateness that a child does when he drags his feet in a futile effort to delay the inevitable. Reider, himself moving with exaggerated motions in an effort to maintain his still questionable balance, said nothing. Either they would follow him, he told himself, or they wouldn't. Either way, it was time to find out if he had what it took to be a combat leader.

X

It took the young platoon leader a few minutes to shake off the physical effects of the near miss. Chief among these were a ringing in both ears, which was why Reisniack, the least affected by the rocket attack, heard the Slovakians first.

The four members of the 3rd Platoon had been moving forward in a loose wedge, with Kittridge behind and to the right of Reider, and Reisniack behind and to the left. As was their habit, Reisniack let out a soft *"Pssst,"* rather than speak, to get his squad leader's attention. Picking up the signal, Kittridge stopped in place, quickly looked around, then turned his attention to his SAW gunner.

With his left hand, Reisniack pointed to his ear, then in the direction in which he had heard a sound. Following Reisniack's finger, Kittridge peered through the trees to see if their foe was visible yet.

It took the acting platoon sergeant a second or two to realize that his platoon leader hadn't stopped. Reider had neither heard Reisniack's warning nor taken note of the fact that the men behind him were no longer following. At a loss as to what to do, and reluctant to call out, Kittridge moved as quickly as he dared up to his platoon leader, glancing nervously between him and off into the distance ahead. When he was within arm's reach, the squad leader grabbed his officer's arm.

This sudden contact caught Reider off guard. With a jerk, his head spun. His lips were parting, and words were already forming in his mouth when his eyes fell on Kittridge, who stood motionless beside him with a finger up to his lips. Only after their eyes met, and he was sure that his novice platoon leader understood, did the NCO remove his finger from his lips and point in the direction Reisniack thought he had heard something. Catching his breath, Reider nodded that he understood. Then he motioned for both Kittridge and Reisniack to come up, on line with him, before going on.

After taking his place to his platoon leader's right, Kittridge looked over to his own right, where Les Kim was. Though hanging back a bit farther, and some ten meters deeper into the woods, Kim had been keeping track of what the others had been doing. With a nod and a wave, Kim signaled his squad leader that he was alert to the unseen danger and prepared to continue on.

Without waiting for Kittridge to come back with a signal that he and his men were ready, Reider continued on. The four men were now in a skirmish line with Reisniack just inside the tree line on the far left, Reider to the right of him, Kittridge keeping to Reider's right, and Kim farther over and slightly behind. With weapons at the ready, and moving with a slow, steady deliberateness, they advanced, ensuring that they kept the man to their left or right within their peripheral vision.

Only now, as Reider finally began to hear voices up ahead for himself, did he realize that his ability to focus on that, or anything else, was still impaired. No sooner had the realization struck him that their foe was just a few meters in front of them, when he was gripped by panic. Suddenly, the young officer realized that he had no idea of what to do next. He had no plan, no clear concept of how he was going to close with those people, or what he was going to do once they had done so. Were they going to fire on them as soon as they had made visual contact? Or was he going to set up an ambush, leaving part of his men in place to establish a base of fire while he maneuvered with the rest? Or . . .

Or what? Reider found himself asking questions he should have addressed before going forward. Unable to answer them, he slowed his pace. He had four men, counting himself. And their foes had, well, he had no idea how many men they had. For all he knew there could be a platoon of them just up ahead. Or maybe there was a full company of the bastards, complete with crew-served weapons and mortars. The realization that he was leading his men into the open arms of an enemy force of unknown size with only part of his force made Reider suddenly appreciate that Custer's headlong charge into the Indian village in June 1876 hadn't been so dumb after all.

It was this last analogy that finally persuaded the troubled young officer to throw his hand up and halt their advance. Dick Kittridge, who had also been pondering what his platoon leader intended to do next, found himself hoping that Reider had experienced a sudden outbreak of sanity. While Reider squatted down, using a tree as both support and cover, Kittridge started to make his way over toward him. They needed to talk, if for no other reason than to get their signals and plan straight.

The young officer sensed the nearness of his acting platoon sergeant, but neither turned to face him or acknowledge his presence. He was still peering off into the distance ahead, trying to come up with a coherent plan, when Kittridge whispered in his ear. "Sir, you want me to go back and bring the rest of the platoon up behind them?"

Turning, Reider looked into Kittridge's face. The young officer was so consumed by his own thoughts and apprehensions that he failed to read the look of concern

that his NCO wore. Yes, Reider thought. That was the
answer. He'd stay here, he told himself. He would provide the base of fire while his platoon sergeant brought
up the bulk of the platoon. That was exactly what they
needed to do.

Combat is an exercise in dynamics. It is a contest between two forces, often unequal, and almost always in
motion. Seldom does one side have the privilege of
carrying out its plans or executing a maneuver while its
opponents, seen or unseen, sit passively. They, too, have
leaders who have plans, a focus, and both the will and
means to achieve them. Rarely does the quality of initial
plans determine the outcome of a confrontation between two armed forces. Rather, it is the ability of the
leaders to assess and respond to the changing situation
they face, and the willingness of the soldiers who follow
those leaders, that often makes the difference. While the
odds still favor the side with superior firepower, even in
the twenty-first century, leadership, particularly on the
cutting edge, makes the difference.

As he stared into Staff Sergeant Kittridge's eyes and
prepared to issue his next orders, Second Lieutenant
Gerald Reider was unaware that he was about to receive
a hard lesson in the dynamics of warfare.

25

The sound of shouting in the distance reminded Nathan of a radio alarm set to a rock station, spewing out noise that is harsh, unwanted, and unwelcome. His natural reaction was to ignore it in the hope that it would go without his having to move a muscle. Go back to sleep, that's what Nathan wanted to do.

But the voices wouldn't go away. In fact, they seemed to become louder, more excited. They were clear now. More distinct and . . .

And they were foreign. With a suddenness that was painful and wrenching, Nathan Dixon regained an awareness of where he was, and what had happened just before he had lost consciousness. A charge ran through his body, causing him to twitch involuntarily from head to toe. The pain that had put him down returned with a vengeance. The taste of his own blood, the sting of his wound, the buzzing in his ears all hammered away at his consciousness at the same instant. Yet, through it all, Nathan's appreciation that he was in mortal danger overcame his physical concerns.

Still, he didn't leap onto his feet or make any sudden move. Not at first. In fact, he didn't even lift his head and look around. Not sure what, exactly, was going on around him, Nathan lay as still as his tensed body would permit. It would not do, after all, to spring upright in front of an armed foe who was just as apprehensive and nervous about what was going on as he was. So Nathan lay motionless as he assessed the voices that had stirred him. The ringing in his ears from the explosion of the rocket complicated this. Since he was unsure how much his hearing had been affected, it was hard to get a fix on exactly how far away the voices were, or how many there were. One thing that quickly did become evident, however, was the fact that they were not in his immediate vicinity. They were being directed at someone else.

Slowly, Nathan opened one eye, then the other. Fuzziness that clouded his brain made this simple task more difficult than it sounds. Like Reider, Nathan was still laboring under the physical effects of the near miss. And like Reider, the seriousness of his position caused Nathan's body to kick in all sorts of involuntary responses. The most important of these, the release of copious amounts of adrenaline, allowed the mind to prepare its domain for either fight or flight, a decision that Nathan was pondering.

When he saw nothing that presented a clear and present danger, the young battalion staff officer slowly began to rotate his head. This action, however, came to an abrupt stop as soon as the collar of his flak jacket rubbed against the bandage covering his wound. All the adrenaline in the world could not trump the pain that radiated from that spot. Unable to bear it, Nathan allowed his head to flop back down, into the wet snow. Pausing to catch his breath, he assessed both his physical situation as well as the negative response to his activities. Reaching behind the back of his neck, Nathan began gingerly to explore his wound. When his gloved fingers came in contact with the bandage, he became confused, and worried. While glad that someone had taken the time to put it on him, the simple fact that he didn't remember that happening collided with the twin realizations that to do so had to have taken time, and that whoever had done it was no longer there.

Throwing caution to the wind, Nathan rolled over on his stomach in preparation to get up, just as he had tried before. This time there was no hesitation. This time his limbs held firm and his muscles responded. All the while he was looking, scanning, and, in spite of the pain, taking in the scene before him.

Another outburst of shouts coming from the field before him drew his attention to that quarter. The crumpled Apache helicopter was still lying there, as before, twisted into an almost unrecognizable heap of smoldering scrap. Unlike before, there were a number of figures standing around it, with guns at the ready. Their lack of uniformity in both dress and equipment pegged the four soldiers Nathan saw as members of the ethnic Hungarian militia. This, Nathan realized, was the first bit of luck he'd been able to rack up so far. Provided they hadn't changed their mode of operation in the past few days, that meant that he was facing a Kommando of ten to twelve militiamen.

Easing himself into a more comfortable position, one that offered a bit more cover and concealment, Nathan continued to watch the militiamen. They were standing in a loose semicircle all facing away from him. The wreckage of the helicopter, which had failed to explode, didn't seem to be of much concern to them. Instead, they were looking down at something on the ground before them. One of the men, with NCO markings on the shoulder flaps of his fatigue jacket, was shouting at the object of their attention. Blinking, it took Nathan another moment or two to sink in that the words he spoke were English, and that the dark heap that the militiamen were staring at was a human being.

One of the Apache's crewmen had survived. This realization galvanized Nathan into action. Twisting around despite the burning pain this caused, Nathan searched for his rifle. He saw it leaning up against a nearby tree. Whoever had tended his wound had been wise enough to recover the weapon and place it where it was both handy and up, off the ground. This thought triggered another, less charitable one. Though he had no idea who had rendered him first aid, and picked up his rifle, Nathan was pretty sure that it wasn't Reider.

Dismissing this involuntary reflection in the time it took him to reach out and recover his weapon, Nathan turned his full attention to the situation before him. For several moments he sat there, still and surprisingly alert, as the militia leader harangued the prostrate Apache crewman. Though he could not hear every word, the young staff officer was able to deduce that the militia sergeant wanted the crewman to get up. All Nathan could see of the crewman were his arms as he flailed about in an effort to do so. Unfortunately his fellow American was failing miserably, despite the nonstop flow of exhortations and curses being directed at him. Seeing that his words were not having any effect, the militia sergeant took a quick step forward, cocked his right foot back, and swung it forward, into the side of the American, with all his might.

Tightening his grip on his weapon, Nathan fought the urge to open fire on the bastard. Even if he were able to take down the four militiamen before they could do any harm to the Apache crewman, Nathan knew he was looking at only a small piece of the overall picture. His total ignorance of the tactical situation kept his passions in check. By his own estimate, there were at least six more militiamen somewhere near at hand. The response of the militiamen he could not see could be fatal, if not to him, then to the hapless Apache crewman. These facts, together with the appreciation that he had no idea where any of the 3rd Platoon was, checked Nathan's urge to respond.

Still, he could not simply sit there and do nothing. Even as he desperately weighed each possible course of action, rejecting them almost as quickly as he formulated them, the militia sergeant had abandoned his efforts to rouse the American before him. Instead, he motioned to two of his companions to pick the crewman up. With no more tenderness than one would show a sack of grain, the two men delegated to this chore stepped forward, reached down, and jerked the Apache crewmen up onto his feet. Like a rag doll, the American's legs gave out, causing him to slump down between his captors. This angered them both, though only one, a thick, brutish fellow on the crewman's left, did anything. While Nathan watched and seethed at his own impotence, the militiaman grabbed the Apache crewman's throat with his free hand, twisted the American's face toward him, and screamed what only could be obscenities at him.

The militia sergeant said or did nothing to check this behavior. Instead, while his men took a moment to adjust their grips, he turned and faced the wood line off to Nathan's right. Pointing to someone Nathan could not see, the ethnic Hungarian started to shout out orders when, distracted by something to his right, he stopped in midsentence. Able to see the man's expression and where he was looking, Nathan was positive that the militia sergeant hadn't seen him. But the astonished expression he wore, and the manner in which he brought the AK that had been dangling off his shoulder up into a firing position, told Nathan that the militia sergeant had spotted someone from the 3rd Platoon.

Now, there was no hesitation, no need to hold back. Ignoring the sting from his wound, Nathan brought his weapon up. With his right thumb, he flipped the safety off as he rested his warm cheek on the cold, hard plastic stock of his M-16. Though the militia sergeant was the most obvious target, Nathan's immediate concern was for the safety of the helpless Apache crewman. The young staff officer laid the sights of his weapon onto the one militiaman who was following the pair carrying the crewmen. He, and not the sergeant or his two companions struggling with their burden, posed the greatest threat to the crewman. Squeezing off a quick three-round burst, Nathan eliminated that threat.

Even before his mark had toppled over, Nathan was shifting the muzzle of his weapon over toward the pair hauling the Apache crewman. Those two, having heard their leader shriek out a warning one second, and then witnessing the death of a comrade right before their eyes the next, had already let go of the wounded American. While Nathan was bringing his sights to bear on them, each was responding to the crisis he faced in accordance with his own particular nature. The man who had been holding up the crewman's right arm dropped to the ground like a rock. Whether by choice, or because the weight of his charge dragged him down with it did not matter. That action saved his life, at least for the moment, leaving Nathan but one target.

With an ease that was out of all proportion to the lethality that followed it, Nathan took aim, drew a deep breath, held it, and slowly applied pressure to the trigger of his rifle. The three-round burst this sequence unleashed caught the brutish militiaman square in the stomach. The impact caused the man to jerk forward, thrusting his midsection out, as if to absorb more quickly the trio of 5.56mm projectiles that were tearing their way through it. Staggered and shocked, the stricken militiaman maintained self-control only long enough to bring his hands up to his fresh wound, look down at it with stunned disbelief, and let out a pitiful moan before falling away.

All this took no more than five seconds. Yet the entire

tactical situation before Nathan was altered. Two of the militiamen were down and no longer in play. The militia sergeant, whose alarm had triggered the action, was on the ground. In all the confusion he had failed to take note of Nathan. Instead, the ethnic Hungarian was focused on the tree line before him, launching salvos of fire at a target Nathan could not see, off to his right. In response to this, well-measured automatic fire was coming out of the woods, kicking up snow and dirt all around him. The Apache crewman, as well as the surviving militiamen who had been carrying him, had all but disappeared into the landscape somewhere between the bodies of the two militiamen Nathan had dispatched.

The report of the automatic fire directed at the militia sergeant, as well as the twinkling of an occasional tracer round, told Nathan that the fire he was observing was coming from a SAW. But whose SAW? Was it Reisniack's, the SAW gunner from the 2nd Squad? Or had Reider brought up the rest of the platoon? Nathan had no way of knowing. Unable simply to stand fast where he was while the action continued, Nathan was about to pull back, away from the edge of the tree line in order to shift to the right and find out for sure, when a fusillade of automatic weapon fire erupted from that direction. The echo of gunfire off the barren trees distorted the report of small-arms fire, magnifying the sound of the battle being waged just out of sight.

Through all the cacophony flooding ears that were still ringing from the rocket's near miss, Nathan thought he was able to count two, maybe three M-16s. Together with the SAW that continued to hammer away, this meant that only one squad was engaged. The rest of the platoon, Nathan realized, was still probably back on the trail, where they had been told to wait. Deciding that he had already wasted far too much time sorting all this out, Nathan again ignored prudence. Standing up, he turned his back on the growing firefight and made his way, as fast as he could, to the trail and, he hoped, two squads ready to be led into combat.

The sudden exchange of fire between Reisniack and the militiamen he had been watching, out in the field to their left, caught both Reider and Kittridge off guard. Reider, who was just finishing up explaining how he wanted his acting platoon sergeant to bring the rest of the platoon up and deploy it, stood upright and turned toward the sound of gunfire. Had anyone had the time to consider the young officer's expression, they would have been surprised to note that rather than sporting a look that betrayed confusion or surprise, Reider's face was a study of frustration and resignation. Like everything else the platoon leader had tried to do over the past few days, his latest maneuver was stillborn. Even as he looked about, trying to get a firm grasp on the new situation that was unfolding before him, a fresh volley of gunfire, from the direction they had been traveling in, rippled through the leafless branches above him.

This new menace from an unseen foe was still not enough to drive Gerald Reider to ground. Instead, he continued to stand, upright, looking over to his right, away from the ongoing exchange between Reisniack and the militiamen in the field. In part his failure to seek cover, as Kittridge already had, was due to confusion. For a moment Gerald Reider didn't know which way was up, or where true safety lay. But there was more to Reider's failure to appreciate the danger his current stance placed him in. He was angry. Frustrated and angry. Clenching his fists, Reider saw this latest debacle as reinforcing the sorry fact that all his efforts over the past three days had been stymied, overruled, or ignored at every turn. As an officer and a leader, he had been neutered by Nathan Dixon's interference and eventual assumption of command. To a man of Reider's temperament and ambitions, this humiliating evisceration was intolerable. So while he looked this way and then that, assessing the situation, Gerald Reider resolved that he was going to hold his ground, right then and there, and not budge an inch until he was physically forced to yield or . . .

Then it hit him, just like that. In the midst of confused gunfire, with rounds zinging this way and that past his head, Gerald Reider realized that he was going to die. The term "mortal combat" suddenly took on a whole new, and very definitive, meaning.

With a calmness he had never before experienced, Reider looked down on the ground at Staff Sergeant Kittridge. Using two dead trees as cover, the squad leader and acting platoon sergeant popped up, fired a few quick rounds in the direction of the new threat, then dropped back down before return fire could be directed his way. While lying on the ground between volleys, Kittridge stared up at his platoon leader. Bewildered, Kittridge said nothing. Yet the expression he wore asked, without saying a word, Why are you standing up like that, in the middle of all this? In response, Reider found himself smiling. If only you knew, Reider thought as he turned away and continued to survey the savaged woods around him. If only you knew.

Off to his right, the young West Pointer caught sight of Les Kim, exchanging fire with an unseen foe. That rifleman's face was set in an expression that betrayed all the fears, concerns, and the horror he felt at being caught in such a terrible place. And yet Kim continued to aim his weapon and fire in a manner more fitting to a range than the heat of battle. The lone rifleman paid no heed to his platoon leader's strange behavior, or anything else. Knowing that his very existence depended on returning fire, Kim was focused on doing just that, as quickly and effectively as he could.

To his left Reider noted that Reisniack was no longer firing. Instead, the SAW gunner was rolling on the ground. Both his hands were tightly clasped over his face, but not tightly enough to stop blood from oozing out between the black fingers of his gloves. This meant that the people in the field had prevailed. Even as he watched his stricken SAW gunner come to rest on his back and commence stomping his feet wildly, Reider could see a figure out in the field spring up, off the ground, and dash forward.

Mechanically, Reider brought his M-16 up to his shoulder. With measured ease, he pulled in his weapon's stock until it was firmly planted in his shoulder. A smattering of rounds, coming from somewhere off to his right, ripped into a tree behind Reider, throwing off a shower of tiny splinters that peppered the rear of Reider's helmet and flak vest. Undaunted by this distraction, the platoon leader took up a good sight picture. Peering through the pinhole of his rear sight, Gerald Reider aligned it with the front post of his rifle's sight. Just above that post, in the distance, Reider refocused his eyes until he could see the chest of the militiaman running toward him. Remembering, at the last moment, that his rifle tended to climb a bit when firing in the three-round burst mode, Reider lowered his aim point to about where the militiaman's belt buckle would be. Ready, Reider held what breath he had before firing.

Three quick nudges, each all but indistinguishable from the others, drove the butt of the rifle deeper into Reider's shoulder. Even before the ripping noise that accompanied the automatic firing of three rounds faded, the young officer saw that his target, who had been mere yards from cover and safety, now lay sprawled out on the ground. The militiaman's forward momentum, unchecked by the two rounds that had found their mark, sent the ethnic Hungarian careening, headfirst, through the snow for a couple of meters before coming to rest.

As before, Reider remained standing as he lowered his weapon. He found he could not take his eyes off the man he had brought down. Unlike the ambush at the road crossing the previous day, when everyone had fired wildly at distant figures and trucks, this had been a deliberate act of murder. Reider had taken the time to select exactly where he was aiming before executing a human being. Though he wanted so desperately to continue exploring his personal reflections on his actions, a round ricocheted off the side of his helmet, reminding him that the situation off to his right demanded attention. Still, the young officer could not help but take one more, longing look at the stricken figure in the snow. If this was what it felt like to kill, he found himself thinking, it was no wonder the church found it immoral and the state made it illegal.

Nathan had found Staff Sergeant Hernandes and the balance of the 3rd Platoon formed up and ready to advance toward the sound of the guns. The appearance of the battalion staff officer had come as a great relief to the Hispanic NCO, for now he would not have to lead his men forward blindly into an ambiguous situation. He didn't realize that Nathan, although he was animated and quick to issue his orders, was just as uncertain of what, exactly, was going on with Reider, the 2nd Squad, or the enemy they faced.

With safeties off, weapons held at the ready, and the word passed on to mark their target before firing, the soldiers of the 1st and 3rd squads advanced abreast of each other, with 3rd on the right, and 1st to the left. Between them was Nathan. Unable to tolerate the pressure the collar of his flak vest placed on his wound, Nathan had shed this bulky piece of body armor before stepping off. With nothing but two spare magazines stuffed into the lower pockets of his BDU pants, Nathan felt unencumbered. This reduction in personal baggage, combined with the agitation he felt, drove him forward with quick, springy steps. Bobbing and weaving, he flew through the light woods into what he hoped was the flank of the ethnic Hungarian position.

Not everyone kept pace with him. This was due less to the weight they carried than to the conviction each man felt, his dedication to duty, and his state of mind. Unlike Nathan, who had already felt the sting of battle, the men in the 1st and 3rd Squads hadn't whiffed freshly burnt gunpowder that day. Their bodies and souls had yet to be seduced by its strange, intoxicating allure. A lust for battle that permitted otherwise sane and civilized men to turn into savages willing to expose themselves to mortal danger while slaying fellow human beings was still building. These soldiers had lingered too long on the trail, close enough to hear the fight, but not near enough to be galvanized by it. So while they moved forward, many found themselves struggling with more than the snow they were plowing through or the pace Nathan was setting. Fears engendered during the wait remained, slowing their pace and threatening to stay their hands.

For Sergeant Dubois, the idea of plunging headlong, blindly, into a firefight was a horrific idea that all but paralyzed him. He was a cautious man, a person who had to see everything and know, in advance, where he was supposed to go and what he was expected to do before sallying forth. That was what made the Old Guard so appealing to him. Everything was so well regimented, so meticulously planned and rehearsed. This rushing around, with little more guidance than "Follow me," was terrifying. Had the habit of blind obedience, another hallmark of the Old Guard, not been so deeply rooted in him, Dubois wondered if he would have gone forward.

Given a choice, he would not have been alone. On the far left of the line rushing forward, Hector Santiago muttered to himself as he fought the urge to let the others go forward, ahead of him. Wide-eyed, the Hispanic rifleman found himself praying unabashedly to the Virgin Mother one moment, and then, with the next breath, cursing the day he walked off the street into the Army recruiting office.

Back then, he reminded himself, it had all made sense. It had been the smart thing to do. The Army gave him an out. It took him away from the barrio and the gang violence that he had become convinced would one day claim his life. In the Army he could finish an education he had never before valued. Perhaps he could learn a skill. Everything, that day, had been possible, all sunshine and promises.

This bitter reflection was cut short. The deep, throaty report of a large-caliber machine gun ripped through the woods from somewhere off to Santiago's right. Reminded that his next moment could very well be his last, he threw himself into a fresh recital of "Hail Mary, full of grace."

"We've got to get the hell out of here, lieutenant!"

The words floated up to Gerald Reider from Dick Kittridge, who was at that moment in the process of slamming a new magazine into his rifle. "That's a 12.7 mike firing," he yelled in reference to the new sound that reverberated off the trees around them. "They'll fucking cut us to pieces, one man at a time."

For the first time since the firing had started, Reider made an effort to find cover. Dropping down on one knee, he took a post behind a tree half as wide as he was. These actions did very little to improve his chances of surviving, though. Not that this concerned the second lieutenant. "We can't," he stated calmly. "Both men, off to the left and right, are down. The SAW gunner, I think, is still alive."

Having become totally absorbed in his own little struggle, Kittridge realized, for the first time since going to ground, that he had taken no notice of what the other men in his squad had been doing. Reider's words, spo-

ken with a casualness that did not match the cruelty of
their message, shocked the squad leader. Lifting his
head up, above the level of the logs that he had been
using for cover, Kittridge looked left, then right. Both
men were down, just as his platoon leader had said. And
though he didn't see any motion from either, Kittridge
had no reason to doubt Reider's assumption about Reisniack.

Sickened by the sight of men entrusted to his care cut
down like that, Kittridge slumped back down and rolled
over onto his back. He lay there for a moment, looking
up at Reider. The young officer was returning fire with
a methodical deliberateness that was out of place at a
time like this. While observing his lieutenant's phleg-
matic response to enemy fire, the professional NCO
came to the inescapable conclusion that he had failed.
He had lost his entire squad. First the Bradley and the
men with it. Then he had abandoned Dave Foss at the
road crossing. And now Reisniack and Kim. He had
been unable to protect them and keep them safe.

He had also failed, he told himself as he watched Reider, to provide wise and timely council to his newly assigned platoon leader. It had taken another officer, a
stranger to the company, to take his lieutenant in hand
and guide him along. When that battalion staff officer
wasn't present, and it had fallen to him to keep Reider
from committing them to an ill-advised course of action,
Kittridge realized he had failed there, too. And on top
of those failures, as the sounds of battle continued to
echo through the woods around him, Kittridge came to
appreciate that he had been unable to prevail, as an
individual combat infantryman, over his enemy.

The eruption of M-16s and SAWs off to his right, and
the sound of Nathan Dixon's voice as he shouted orders
and directed the fire of the rest of the platoon as it
closed in for the kill, failed to stir Staff Sergeant Richard
Kittridge. An overwhelming sense of anger, frustration,

loss, and the stress of the past three days, were all too much. Gripping his rifle tightly with both hands and rocking his head back and forth in the snow, Kittridge broke down and began to weep.

26

Slowly, Nathan made his way back to the trail where he had dropped his flak vest. He had informed Staff Sergeant Hernandes that he wanted to recover that item before it became dark. When that NCO volunteered to send one of his men back for it, Nathan declined the offer. The truth was that Nathan needed to have some time alone. With the third day of this odyssey fast coming to a close with no end in sight, and in light of the disastrous results of their confrontation with the militia unit, Nathan was faced with the realization that his own ability to carry on, much less lead and inspire the dispirited troops under his command, was fast ebbing away.

In the silence and solitude of the woods, an old quote, from the Duke of Wellington shortly after the Battle of Waterloo in 1815, came to mind. In response to a lady who had been speaking of the glories of his triumph over Napoleon, Wellington commented that the only thing more dreadful than a great victory was a great defeat. This sentiment pretty much summed up how Nathan felt about the outcome of the skirmish between the 3rd Platoon and the ethnic-Hungarian Kommando they had run up against. It had been anything but a great victory.

Even now, a full hour after the last shot had been fired, Nathan was still assessing the true costs of their latest encounter. These far transcended the physical injuries sustained and the psychological impact those casualties had on the other members of the platoon. One of those losses was the thin thread of hope that helicopters would swoop in, snatch them up, and whisk them away to safety. That dream had been cut short by the actions of the militiamen. Even worse, the platoon's ability to march its way out was now compromised not only by the casualties it had suffered, but by the addition of prisoners, both wounded and unwounded, the victory had produced. Hope, that glimmering, immeasurable commodity that drives men on to accomplish things that logic tells them is impossible, disappeared.

Were he nothing more than a simple rifleman, with no concern other than caring for the weapon he carried and following orders, Nathan could have slumped down on the ground, let his head hang down, and bemoaned their fate as so many of his men were doing. But Nathan was an officer, a leader. Out here, in these woods, he was the senior American present, a point he had taken great pains to stress during his confrontations with Reider. Nathan was their leader. As such he held the key to their success. His responsibilities did not end with the development of a plan that would carry them through. Even more fundamental than that aspect of leadership, even more critical when faced with adverse conditions and odds, was the requirement placed on a leader to provide the spark necessary to ignite the souls of the men under his command.

Soldiers, be they professionals or conscripts, hardened veterans or part-time militia, had to be inspired. Men asked to place their lives on the line and prevail over their foes had to be led. Leaders, either through physical example or with appeals to the emotions of their subordinates, were still necessary in the age of the computer chip. At times, a leader found he had to be a cheerleader, employing words of encouragement or inspiration to achieve his ends. At other times, circumstances dictated that he be a slave driver, lashing his men onward with unbridled threats or even abuse. More often than not, a leader found himself bouncing back and forth between these two extremes within the span of minutes, or even seconds, depending upon whom he was addressing or what needed to be done.

All of this, of course, places great demands on anyone who leads. The strength, drive, judgment, and fortitude necessary to function effectively in that role must come from within. This is especially true when the leader is isolated from his own commander, unable to seek guidance, comfort, and encouragement from his immediate superior. The combat leader must reach deep within himself and summon the courage and fortitude needed to see him through. A combat leader cannot abdicate his responsibilities or simply excuse himself from them if, for some reason, he feels unable to carry on. While wisdom and logic sometimes dictate such a course, especially when the leader is wounded, such a relinquishment of authority in the face of the enemy has never been a viable option to Western warriors. It is more than simple machismo that drives a man to carry on when common sense dictates he step aside. It's just the way things are.

When he reached the trail, Nathan was able to locate his flak vest without much difficulty. But rather than bend over and snatch it up, Nathan plopped down upon it, using it as a seat cushion. Closing his eyes, the young battalion staff officer unsnapped the chin strap of his helmet. Slowly, Nathan leaned forward in an effort to relieve the pain his wound was causing him. In the process his helmet fell away of its own accord. Nathan ignored the crunching noise the helmet made. Instead, he slowly removed the glove on his right hand. Clearing his mind of all thoughts, he took a few moments to explore the bandage about his neck by feeling it with his fingers. Though it smarted to do so, Nathan applied pressure on the wound, in part to see just how much pain he could tolerate, and in part to see if the bandage was soaked through with his own blood.

Nathan was in the midst of this self-examination when a voice called out to him. "Sir, could I have a word with you?"

Startled, Nathan looked up to see Staff Sergeant Hernandes standing mere feet from where he sat. The sight of this man so close to him, without having been detected, demonstrated to Nathan just how badly his hearing had been affected by the detonation of the rocket that had missed him. Recovering as quickly as he could, Nathan nodded. "Yes, of course." He gestured with his left hand to the ground before him. "Have a seat."

After looking around, Hernandes found a suitable spot and settled down. "Sir," the NCO started, "the platoon's pretty well beat up."

Nathan, who had continued to probe his wound, had his head cocked back. He looked over at Hernandes out of the corner of his eye. The man's face, like his voice, betrayed no emotion. "We were lucky the other day, with Jefferson. His wounds were light enough to ignore and go on. I'm afraid we can't do that now."

Nathan moved his head slowly till he faced Hernandes square on. "I know that."

"Smollett has done the best he could, but I'm afraid he's out of his league. The round Reisniack took to his face shattered his jaw and tore things up. Not only is the lower jaw hanging by a thread, Smollett is unable to do anything about the internal bleeding. He's afraid if we move Reisniack, we'll lose him."

"What about the other man?" Nathan asked as he continued to explore his own wound.

"Kim's kneecap was pretty much blown away. There's not a lot of bleeding, but the man is in a great deal of pain. Every time we move him, he howls."

"And Kittridge?"

Hernandes paused before responding. Dick Kittridge was more than a fellow NCO and squad leader. He was a friend. The Hispanic NCO had no way of knowing, for sure, if his companion's mental collapse was a temporary condition that would pass, given a chance. Hernandes had already justified, in his own mind, Kittridge's behavior. So the leader of the 3rd Squad hesitated while he carefully chose his words, never suspecting that Nathan had already come to a conclusion.

"Dick," Hernandes started slowly, "I mean Sergeant Kittridge, will be right as rain, sir, as soon as he gets a chance to rest and sort things out. You'll see."

Nathan looked back at the NCO seated before him. Though hardly ready, physically and mentally, to resume his role, the young staff officer once more took up the mask of command and became the leader of this forlorn band of infantrymen. "We haven't the time or luxury of doing that, Sergeant Hernandes," Nathan stated in a manner that made it clear to the NCO that a decision had been made. "You're now acting platoon sergeant."

Though in his heart he wanted to appeal this verdict in favor of preserving his friend's position, as well as his career, Angel Hernandes knew Nathan was right. Reluctantly, the Hispanic NCO nodded his assent.

"What of the militiamen?" Nathan asked in an effort to change subjects as quickly as possible. "What kind of shape are they in?"

Hernandes drew in a deep breath, cleared any lingering thoughts he still entertained concerning Kittridge, and presented his assessment. "Two of them are lightly wounded and will be able to walk on their own. One is definitely a stretcher case, and the other could go either way."

"So we have four men that have to be carried, and sixteen men, counting you and I, to do the carrying," Nathan summarized.

"That's if we count the two uninjured Hungarians," Hernandes countered.

Finally ready to stir from his spot on the ground, Nathan gave his new number-one NCO a cold, hard stare. "Oh, they'll carry their own, sergeant. Either that, or we'll leave them here to freeze to death."

The Hispanic NCO nodded his consent.

"By the way," Nathan asked when he was on his feet. "Do any of them speak English?"

Hernandes, also on his feet by now, hesitated. "I think one of them does, but I'm not sure. He keeps watching us and straining to hear what's being said as if he does."

"Well," Nathan stated flatly, "Let's go see what we can get out of him. Perhaps he can lead us someplace where we can hunker down for the night and sort ourselves out."

The young officer was in the process of bending over, slowly so as to minimize his pain, when Staff Sergeant Hernandes squatted down and recovered both Nathan's helmet and flak vest. "Here, sir. Let me."

Touched by this show of kindness and sympathy, Nathan straightened up. Perhaps, he thought, all was not lost.

All eyes were on Nathan when he reentered the small circle formed by the members of the 3rd Platoon. Nathan knew this. He knew they were watching him in an effort to gauge his determination, his ability to carry on, his capacity to lead. Now, more than ever, the soldiers who made up the 3rd Platoon appreciated the terrible fact that their collective survival depended on his competence and skills.

Some, like Everett Cash, were skeptical about their chances. In Nathan's absence Cash had freely expressed his views with Hector Santiago. He voiced his opinion loud enough for Sergeant Bobby Dubois to hear. Dubois, still shaken by the unwelcome realization that he, himself, had failed to rise adequately to the crisis they had faced, did nothing to silence Santiago's biting remarks. Only Nathan's appearance brought Cash's harsh rhetoric to an end. Yet even as they watched, both Dubois and Santiago glanced between the officer and Cash, who viewed the battalion staff officer with the same contemptuous stare as he did their common foe.

Unaware, and unconcerned with such thoughts among his own, Nathan followed Hernandes over to where the ethnic Hungarians were gathered. "He's the one," the newly appointed platoon sergeant announced, pointing to one of the two unwounded militiamen.

With a wave of his hand, Nathan motioned to the man Hernandes had indicated. "You, on your feet."

The militiaman, feigning ignorance, continued to sit where he was while deliberately looking away from Nathan. For a moment, Nathan said nothing as neither man moved. Then, with a speed that surprised everyone, Nathan brought his right foot up, cocked his leg like a hammer being raised, and brought the heel of his boot crashing down into the side of the militiaman's head. Even as the prisoner of war rolled over onto his side in the snow, Nathan advanced on his victim and lifted his foot again in preparation to follow up his first blow. "I said get on your feet, you motherfucker," Nathan growled as the militiaman struggled to recover. Lifting his hand, in part to signify his submission, in part to ward off the next strike, the militiaman staggered about. "Stop!" he called out in desperation. "I speak English."

Slowly, Nathan planted his foot back on the ground, calling on all his strength as he did so, to mask the agony his actions and wound were causing him. When he was composed, and the militiaman was on his feet and facing him, Nathan advanced. "You're a heavy weapons unit," Nathan snapped. "Not an infantry Kommando."

Still dazed, the militiaman responded without hesitation. "Yes, support squad."

"You brought your weapons here on foot," Nathan continued, framing his question in the form of a definitive statement, and thus creating in the confused mind of the militiaman the illusion that Nathan already knew the answer.

"Yes, we carry them here, by hand. All of them."

Realizing that he had the upper hand, for the moment, Nathan pressed on. "You will lead us to your safe house now."

This caused the English-speaking militiaman to hesitate. While still holding his hand to the side of his face, the ethnic Hungarian looked into Nathan's eyes. This was met with a cold, unfeeling stare. Nathan pointed to the wounded militiamen without breaking eye contact. "These are your comrades, your friends. If you do not lead us to your safe house, now, we shall leave them here, to freeze to death during the coming night, or die at the hands of the Slovakian Army."

Seeing no compassion in his captor's eyes, the ethnic-Hungarian militiaman gazed over at his wounded comrades, lying in the bloodstained snow. When he finally looked back at Nathan, his defiance was gone. For a moment, the militiaman hung his head low before Nathan, staring at the ground between them. Then he lifted his head. "For my brother, and his friend, I do that."

Concealing both the relief and satisfaction that this capitulation brought, Nathan turned to Hernandes. "There should be food and medical supplies there. We'll hunker down for the night where it's warm and figure out what to do next." Nathan deliberately announced this last decision loud enough so that every man present could hear it. At this point, given their sorry state, the young staff officer felt that a carrot, and not the stick, was what he needed to rally his men and get them moving again.

He was right. Even before the new platoon sergeant acknowledged Nathan's order and turned to organize the platoon for movement, they were stirring. Only one man continued to sit, off to one side, and watch as if he were a disinterested spectator with nothing to do with the goings on. Feeling more depressed than he had ever felt before in his life, Gerald Reider made no effort to get up. What, after all, was the point? As with Kittridge, this last fight had inflicted a wound on him that cut as deep as those sustained by Reisniack and Kim. Though no blood oozed from it, it was just as crippling. Second Lieutenant Gerald Reider was, psychologically, a broken man.

27

SOUTHWESTERN SLOVAKIA,
LATE EVENING, FEBRUARY 7

Throughout the evening no one spoke unless he had to. Each squad, settled into its own corner of the small, stone farmhouse, kept to itself. Within these small knots of men, those soldiers who dwelt on the day's events kept their own counsel. In part, this was due to their exhaustion. Irregular rations, physical exertions, lack of sleep, and the psychological stress of combat had taken their toll. While the effects of each of these degenerative elements varied from individual to individual, overall, each man in the 3rd Platoon was pretty much whipped. There was another, more subtle reason why no one went out of his way to discuss what had happened, or speculated on their chances of successfully making it back to the battalion. They all understood their collective plight. In this small, select gathering of soldiers, they had all pretty much seen and heard everything there was to see and hear. Nathan Dixon's view of the world was no different from theirs, and his sources for gathering information concerning his situation no better. Each man, even the lowest-ranking individual present, suspected that their situation, after the destruction of the Apache that afternoon and the heavy casualties they had sustained, wasn't going to improve anytime soon.

While their men wolfed down food in silence almost as quickly as it was passed out to them, Nathan and Angel Hernandes sat at a table in the middle of the room. The map they had been poring over lay between them, lit by an oil lamp that had not been properly cleaned in months. Even as Specialist Smollett finally finished with tending to the more severely wounded and cleaned Nathan's wound, the battalion staff officer and the senior NCO discussed their plans for the next day.

It was an awkward way of conducting business. With his forehead pressed down onto the tabletop to keep his head and neck steady, and his hands tightly grasping the edges of the table, Nathan spoke to Hernandes in low, guarded tones. "Listen, I'm less thrilled about the choices we have to make than you. But I don't see any other way out of this."

Leaning back in his chair, Hernandes folded his arms. His chin almost touched his chest as he watched the medic carefully suture the gash in Nathan's neck. With nothing in his bag or in the sparse medical chest the militiamen had pulled out of their stores to kill the pain, Nathan had to endure this ordeal cold, stone sober. Even as he spoke, Hernandes could see the officer's knuckles turn white, and his words become labored as Nathan struggled to ignore the pain. "It would be . . . simply . . . a matter of time before . . . a Slovakian patrol got around to checking . . ."

Pausing, Nathan closed his eyes and drew in a deep breath as Smollett pierced his skin with the point of his needle on one side of the gash, then the other. Slowly,

Nathan picked up where he had left off as the medic drew the thread through, brought the needle around, and gently tugged on it. "To stay back at the woods, waiting for someone from Brigade to find us," Nathan blurted out during this break, "would have been dumb."

Hernandes nodded. "I agree. But I think leaving the bulk of the platoon here, while three men take off in search of Brigade, is equally unsmart."

Nathan didn't reply right away, waiting instead for Smollett to push the needle through the torn skin of his neck first. The burning pain that racked Nathan was almost too much for him to bear. Simultaneously he pulled, with all his might, inward and upward on the edges of the table while pressing his head down onto its rough surface. Had the table not been a sturdy, well-constructed piece of furniture, Nathan would have folded in on himself.

But the table held, and Nathan was finally able to respond. "You know these men. They respect you and will follow you. Your place is here, keeping them together."

To this Hernandes made no response. He knew Nathan was right. He also appreciated the risk the young officer was taking. If, in his absence, something happened to the 3rd Platoon, Nathan would be branded a coward, an officer who had run out on his men. The loss of a promising career, compared to that, would be trivial.

"If we were east of where Fort Apache was, in the contested zone," Nathan justified, as much to himself as to Hernandes, "I would have let you go. You know that area. You and your men have been operating there for months. But the sector between Fort Apache and the Brigade base is staff officer country, where REMFs like me run back and forth all the time." This attempt at humor was cut short by another, fresh stitch.

As before, Hernandes merely nodded in assent, even though Nathan could not see this, as he watched the medic tie off the wound and begin to clean it up. "Tilton's a good choice, but are you sure," Hernandes asked, "you want Cash?"

Sensing the end of his ordeal with Smollett was near when he felt Benadine flow down his neck in little rivulets, Nathan relaxed. "He's tough. He may not like officers, especially white officers, but he's tough. I think he'll keep going, and keep up, just to show he's better than me. Besides, my choices are limited. You need the SAW gunners, and I need to travel light. Flak vests stay. Each of us will carry two spare magazines, a canteen, and our medical pouches. I'll take Reider's GPS and my map. That's all."

The mention of his platoon leader's name caused Staff Sergeant Hernandes to make a face. "I know you have other things to consider, sir," the Hispanic NCO stated slowly. "But what about the lieutenant? He will be, after you leave, the senior man present. Isn't that going to be a bit, uh, awkward, for the two of us?"

At this point, the medic interrupted. "Sir, could you sit up and stay still. I'm ready to bandage your neck."

Happy to comply, Nathan sat upright. "Just don't make it too tight," he advised the medic. "I'd hate to be fragged by my own medic."

Both Smollett and Hernandes could not help but smile at this unexpected stab at humor. "If you asked me for my professional opinion, sir, I think it's a bad idea for you to go," Smollett ventured.

With his eyes closed, Nathan sat still while the medic's fingers worked their way around his neck, unrolling a clean, fresh bandage. "Well, I'm afraid I'll have to ignore your medical advice, specialist. I'm going."

"Officers," Smollett mumbled. "I'd rather work on ten bitching and moaning buck privates than one dedicated officer. They never do what's good for them."

Picking up the lighthearted tone of the conversation, Hernandes threw in. "Didn't you know it's part of their oath as officers? Not only are they obliged to defend and uphold the Constitution, they must dedicate their lives to busting the hump of every medic they come across."

"That's right, Smollett," Nathan added. "So don't you forget it."

"In that case, sir," Smollett replied after winking at Hernandes, "I need to retie this bandage. I think it's way too loose."

Having felt the medic tie off the loose ends, Nathan opened his eyes, placed his right hand up to feel Smollett's handiwork, and waved him off with the other. "Trooper, I think you're finished here, thank you."

With a nod from Hernandes, Smollett gathered up his equipment. "Sir, it's been a pleasure."

Taking great care not to cause himself any undue pain, Nathan nodded. "I wish I could say the same."

Before leaving the two men alone, Smollett gave Nathan a handful of aspirin for the pain. Nathan promptly took four of them, without benefit of water.

With the medic gone, Hernandes returned to the last point he was trying to make. "Sir, Lieutenant Reider?"

"Oh, you needn't worry," Reider stated in a low, almost hushed voice as he emerged from the shadows. "I know the score."

Hernandes, caught off guard by the appearance of his erstwhile superior, stared at his platoon leader with wide eyes. Nathan, on the other hand, merely glanced at the West Pointer. "What, exactly, is it you understand?" Nathan asked calmly.

Making an effort to get up, the acting platoon sergeant leaned forward toward Nathan.

"Perhaps I should go check the outpost."

Nathan brought his hand down and faced the NCO. "No. This concerns you as as much as anyone else. It's best if you stand fast."

Though visibly uncomfortable with the idea of becoming caught between these two officers, Hernandes eased back and watched as Nathan turned his attention on Reider. "You understand the situation, lieutenant," Nathan stated flatly, "and what needs to be done if any of us are to survive."

Reider nodded. "Yes, of course."

"And you understand my concerns, vis-à-vis the leadership issue," Nathan declared.

"Look, Lieutenant Dixon," Reider replied in a tone that betrayed his frustrations as he advanced to the table, grabbed a chair, and swung it around under him. Sitting on it backward, with his hands gripping the top of the backrest, Reider stared down at it. "I screwed up. I know that now. I know that I wasn't ready to lead this patrol." Pausing, he looked up, first at Hernandes, then at Nathan. "I let my pride, and arrogance, I guess, get in the way of common sense and logic."

"There's no need to apologize, Lieutenant Reider," Nathan started to say, "I'm sure . . ."

Reider didn't permit his superior to finish his thought. "I'm not apologizing." For a moment, the two officers stared at each other, with Nathan showing a bit of confusion. "What I mean to say," Reider explained, "is that I understand what you were trying to tell me this morning. I have a lot to learn, from you, from my NCOs, from people who have done this sort of thing before. That my attitude kept me from tapping into that knowledge is a personal problem, one I need to deal with. But," he hastened to add, "that doesn't mean that I'm a complete idiot when it comes to tactics."

"I never said you were," Nathan countered.

"You never gave me a chance."

With a slight nod of his head, Nathan acknowledged the point. "Touché."

"What I am trying to say, Dixon," Reider stated but then paused to reflect on what he was about to say. "What I am asking, is that you let me do my job. I may not be the fastest learner in the world, but one thing I have come to appreciate over the past three days is that I don't have all the answers. I don't even know what half the questions are. But I've watched you, listened to what you've said and done, and believe I can hold out here, working with Sergeant Hernandes, while you're gone."

This brought a smirk to Nathan's face, one that, for a moment, infuriated Reider, for the young second lieutenant thought the older officer was gloating. But this thought quickly disappeared as Nathan spoke. "I wish I had all the answers. And I wish half the decisions I've made since setting out on this adventure had been good ones."

Then Nathan's expression changed as he looked into Reider's eyes. "The cold hard facts are that I'm as lost as you are. I'm making up my plans as I go. I can no more guarantee you that Brigade will be where it was than I can that I will make it there, in one piece, in time. The only difference between you and me, from day one, was that I had the advantage of having a little more experience than you. I've had a chance to learn what's up and what's down in this shit hole of a country while everyone else was learning. Hell," Nathan proclaimed as he leaned back in his chair and threw his hand up, "if you make it out of this alive, you're going to be more qualified as a combat leader than ninety-nine percent of your fellow classmates."

A hush fell over the room, and Nathan and Reider looked at each other, waiting for the other to speak. It was Hernandes who finally broke the silence. "Lieutenant Dixon," he stated dryly, "I have no reason to doubt that Lieutenant Reider and I can work together."

Drawing in a deep breath, Nathan answered, without ever taking his eyes off Reider. "I am confident, sergeant, that the two of you will do well."

With that, Nathan stood up and looked down at his watch. "I want to leave at oh four hundred hours. Wake me and the others going with me at oh three hundred. We'll need to eat and go over our route before we set out."

Hernandes nodded. Then he glanced at Reider. "The lieutenant and I will take turns sleeping as soon as I make the rounds with him and check the Ops and wounded."

"Your people are pretty well beat up, lieutenant," Nathan warned Reider as he gathered his things off the table. "Don't cut them any slack. This is neither the time nor place to start cultivating the image of being a nice guy."

Reider nodded. "I understand, sir."

Looking up, Nathan found himself wondering if he really did. Because if the young second lieutenant before him didn't, then the staff officer realized that his decision to give in to Reider's appeal would be the biggest mistake he ever made.

Before dawn, those soldiers of the 3rd Platoon lucky enough still to be sleeping were roused for stand-to. This military ritual is repeated daily, or whenever a commander considers his force to be in imminent danger. It requires that all members of the command be at their assigned fighting positions, with all weapons up and covering assigned sectors of responsibility. On occasion, a commander will use this time to tour those positions to inspect the readiness of his troops, the conditions of their weapons, or the adequacy of the dispositions he has made. On this morning Gerald Reider, accompanied by Staff Sergeant Hernandes, made the rounds to check all three.

The safe house that had been the base of operations for the ethnic-Hungarian Kommando that 3rd Platoon had run into was no different than many of those that dotted the area. It was an ancient structure, set well back from a little-used road. It looked more like a miniature fortress than the home of a peaceful farmer. The fact was that the people who built the place at a time when the United States was nothing more than an unexplored wilderness needed a sanctuary strong enough to protect themselves and their animals from outsiders. This particular farmstead had escaped destruction by Protestant and Catholic armies that tramped around the countryside for thirty years in an effort to determine which true God was *the* true God. The gates of the farmstead had been locked securely in a vain effort to keep those infected with plague from spreading that dreaded disease to the occupants of the place. In the mid-1700s, Prussian and Austrian eagles had passed its doorstep as the monarchs of those kingdoms fought for the control of land they would never step foot on. Later, Cossacks would ride by and loot the place, once in 1813 after driving Napoleon out of Russia, and again in 1945, while pursuing the armies of another dictator who had dared to violate Mother Russia.

While darkness gave way to another gray, cheerless dawn, Gerald Reider followed Staff Sergeant Hernandes as they made their rounds. In the process, the young officer considered both the assets he had in hand and the terrain on which his platoon had to be prepared to defend itself. The farmstead itself was small and modest. It consisted of two structures, one of which was a two-story house and the other a barn. Both were constructed of stone and masonry walls that were a good twelve inches thick. The walls that enclosed the small area that separated them did not stand alone but rather were extensions of the structures themselves. This arrangement formed a rectangle, with the house occupying the southeastern corner of the box, facing the road, while the barn sat in the northwestern corner. The six-foot-high wall that connected them formed the remaining sides of the rectangle.

Around this artificial island of whitewashed stone were fields and orchards. To the front of the house, nothing stood between it and the road except three hundred meters of open ground. Stone walls, standing waist high, broke this intervening terrain up into several small fields and lined the well-rutted path leading up to

a gate that stood just to the right of the house. The last
of these walls was just under one hundred meters from
the road itself. Here, adjacent to the path, Hernandes
and Nathan had placed a two man OP/LP the night
before. Under the cover of darkness, the men assigned
to this position had had little to worry about when they
were there, and while moving to and from it as that duty
was rotated. With daylight fast approaching, however,
Reider could see that anyone left out there was both
terribly exposed and isolated. If forced to make a run
for the farmhouse, they would have no choice but to
vault the walls that lay between their position and the
rest of the platoon. Supporting fire from the house
would have, in Reider's opinion, little chance of staving
off the inevitable. Either the men in the roadside OP
would be pinned, unable to move or defend themselves,
or they would be picked off as they popped up to jump
the walls in their way. After pointing this out to Hernandes, both men agreed that they would abandon this
post during the day. If it turned out that they were still
there in the evening, the OP/LP would be remanned
after darkness.

To the east, or left, of the house as one looked at the
place from the road, stood a small orchard. Unlike the
fields before it, the orchard was surrounded by a three-
strand barbed wire fence held up by rough wooden
posts. Even if this fence had been in good repair, it
would not have been much of an obstacle. Neglect and
abuse, due to the long absence of a tenant in the house,
made it even less so. Here and there strands of barbed
wire had snapped, coiling themselves up near the posts
and leaving wide gaps. The only thing the orchard did
was break up a clear field of fire, from the house, into
and past that quarter.

To the rear of the farmstead were open pastures with
nothing breaking them up other than a small pigsty
tucked in next to the outer wall of the barn. In the distance, at a range of about 150 meters, was a hedge, be-

ond which were woods. These were the same woods
that the 3rd Platoon had been in, several kilometers
away, when they had spotted the Apaches and then engaged the militia Kommando. It was out of these woods,
and across the pastures behind the house, that the platoon, carrying its wounded and escorting its prisoners,
had moved the night before. In the light of day, Reider
was shocked to note how much the path they had beaten
down in the snow while doing so stood out. This triggered the realization that this path extended beyond the
hedge, through the woods, and out to the tree line they
had fought in. Not only was the wreckage of the Apache
still sitting there, exposed to the casual observation of
anyone who happened to wander by, but nothing had
been done to hide the bodies of the militiamen they
had killed. Mental exhaustion, confusion brought on in
the aftermath of battle, and concern over their own
wounded had caused Lieutenant Dixon to abandon the
site without making an effort to conceal what had happened, or in which direction the participants had de-
parted. The fruits of this error, Reider realized, were
ones he just might have to reap.

Faced with a threat coming at them at the front of
the house, from the road, and one emerging from the
woods to the rear, Reider had to make plans to counter
either or, in a worst case scenario, both. On one hand,
the manpower he had available for this was rather slim.
With Nathan Dixon taking one man from the 1st and
3rd squads each, that left those units with three men.
The 2nd Squad, with Reisniack totally incapacitated,
Kim limited in his ability to move about, and Kittridge
still not recovered from his breakdown, would be of little use in a fight other than guarding prisoners. To this
pitifully small lot, Reider could add Sam Pavlovski, the
XTO, and Jeff Jefferson, the unemployed assistant Javelin gunner. Counting himself, he had nine able-bodied
combatants, two of questionable value, and one medic.

To the good, Reider discovered that he did not lack

for firepower. As is the normal practice, the proportion of automatic and crew-served weapons to men increases as a unit takes casualties. Rather than leave Reisniack's SAW behind at the tree line, or leave it lying around the house, Reider had Staff Sergeant Hernandes assign an ordinary rifleman to take it. In addition the ethnic Hungarian unit they had come across was, as Nathan had suspected from the start, a heavy weapons Kommando. The safe house where they'd gathered before sallying out to inflict retribution on their Slovakian foes was a virtual treasure trove of weapons. Despite the fact that they had disabled and abandoned the 12.7mm machine gun after the previous day's firefight, there were more than enough weapons cached at the farmstead to deal with just about any contingency. From antitank mines to shoulder-fired antitank rocket launchers, Reider and Hernandes found they had just about everything they needed. There was even an 81mm mortar with plenty of ammo, still in its shipping crate.

In the process of sorting through what could be of use, Reider became aware that their own ammunition was starting to run rather low. Over the past three days the 3rd Platoon had been engaged in three separate engagements, though not everyone in the platoon had been involved in all three. They had expended varying amounts of the basic loads that they had carried away from Fort Apache. Some, like Sergeant Bobby Duboi and his SAW gunner, Henry Smith, had hardly fired a shot. Les Kim, on the other hand, was down to less than two magazines. The redistribution of the ammunition completed shortly after their arrival at the safe house served only to accentuate the shortage.

In looking at the tactical dispositions, Reider found there was little he needed to change. The layout of the farmstead, as well as the terrain surrounding it, pretty much dictated how the soldiers within the platoon were dispersed. The 3rd Platoon faced two threats, each of which would be very different. The road presented the platoon with what is called a high-speed avenue of approach. A mounted attack, supported by tanks, could materialize out of nowhere and, in minutes, be knocking at the front gate of the farmyard. Conversely, anyone who followed the trail the 3rd Platoon had used the previous day would have to do so on foot. Of the two possibilities Reider imagined that he would prefer the latter, dismounted threat. There, the 3rd Platoon's firepower would be of some use. Against armor they would be all but defenseless.

To deal with either or both these possibilities, the squads had been deployed based on Nathan's assessment of their abilities. Having determined that the side of the farmstead facing the road posed the greatest threat to the platoon, he had posted the 3rd Squad to cover it shortly after they had arrived there. The 1st Squad, belonging to Sergeant Dubois, was to watch the back door. In the evening, when they were alone, Nathan had confided in Hernandes that he had greater confidence in his squad than the one led by Dubois. By the time Reider was brought back on board, neither man felt the need to inform the 2nd Lieutenant of the logic behind this choice, and he didn't think to question it.

That does not mean that there was nothing left for Reider to do, or that he was constrained from improving on it. A unit in the defense is not a unit at rest. Few commanders are gifted enough to see everything in a single glance. When a unit moves into a position it has not had time to recon, the leader of that unit throws his subordinate elements out as best he can based on a quick assessment. As time passes and the leader has an opportunity to study, in detail, both the positions themselves and the avenues of approach into that position, he makes adjustments. Fields of fire that cover the avenues of approach are established for each weapon. During these detailed studies, dead space, terrain features that block line of sight that lies within a unit's assigned sector, are identified. If a position cannot bring effective fire upon that dead space itself, other personnel or weapons are shifted about so that terrain that would give the enemy cover or an advantage is either eliminated or neutralized. Within a position, the defender prepares where he will be fighting from, selects and prepares alternate positions capable of covering the same ground, and, as time permits, recons other positions that cover secondary avenues of approach.

Preparing a position also means enhancing the survivability of the soldiers who will be fighting from those positions. In an open field this is accomplished by digging in, preparing a fighting position that is below the surface of the ground. While doing so, the soldier must fashion his position so that he can use his weapon. While a deep foxhole will go a long way toward ensuring that a man will survive incoming rounds, a prepared position that has no firing step, or is not fashioned so as to prevent a crew-served weapon from being operated effectively, is worthless. So preparing a fighting position is a delicate balance between protection and exposure.

Fighting from a structure presents challenges of their own. Modern weapons possess the ability to level the average structure in no time. Debris thrown off during this process can be, and often is, as deadly as the projectile that created it. Yet structures such as the farmhouse and barn offer a unit that is poor in resources and manpower an ideal place to hold. Had the house been made using standard building material available in the United States to create communities overnight, it would have been foolish to stay there. But the entire farm complex was built like a fortress, with materials capable of dulling the lethal edge of the most modern weapons. One simply had to know how to use this advantage.

A firefight is a brawl, a vicious engagement in which the quick and the dead are sorted out based on experience and the ability to respond well in chaos. A leader who finds himself in the midst of combat makes deci-ions based on fragmentary knowledge, snap judgment, and assumptions. Setting up and preparing a defensive position, on the other hand, is more akin to solving a problem in geometry. The commander preparing a defensive position goes about this task as an engineer would. He generally has the time to survey carefully the land he is expected to hold, consider the men, material, and weapons at hand, and take into account the forces that could be pitted against his creation. Establishing kill zones, selecting the angle of a weapon's sector of fire, judging the ability of various materials to withstand attack by high explosives, and other considerations critical to this task are all drilled into aspiring officers at West Point or in ROTC. This skill is further honed and practiced during their basic course at Fort Benning. So, as Gerald Reider assumed responsibility for the position that Nathan Dixon and Staff Sergeant Hernandes had laid out the night before, he was finally presented with a military problem for which he was truly prepared.

Taking his time, Reider toured the farmstead. He looked out of every window, taking in the view that it provided, noting what terrain features blocked his line of sight. As he went into another room, and looked out other windows, he would look back at the troublesome location previously noted to see if this new perspective provided a better shot into the dead space. When he was finished with his inspection of the positions themselves, Reider ventured out into the space between the road and the farm to look back at the farmstead so as to gain an appreciation of how the enemy would see it. Little by little, he built up a complete appreciation of what needed to be done.

While his officer was off, doing officer things, Staff Sergeant Hernandes was busy trying to make up for their lack of antitank weapons. In this the cache of weapons stockpiled at the farmhouse by the militia Kommando proved to be invaluable. On the downside, all of it was obsolete, weapons built during the Soviet era to counter a threat that no longer existed. As a member of NATO, Hungary was anxious to make room in it's ammo dumps for newer, more capable Western munitions. Rather than incur the cost of demilitarizing the Russian-built weapons and munitions, the Hungarian Army had provided it, gratis, to its ethnic brethren north of the Danube.

Chief among the weapons found by Hernandes were antitank rocket launchers of the old RPG type, and antitank mines. The NCO used the better part of the morning to train, as best he could, Jeff Jefferson, the assistant Javelin gunner, in the use of these RPGs. Since the batteries in the platoon's manpack radio were all but drained, Sam Pavlovski, the RTO, was also drafted to be a tank killer. Once these two men had demonstrated a basic understanding of how their newly assigned weapons worked, Hernandes had them preposition both launchers and antitank grenades. As the RPG had a considerable backblast, Hernandes was careful to assign them positions that would not interfere with other members of the platoon. He also took great pains to caution both his newly minted RPG gunners to use their earplugs. "If you do nothing else right, stop up your ears."

To this Pavlovski dryly replied, "If that's the only thing we do right, then my ears are the last thing I'm going to be worried about preserving."

With that chore taken care of, Hernandes moved on to laying mines. There are two ways of doing this. One is to dig a hole, place the mine in the hole, arm it, and cover it with the soil from the hole. The second technique is known as a surface lay, or hasty minefield. In this, the mine is simply placed on the ground, armed, and left. While this method is faster, the attacker, if he is alert, can see the mines and avoid them. Of course, a hasty minefield, properly placed, also has the advantage of slowing an attacker up by causing him to turn or back up while in the kill zone. All these maneuvers cost time,

ime that antitank gunners can use to perfect their aim
r, if necessary, take a second shot.

The ground, partially frozen and covered with pristine
now, ruled out burying the mines. While Pavlovski and
efferson brought the mines up, out of the crude cellar
where they had been stored, Hernandes placed them on
he ground and armed them. He selected three loca-
ions in which to deploy these weapons. The first was in
he path leading up to the farm, midway between the
oad and house. A vehicle coming up that path would
e caught, even if the driver or vehicle commander spot-
ed the mines, between the walls, on either side, the
nines to the front, and vehicles behind him. If he
acked up, he would cause a traffic jam that left his
ehicle, and all the others, open to continuous attack.
f he turned left or right, he not only exposed his more
ulnerable flanks to antitank fire, he faced the prospect
f climbing over the stone walls, a task that would dis-
upt his ability to return effective, well-aimed fire.
Though Hernandes had no way of knowing which of
hose options the lead vehicle would go for, all of them
ought time, a commodity that usually favors the de-
ender.

Generally a failed attack along one axis of attack is
ot repeated. So once the main belt of mines was set on
he trail leading up to the house, Hernandes used the
alance of the mines on either side of the stone walls
urrounding the fields facing the road and, as an insur-
nce policy, in the orchard to the right of the house.
his took much of the remainder of the morning and
good part of the afternoon to accomplish.

With his platoon sergeant occupied with those tasks,
eider continued to move about, from position to po-
ition, inspecting the individual preparations that the
oldiers assigned to them were making. Unlike actors in
Iollywood, soldiers are taught to avoid fighting from
indows whenever possible. In the first place, these
eady-made portals are big, offering minimal protection

to someone firing from one. Second, windows are easily spotted by an attacker in the distance. It is a simple matter for the commander of an attacking force to direct return fire using them as reference points. So, if time permits, soldiers prepare loopholes, or small openings in the walls of structures, that are low to the floor or ground and placed in seemingly innocuous locations.

Using their bayonets to chip away at the ancient mortar between the stones, the soldiers of both the 1st and 3rd Squads painstakingly created slots that were not only large enough for the muzzles of the weapons, but also permitted them to observe their assigned sectors. With the overall scheme of their defense committed to memory, Reider made sure each loophole, and the soldier using it, did its job. While conducting these inspections, he also used the time to become more familiar with his men. Though most worked in silence, and few responded to his questions with more words than were necessary, Reider found that just watching his soldiers go about their tasks told a great deal about them. Were there not other things to do, and if their situation hadn't been so serious, it would have been an enjoyable study in human nature for the young officer.

But events and circumstances continued to move on, just as they had for the past three days. Soon Reider found himself faced with his final exam in military leadership.

28

Finished with his rounds, and sensing that his men wanted to be rid of him for a while, Gerald Reider made his way into the crude cellar of the farmhouse. Besides the weapons, equipment, food, and other stores kept there by the Hungarians were the wounded and prisoners. These were being watched by Kittridge, Les Kim, and, when he wasn't performing his duties as a medic, Isaac Smollett.

Though far from an ideal setting for a makeshift aid station, it had the advantage of being both safe and out of the way. The walls of irregular stones, seemingly stacked one on the other in a haphazard manner, were covered with centuries of cobwebs and dust. The overhead beams and floor supports were rough cut and black from age. Since this part of the farmhouse was never meant to be anything more than a place to store things, the low crossbeams and exposed floorboards of the rooms above forced anyone moving about in the cellar to bend over almost double.

In the rear of the cellar was a crude hole in the wall that led to another chamber. This was where the militiamen had hidden their weapons and stores. Since it was important to keep their prisoners as far away from those items as possible, the 3rd Platoon's wounded and their guardians had settled there, on either side of the passage leading into the storage chamber. The militiamen who had been captured, including their wounded, had been placed up against the front wall.

Making his way down the steep ladder, Gerald Reider found he had to step aside quickly as Jefferson, hauling the last of the antitank mines, made his way to the ladder without looking. Sweating from his exertions, the assistant Javelin gunner said nothing as he passed Reider. While he was watching Jefferson climb, a voice called out to the young officer from the front of the cellar. "It does my heart good to see that those things will finally be used against the Slovakian pigs."

Reider looked over at the Hungarian prisoner Nathan had roughed up the previous day. "How do you know one of your compatriots won't find them first and set one off?"

The Hungarian laughed. "No. They are for tanks. A man can jump up and down on them and nothing happens."

Reider gave the man a leery look. "Well, you won't find me testing that theory out." Turning his back, he made his way over to where Smollett sat, dozing off. With his back to the wall, he was seated next to Reisniack, who lay on his side on a bed of blankets. Concerned by the SAW gunner's labored breaths, which made a gurgling sound every time he inhaled and exhaled, Reider shook the medic. "Smollett, is he supposed to be like that?" Reider asked, nodding his head over at the wounded man.

Startled, Smollett stared wide-eyed at his platoon leader. After taking a moment to look up, the medic heaved a sigh of relief. "Yes, sir," the exasperated aidman finally replied. "As painful as it is, if he doesn't stay on his side, he'll drown in his own blood."

This answer made Reider grimace. "Isn't there anything you can do?"

"Well," Smollett answered as he shifted himself about on the hard ground, "if I were in a well-equipped dispensary, with a qualified physician's assistant looking over my shoulder, I could try. But," he continued in a tone that betrayed his resignation, "I don't dare do anything fancy here. I'm afraid I'd start something and, in the middle, find out that I'm in over my head." Pausing, the medic looked over at Kim, who was sound asleep, and then at the wounded militiamen. "As it is, I'm barely staying afloat."

Not knowing what to say by way of response, Reider turned away and looked over to where Kittridge sat. Like Kim, Kittridge was sound asleep. "How's he been?"

Though not actually a member of the 3rd Platoon, Smollett was the medic who was normally assigned to accompany them whenever they went out into the field. In the process he had grown to know these men, counting many of them among his best friends. It therefore pained him to see those who were gathered around him, in this cellar, in the condition they were. This was especially true of Kittridge, who was just as much a casualty as any of the men there but didn't have a red badge of courage to show for it.

"Physically," Smollett started as he stared at the staff sergeant, "he's no better, or worse off, than the rest of the platoon that's not gathered here in the cellar. But . . ."

"Can he fight?" Reider asked when the medic failed to finish his assessment.

Without taking his eyes off the man in question, Smollett shook his head. "I'm not qualified to make that sort of call. If he were bleeding, I could help him. If his pain were physical, I could give him something to make it go away."

Sensing that the medic wasn't going to give him a definitive answer, Reider dropped the issue. "Keep an eye on him." With that, he started to make his way to the ladder.

He had his foot on the first rung of it when a voice from the front of the cellar called out. "You let us fight?"

Stopping with one hand on a rung of the ladder, and one foot up, Reider peered into the dark corner of the basement where the militiamen were being kept. "What?"

"You let us fight when they come?" the English-speaking militiamen repeated. "The Army will come. Their Army. They will kill us all, you know."

"And you wouldn't, I suppose," Reider replied sarcastically.

Shrugging his shoulders as best he could with his hands bound behind his back, the ethnic Hungarian cocked his head to one side. "Well, not to worry. We take care of business first, pleasure second."

It took a moment for the militiaman's meaning to sink in. When it did, it angered the young officer. Stepping down off the ladder, he made his way over to where the militiaman sat. "You sorry piece of shit! Those are my men you shot up yesterday."

"What do you expect?" the militiaman replied, without the slightest hint of remorse or sorrow. "You are in the way. We only wish to resolve this issue. I do not know why you are here. Do you?"

Blinking, Reider found himself searching for an answer, but found nothing of any substance. Instead, he fell back on the rhetoric that had been played up in the media, and had been used by the president to justify NATO intervention. "Our mission is a humanitarian mission, to keep the peace and protect innocent lives."

The militiaman laughed. "I tell you what your own

soldiers wish they could tell you. Bullshit. You have no business here, in my country, telling my people what they can and cannot do. We wish to free ourselves of the Slovakians. They wish to eradicate us from the face of the earth. If you were so concerned with our future, you would give us weapons and let us settle this matter and not pass this ancient hatred on to our children."

"But they are *killing* your children," Reider countered. "Don't you want to see your children grow up?"

"Yes," the militiamen hissed. "But as free men. I want them to be free to speak the tongue of their ancestors, to rule land that is Magyar, not Slavic. You, an American, must understand such a simple wish. Did you not fight the English for your freedom?"

"We didn't kill women and children," Reider shouted.

"We have no choice."

By now the two men were glaring at each with mere inches between them. During the long, trying days of wandering around, an anger had built up within Gerald Reider, an anger that threatened to explode. His wish to lash out at the militiaman was compelling. Had not the *pop-pop-pop* of an M-16 firing drifted down into the cellar from above, Reider might well have let his passions override his common sense.

As it was, even while he was backing away as quickly as he dared, making his way back to the ladder, he saw the ethnic-Hungarian militiaman smiling. "See," the man said, pleased with himself. "They are here."

There was no one in the kitchen when Reider emerged from the basement. All he heard were the excited voices from the floor above. Pausing, he waited for another burst of gunfire to direct him toward the danger. He had no desire to go running around ignorant and haphazardly. He had already done enough of that over the past few days and had found that doing so was, more often than not, disastrous. With no one like Dixon there to pull his chestnuts out of the fire, the last thing Reider wanted to do was screw this up.

He was seated there, on the floor, half out of the opening leading to the cellar, when Staff Sergeant Hernandes, followed by Jefferson and Pavlovski, came running into the room from outside. "In the rear," the NCO yelled, guessing what Reider was waiting for.

"Who?" Reider asked quickly as the two tank hunters continued to scramble for the stairs going up, and Hernandes made for the back door. "How many?"

"Fuck, sir! I don't know," Hernandes shouted without breaking stride. "We were out front, laying mines."

Seeing that he would have to go himself to find out, Reider sprang up, off the floor, and out the door behind Hernandes. Both men made straight for the section of the barn where Dubois and Henry Smith, his regularly assigned SAW gunner, were posted. Both of those men, crouched prone on the floor and staring intently out their respective loopholes, paid no heed to the appearance of their platoon leader and acting platoon sergeant. Squatting down next to Dubois, Hernandes leaned over and looked out the squad leader's loophole. "How many of them are there?" the senior NCO asked.

"I don't know," came the short, sharp reply.

"Well, how many do you see, or do you think there are?" insisted Hernandes.

This time Dubois looked up at Hernandes. "I said, I don't know."

Reider watched from a few feet away, as his platoon sergeant blinked his eyes in surprise. "You're shooting, and you have no idea what you're shooting at?"

"We didn't start the shooting, damn it," Dubois snapped. "Santiago, in the other room, did. How the hell am I supposed to know what the hell he saw."

Hernandes leaned closer to Dubois. "You're his squad leader."

Nervous and utterly ignorant of what was going on outside the barn, Reider intervened. "Save that for later,

Sergeant Hernandes. Go back to the house and check the front. Make sure we're okay there. If we are, bring one of the tank killers back here. I'm going over to see what Santiago is firing on."

For a moment, Hernandes looked at Reider. Though his face betrayed no emotions, no sign of what was going on in his head, Reider guessed that the man who was supposed to be his number two was weighing the orders he had just been given. This both angered and frustrated him. Had Dixon told his senior NCO not to obey his orders if they might be dangerous? Or was this hesitation purely a natural response by the more experienced soldier who had grown leery of his new platoon leader's judgment?

Finally, Hernandes nodded. "Right" was all the NCO said as he gathered himself up off the ground and made his way past Reider. Looking back at Reider, Dubois stared at his platoon leader, knowing full well what had just transpired between the two.

Relieved that this crisis had passed, the young officer moved on to the next awaiting resolution. "Keep your eyes open, Sergeant Dubois," Reider reminded the nervous NCO as the platoon leader got up and made his way over into the other section of the barn.

The barn was a single-story structure, built in the same robust manner as the house and divided into two sections, one for animals and one for equipment. Dubois and Smith had set up in the portion of the barn that formed the outer corner of the farmstead. There were two sets of loopholes in that part of the barn, one for each man facing into the woods, to the rear of the farmstead, and another pair covering the flank. Santiago had been working on a third, for another rifleman, but this one was far from complete. Reider went straight for the open loophole, dropped to the ground, and brought the muzzle of his rifle up to the hole without actually pushing it through. He took the time to settle himself and to make a quick scan of the woods before speaking.

When he saw nothing, Reider asked the rifleman next to him, "What are you firing at?"

"They were out there," the man insisted with a plaintive tone. "I saw them."

"Who did you see? How many?"

"I don't know. Two, maybe three. I don't know."

It was clear to Reider that the man was both nervous as hell and confused. Convinced that he wasn't going to get anything of value by pressing him, Reider silently observed as much of the woods to his front as he could see. He was still there, searching for any sign of movement, when Hernandes reappeared with Pavloski in tow. Both men headed to where Reider was, though only the NCO squatted down, next to his officer. "The front's clear so far, sir," he whispered.

"I haven't seen anything here, either," Reider replied as he continued to search.

Knowing the men in the platoon far better than Reider, Hernandes got up and went over to Santiago. "Are you sure you saw something?"

Frustrated by this line of questioning, the rifleman rolled over on his back and looked up at his fellow Latino. When the pair exchanged harsh words in Spanish, Reider looked up over at the two in time to catch the NCO raise his right hand as if he were going to slap the man he was arguing with. "At ease, sergeant," Reider commanded.

Without looking back at his platoon leader, Hernandes glared down at Santiago as he kept his raised hand up, holding his threat for a moment longer. Only slowly did the NCO bring it down without taking his eyes off the man before him.

Reider turned toward the RTO, who was standing back, watching the confrontation, and motioned him to where he was. "Come over here and cover this hole." Glad to be doing something, Pavlovski quickly took over the loophole after Reider backed away from it.

By the time the young officer was on his feet, Staff

Sergeant Hernandes was standing in the door of the barn leading into the small, enclosed yard. Slowly, Reider made his way over to him. At first Hernandes didn't look Reider in the eye. His face was still red. The young officer didn't know if this was from his anger at Santiago or the embarrassment at being caught by his platoon leader arguing with one of the men. Whatever the reason, it was not important at the moment. "Do you think he saw something?" Reider asked.

Hernandes shrugged. "The men are all strung out, sir. They're tired, nervous as hell, and scared. Maybe he did see something. Maybe he didn't."

This was not the answer he was hoping for. He had come to expect quick, straightforward answers that provided solutions from the NCOs in the platoon. To hear his platoon sergeant reply in a manner that bordered on abject resignation was unnerving. "What do you think we should do?" Reider found himself asking, genuinely at a loss as to how to proceed after seeing what he just had.

Hernandes, having composed himself, shook his head. "Well, it's a cinch I'm not going to send anyone out there, stumbling around, looking for someone who may not be there." When the NCO looked up into Reider's eyes, the young officer could see the exhaustion, tainted with frustration, in them. "With everyone, including me, hovering somewhere on the edge, we'd be just as likely to shoot our own men."

"So you're suggesting we do nothing?" Reider asked incredulously.

"We've done just about everything that is within our power, sir," Hernandes tried to explain. "Lieutenant Dixon will make it, or he won't. The Slovakians will find us here and attack, or they won't. Someone will come along and bail us out, or they won't." Pausing, Hernandes looked up at the gray sky above them. "The sun will shine, or it won't." Lowering his chin, the exhausted NCO looked at Reider. "Regardless of what we do from here on out, whether or not we live through this or die where we stand is pretty much up to other people. Only God knows for sure how this will turn out. There's not a whole hell of a lot either us can do to change that." Finished, the NCO turned and walked away, leaving Reider in the small farmyard alone.

With no one he could turn to, no one from whom he could seek advice or comfort, at that moment, Gerald Reider discovered just how lonely being an officer could be.

29

SOUTHWESTERN SLOVAKIA,
DAWN, FEBRUARY 9

The first attack came shortly before dawn. Evens Tobias, who had been manning LP/OP near the road, came stumbling into the house, panting and breathless, shouting *Tanks!* as loud as he dared. Gerald Reider, who had found it next to impossible to sleep, was wide-awake and making his way up the stairs with Tobias on his heels. As an afterthought, the young officer paused only long enough to turn and order the man to go out back to rouse Dubois and his men. Though he understood the order, Tobias protested. "My fighting position's up there, sir. In the corner room."

"First," Reider snapped, "warn the 1st Squad."

Tobias was in the process of backing down the narrow staircase when a volley of small-arms fire erupted from the direction of the barn. The soldier looked back up at his platoon leader. "Sounds like they're already awake," Tobias stated dryly.

Caught off guard, Reider hesitated, unsure if he should first go up and check out what the tanks Tobias had seen were doing, or go back down the stairs and out to the barn to find out what was happening there. The issue was decided for him when a series of explosions erupted in the farmstead's courtyard. "Get to your post," he shouted at Tobias as he pushed his way past the soldier and made for the back door.

On his way through the kitchen, Reider literally ran into Staff Sergeant Hernandes, who had been in the cellar after checking on the wounded and prisoners. "We've got tanks on the road," Reider quickly informed his platoon sergeant, "and God knows what out back. Get back upstairs. I'm going back to the barn."

Without a word, Hernandes disappeared through the doorway leading to the rest of the house. Reider turned to pull open the back door. He had no more than grabbed the door handle with his left hand and pushed it down to open it than a blastwave blew open the door. Unprepared for this, the force of the explosion jammed Reider's arm back and out of the way. In quick succession, it smacked against the toe of his boot, then against the lip of his helmet, which knocked his head out of the way. Thrown off balance, the young officer was reeling from this shock when a figure appeared in the doorway.

"Dubois is hit!" the man yelled. "We need Smollett!"

Without thinking, Reider lifted his left hand to stop the man. When the soldier plowed into it, a wave of pain shot up Reider's hand. It had been sprained, or perhaps even broken, when the door had been blown in. Working through his agony, Reider shouted at the soldier he was now holding at arm's length. "Get back to your position, *Now!*" After pausing for no more than a second, the soldier turned and disappeared back out the door, leaving Reider free to shake out his left hand in an effort to alleviate the pain, while turning to yell down into the cellar. "Medic! Man down in the barn." Not waiting for a response, Reider again swung around and made for the now open door leading into the small courtyard.

The sound of the 1st Squad firing furiously echoed off the small, enclosed space. Emerging through the doorway, Reider was angered when he ran headlong into someone. "I said get back to your position," the exasperated platoon leader screamed at the man.

In panic, the soldier jumped back, let out an astonished exclamation, and stared at Reider as he brought the AK he had been holding at his side up to fire. It took a bit less time for Gerald Reider to realize his error. In a single motion that would have made a western gunfighter proud, the young officer brought his own weapon up, flipping the safety off as he did, and jammed the muzzle of his weapon into the midsection of the astonished Slovakian soldier. Jerking his finger in quick succession, Reider pushed forward, keeping his rifle against his foe's body as each bullet he fired ripped through the Slovakian. Only when the man fell over backward, sprawling in the mud of the courtyard, did Reider cease fire.

He had little time to savor this bloody victory. Even as the Slovakian before Reider was going down, another appeared. Confused, this Slovakian also took a bit too long to assess the situation. With his AK held at the ready, the Slovakian watched his leader, the man who had run into Reider, backing up. Only when the leader fell away, revealing Reider, did this new man understand what was going on. Reider, with his weapon still held at waist level, merely had to bring the muzzle of his weapon over a bit to one side before sending a hail of projectiles at the second Slovakian.

Hit twice, this enemy soldier jerked the trigger of his AK, sending a wild stream of small-arms fire spraying all over the yard. Diving for the ground, Reider found himself seeking cover from this wild fusillade of gunfire behind the corpse of the first man he had shot. With his face buried in the mud and his head jammed against the lifeless body, Reider struggled to catch his breath.

Only when the firing ceased did the young officer lift his head. When he did, he found himself confronted by a third Slovakian who had just finished scaling the high wall that was adjacent to the orchard on the other side. Panicked, Reider searched for his weapon with his right hand as he watched the Slovakian turn and survey the situation in the courtyard before advancing. In the process of doing so, he saw the bodies strewn about and caught sight of Reider's desperate efforts to bring his own rifle to bear. This time, the Slovakian had the drop on the young officer.

The first burst of gunfire unleashed against Reider was wide of the mark, giving the young officer a chance to bring his own weapon up to his shoulder. The time that he needed to bring his M-16 into play far exceeded what the Slovakian required to adjust his fire. Yet Reider did not surrender to the inevitable. He was acting instinctively. This was not a classroom drill or an evaluated field exercise. It was the basest of armed conflicts. This situation required no thought, no assessment or planning. It was a simple man-against-man confrontation, one in which one would survive.

This morning it would be Reider who walked away, but not because of what he did. In the middle of his struggles to get off a shot, the Slovakian soldier before him was thrown back, against the very wall he had just scaled. Not quite sure what had caused this, and unwilling to gamble that it was only a momentary advantage, Reider fired twice into the Slovakian even as he was falling to the ground. Only when his foe's only response was a moan and a twitch did the young platoon leader turn to see who had fired the first shot.

In the doorway of the house, a figure stood, holding his rifle up. Smollett, seeing his platoon leader looking around, yelled in anguish. "I'm supposed to be *saving* lives!"

Reider rose up off the ground as quickly as he could. When he was on his feet, the young officer nodded. "Well, you just did. Now get into the barn and see to Dubois." Without waiting, Reider faced the wall over which the Slovakians had come. For the first time since the grenades went off, he was able to make an assessment and actually plan his next move. The stinging in his arm, and the memory of the grenade blasts that had caused it, cued Reider as to what he needed to do next. Bounding over to the wall, he leaned his rifle against it and pulled a grenade off the side of his ammo pouch. Pulling the pin with his left hand, despite the pain, Reider held the grenade in front of his face as he watched as the spoon flipped off and the hammer snapped down onto the primer. When it was armed, the young officer took a step away from the wall, cocked his arm back, and lobbed the grenade over the wall. Quickly he flattened himself against the wall.

As he waited for what seemed to be an eternity, terrible thoughts began to creep into his mind. What if it was a dud? Like everything else the Army bought, he knew grenades were manufactured by the lowest bidder. Maybe he had thrown a Friday grenade? What if the Slovakians threw the grenade back? Reider had seen that in the movies. Only a detonation on the other side of the wall, which he felt as little more than a vibration, followed by a scream of pain, put these fears to rest.

Having clearly scored success with one, Reider was quick to follow up with a second grenade. This one, thrown with a little more force, was meant to go farther out, away from the wall, in an effort to catch anyone who was retreating or hanging back in support of those going over. While the explosion of this follow-up grenade was not accompanied by the cries of fresh victims, Gerald Reider thought he could hear a number of excited voices on the other side of the wall. Though anxious to send them fleeing and ending this threat, he had no more grenades. In a desperate long shot, the young officer dropped down on his knees and searched the body of the Slovakian next to him. This yielded two grenades, both of which he sent sailing over the wall in quick succession, one to the left of where he had thrown the first, and the next a bit to the right.

After the second grenade had gone off, Reider waited as long as he dared, listening for any signs that there were still enemy soldiers on the other side. The steady rattle of gunfire from the barn made this difficult. On one hand, Reider knew it was a gamble to turn his back and leave this quarter of their position unwatched. Yet he could not linger there forever. Not only was he the platoon leader, he was also the only man in the place who was free to move about. Everyone else had a fighting position, an assigned sector of responsibility. As a leader, it was his job, in combat, to step back and keep an eye on the overall situation, directing the fire of his men and adjusting their positions as the situation required. With no good choices open to him, Reider opted to select the least of the bad ones before him. Taking a deep breath, he left the relative safety of the wall and made for the section of the barn where Dubois and Henry Smith were situated.

As dark as it had been in the small yard, it was all but pitch black in the barn. Only a pinprick of light, off to one side, was visible. Having forgotten the name of the other man posted here, and remembering that Dubois had been hit, Reider called out the name of the only man he was sure would reply. "Smollett."

The small beam, emanating from a penlight, briefly flashed up, in the young officer's direction. "Over here."

Making for the source of the light as quickly as he dared in the dark enclosure, Reider knelt down when he sensed he was next to Dubois. "How is he?"

"I think the bullet just grazed him, here," Smollett explained as he shined his small penlight on a red gouge that creased the squad leader's upper arm.

Having sorted out where Dubois's head was, Reider looked into the space where he assumed that man's eyes would be. "Can you use your arm?"

"It hurts like a mother," Dubois whined.

Angered by the sergeant's tone of voice, Reider looked back up at Smollett. "Slap a goddamn Band-Aid on it and get him back into the fight!"

Not waiting for any sort of response from either man, Reider made his way over to an unoccupied loophole visible only because the darkness on the other side wasn't quite as dark as that within the barn itself. He was easing down into position to observe from it when Henry Smith cut loose with a burst. "What are you shooting at, soldier?" Reider yelled after the echo of the automatic fire faded.

Easing back from the butt of his weapon, Smith looked out his loophole, then at Reider. "I don't know, sir. There was movement out there, then someone opened fire. Sergeant Dubois went down right off."

"Have you hit anything?" Reider shot back. "Have you seen anyone?"

Again Smith took a moment to consider this last question. "I'm not sure, sir."

It quickly became obvious to Reider that whoever had fired on the 1st Squad was not interested in overpowering, at least not with a frontal attack. The gunfire that wounded Dubois and that Smith was responding to had been meant to hold the attention of his men here while the Slovakians he had run into in the yard slipped over the wall and took the 1st Squad in the rear. From the other section of the barn, Reider heard a smattering of rifle fire. "Hold your fire," Reider told Smith before backing away from his loophole. "Keep your eyes open, and don't fire until you have something to shoot at."

Responding with a crisp "Roger that," Smith settled down to watch and wait.

Rising to his feet, Reider made his way back to Dubois

and the medic, who was finishing up. *"Sergeant!"* Reider barked. "Get control of your people. We had infiltrators in the yard behind you. I'm going to shift one of the men in the other room and watch that area from there. Is that clear?"

Dubois drew a deep breath before he slowly answered with a curt "Yes, *sir.*"

Though he was peeved at the manner in which this squad leader was reacting, Reider didn't feel as if he had the time to deal with that particular issue at the moment. Instead, he continued over to the other side of the barn, where he repeated his order to cease fire and not to fire unless there was a target worth engaging. He tapped Jefferson, at random, for the task of displacing to the door of the barn and covering the yard. "Make sure," he told the assistant gunner, "you're looking at a Slovak before you fire. Clear?"

Nervous and dry-mouthed, the soldier simply nodded.

With that, Reider was up and making his way back into the house. As he passed through the yard, he kept an eye on the wall from which the enemy, and its barrage of grenades, had come. It was at that moment that the Land Warrior systems of the 2nd Squad came to mind. Though they had dragged them back, along with the wounded, from the tree line the day before, Staff Sergeant Hernandes had not redistributed them. The batteries of the night sights and computers, like that of the platoon's radio, were all but drained.

Rushing into the kitchen of the house that he had left mere minutes before, Reider hesitated. Should he go up and check in with his platoon sergeant and 3rd Squad first, or head down into the cellar to retrieve one of the Land Warrior packs and sights? Not having taken the time before to assess what was going on out front, Reider opted for the former. Things were quiet up there, something that was, strangely, more unnerving than all the racket that had gone on at the rear of the house.

* * *

On the second floor of the farmhouse the young officer found Staff Sergeant Hernandes kneeling, peering out of a window. All the glass, as well as much of the wooden frame as could be removed, were gone from the window. Next to him Reider saw a man clutching one of the captured RPGs, also staring intently in the direction of the road. Through the window, Reider could see a glimmer of light in the distant sky. Dawn was breaking.

From the doorway Reider called out in a low voice. "Seen anything yet?"

Without diverting his eyes from their task, Hernandes whispered, "No, nothing, nada. What about 1st Squad? What happened out there?"

Easing his way forward, Reider took up a position on the side of the window that Hernandes was on. Carefully, the young officer looked out, over the sergeant's head. Quickly platoon leader filled in platoon sergeant, skipping the details of the engagement and passing on only those facts he deemed relevant. Not included in Reider's recounting of the situation were Sergeant Dubois's conduct or his own exploits in the yard.

When his platoon leader was finished, Hernandes grunted. "I guess Dubois and his boys really did see something yesterday."

"Yeah," Reider responded. "They were checking us out, setting us up." Due to the ringing in his ear that had persisted after enduring the near miss from the helicopter's rocket, not to mention the grenades that had almost knocked him down mere moments ago, Reider spoke in a voice louder than he thought he was using. Hernandes considered mentioning this, but said nothing. Instead, he kept watching. Finally he eased back from the window, resting his buttocks on the heels of his boots. "You suppose we've spoiled their plan and that they've got to pull back and sort things out?"

"That's what I'm thinking, Sergeant Hernandes."

"Well, if I were them," the NCO went on as he shifted himself around until he was sitting on the floor with his back to the wall, "I'd come at us in one of two ways."

"And they are?" Reider asked as he continued to scan the landscape that was becoming visible as the sun began to show itself.

"If they really want a piece of us," Hernandes began, "they have a couple of options. If they have BMPs or BTRs as well as tanks, they can make a mounted attack. On the other hand, if time's not a big problem for them, they can sit out there, in the distance, and pound us into the dirt."

Reider nodded. "I know which one I'd vote for. What about you?"

Before he answered, Hernandes leaned forward and turned his head until he could see the early morning sky out the window. When he saw patches of clear sky, he muttered, "Ground attack, for sure. And soon. Otherwise," he added, "they'll be leaving themselves open to air attack."

Reider took in a deep breath. "Ground attack it is. I'll pass the word to 1st Squad. I don't think they'll be bothered much back there again, but you never know."

"If anything," Hernandes quickly added, "whoever they threw back before will open up a lively fire, just to keep 1st Squad pinned back there."

Straightening up, Reider looked around the room, catching sight of the stack of pre-positioned RPGs. "I've got some things to check out. I'm going to send Jefferson back to you. If there's a mounted attack, you'll need him here."

Staff Sergeant Hernandes was about to add that they would need a lot more than one more man if it came to that, but didn't. Things were looking grim enough without adding that sort of comment to their already gloomy outlook.

*   *   *

By the time Reider made his way down into the cellar, Smollett had returned. He had just finished checking the Apache crewmen and was moving to where Reisniack was lying. The medic glanced up at Reider when he appeared, but said nothing, leaving the young officer wondering if he was still upset over what had happened at the rear of the house.

Looking around, he saw Kittridge off to one side, leaning against the wall. The NCO's M-16, with the Land Warrior sight still attached, was sitting on the ground next to him. With his knees drawn up to his chest and his arms wrapped around his legs, the former squad leader sat staring at the floor before him. "Sergeant Kittridge," Reider called out, "grab your weapon and one of the Land Warriors that's still working and follow me."

The sergeant said nothing.

"Sergeant Kittridge," Reider repeated a second time, speaking slowly and a bit louder, "take up your weapon and a functional Land Warrior and get up here."

Still the NCO said nothing. Nor did he move, not even his eyes.

"I will gladly go in his place," the English-speaking militiaman chimed in. "Killing a Slovak in the morning is always good sport."

Reider turned on the man. "You shut the fuck up!" Then, moving closer to Kittridge, Reider repeated his orders. "Sergeant," the young officer shouted when he was inches from the man's head, "get off your ass and take your weapon."

From behind, Smollett answered for the despondent NCO. "Shout all you want, LT. It won't do any good. He's finished."

Flushed with anger, Reider turned on the medic. "The man's a professional soldier. He'll do what he's told."

"The man," the medic shouted back, "is a human being, a very broken human being. He's taken all the abuse you or anyone can heap on him. So leave him alone."

For a moment, the two men stared at each other. One man was responsible for orchestrating the conduct of others in an effort to kill their fellow man. The other was dedicated to saving lives. Neither man truly understood the other. And neither cared to give way to the other. Only the intervention of another voice from across room ended this silent impasse. "I'll go."

In unison, both officer and medic turned to face Les Kim, who was struggling to get up off the floor. "I'll go, sir," the little Korean-American repeated. "I'm getting tired of sitting around in this hole listening to you guys up there have all the fun." These words, meant to be lighthearted, were broken up and strained as waves of pain and agony from Kim's wound racked his body.

Smollett made an effort to move over and block Kim's way. "Les, don't be an idiot. What good are you going to do up there?"

Waving the medic away, Kim began to hobble over to the ladder. Once there, he paused to catch his breath. Looking at his friend, Kim managed to muster a faint smile. "Down here all I'll be good for is absorbing grenade fragments when those shits make it into the house. At least up there . . ." The wounded man didn't finish. He stopped, turned his face away, and stared up the ladder, through the hole in the floor above. "Well, let's just say I'm going, and leave it at that." Pausing only long enough to shift his rifle so that he could climb the ladder, the wounded man began to make his way up, one agonizing step at a time.

When Kim was up and out of the way, Reider made his way over to the ladder. As the young officer lifted his left hand, a pain shot down his arm. Hesitating, he let the pain pass. Reider thought about asking Smollett if he had something that he could wrap his sprained hand and wrist with, but decided against it. Despite everything that had transpired since leaving Fort Apache, Second Lieutenant Gerald Reider still suffered from a sense of pride that kept him from doing the smart thing.

30

SOUTHWESTERN SLOVAKIA, MORNING, FEBRUARY 9

I t took the Slovakians more than an hour to sort themselves out and regroup. When they did come, they came as Hernandes had predicted, mounted, and in force. As before, Gerald Reider wasn't at one of the primary fighting positions. He was back in the small kitchen, not far from where he had been at the start of the predawn attack. The young officer was still in the process of settling Les Kim into his position. Unable to move about and gather up material with which to protect himself from where he was to fight, Kim sat on the floor while Reider scrounged around looking for anything that gave even the appearance of being capable of stopping a bullet or soaking up some shrapnel. The impact of the first high-explosive round smacking into the farmhouse shook the building and knocked loose anything that wasn't fastened to the walls and put a stop to Reider's efforts.

Placing his hand on the wounded man's shoulder, Reider looked into Kim's eyes as he pointed out the door. "Watch the yard out there. Sound off if you need help."

With the same grim expression everyone in the platoon wore that morning, Kim blinked twice and acknowledged this order by nodding. With nothing more to be done here, Reider turned and began to make his way to the stairs, when a second round plowed its way into the house and exploded.

By now the dust of ages and pulverized plaster was mixing with the fumes generated by the detonation of high explosives in a confined space, filling the entire structure with choking clouds of dust. By the time Reider reached the top of the stairs, the acrid odor was so overpowering that he began to wonder if the Slovakians were using gas. That, he thought as he continued on, would be stupid.

The next round slammed against the house just as Reider reached the top step. While the sturdy structure absorbed the impact, passing it on with little more than a slight tremble, the concussion of the explosion swept though the house, knocking Reider backward, sending him tumbling down the stairs. Rolling and bouncing back and forth, from side to side, the young officer desperately clawed at the walls on either side of him in an effort to find something to grab and arrest his descent. His efforts were in vain. Even as he came to an abrupt stop on the ground floor, another round plowed its way into the house. By now the smoke was so thick that he could not see the top of the stairs, even though he was looking up at them. This is insane, he thought to himself as he struggled to gather himself up. In the process, he quickly discovered that his falls and tumbling about not only had aggravated his sprained left hand and wrist, but now he found he couldn't put any weight on his right foot. Very little pain registered from the limb. It simply wouldn't support him. Faced with the need to get up to where he could see what was going on, Reider found he had no other choice. Rolling over onto his hands and knees, the graduate of West Point started to crawl up the stairs.

Suddenly the whole world seemed to slow down. Everything, except the thoughts that tumbled through his mind, crept along at a tortuously slow and pathetic pace. Round after round pounded the house, adding to the thick dust that irritated his eyes and filled his lungs. There's got to be a better way to do this, he found himself thinking. With all the computers the Army boasts of, automated systems, and gee-whiz gadgets, there had to be a better way to wage war.

Unable to put much weight on his left hand, he had to use his elbow when it came time to push up on that side to the next step. In the process of doing this, he began hacking, an action that drew more of the dust and fumes into his mouth, nose, and throat. Suddenly an image of his father appeared out of nowhere. Reider couldn't remember ever seeing his father dirty. He came home from his downtown Manhattan office just as neat and trim as he had been when he had left in the morning. Even when his father had come from his health club, the most Reider had ever seen was a few odd beads of sweat on his father's brow. How his old man had managed to make his way through life without ever getting his hands dirty was beyond him.

More shells slammed into the house. With each the house shook, sending a fresh wave of hot air and debris rolling over Reider, threatening to smother him anew as he struggled up the narrow stairway. Bowing his head down till his face was but inches from the stairs themselves, Reider continued to force his way upward as if he were fighting the howling winds of a hurricane. By the time he reached the top of the stairs, the only way he knew for sure that he had done so was when he reached out, with his right hand, to grab the next step before him and found nothing but air. Pausing there only long enough to get his bearings, Gerald Reider remained on his stomach as he slowly made his way into the room where he had left Staff Sergeant Hernandes.

When defending a building of any sort, one does not simply cower behind the walls of that structure and hope for the best. Even high-explosive rounds that detonate on impact and do not penetrate or knock out a section of the wall generate damage on the inside. The blast from a projectile sends shockwaves through whatever material it has made contact with. If the structure is sturdy and well built, most of this shockwave is absorbed and dissipated by the material and structure. Some, however, causes the side opposite the impact to fragment or splinter. This fragmentation is known, in the military, as spalling. The debris, or spall, thrown around, can be just as deadly to an occupant of the structure as the fragments of an exploding projectile itself.

Defenders in a building, therefore, must protect themselves from this by erecting interior bunkers. Unlike those built on open ground, these bunkers are constructed with an eye to protecting their occupants from blasts that occur in the room, as from a hand grenade, or spalling thrown off from a round that slams into a wall and sends bits and pieces of that wall flying around. While the wall the defenders are facing pretty much provides cover from direct fire to their front, the walls of their bunker protect their flank, rear, and overhead. Of course, the downside of this arrangement is that if an enemy round hits the wall directly in front of where this bunker is, the bunker and its occupants absorb the full fury of the blast and resulting spall.

As with their exterior counterparts, the ideal material for building a bunker in a room is sandbags. When these aren't available, the furniture of the room itself is used, with well-built tables, mattresses, and sofas being the items of choice. The 3rd Platoon, besides carving out loopholes, had searched the entire farmstead for anything that could be used. In this Staff Sergeant Hernandes had left no stone unturned. Besides using the furniture, boards, and a few cinderblocks left in the corner of the barn, he had detailed two of his men to empty the many ammo boxes that had been hidden in the cellar of their content. These boxes, in turn, were filled with dirt and hauled up the stairs, providing some of the bunkers with sound, sturdy walls. For overhead cover, every interior door in the farmhouse was pulled off its hinges, laid over the tops of the bunkers, and covered with loose dirt or a mattress. Only a small opening, big enough for a man to crawl through, was left. It was toward this opening, in the bunker where Staff Sergeant Hernandes was supposed to be, that Reider now made his way.

Doing so, as just about everything else had, sounded a lot easier than it was. The slow, almost random shelling of the house had transformed the room into a virtual obstacle course. Debris littered the floor, making it difficult and painful for Reider to inch his way over hot fragments, sharp splinters, and jagged bits and pieces of masonry. The only plus there was to entering one of the front rooms was that the open windows, and the holes freshly blasted in the walls, provided ventilation that had not been available to the interior portions of the house.

The small bunker where Reider found Staff Sergeant Hernandes was shared by Jefferson. The two men, lying flat on their bellies, were situated on either side of the loophole at the front of the bunker. In order to allow Reider to make his way up to that hole, Hernandes and Jefferson had to partially roll over onto their sides. When their lieutenant was situated, both men eased down on top of him.

"Besides the two tanks tucked away in the woods on the opposite side of the road, what do we have?" Reider asked after surveying the fields before him.

"Nothing yet," his platoon sergeant responded as he continued to look out over Reider's shoulder. "But I expect that to change soon. They're trying to get a rise out of us, so that they can target us."

This comment was accompanied by the shock of another round striking the wall of the room Reider had just crawled through. As dirt from above drifted down upon them through cracks in the door that was serving them as overhead cover, Reider looked over to Hernandes. "If you ask me, I'd say they pretty much have us targeted."

Jefferson, staring out at the tanks, grunted. "I hope those RPGs we left out there are still in good shape. Not that we're going to get to use them if they keep this up."

"What are the chances of hitting the tanks from here with them?" Reider asked, unfamiliar with the weapons they were depending on.

"Even if we hit the bastards," Hernandes explained, "the odds of doing any serious damage are close to nil."

"So we wait," Reider replied.

"Yes, sir, we wait."

It took the pair of T-72s a little more than five minutes to lob a dozen or so 125mm HE shells apiece at the farmhouse. All of the rounds hit, somewhere, on the ancient stone structure, though from where they sat, it didn't seem to make much difference. As there was nothing definitive to engage, the gunners had used the windows as aiming points, relying on the natural dispersion of their tank cannon to pepper the front of the structure near the windows they were firing at. Those rounds that did manage to sail through the open windows impacted on the far walls, sending shell fragments as well as splinters and chunks of masonry flying about the room. Only when he felt that firing additional rounds would be a waste did the Slovakian commander instruct the tank commanders to cease fire and order his three BMPs forward. Even then, the gunners of the T-72s stood ready with their eyes glued to their sights, waiting for someone in the house to show himself.

No one in the house moved for several long moments when the shelling stopped and the BMPs broke cover. Everyone who had a loophole to watch from held their breath as the three Slovakian BMPs crossed the road abreast and approached the first line of stone walls. If the BMPs continued on as they were, Jefferson and Reisniack would have to pop them as they climbed up, over the intervening walls. With the pair of T-72s patiently hanging back, waiting for something of value to shoot at, Staff Sergeant Hernandes guessed that each of his antitank gunners would get one shot off before the tanks tore the farmhouse apart, stone by stone. But if the Slovakian infantry fighting vehicles queued up and used the narrow trail between the walled fields, the land mines that had been set out there would come into play. Even if just one of the BMPs was stopped by a mine, the outcome of the battle would swing back into 3rd Platoon's favor.

In silence, the three men crammed into a bunker built for two watched. Once across the road, the three BMPs continued forward. None of them made an effort to line up, single file, as they would need to if they were going to use the trail leading up to the farm. Even the sound of small-arms fire, floating into the room from the rear of the farmstead, didn't distracted Reider or Hernandes. The two men had expected this. The Slovakians who had tried, and failed, to make their way into the farmhouse by stealth earlier in the day were now doing their best to draw the defenders away from the main effort.

Then, looking more like remote-controlled toys than machines of war, the two flanking BMPs slowed, stopping just short of the first wall while the center

BMP pushed on. When that BMP reached the walls, it squeezed itself in between them and began to make its way up the narrow, confined trail. Unable to contain his elation, Hernandes pounded the floor under him with his fist and let out an exuberant "*Yes!*" Even as he was expressing his joy, the left BMP made a slight turn and moved to follow the first.

Assuming that the other BMP would follow suit, Hernandes turned to Jefferson. "Okay, get out there and get ready. Your target will be the third BMP in line, whether it follows the other two or stays where it is. Don't shoot till the lead BMP hits a mine. And for God's sake," Hernandes added quickly, "don't show yourself until you're ready to fire."

Jefferson was already in motion, and halfway out of the bunker, before Hernandes finished. In the process, he accidentally bumped into Reider's right leg. This inadvertent contact sent waves of pain up the young officer's leg. Though he wanted to scream out at Jefferson, Reider held his tongue. To say anything that would slow Jefferson up was not what they needed at that moment.

With Jefferson gone, Hernandes motioned to Reider. "After you, sir."

Still fighting the pain, Reider shook his head. "No, you first" was all he could force out.

In no mood to argue, and in a hurry to get over to check on Pavlovski in the next room, Hernandes squeezed his way out of the bunker as quickly as he could. By the time Reider had done likewise, his platoon sergeant was already gone from the room. Jefferson, with an RPG resting on his right shoulder, was hanging toward the back of the room, peering out the battered window and paying no heed to his platoon leader. Not that the young officer minded. In fact, he preferred it this way, since he didn't want anyone to see him should his first effort to stand up and put weight on his foot prove to be embarrassing.

Once he had managed to drag himself till his back

was flat against the rear wall of the room, Reider slowly began to push himself up off the floor. As he did so, he put all his weight on his left leg and both arms, holding his right leg as still as he could. This, of course, meant that he had to use his left wrist. Though painful, it was the least of his worries.

Just as he finished stretching out in a full, upright posture, a dull explosion from outside echoed through the room. Looking up, out the window, Gerald Reider saw the lead BMP shrouded in a cloud of black and gray smoke. Off to his side, Jefferson stepped forward, yelling as he went. "Get out of the room, sir. You're in my back blast."

Glancing over at the assistant gunner, Reider saw that the man already had his eye pressed up against the sight of the RPG and was in the process of kneeling down before the open window. Sensing that Jefferson was going to fire whether he moved or not, Reider brought his right foot down, turned, and dived through the doorway into the hallway.

Two blasts in quick succession, accompanied by waves of intense heat, swept over Reider as he lay on the floor of the hallway just outside the room he had been in. The second, more powerful, showered him with fragments of masonry and filled the already suffocating air with fresh clouds of smoke and acrid fumes. The force of both explosions had smacked the soles of his boot, aggravating the injury to his right foot.

Unlike the previous shelling, when each blast had been followed by a brief, stunned silence, the rattle of small-arms fire, emanating from the room into which Hernandes had disappeared, filled the house. Feeling more like an abused rag doll, Reider rolled over onto his side and sat up. He was about to pull himself up off the floor by grasping the frame of the door before him when he heard the now familiar zing of bullets pass over his head and smack the wall behind him. Either the tanks, or the surviving BMPs below, were using their coaxial machine guns. So, rather than rise into their line of fire, Reider used his grip on the door frame to pull himself forward, back into the room he had just bailed out of. He needed to see what was going on.

The tank round that had hit just below the window had knocked a fair-sized hole in the wall, making it possible for Reider to look out into the fields below without getting up. The lead BMP was motionless, having come to a stop shortly after rolling over a mine. Thick black smoke, punctuated by an occasional tongue of flame, poured out of the open hatch on top of the turret. That vehicle, Reider told himself, was dead. The third BMP, while also halted, didn't seem to be badly hit. Yet he could see no movement from it. All its hatches were still buttoned down, and the long, thin 30mm cannon remained cocked to one side. Only the second BMP, sandwiched between the two derelicts, showed any sign of life. Gerald Reider sat where he was, watching for a moment as the BMP backed up, turned a bit, then backed up more, twisting around in the narrow space between the walls. He could almost imagine the desperation of the driver and the track commander as they struggled to extract themselves from the hellish situation in which they now found themselves. Reider was just about to start feeling sorry for them when a tank from across the road cut loose with another burst of machine-gun fire that peppered the wall around the doorway where he was seated.

Curling into a ball, Reider flopped over onto his side as he was showered with fragments of plaster and bits of masonry kicked loose by the wild firing. When it ceased, he remained scrunched up for a moment just to be sure it was over.

It was while he was unraveling himself from the fetal position he had assumed that Reider began to appreciate that something was not right. Looking around, he realized that he had been so fixated on assessing their tactical situation, that he hadn't bothered to see what had become of Jefferson. Looking through the whiffs of smoke that filled the shattered room, Reider quickly came to the conclusion that Jefferson was no longer there with him. Since he knew Jefferson hadn't gone over or past him, Reider was about to look into the bunker over in the corner of the room when he noticed that the walls around him were smeared with dark streaks. Squinting, Reider leaned forward to get a closer look. As he did so he placed his right hand onto the floor. When his gloved hand began to slip out from under him, Reider looked down. In horror, he watched as the five black fingers of his glove sank into a formless mass of bright red goo. Pulling his hand away, Reider looked up, again, and came to the realization that the red streaks on the walls were blood, and the goo on the floor was all that remained of Private First Class Jeff Jefferson.

In panic, Gerald Reider pushed himself back and out of the room as quickly as he could. He reentered the narrow hall just in time to run into Hernandes. Looking up at his platoon sergeant, Reider saw that his senior NCO had a man on his back in a fireman's carry. In his free hand he clung to an RPG. Without pausing to explain to his superior, Hernandes continued on, shouting as he went. "We need to get the hell out of here before it comes down on us." As if to add emphasis, another explosion rocked the farmhouse and sent a fresh wave of gray smoke billowing out of the room Hernandes had just left. "LT, Jefferson," the platoon sergeant screamed. *"Get the fuck outta here!"*

Reider pulled himself up and, as best he could, made for the stairs right behind Hernandes. "Jefferson's dead," Reider yelled.

This announcement did nothing to slow Hernandes down. "So is Larkin," he replied as he took the steep steps as fast as he dare.

Unfamiliar with all the men's names, Reider instinctively yelled, *"Who?"*

"My SAW gunner."

By the time he said this, Hernandes was on the ground floor and halfway into the kitchen. Reider, despite his pain, was right on his heels. In all the excitement, he hadn't noticed that he was being followed by Evens Tobias. The only way he discovered this was that Reider paused to grab Kim, who was watching Hernandes as that NCO flew out the back door. Tobias, not expecting Reider to stop, plowed into the rear of his ailing platoon leader, sending him sprawling onto the kitchen floor at Kim's feet. Instead of being angered, Reider felt relief when he saw there was someone else with him. "Trooper," he yelled as he pointed toward Kim, seated next to him and looking around anxiously, "grab that man and follow Sergeant Hernandes!"

The sound of another round smacking into the front of the house caused Tobias to look first at Reider, then at Kim, then back at Reider, and finally over the young officer in the direction of the doorway that opened up into the yard and safety from the tank fire. All the while the man's face was frozen in fear and indecision. Reaching over, Reider grabbed the rifleman's boot. "Damn it, grab Kim and get him out. I can't do it."

The physical contact, as well as the sound of the house collapsing around his ears, galvanized Tobias into action. Dropping his rifle, Tobias reached over, jammed his hands into the armholes of Kim's flak vest, and jerked the man up. Though he saw it coming, and knew what would happen, Kim couldn't hold back the scream that Tobias's rough handling caused him. Still, had he been given a chance, faced with the prospect of being left behind, Kim wouldn't have protested.

With that taken care of, Reider moved over to the hole in the floor leading down into the cellar. Sticking his head into the opening, he yelled down to Smollett. The medic, wearing an expression no different from anyone else's, looked up at his platoon leader. "Stay with the wounded. No time to move you. You're safer down there." With no time to explain and no need to say anything else, Reider pulled away and made his way out of the kitchen on his hands and knees.

Once out of the house, Gerald Reider was able to get himself up off the ground. Looking around, he heard Hernandes call out to him from the barn. "Over here."

As Reider hopped his way over to their last bastion, Hernandes realized for the first time that his platoon leader was wounded. Dashing out, the NCO grabbed his lieutenant by the arm and helped him the rest of the way.

Once in the barn, seated on the floor near the open door, Reider took a deep breath. Free of the smoke, dust, and fumes of the house for the first time in what seemed like an eternity, he paused to close his eyes and enjoy the relatively clean air of the barn. Around him, everyone who had bailed out of the farmhouse was doing likewise. Then, one by one, they looked at one another, over to where Dubois and Henry Smith lay, manning their loopholes, then at Reider. In each of their faces, the young officer could see the same question. "Now what?"

Looking out the barn door, Reider could see the wooden gate, which was still closed, next to the house. He watched as the house, pummeled by shell after shell, shook. Above the crash of high explosives Reider could make out the sound of a diesel engine somewhere, beyond the gate. The second BMP he realized, was still out there, maneuvering under the cover of tank fire.

Slowly, Reider turned toward Hernandes, seated a few feet away from him. "We'll make our stand here," the young officer announced in a low, calm voice. "If the BMP comes crashing through the gate, sergeant, take it out with your RPG. Tobias," he stated as he looked up at that soldier, "take Hernandes's rifle. You and I will cover him. Kim," he continued as his eyes moved on to the next man, "see if you can make your way over there, against the wall, between Sergeant Dubois and his SAW gunner. Only face this way, toward the door. If the Slovakians come charging in here, over us, they're all yours." Then, slowly turning his head, making eye contact with each man as he did so, Reider asked, "Any questions?"

When no one responded, everyone quietly went about preparing himself for the next round. Lying flat on the ground, with the RPG angled so that the backblast wouldn't do too much damage to the rest of the platoon, Staff Sergeant Hernandes took up a good firing position and trained his weapon on the gate just a few yards away. Standing on the same side of the door above his squad leader, Evens Tobias brought his rifle up to his shoulder and peeked around the door frame, watching and waiting for a target. Making his way over to the door, opposite Hernandes, Gerald Reider did likewise. To the rear of the barn, Sergeant Dubois and Henry Smith continued to peer out of their loopholes in search of an enemy that had gone to ground. Kim, the only man who didn't have a definitive sector of responsibility, sat where he was told to, with his eyes closed, trying hard to remember all the words of the Lord's Prayer. Once set, they settled in to wait.

When tanks stopped shelling the house, the silence that followed was deafening. Even the strain of the BMP's engine could not be heard. Whether or not the BMP was still out there, closing, was all but impossible for Gerald Reider to tell. What hearing he had left after his run-in with the attack helicopters had pretty much been finished off during his ordeal in the farmhouse. Craning his neck around the corner of the door in an effort to see more of the yard, the young officer scanned and listened. Across from him, Staff Sergeant Hernandes eased his head back from the sight of his RPG even as Tobias lowered the muzzle of his weapon while still keeping it tucked into his shoulder. "What do you suppose they're up to?" he asked, unable to bear the silence any longer.

Neither Hernandes nor Reider said a word. Instead they looked at each other for a moment. Separately each man began to suspect that the soldiers in the last BMP had dismounted. As the minutes ticked away and they sat there, both men were left with nothing to do but wonder when and where the Slovakians would pop up next.

They were still pondering this when the sound of a rifle butt pounding on the other side of the gate caused the pair to jump. In unison every man facing the gate resumed his former posture, ready to fire as soon as he had a viable target. Only when they heard the words, "Hey, is anyone in there alive?" spoken with an accent that only a Texan could affect, did they ease off their triggers and come to the realization that their long nightmare was over.

EPILOGUE

When Nathan Dixon saw Christina Donovan pass through the flaps of the hospital tent he had been waiting in, all traces of anger at being made to wait disappeared. Her smile, like the morning sun rising over the western prairie, brought warmth and cheer where there had been only darkness. "Here you go," she announced, plopping a partially filled duffel bag on the bed he was sitting next to. "It seems a little cut on the back of the neck is good for only two days in bed and a medium-sized attaboy from a field grade officer. You'll find a clean set of BDUs, your spare boots, cold-weather parka, hat, and shaving kit in there. Packed it all myself."

Smiling, Nathan looked up at the woman who had so

captured his heart. "And what about my unmentionables? Did you remember them?"

Leaning over, she whispered in his ear. "Dear sir, I hardly consider white cotton boxers worth mentioning, let alone remembering."

Unable to help himself, Nathan took a deep breath while Christina lingered with her face just inches from his. It amazed him how she could always manage to smell so good in a unit where diesel fumes and the odor of dirty socks were the order of the day.

"Well, now," Nathan enjoined as he cleared his throat and Christina pulled away. "How'd you manage to talk the major into letting you come back here and pick me up?"

Chris smiled. "Oh, it's the usual story. You know how we poor bugs and gas pukes always wind up getting stuck with all the dirty little details no one else wants."

Nathan chuckled. "Yeah, I'll bet. I can see how upset you are over being here."

Christina didn't respond. Instead, she sat down on the empty cot across from Nathan's. As she did so, her expression turned serious. "The major has a message for you."

Sensing that the time for joking was over, Nathan sighed. "Go ahead. Tell me how I've managed to screw up in absentia."

Looking down at the floor, Christina paused for a moment. Then she looked up into Nathan's eyes. "It seems the report you sent along doesn't jibe with any of the stories the survivors of the 3rd Platoon have been telling the battalion commander. They claim you did a bit more than simply tag along and observe that new lieutenant."

For a moment the battalion staff officer considered feigning ignorance. But he knew better than to do so. The truth, he suspected, would eventually rear its ugly head. Still, he didn't feel any need to help it along, at least not here, not now. "By the way," he replied, by way of changing the subject, "how is Lieutenant Reider?"

Sensing that the man she longed to know better had no desire to talk about what had happened out there, Chris Donovan obliged him. "He was evacuated back to Germany yesterday. He broke an ankle and sprained a wrist during their last stand."

When Nathan began to chuckle to himself, Chris Donovan looked at him as if he had lost his mind. "What's so funny about breaking an ankle?"

"Don't you see?" Nathan explained. "Imagine what it's going to be like when he's a general. Some admiring young officer looks up at him and asks, 'Sir, how did you get your Purple Heart? Was it a grenade fragment? A bullet? A bomb?' Reider will have to look him in the eye and say, 'No son, I fell down a flight of steps during a firefight.'"

In a flash, Christina broke out in a broad smile with the deep, lusty laugh that so turned Nathan on.

Everything, the young officer told himself, was going to be okay. Everything.

Coming soon from Forge books,
New York Times bestselling author
Harold Coyle's apocolyptic novel,

DEAD HAND

Under the Soviet regime, the communist leadership developed a system to launch all their nuclear missiles even if every member of the Russian government was incinerated. The system was entitled Dead Hand, triggered by any attack on the Russian perimeter. But when an asteroid strikes Siberia with the force of a thousand Hiroshimas . . .

EASTERN RUSSIA
MARCH

Like the slow steady pealing of a church bell announcing the death of a parishioner, the massive steel blast doors reverberated with each new explosion. Some of the more nervous officers and soldiers still at their stations jumped each time a new eruption shook the doors that separated them from the vicious combat on the other side. When the sound of one particularly violent detonation rippled through the launch control center, even the steadiest of them dropped all pretenses of the calm demeanor that was a hallmark of the elite Russian Strategic Rocket Force. Comrades who had shared and endured so many hardships on the fringes of Siberia exchanged nervous glances. Now, with the rattle of small arms fire growing closer and the acrid smell of cordite seeping into the room that controlled the ICBM fields of their regiment, one by one the mutinous soldiers turned to stare at the console where their commander should have been.

Unlike them, he was not at his assigned place of duty. His seat was vacant, as it had been since the first report that commandos, loyal to the government in Moscow, had managed to break into the subterranean complex where the control center was located. Nor was the deputy commander. Knowing that he would never be able to idly stand by in the stifling confines of the control center and passively wait for the end, the deputy had abandoned his post to personally direct the defense of the complex. Nothing had been heard of him after the large blast door had been shut behind him. Only the growing sounds of fighting suggested that those mutineers tasked to defend the control center were losing ground.

It wasn't until the roar of battle was replaced by the sound of hushed voices just outside the blast door that the next senior officer, a major, rose from his seat. Slowly, almost haltingly, the major made his way to the rear of the room where the commander of the regiment sat alone in his office. Following protocol the major knocked on the door before pushing it open and slipping into the darkened room. His colonel, who had led them into open revolt to protest the abysmal living conditions his men were forced to live under, was bent over his desk holding his head in his hands. "Sir," the major announced, "it is time. I need the codes in order to . . . "

"To do *what?*" the colonel bellowed as his hands fell away and he glared up at the major. "Murder our fellow countrymen?"

Undaunted by his rebuke and spurred on by the ominous activities just outside the blast door where he suspected the commandos were laying charges to blow it open, the major did not back down. Instead, he cleared his throat as he prepared to press for the codes the men waiting in the control room would need to launch their missiles.

The colonel, however, did not give him a chance. His blurry eyes, framed by a puffy white unshaven face, was contorted by anger. "Or perhaps," the colonel sneered, "we should launch our missiles at the Americans and let them rain death and destruction down on our people for us."

"But, our threats. Our plans?" the major stammered. "I fear the commandos are preparing to blast their way into here. If we don't act now . . ."

"Go away," the colonel moaned as he let his head drop back into the open, waiting hands as if his neck could no longer support it. "Close the door and leave me be."

Determined not to leave until he had both the keys and the codes necessary to launch their missiles, the major snapped to attention and drew his pistol. "Colonel," he barked with as much conviction as his parched throat allowed, "we believed in you when you stated that you would force Moscow to honor its obligations to us and our families. We have endured three days and nights without sleep as we stood by and watched those bastards throw everything they had against us. Like myself, the others are prepared to carry out the just and righteous retribution that you, yourself, promised to deliver if our demands were not met. It is time to do so. I insist that you hand over the codes."

This time, when the drunken colonel lifted his head and looked into the eyes of the defiant major, the colonel laughed. "*HA!* The joke is on you, major. I have no codes." As he leaned back in his seat, his right hand reached out and grabbed a bottle of vodka sitting on the desk before him. "Never had the bloody things. The deputy knew that. Why do you think he left to die out there?"

Stunned by this unexpected revelation, the major's

jaw dropped open. Slowly he lowered his pistol and looked about the room as if trying to collect his thoughts. When he finally turned back to face his commander the colonel was taking a long hard pull on the bottle. "This," the shaken major asked incredulously, "has all been a bluff?"

Finishing before he bothered to answer, the colonel pitched the bottle across the room, where it shattered against a world map that covered most of one wall. "*That*," he yelled, "is all we're able to hurl at those bastards in Moscow who have starved our families and left us here to rot. *That's* all we ever had. You should have known that! We have no launch codes here! You're a fucking major for God sakes! How could you have been so damned stupid? You know how the system works." Leaning forward, the colonel's expression became a scowl. "Now go away you fool and join the other fools who were gullible enough to stay with the colors while the crooks in Moscow broke promise after promise to us while they built dachas for themselves and sent the money that belonged to us to Swiss bank accounts. Go and leave me alone. Perhaps," the colonel added, "if you're lucky the commandos will kill you rather than take you prisoner."

Still stunned by the fact that he had gone into open rebellion against his own country led by a man who had never intended to back his threats with action, the major turned and walked out of the office, pistol in hand.

Alone again, the colonel opened a lower desk drawer that contained two unopened bottles of vodka, a pistol, a hand grenade, and some ledgers. Reaching into the drawer he pulled out one of the two bottles. As he twisted the cap off, he looked into the drawer at the pistol and the grenade. A smile crept across his face as he put the newly opened bottle down and bent over. Taking the grenade, the colonel firmly grasped it so that the spoon could not fly off when he pulled the pin. When he was ready he gave the pin a firm yank with his

ree hand. Tossing the pin over his shoulder, the colonel leaned over again. Carefully he nestled the pinless
grenade between the ledgers in the drawer with the last
bottle of vodka. Keeping the spoon down, he slowly
pushed the drawer in until he was sure that he could
release the grenade and the spoon would be held in
place by the bottom of the drawer above the one it was
in. When he was ready, he slowly withdrew his hand.

Satisfied that all was set, the colonel eased the drawer
in a bit further until just the bottle of vodka, laying on
its side was visible. "There," he stated with glee. "A gift
or the victors."

With nothing more to do but wait, the colonel leaned
back in his seat, retrieved the freshly opened bottle of
vodka on his desk, and settled in to enjoy his last moments on earth. He had no desire to pray. His wife was
the one infected by the wave of religious fanaticism that
was currently gripping their staggering country. Nor did
he intend to pen an excuse or explanation of his actions
or his former masters. They knew why he had done
hat he had. That was why they kept well fed and paid
men, like those preparing to force their way into the
control room with orders to kill everyone in there, close
at hand. Every commander in the Strategic Rocket Force
knew that. Like his fellow regimental commanders, his
only duty over the past few years had been to keep his
people mollified as best he could no matter what happened, or suffer the consequences. There would be no
compromise, no negotiations. He even suspected that
he major who had been in his office knew what was
coming. The only problem with the major was that he
was still a bit too young. The system, or what passed as
ne nowadays in Russia, simply had not had enough
me to squeeze the last vestige of hope from him.

With little left to do now but wait, the colonel contin-
ed to do his best to drink himself senseless. He was
well into his new bottle of vodka when a blast, just out-
de his door in the main room, announced that the

commandos had penetrated the last barrier. As the sound of gun shots, exploding grenades, shrieked orders, and screams of pain filled the colonel's dark office, the regimental commander suddenly had a funny thought. Looking down at the booby trapped desk drawer he smiled. "Well," he exclaimed, ignoring the sound of boots pounding their way up the concrete stairs that led to his office. "It seems I have created my own dead hand." Then looking up at the partially opened door, he lifted his bottle in a mock toast. " I only wish those shits in Moscow could have been here to enjoy my last, little joke."

Seconds later, it was all over.

All except for one last vengeful swipe by the dead.